Praise for the Nicki Valentine Mystery Ser

FINDING SKY (#1)

"Nicki Valentine, the heroine of O'Brien's engaging cc
her hands full as a widowed mother of two...When he
Kenna, phones to tell her that Beth, the 18-year-old mc
the baby Kenna plans to adopt, has disappeared, Nic
chance to put what she's learned in her PI trainir
work...Nicki proves a resourceful sleuth as she gets ol
the missing teen. The conclusion will leave readers eager for the
next installment."

– *Publishers Weekly*

"Author Susan O'Brien deftly combines motherhood and mayhem
in this lively tale of a single mom tracking down a missing teen.
Lots of fun!"

– Laura Levine,
Author of the Jaine Austen Mystery Series

"Has a heart and soul and the minute I started reading it, I knew it
was something special. Nicki Valentine, the sleuth at the center of
the mystery of a missing pregnant teen, felt like an old friend to me
and the lengths to which she will go to help a friend is just one
example of her integrity and loyalty. I can't wait to read more about
Nicki and her journey as a single mom and modern-day Nancy
Drew."

– Maggie Barbieri,
Author of *Once Upon a Lie* and the Murder 101 Mystery Series

"This debut mystery offers menace without violence, intrigue, and
the realistic depiction of a single mother struggling to find an
identity outside of motherhood. The hint of romance and element
of humor further ensures that this novel will attract a following of
cozy-reading fans for the upcoming sequel, *Sky High*."

– *Kings River Life Magazine*

FINDING Sky

**Books in the Nicki Valentine Mystery Series
by Susan O'Brien**

FINDING SKY (#1)
SKY HIGH (#2)
(September 2015)

A Nicki Valentine Mystery

FINDING Sky

Susan O'Brien

HENERY PRESS

FINDING SKY
A Nicki Valentine Mystery
Part of the Henery Press Mystery Collection

First Edition
Trade paperback edition | October 2014

Henery Press
www.henerypress.com

ISBN-13: 978-1-940976-30-3

Printed in the United States of America

To Pete

ACKNOWLEDGMENTS

I am forever grateful to everyone who helped *Finding Sky* (and me!) come this far.

My loving, supportive, fun family—Pete, our children, Mom, Dad, Sarah, David, Peter, Gayle, and our extended families.

My steadfast friends—Noelle, the St. Anne's Healing Prayer Group, Audree, Alice, Sue, Eileen, Michelle, Terry, Shevene, and many others.

The extraordinary Henery Press team—Managing (and Simply Amazing) Editor Kendel Lynn, Art C. Molinares, Stephanie Chontos, Erin George, Rachel Jackson, and the entire Hen House.

Generous experts—John L. French, Sgt. Ken Dondero, Dan Wright, Abbe Levine, S. Pierre Paret, and Terri L. Chadwick. (This is a work of fiction, so they aren't responsible for any mistakes or liberties taken.)

And my ultimate source of blessings and peace—God.

Countless individuals have knowingly and unknowingly provided encouragement, strength, and inspiration. I'm thankful to every one of them, especially the readers, who are making my dreams come true!

One

If it hadn't been for the herd of wild animals thundering through my kitchen, I wouldn't have agreed to my best friend's plan so quickly. I don't live on a Montana ranch or an African preserve, but my suburban Washington, D.C., home more than qualifies as a zoo, especially on playgroup days.

"Mommy's on the phone!" I yelled as four kids screeched by, seemingly oblivious. Two of them were mine, so I blamed myself for their manners. But where was Irene, the other mom? I hoped she wasn't using Jack and Sophie's bathroom upstairs, which looked like it had been hit by a monsoon. That's what happens when you bathe children while devouring *People* magazine. Things get out of hand. It had been the most peaceful time of day so far.

"What were you saying?" I asked Kenna while trying to zero in on the kids' destination with my Supermom sense of hearing. I felt guilty for being distracted when she called, as usual, but she'd understand soon enough when she adopted her baby.

"I said Beth is missing!"

This would have shocked and devastated me, except I had no idea who Beth was. Throwing playgroup etiquette to the wind, I hollered, "Irene! Can you watch the kids for a minute?"

She emerged from the basement with a rocking horse a child must have wanted. Her wide-eyed expression could have been due to my booming request or the mountains of unfolded laundry she'd witnessed downstairs. I consoled myself with the fact she hadn't seen the kids' bathroom after all.

"Sorry," I mouthed. I pointed at the phone and shrugged apologetically.

She shooed me back to my conversation and headed in the general direction of a huge crash and hysterical laughter that carried from somewhere upstairs.

"Kenna, who is Beth?"

"She's the birth mother," she croaked.

"Oh my God."

In all our talks about adoption, she'd never mentioned the birth mother's name. I'd been so elated that she and Andy had been "matched" with someone—especially after four miscarriages and a year in adoption limbo—that I'd focused on the big picture, not the details. That was partly because Kenna did the same thing. When I suggested we shop for baby supplies, for example, she said, "Let's wait until things are final. Anyway, you have all your old baby stuff."

Uh, not really. I couldn't break it to her that when Sophie turned three, I'd given away every last piece of baby crap I owned. I cherished the memories of my precious infants, but if I had to climb over one more baby gate or catch even a whiff of Eau de Diaper Pail, I might go insane. I needed to move on...into a world that wasn't a poop-scented obstacle course. I'd be happy to get her fresh, new necessities.

"What do you mean *missing*?" I asked.

"She hasn't shown up for anything this week. Not checkups, not counseling, not even classes."

"What kind of classes? Childbirth?"

"No. Summer school. She's trying to graduate. She's only 18."

Wow. I had no idea the birth mother was so young. It dawned on me there must be a lot we hadn't discussed. After twenty-five years of best friendship, it felt a little awkward.

"What does the adoption agency say?"

"They think she ran away. Her parents do too. They told the agency she's done it before, and she'd do it again."

"A pregnant girl, about to give birth, on the run?" I pictured myself at thirty-eight weeks. I could barely get off the couch, never mind flee. And I certainly wouldn't have gone undetected.

"She was so committed to this adoption plan. There's no way–" Her voice broke. "No way..."

There were only so many disappointments a person could take, even someone with Kenna's unfailing buoyancy. I finished her sentence in a near-whisper. "No way she changed her mind?"

"Mmm hmm." Sniffles. "I know she didn't run away. Something happened. You have to find her."

Me? She couldn't be thinking what I thought she was thinking.

"Kenna. I'm sure the police are working on this," I said to comfort both of us.

"They are, but they think she's a runaway. And they're preoccupied. They're not going to do enough."

By preoccupied she meant focused on a local case making national headlines. A terrorist plot to bomb D.C.-area venues had been thwarted, but several suspects were at large. The pressure was on. Like many crimes, it fascinated me, and that's why I was becoming a PI. I wanted to solve cases someday—someday when my kids were in school full time and I had a millisecond to think straight. That is if years of playing Candy Land and watching *Barney & Friends* hadn't obliterated my brain cells.

"If she's 18," I said, "and her parents think she's a runaway, maybe the police won't suspect anything else. But she's pregnant. That's a big deal." I probed a little. "Are there any other reasons you think she's in trouble?"

"She told me some things." They'd been talking? Another surprise. "There's so much to..."

Her voice was drowned out by an oncoming train. Four children, linked hands-to-shoulders, were *whoo whooing* toward me on an imaginary track with Irene as a derailed caboose.

"Shhhhh," Irene begged. "Your mom's on the phone."

I pressed a hand over my free ear and raised my voice. "I can't hear you, Kenna," I said. "Playgroup ends in a few minutes. I'll call you the second it's over. We'll figure this out."

I had no idea if that was true. But more than anything else, I wanted it to be.

After twenty minutes of gathering toys, strapping on shoes, and saying goodbye, Irene finally dragged her little guys, Ryan and Will, out the door. I made my regular silent vow to quit playgroup, which I never kept. I dreaded adding mayhem to my life, but four-year-old Sophie and six-year-old Jack thrived on socializing. At least it got me to vacuum occasionally.

I stuck juice boxes in their hands and a DVD in the machine. Guaranteed thirty minutes of relative freedom, I dialed Kenna.

"It's Nicki," I said to her voicemail. "Playgroup's over. Call me."

I maneuvered around race cars and action figures to peek out the front door at her driveway. Being neighbors means knowing what the other person is up to in a non-nosy, *hope-you're-home-so-we-can-talk-about-today's-news* kind of way.

Her red convertible Solara wasn't in its usual spot, so I assumed she was running errands. Sunday was her day off from teaching aerobics at a health club. It was a nice supplement to Andy's work as a reporter, and it kept her in disgustingly good shape.

Way back in middle school when we met, I was insanely jealous of Kenna's long legs, wavy blond hair, gray-blue eyes and fair skin—just the opposite of my short, dark self. Over time, things have stayed exactly the same. Once we went to a neighborhood Halloween party as Nicole Kidman and Tom Cruise. Convincingly. We won "best costume." Yet it didn't feel like a prize to me.

I stepped into the July humidity and put my life at risk. The warnings in effect were staggering—air quality, West Nile, Lyme disease, terrorists. Years ago we'd even had a local outbreak of malaria, not to mention snipers on the loose.

I relaxed as much as possible until Kenna pulled in. She looked striking as usual. Shades on, hair glistening in the sun. It wasn't until she pushed back the glasses that I noticed her splotchy complexion, a sure sign she'd been crying, since she doesn't break out. I raced across the lawn to meet her.

"Come over," I urged. "Let's talk."

We sat on opposite ends of my wicker porch sofa, Kenna's legs stretched over floral pillows, mine tucked beneath me. She clutched a large fast-food cup, a clear violation of our recent pact to give up soda. Looking at her made my heart sink. Usually her eyes sparkled with energy. Today they were blank and downcast. I almost hoped she was sucking on forbidden caffeine.

"I can't believe this. What did you mean when you said Beth told you some things?"

"We've been talking on the phone every week to get to know each other and make sure everything feels right. The agency set up calls after her checkups." She sniffed.

"Was Andy on the phone too?"

"At first. Then he'd hang up so we could talk about girl stuff."

"Like what?"

"Like Beth's relationship with the birth father, Marcus." She took a deep breath. I waited for her to go on. "He's in a gang. She had a huge crush on him and wanted to turn him around."

"Uh oh." How many guys had I tried to "turn around"? I'd never been successful. And turning around a gang member sounded a wee bit risky.

"Yeah. She slept with him, and he dumped her. He wouldn't even admit the baby was his."

"Oh my gosh."

A pang of empathy hit my gut. Adolescence is packed with insecurity and emotion. To deal with it along with pregnancy must be torture.

I chose my next words carefully, mindful we were discussing the baby's birth father. I'd learned from experience how much father-related criticism can hurt. My husband Jason died in a boating accident with a lover I didn't know about, but no matter how many times I've badmouthed him, I don't want anyone else to do it. He's still my kids' dad. So I went with a simple question: "How did Beth take it?"

"She was hurt. But she's amazing. She found an adoption agency and made a plan, even though her parents didn't approve."

"Wow. That's impressive. Remember us at her age? I don't think I could have done that. Was she afraid of Marcus at all?"

"I asked her and she said no, even though she admitted his gang is violent. She thought deep down he cared about her, or at least about the baby."

Yikes. Gangs were in the local news all the time. Being miles from the inner city didn't make us immune.

"I hope she has friends to help her."

"There's at least one. She went to every appointment with her best friend April."

"That's a relief. Do you know Beth's last name?"

She shook her head. "No. But I have this." She pulled a crinkled white envelope from her purse and passed it over.

I reached inside. A wallet-size portrait of a young woman spoke for itself. She had bright green eyes, honey-colored hair and a closed-mouth smile that somehow managed to look sad. Layers of makeup couldn't begin to hide her natural beauty. I guessed she was on the fringes of the in-crowd—too rebellious to be a follower, too pretty to be an outcast.

"This is Beth? She's beautiful."

"I think so too. It's from last year."

"You got it from the agency?"

"Yeah, with a bunch of information about her. I'm putting it together for you. It's got her height, weight, medical history, a little bit about her family and hobbies."

I felt a mental twinge, probably disappointment that she hadn't shared any of this until now. Usually we talked about everything in excessive detail. I exhaled and let it go.

"Okay," I said. "Do you know where she goes to school?"

"It can't be far from the agency. She stopped there after school a lot."

"First Steps Adoption, right?"

She nodded, and just then I heard my sweeties belting out the *Dora the Explorer* finale song. From experience, I knew they were also jumping on the couch in celebration.

"Want to come in?" I asked.

"Auntie Kenna! Auntie Kenna!" Jack and Sophie shrieked as we entered the family room. Sophie hopped from couch to coffee table, brown curls bouncing, right into Kenna's outstretched arms.

"Nice catch," I said. There should be awards for such childcare skills—best retrieval of an airborne child, least traumatic hair rinsing method, fastest removal of a bandage, most creative use of furniture as an indoor playground.

"You guys aren't going to believe it," I said. Their eyes doubled in size.

"What?" Sophie asked.

"You get to watch another show." That broke my hour-a-day rule, but it was unavoidable.

"Hooray!" Sophie shouted.

"Which one?" Jack was skeptical. No baby shows for him. I was lucky to get away with *Dora*.

"Let me see." I grabbed the remote and searched for something that wouldn't cause nightmares or expand their bad-language vocabulary (currently limited to *stupid, idiot,* and *butt*). A *Zoboomafoo* rerun elicited cheers, so I stopped there.

"Your mom loves *Zoboomafoo*," Kenna teased. I was so glad to see her perky side that I didn't mind the teasing. So what if I have a tiny crush on certain TV hosts? I'm a thirty-six-year-old stay-at-home mom. My options are limited. And those Kratt brothers *are* cute.

"*Zoboomafoo* is great," I agreed. "Sophie, sit on the couch, sweetie." Kenna lowered her next to Jack, and their matching brown eyes glazed over in seconds. I trusted their brains would survive the extra assault.

Kenna followed me down the hall to the only fully organized area of my life. French doors with childproof locks led to a study, complete with a bay window, banana-yellow paint and white, built-in bookcases lined with textbooks and mementos. A model airplane crafted by my late father, a retired pilot, hung from the ceiling.

Kenna sprawled on a creamy velvet chaise. I sat at an antique desk incongruously topped with a high-end computer, a graduation gift to myself when I finished an M.A. in forensic psychology. Sometimes the Internet felt like my only connection to the outside world. I logged on.

"Why are you doing that?" Kenna asked. She hated computers and refused to get comfortable with them. I understood, since the idea of gyrating my spandex-covered ass in front of a class of hardbodies didn't agree with me. We each had our comfort zones.

"I'm looking up Beth's school." I typed and clicked away.

"We don't know where she goes."

"We will in a second." I found First Steps' address and a list of nearby high schools. One was in the same city as the agency, and according to a mapping site, they were just a mile apart. "I bet she goes to Woodridge High School."

I explained why, and Kenna agreed. "Now what?" she asked.

I ran my hands through my shoulder-length hair, stalling while I figured out how to respond. Despite how much I'd studied criminals, I had no practical experience. Even if I figured out Beth's last name, where she lived, who her friends were, and what her life was like, what could I do with that? Did I really expect to track down a teen while my kids were at day camp?

"I want so badly to help. But you and Andy should hire a private investigator. I could put you in touch with one of my teachers."

"As much as I'd like to give you an excuse to talk to Dean, no."

Dean, a muscular blond instructor at the PI Academy, was the only man who tempted me to abandon my anti-relationship stance. He set off an involuntary chemical reaction that made me blush if I so much as raised my hand in class.

"We can barely afford this adoption as it is," Kenna said. "Andy isn't convinced that Beth is in danger. And I trust *you*."

It was hard to argue those points, except for the misplaced trust part. What if I ruined the investigation, our friendship, or, at worst, the adoption? I glanced at Kenna for reassurance. Our eyes didn't connect because hers were becoming puddles. I scooted out from behind the desk, crossed the room, and gave her a tight hug. A sob escaped her, the kind that only surfaces when someone's there to respond.

"It's okay," I said, even though I wasn't sure.

"Maybe I'm crazy. Maybe I'm wrong. But I just feel so responsible. Who's really going to look for her?"

If I hadn't already been convinced, she would have swayed me. It was rare for Kenna to feel weighed down by anything. Unlike me, she didn't worry obsessively or battle with her conscience over every little decision. I loved how she enjoyed life, went with the flow. If she felt we had to do this, we did.

"You talked with Beth, and I trust *your* judgment," I said. After all, there's nothing like a woman's intuition. Mine was setting off alarm bells left and right.

I spent the rest of the evening making the kids a gourmet meal (meaning I used the stove instead of the microwave), praying intermittently that Beth would be okay, and—shock of all shocks—emailing Dean after the kids were tucked in. It's amazing what a best friend in trouble can do for your motivation. Plus, he couldn't see my flushed cheeks through the computer. Here's what I wrote:

Hi Dean,

It's Nicki Valentine from your PI training class. I know it sounds ridiculous, but I'm helping a friend look for a missing person. She can't afford a PI, and she doesn't know where else to turn. I hope you'll have a few ideas for me. Would you mind hearing about the situation whenever it's convenient for you? Thank you so much.

Nicki

I spell-checked the email, added my phone number, and read it a billion times. Confident it didn't include glaring errors or evidence of lustful fantasies, I clicked *send*. I wasn't sure what to do next. This late, I'd usually eat a meal in peace, study, bounce around to hip-hop music, or watch reality TV—basically anything I couldn't do around the kids.

Tonight was different. Just yards away, Kenna was probably collecting every scrap of paperwork she had about Beth, afraid of what was happening—and what might not happen. It reminded me of her pregnancies. Hopeful elation followed by crushing disappointment. But this time it was tinged with conflict with Andy. I wanted to go to sleep and pretend it wasn't real, or, alternatively, burst through her door and comfort her.

I rolled my desk chair to the window and pulled back the sheer curtains a touch. I could see the side of Kenna's house and yard, lights ablaze in the kitchen and living room. Even the stone patio, where we'd had so many conversations about marriage and motherhood, was lit.

Our houses were like fraternal twins—same builder, different outcome. Hers was an elongated rambler while mine was a three-story colonial. Both had crimson bricks and white shutters. We'd bought them when the neighborhood and our marriages were new. If you'd asked me then, I'd have put money on my home, not my marriage, falling apart first.

Thank God Jack and Sophie had been too young, just two and two months, to sense the enormity of Jason's death and my pain. If anything, they'd been more aware of the loss of my dad, "Grampy," who lived with us after the accident, caring for them while I took night classes. He and my mom had divorced after he retired, finally accepting that his busy career hadn't created an unhappy marriage—it was respite from one. So much travelling had only prolonged the inevitable.

When he died of a heart attack two years later, I was all too familiar with shock, grief, and the awkward acceptance of money from tragedy. I wanted to keep our home forever because of its memories, but I wanted to escape it for the same reason. Kenna kept me here.

I slid back to the desk and distracted myself with research. The Internet had endless information about area gangs. One story described a pregnant gang member who was killed for becoming an informant. Beth didn't sound like someone who would join a gang, never mind snitch on one. Several articles referred to a regional gang task force, which was impressive yet worrisome, because if the problem got this much attention, it had to be big.

My next stop was the First Steps Adoption site. Images of adoptive parents and children beamed from page after page, reflecting experiences that seemed miraculous. I wanted so much for Kenna and Andy to be this fulfilled. The section devoted to birth parents was tiny in comparison. I couldn't imagine what adoption was like for them. For Beth.

A mental break was in order. I propelled myself across toy-littered carpets and sticky hardwood to the kitchen, reciting the mother's creed: "I'll clean it up tomorrow."

The refrigerator was filled with kid-size, vegetarian options: squeezable yogurt, baby carrots and mini bagels. I needed something big, warm and comforting. Yeesh. That sounded like a man. Maybe I was having some sort of psychological revelation. Instant soup would have to do for now. I put water on the stove and tiptoed upstairs to check on the kids.

Entering Sophie's room was unnecessary. Her curls were unmistakable against a white pillowcase, her breaths loud enough to hear. When awake, she's always in motion. Her nighttime stillness awes me.

A nightlight illuminated Jack's slender figure under a jumbled blanket. All but the top of his silky head was covered. Maybe he'd convened a secret meeting with his caped bear, Super Teddy, before falling asleep. I lowered the blanket slightly, willing him to rest despite the cool air he must have felt around his cheeks. He squeezed Super Teddy to his chest and sighed deeply.

Minutes later I had steaming, tofu-broccoli soup beside me and my fingertips on the keyboard. I needed to think about something less emotional, like the legal aspects of adoption.

I clicked on First Steps' "FAQ" link and alternated between slurping and scrolling. It felt like an invasion of Kenna and Andy's privacy, but I needed to understand how things worked. I already knew they'd provided proof (including a reference letter from me) that they were responsible, healthy adults, committed to each other and raising a child. A social worker had inspected everything from their home to their bank accounts. They'd also made a "profile" for birth parents to review, complete with pictures of their house, hobbies, relatives, and neighborhood playgrounds and pools. *But what if the birth father didn't want to relinquish? What were his rights? What if the birth mother changed her mind, even after the baby was born?* These questions must have been asked often, but they weren't addressed online, probably because their answers were too complicated. The site did say the wait for a child, from application to placement, was typically about a year—exactly how long Kenna and Andy had been working with the agency. I couldn't imagine them starting over.

The warm soup made me drowsy. I moved the cursor to sign off just as the computer emitted a familiar sound. I had new mail. *Please let it be Dean*, I thought. Maybe help was in sight.

Two

I don't know what I expected Dean to say, but it wasn't this:

Nicki,
I have a busy day tomorrow, but you're welcome to meet me at the Academy for lunch. Bring whatever information you have. How does one o'clock sound?
Dean

It sounded perfect in one way. The kids would be at camp from twelve to four, but otherwise, I wasn't sure. Could I maintain an hour's worth of one-on-one conversation without visibly overheating? What would I wear? Should I offer to bring lunch? I shook my head to dispel anxiety. *Concentrate on Beth*, I told myself.

I forced my fingers across the keys, accepting his offer and insisting on providing lunch. This was both polite and practical, since I didn't want my picky vegetarian diet to be a concern. Going veggie had been an act of teenage rebellion that sufficiently annoyed my parents, but now my heart was in it—hopefully to its benefit. I left Kenna a voicemail with a few adoption questions, hoping my call didn't wake her or Andy.

The fatigue I'd felt moments before was replaced with buzzing nervous energy. I turned off everything downstairs and headed for my closet. I pushed through one item after another. *Mommy outfit. Mommy outfit. Mommy outfit. Stained mommy outfit. Wrinkled mommy outfit.* Good grief! Did I own anything except jeans, T-shirts, and sweats? How about a freaking iron? I shoved aside some lingerie-like shirts I'd bought years ago in a fit of anti-frumpiness. A lot of good they'd done.

I was about to give up when I ran across a stretchy, black, v-neck tank top. Hmm. It was really designed for exercise, but if I paired it with my casual black rayon pants, it might be okay. I hung the items over the closet doorknob and went in search of a black thong and bra. I found them abandoned in the back of my underwear drawer under an unopened pack of pantyhose. A true reflection of my life. Full outfit assembled, I crawled into bed.

It was one of those terrible times when you blink and it's over. I'm not talking about sex, of course. Just one of those rock-hard sleeps that completely robs you of any sense of lengthy rest. The fact that Sophie was next to me babbling about her plans for the day meant it was somewhere between six and seven. Jack would sleep for another hour if I read Sophie stories and reenacted them as various characters. By breakfast, I'd been an ant, a baby, and a dump truck—and also added "actress" to my résumé.

We survived the morning unscathed despite roughhousing, imaginary sword fights, and a battle over who would get the first turn playing UNO. I was so busy refereeing that I didn't have brain space for worrying. At 11:30, I started the pre-camp routine with sunblock slathering. Jack was mid-scream ("I hate this!") when the doorbell rang. Sophie ran to get it.

"Don't open it until I say it's okay," I warned.

"It's Auntie Kenna," Sophie announced. "But the door is locked."

I grabbed my keys from the kitchen counter and hurried to the deadbolt. Jack was stuck holding his arms away from his sides, hoping the white gunk would dry quickly. I turned the lock and let Sophie turn the knob.

"Hi, Auntie Kenna. What's that?" she asked. Kenna was holding a manila envelope.

"Hi sweetie. Some papers for your mommy." Her smile was strained.

"Thanks," I said, taking the package and giving her a hug, careful not to smear sunscreen on her back. "I'm sorry. I'm getting them ready for camp."

"It's okay. I put a note inside. Thanks for your message last night. Call me later."

"I will," I said. "I'm meeting with Dean about this at one." I held up the envelope.

"What?" She was incredulous.

"I know. I hope it helps."

"What are the papers about?" Sophie asked.

"A very nice girl," I said while giving her a squeeze. "Just like you!"

My stomach did its usual flip as the kids climbed out of the van at camp. It was a relief to get a break, but my worry level always raised a notch when we were apart, at least for the first few minutes. A camp counselor walked them into the community center while I waved goodbye and called "I love you!" They blew me off, but at least it was the last thing they heard in case any of us died that day. Sad to admit, but that's how my anxious mind works.

After stopping at home to freshen up, it took about fifteen minutes to get to the PI Academy, including a pickup at my favorite pizza joint. I wasn't sure whether to be offended or relieved that none of the staff recognized me. Makeup, blown-out hair, decent clothes, and lack of dependents apparently transformed me into a new person. Go figure.

I parked with a few minutes to spare, which I used to rip open the packet from Kenna. She'd copied a ten-page intake form Beth had filled out at First Steps. Last names were blacked out, but everything else— from Beth's birthday to her pre-pregnancy weight to her parents' first names—was there. Bubbly writing listed her hobbies as dancing and soccer and her personality as "friendly but shy." A sticky note from Kenna read, "Thanks, Nicki."

I balanced pizza, bottled waters, and salads as I walked toward the Academy—an optimistic way of describing a strip-mall office shared by Dean and several other investigators. Each was some kind of expert, which meant they could collaborate on cases and teach various subjects. Dean's specialty (other than looking like Brad Pitt on steroids) was technical surveillance countermeasures, or TSCM, a fancy term for debugging. His part of the sixty-hour PI training, in all honesty, would have been mind-numbing if it hadn't been for his fascinating appearance. But he was president of the school and had tons of experience. I knew because I'd read the company brochure several times. Okay, I'd mostly stared at his photo and read his bio twice.

I used my butt to push open the glass door, hoping Dean wouldn't spot me from the little reception area. I was blessed with the sight of the twenty-something receptionist, Amber, alone and smiling at the front desk. Her hot pink lipstick went perfectly with her unnatural tan, bleached hair and acrylic nails. She was gorgeous in a kinda trashy way.

"Hey Amber," I said. We'd met a few times on my way into class. "I'm here to see Dean."

"He told me you'd be here. Give ya a hand?" She chomped on a piece of gum.

"Oh no. I'm fine." Hopefully my food-container pyramid wouldn't topple.

"Okay. Well, he's in the back." She swung her feathery layers toward the area where classes were held. "Go right ahead."

Gray industrial carpet led past closed office doors to the darkened conference room. Dean sat at the end of a U-shaped table configuration, flashing slides onto a wall-size screen. They were changing so quickly I could only make out a blur of words.

"There," he said, stopping on one that said *Infrared Bugs.* Sounded like a sci-fi flick. He turned to me, and his smile pierced the dark. I made a mental note to buy teeth whitening supplies. "I'm trying to get organized for a presentation tonight."

"Oh. I'm sorry if it's not a good time," I said. "I really appreciate this."

"No problem. I'm glad for a break. You brought pizza?"

"I did. And salads. Is that okay?"

"Love it. Have a seat."

I set everything to his left, skipped the chair between us, and sat down. My hands were a little shaky, but I busied myself arranging the meal while he flipped on lights, obliterating the projector's soft, forgiving glow with fluorescent-bulb brilliance.

"So your email said you're helping a friend look for a missing person. I assume the police are already involved." He helped himself to a slice of pizza.

I told the story as he plowed through three slices straight and dug into his salad. I guess I didn't need to worry about my looks. He only had eyes for the food. All those muscles probably needed a lot of fuel.

He paused to ask a couple questions: "What does your friend's gut tell her happened?" ("Something bad.") And "Aren't you hungry?" ("I'm too worried to eat.") Getting lettuce stuck between my teeth was among my concerns, but he didn't need to know that.

He launched into a mini-lecture on missing persons while I took notes. Some things I knew (time was of the essence) and some things I didn't (police have to notify the FBI when someone under twenty-one is missing). He handed me a stapled sheaf of papers, and I couldn't help noticing even his hands were well defined. I stopped myself from imagining what they could do.

"We won't cover this stuff for a couple weeks. But I thought it would help now."

I started flipping through it. *Skip tracing. Internet resources. Runaways*. That's when I noticed my nails. Nervous picking meant they were barely there, and I'd forgotten to file what was left. I tucked them under the pile's edges. "Thank you so much, Dean." I stood to go.

"Sure you're not going to eat?" he asked. We glanced at my untouched food.

"That's okay." I waved toward the pizza and salad, grazing my water, which cascaded across my notes and over the table's edge. Dean caught it too late and set it upright. I grabbed some napkins and dabbed the notes, and then knelt to work on the floor.

"I'm so sorry," I said from under the table. I was looking at the mammoth spill but concentrating on my mammoth ass, which was poking out toward Dean. Thank heaven for thongs. Nothing worse than a mammoth ass with panty lines. When the puddle was reasonably dry, I wiggled out backward. Lovely. I stood, straightened my pants, and managed to look at him sideways. He was grinning. At least he wasn't screaming in horror.

"No problem," he said. "It's just water. Are your notes okay?"

"I think they survived." *My dignity, not so much.* I dropped the sopping napkins into a bag-lined trash can along with the bottle. "Whoops. Do you recycle?" The kids begged me to help save the environment, and I was trying to do my part, no matter how inconvenient it was.

"We do," he said. "I'll take it for you." I retrieved the bottle and handed it to him.

"Thanks. And I'll leave the extra pizza for you," I said, collecting my drippy papers.

"At least take your salad." He handed it to me and stepped toward the door. "Let me walk you out."

Relaxed khakis and an oxford shirt couldn't contain his muscles, everywhere from his triceps to his glutes (words I'd picked up from Kenna). I followed them back down the hall toward Amber.

"Good luck with your presentation tonight," I told him. I waved goodbye to Amber.

"Thanks," he said. "I'll see you in class, but keep me posted. Email or call if you need to. Okay?"

I agreed. He held the door while I stepped into a heavy, warm blanket of air. Outlines of everything from trees to cars were obscured by steaminess. My thoughts were fuzzy too. So much to do, confusion about where to start, and a separate priority: mommying. It's times like these that call for a husband, a partner, a helper. Heck, I'd even take a part-time nanny.

I glanced at Dean to say goodbye and got stuck in his turquoise stare. It was like visiting an exotic beach. Clear, blue waters beckoned, made me want to gaze and eventually dive in. Blood rushed to my cheeks, and I tried to turn away before he'd notice.

"Thanks again," I called as I hurried toward my minivan. I had less than two hours to finish one more critical task, alone.

Here's my opinion. Every stay-at-home mom's car deserves to be pimped with a retractable roof, thumping speakers, *Sex and the City* DVDs, and a valium dispenser. It's not right that our excitement-deprived lives have to include boring rides.

I try to make up for it with a monster sunroof that douses me with sun and wind. The minute the kids hop out, it slides back, and the tunes go in. I don't don a backward baseball cap and gold chains or anything, but a little Nelly distances me from reality. I just have to remember not to blast 50 Cent in the carpool line.

Today I was in need of support and inspiration. I slipped in a CeCe Winans gospel CD, double checked that my cell was on, and headed for Washington.

I know it's overprotective, but I hate to be more than a few miles from my kids. Driving twenty minutes to Beth's school was uncomfortable but necessary. If I was ever going to be a PI, I'd have to separate from my kids as easily as they separated from me. Maybe I needed a transition object, like Super Teddy riding shotgun.

I exited in the ritzy downtown section of King County. It was odd to imagine throngs of stroller-clad moms lunching and shopping there. Upscale stores were never in my budget. I barely had an outfit nice enough to *shop* for nice outfits.

The skyline rose in graduated steps, from low-slung car lots to oversize stores to high-rise luxury hotels. There was a sudden dropoff where the county meets 495, and then a sense that opulence might never make it across the highway. Strip malls and squat apartment complexes gave way to a mix of older homes, renovations and dilapidated businesses. I'd always wanted to stop at a place advertising psychic readings, but I didn't have the courage, and I wasn't focused on my future today anyhow.

Eventually I turned left into Woodridge's asphalt lot, peppered with sensible sedans and bumper-stickered hand-me-downs. I parked between a curb and a dented, rusty Explorer—probably some teen's precious ticket to freedom. Many of my best adolescent experiences had been in junkers. Cruising with friends to LL Cool J, sneaking off to the beach when my parents were out of town, making out. Privacy was so hard to come by that location didn't matter. An ugly car was paradise compared to no place at all.

I wished the reflection in the rearview mirror matched my teenage self better. I still had skewer-straight black hair and big brown eyes. But my starter wrinkles and thinning skin were giveaways. I'd never pass as a student.

Butterflies filled my stomach, maybe because a police cruiser was in the lot, or maybe because high school affected me the same way it did decades ago—it made me feel inadequate.

A man leaving the main entrance held the door for me and nodded hello, apparently okay with an unfamiliar woman entering the building. Did I look like a teacher or, *horrors*, someone old enough to be a teen's mom? I smiled politely and kept moving. *Don't ask where the library is*, I thought. *He might ask questions, and then I'll have to lie.*

Being misleading ("pretexting" in PI talk) is simply part of an investigation. But it's completely unnatural to me. Usually I let morals—combined with fear and guilt—dictate my life. Maybe pursuing a risky, sneaky career was a sign of trouble, desperation, or insanity. Something to ponder when I had more time. Or a therapist.

I spotted the library after wandering through walls of colorful lockers and white-painted bricks. I even peeked into classrooms and the dreaded cafeteria, where a few kids and teachers were hanging out.

That really made my heart race. Who could forget walking into a room teeming with students, feeling on display and judged? Kenna and I had been semi-popular. I could scarcely imagine being ostracized or worse.

Thinking of Kenna jolted me back to the present. I entered the library and was relieved not to see anyone else. The place was so still I thought it might be empty.

Yearbooks lined a back wall beneath construction paper letters that announced "Woodridge—A Tradition of Excellence." I ran my finger down the line of leather-bound volumes, finding the last four years. I lugged them to the nearest chair and hunkered down.

I scoured Beth's eleventh-grade class, comparing each girl's portrait to hers. Finally I reached the letter M, and there she was. *Beth Myers*. I let her name sink in. Then I flipped through the other books to find her again.

Beth had entered high school just like I had: gawky, with braces and breakouts. Four years had smoothed her skin, lengthened her hair and straightened her teeth. But she didn't look any happier.

Each year she'd joined the diverse and attractive dance team. In every photo, she stood next to the same girl, April Johnson. She was pretty too, with light blue eyes and shiny black hair that belonged in a commercial.

I looked for Marcus and found three junior Marcuses and one senior, Marcus Gomez. I recorded all four names, but instinct told me it was Gomez. He had an indefinable charismatic quality. I tried to put my finger on it. Confidence? Cockiness? An impressive physique? He had broad shoulders, dark eyes, bronze skin, a fuzzy mustache and sharp features. I could imagine Beth being overwhelmed by him. Just looking at his picture drew me in.

On the way out, I stopped at an information rack and picked up a school calendar. I was surprised sports tryouts and practices started in the summer, not the fall. I couldn't help checking an old cafeteria menu too. Pizza and French fries were still staples, but so were encouraging options, like hummus and zucchini. I had one foot out the door and was about to escape lie-free.

"Excuse me," a woman said. Damn.

"Yes?" I turned and saw her at the front desk. Either she'd beamed herself there or librarians really know how to be silent.

"I noticed you by the yearbooks. What are you looking for?"

I hated and loved how fast my answer flew out. "I'm a sports reporter. I don't want to miss any events or misspell any names."

"Oh."

Before she could continue, I hightailed it out of there, sweating long before I reached the afternoon heat.

It wasn't until I pulled out of the parking lot that I realized the lie wasn't necessary. The truth might have been helpful. *I'm looking for a girl named Beth Myers. She's missing. Do you know her? How about April Johnson? What about Marcus Gomez?*

I recalled that at one time in life, I was good at telling lies, and I hadn't minded at all. It was in high school. Few things had mattered more than having fun and staying out of trouble. Something to remember when investigating kids.

I made my way back toward downtown, retrieved my phone from its cupholder storage spot, and eyed the drivers around me. A turbaned man in an ancient Chevy. An Asian woman in a champagne SUV. A shirtless guy in a yellow Jeep. Everyone appropriately focused on the road. Normally I didn't make calls while driving, but if I waited until Jack and Sophie were home, I'd end up saying "What?" and "Hold on a second" endlessly, so I compromised by waiting for a red light, speed-dialing Kenna and using my Bluetooth speaker.

"I just left the high school," I told her. "The birth mother's name is Beth Myers."

"Really? It's so weird to know that."

"I'm sorry. You were going to find out anyway, right?"

"Yeah. Our adoption was semi-open, so we didn't share last names and addresses and stuff, but we were going to eventually. I just wasn't quite ready."

"I'm sorry. I feel awful. I shouldn't have blurted it out like that. I'm hurrying because I'm at a red light. Do you want me to give you some time and call back in a little while?"

"No. It's okay. Keep going."

I told her what I knew and agreed to touch base after dinner. I wanted to review Dean's advice, and she needed to consult Andy.

It always struck me when people had to run something by a spouse. I didn't have that responsibility—or that luxury. I always got my way, but it was a heavy burden to make every decision, and I still had to compromise with myself. I wanted to ask Kenna, my go-to advisor, *Is it okay to be dishonest for a good cause? What about invading Beth's privacy? Am I being horribly insensitive to everyone involved?* But she needed my help, not my confusion.

Uneasiness drew me like a magnet to the kids' camp and their sweaty, sunscreened faces, stories about the day, and nonstop needs. They make it impossible to focus on anything else. A challenge, yes, but also an incredible blessing.

The minivan went from empty to full. Backpacks and lunch bags crowded the kids' feet. Art projects made their way forward and sprinkled glitter on the empty passenger seat. The silence was broken by Sophie's, "I'm thirsty!" and Jack's, "Reggie said atomic wedgie today. What the heck is an atomic wedgie?"

I fished a water bottle out of the summer "supply" bag between the front seats, a disorganized tangle of goggles, lotion, drinks, pool passes, dive sticks and half-read magazines.

"I want to go home," Jack said. "I'm pooped." This was his new favorite expression, since it involved legitimate use of a bathroom word.

"I'm pooped too," Sophie laughed. "Can we listen to *Aladdin*?"

"Yes. Buckle up."

Both kids struggled into seatbelts and made song requests. I uncapped the water, handed it to Sophie, found the *Aladdin* CD, negotiated an agreement on song twenty-three, gingerly defined atomic wedgie, prayed my definition would not be tested, and headed home.

By eight o'clock, *I* was pooped. I'd just tucked the kids into bed when the doorbell rang.

"Who is it?" Jack yelled from upstairs. I hoped Sophie wouldn't come running down. I needed the peaceful miracle of bedtime.

I peeked out the doorside window and saw Kenna.

"It's just Auntie Kenna, sweetie," I called softly to Jack. Maybe Sophie had already conked out. "Relax and go to sleep."

"*I* have to relax," Kenna said when I let her in. She pushed two beer bottles toward me. "Got an opener?"

"Of course."

We walked into the kitchen and she rummaged in the fridge while I cracked the beers. Another benefit of being neighbors—no driving home.

"Ugh," she said. "Don't you have any junk food?"

"Look in the pantry. There are cookies," I defended myself. "And there's ice cream in the freezer." No need to mention it was low fat, soy, and more "ice" than "cream."

"Never mind. I need something that goes with beer."

"Popcorn then. You know where it is."

Kenna found the organic, no-oil-added popcorn and stuck a bag in the microwave. I caught her rolling her eyes as she read the label. For an aerobics teacher, her diet was surprisingly all inclusive. One of the perks of her job, I guess.

Popping kernels filled the room with an aroma better than any taste could be. I wondered whether it would soothe Jack to sleep or lure him downstairs.

I got the feeling Kenna's casual presentation was self-protective. Nothing could be more emotional than what we had to discuss. Children. Motherhood. Loss. It was nothing new to her, and that was the problem.

I poured popcorn into ceramic bowls and we crunched away.

"So." I gave her an opening.

"I think I'm going to have a nervous breakdown." That was a brave start.

"What do you mean?"

"I've hit my limit. I can't stop crying. I have chest pains."

"Chest pains?"

"Stabs of anxiety. Every time I think of Beth on her own." Her hand on her heart was proof.

"I know those. They're awful. I got them after Jason and my Dad." I still didn't like saying *died*. "Is Andy being supportive?"

"Yes, but he's less worried about Beth than about getting our money back for another adoption."

"You could lose the money you invested in this one?"

"It's more like we'd have to pay some fees again. I don't want to get into that, though." She waved a hand dismissively. "I want to find Beth."

"How does Andy feel about us looking for her?"

"He thinks she's running from the adoption, so to him it's pointless."

"But he didn't ask you to stop?"

"No. He must be too scared to ask. He knows I'm over the edge." She laughed.

"And he loves you."

She tugged a folded paper from her back pocket. "Here's everything I could think of about Beth. I took notes during our conversations so I could remember what she said. You know, in case the baby wants to know someday."

"That's so nice." I skimmed them, and random details stood out. *Argues a lot with mom. Only child. Loves Disney World. Scared of snakes.* The more I knew about Beth, the more I sensed her vulnerability and knew I couldn't give up on her, even if it meant making questionable calls.

"I'm sorry I didn't tell you all the little stuff about Beth before," Kenna said. "It's just that if I let it out..." She looked around as if searching for words. "It would have made it so real. There would have been so much more to take back..."

"It's okay," I said. "You did what you needed to do to protect yourself. I totally understand."

I gave her a hug and pointed to a stack of papers on the kitchen table. "That's everything I learned today. Or everything I *need* to learn."

"From Dean?"

"Yup." By now most of it was dry, albeit a little wrinkly.

"How'd he look?" Another effort to lighten the mood. I ran with it to make her laugh.

"Doable."

Three

Kenna and I made some crazy-ass decisions. I don't know what gave us the courage—the beer, desperation, or a history of making prank calls as kids. First, we called every Gomez near Woodridge High and asked for Marcus. Kenna had confirmed Marcus was a senior, and Marcus Gomez was the only senior "Marcus" in the yearbook.

We would have called all the Johnsons, asking for April, but there had to be hundreds. We got the expected variety of responses: *Who? Wrong number. Click.* And finally, *He's not home,* in a drowsy woman's voice. That was perfect, because we didn't want to talk to him. Not yet. I wrote down his address along with Beth's, which we found using her parents' first names from the adoption application and her last name from the yearbook. It felt like a good but slow start.

So we took it a step further. Kenna agreed to stay at my house while the kids slept. I agreed to do my first stakeout. I'd hardly sipped my beer, but I gave it time to wear off anyway, hoping that would change my mind. Meanwhile I gathered a camera, fill-in-the-blank stakeout forms from PI class, a juice box, and organic animal crackers. Not high-tech surveillance supplies, but better than nothing. Someday I'd have cool stuff like night vision goggles and hidden microphones, which I was pretty sure they sold at Toys "R" Us these days.

That brought something to mind. Hadn't binoculars come in a Scholastic books package for Jack? Had they been part of a Scooby-Doo club? I crept into his room and dug through his toy chest as quietly as possible. Each time I lifted a toy, it sounded like a muffled avalanche.

"What are you doing?" Kenna whispered from the doorway.

I spotted Jack's collection of detective supplies. A flashlight. A magnifying glass. A notepad. I held the binoculars triumphantly over my head.

"What in the world?" Kenna said. For some reason they were designed to look like a square jigsaw puzzle. I had to extend the pieces to make them work.

"Binoculars," I told her, doing my best not to wake Jack. "Undercover. They might come in handy." I put them to my eyes. I went from seeing Kenna's whole body to seeing her waist, where khaki shorts, a white T-shirt and a cute polka dot belt met. The toy worked. I grabbed the flashlight and notepad for good measure.

"I think I'm prepared. But I have to pee." I'd heard more stories about PI pee than necessary. They all shared a common moral: Peeing in a car is annoying for men and nearly impossible for women. I'd never admit it freely, but when my kids were potty training, I'd rigged a decent travel system using a kiddie toilet and plastic bags—good enough for an adult to use in an emergency. When you're a single mom with curious toddlers, bathroom stalls are not your friends. I still had that potty somewhere, bleached and ready for the next road trip.

"Anything else you need?" Kenna asked when I was ready to go.

I looked at my bulging backpack. Leave it to me to over prepare. Heaven forbid I'm stranded without wipes or an extra outfit at the appropriate moment. I had so much stuff that I'd have trouble finding what I needed. "A gun?" I joked.

"You'll be fine," she said. "You're just taking a look. And the neighborhoods aren't that bad."

That bad? I hadn't been worried about the neighborhoods. *Aren't that bad* meant kind of bad. Too late now. I threw on the pack, wiggled my feet into Nikes, and reviewed the directions I'd printed out. They made sense, but I'd probably screw them up somehow.

"If Marcus goes anywhere, remember the turns so you can find your way out," Kenna cautioned, as if reading my mind.

"Great idea." I tried to remember where I'd stashed my pen.

"I feel so much better knowing you're doing this," she added. Well, that made one of us.

I walked out the door saying I'd check in frequently, a promise I wouldn't keep.

* * *

My first stop was Beth's townhouse. I expected it to be rundown, showing outward signs of whatever family trouble might exist inside. Instead, the end unit looked prim and proper, with its trimmed mini-lawn and bushes, brick façade and flower boxes brimming with orange fluffiness. Behind it was a neighborhood tot lot.

I parked in a nearby visitor spot to get a better feel for the place. I imagined Beth going up and down the cement sidewalk or driving up the asphalt driveway into the garage. I didn't get a cheery feeling from the house, but I couldn't find anything wrong with it either. The windows were dark and the curtains were drawn, which was normal at 11 p.m.

The surrounding houses were similarly quiet and well tended. Neat landscaping. Coiled hoses. Empty driveways. Some had flags with summer themes. The messiest yard held scattered plastic toys, a tricycle and a kiddie pool. If I lived nearby, that would probably be my favorite neighbor—the parent who couldn't pull it together before collapsing into bed. The street felt safe, as though any disturbance would stand out.

After twenty minutes of uneventful observation, I put the car in drive. Off to look for a gang member.

Marcus's neighborhood was fabulous if you appreciate fixer uppers, BEWARE OF DOG signs, and loud, customized cars. I drove just fast enough to avoid being a target for potentially bored, armed teens. As I neared his street, I had to slow down and get my bearings. I resisted the impulse to wave at three guys on the corner. Instead I stared straight ahead and hoped they didn't notice me.

I turned right, and three blocks later I parked across from Marcus's '70s-style split-level home. I doubted its window bars had been an original option. It was surrounded by a chain link fence perfect for little ones or pets. (No running into the street!) But here, maybe it kept people out.

I shut off my headlights and sat in darkness. The ignition emitted a tiny green glow I'd never noticed before, probably because there are street lamps galore in my neighborhood, something I'd taken for granted. I left the keys in place for light and a quick escape.

I felt around the backpack while my eyes adjusted. I wanted a surveillance log, which I'd forgotten to use at Beth's house. After a minute of digging frustration, I dumped everything on the passenger seat and found one.

I lowered my head to get a closer look, accomplishing hiding and writing at the same time. I listed details about the time and location, including license plate numbers on the cars around me. I noted that Marcus's front door was open with only a screen door as a barrier. Did the house need fresh air? Was there nothing inside to protect? The hall light was on and the windows were dark except for a basement half-window in the rear corner of the house, which cast soft yellow light onto the weeds outside. I wanted to sneak up and look inside, but that was way out of my league.

I was just starting to settle in and munch on animal crackers when I noticed something in the rearview mirror. The teens from around the corner were heading my way, and upon closer inspection, one had Marcus's solid build and light mustache. I stuffed my notes under the seat, relocked the doors, and crouched down. Slowly, I squeezed between the kids' seats to the back of the van, where I hoped tinted windows would shield me from view.

As soon as I got to the third row, I wished I'd brought my cell phone. How many times had victims called the police while being carjacked? At least the van didn't have a trunk for anyone to stuff me in. I pressed my face into the gray, brushed fabric bench. My outfit was dark and my tan was decent, so I imagined blending in, as if visualization would help. Anxiety and lack of air conditioning made the van uncomfortably warm and slightly stifling. I turned my face sideways and took a slow, deep breath. Voices were coming closer.

"We need a ride," one guy said.

Footsteps moved past me and stopped.

"Keys in the ignition," said another. Uh oh. My mistake. "Lotsa shit in the front seat." Oops again. Good thing the binoculars looked like a jigsaw puzzle.

Someone jiggled the door handle, sending a zing of fear through my limbs and gut. What if I'd pressed *unlock* instead of *lock*?

"Come on, man. We don't need that heat. We'll use my ma's car."

I didn't move until their voices faded away. Then I lifted my head just enough to use the rear passenger window. The teens, similarly dressed in baggy jeans and tight T-shirts, went into Marcus's house and closed the front door. I waited nervously, thinking about him. If he'd done something to Beth, would he be walking around, socializing and laughing? Sure. Violence was a way of life for gang members. Sad to say, many of them had grown up with it.

Finally they emerged, cigarettes lit, one carrying the remains of a six pack. I tried not to judge. If you watched a rerun of my teen years, many scenes would look like this. I didn't smoke, but I was ready to party. Dad would have been transporting passengers somewhere, and Mom would have been home, asleep. Two clueless parents, one drunk teen. I still marvel that I survived.

I crawled to the second row for a better view. The guys were sauntering toward a red Grand Marquis with impressive patches of rust. Marcus took the driver's seat while the others surveyed their surroundings before hopping in. The car was a few spaces from mine, but its stereo might as well have been on my roof. Hardcore rap pulsed through the van, vulgar and packed with enough lingo to confuse most adults. I waited for them to drive two blocks before pulling out with my lights off.

I fumbled around, hoping to write down the new street name, but I was too slow. I'd have to remember it. *Left on Baylor*. Wait. Coming back, it would be a right on Baylor. *Right on Baylor, right on Baylor. Left on Willow. Right on Payne.* Ahhh! I lost track. I had the sinking feeling they were heading deeper and deeper into the neighborhood. Maybe they were cruising gang territory.

That theory was nixed when I noticed heavy traffic and a lack of parking spots. Teens marched down a sidewalk like ants to an anthill, toting drinks to a crowded front porch and dimly lit home. I squinted at the disheveled abode and its neighbors, trying to determine the address, but it was too dark. I wasn't even sure the houses *had* numbers. They might have peeled off with the paint.

Marcus was three cars ahead, creeping along, with no place to fit his boat of a vehicle. One pal leaned out the passenger window, gesturing toward the party. I slid down my window to hear what he was yelling. Instead I heard several loud cracks. The Marquis veered right, scraping the front of a shiny sedan, and then came to rest against a black pickup's bumper, while mayhem erupted on the porch. Teens ran screaming to and from the house, car doors slammed, and kids tore down the street using all forms of transportation, including a skateboard.

Two cars were stuck behind Marcus, whose angled car was oddly still, blocking both lanes. I couldn't see the other drivers, but judging by how many passengers they'd stuffed in their back seats, they were either kids or clowns.

I had three desires. I wanted to call 911, but I didn't have a clue where I was. I wanted to help Marcus in case he was shot, but I was afraid to get out. I also wanted to back up and get the heck out of there. It was time to get creative.

No one was behind me, so I gave an extended honk, hit reverse, and heard the contents of my front seat fly forward. I continued backward until I reached the corner, where I threw my wheel to the right and parked under a street sign that identified my location. Not bad. The cars in front of me backed up too and fled the scene.

I felt frantic, but everything was in slow motion. All I could think of was Marcus. I threw open my door and dialed on the run. I have no idea what information was requested or given, but I babbled all the way to his car, where the sight of him slumped over the steering wheel, perfectly still, stopped me. He was alone, apparently abandoned while his friends ran for cover. I was too afraid to confirm it by looking around. If anyone was nearby, particularly with a gun, I didn't want to know.

I crouched, hauled open the car's enormous door, and looked at Marcus's chest. I thought it was rising and falling.

"I think he's alive," I told the 911 operator. Then I noticed the dark stain on his lap, growing as drips fell from somewhere above. "But he's not okay. He's definitely not okay."

Neither was I, although my discomfort was nothing compared to Marcus's suffering. I'd never seen so much blood, and the thought of finding its origin was scary. I rose slowly and leaned behind him.

Supported by the back of his seat, I peered around to the other side of his face, where a bullet had struck his temple. The open flesh reminded me of the time Sophie cracked her chin on a counter, and the gash looked like cut, raw meat, something my vegetarian brain wasn't used to. Just like with Sophie, I thought I should cover the wound for both our sakes.

I didn't have any spare cloth, and I didn't think I should waste time checking Marcus's trunk. I wavered between ripping off my shirt or pants and then had a brainstorm. I'd use my cotton bra. (Socks or underwear seemed unsanitary.) It wasn't huge, darn it, but it would do. I unhooked the clasp, pulled it through a sleeve, and pressed a B-cup to his head. He moved, and I yelped. His eyes flew open, slid toward me, and closed again. Sirens rang in the distance, and I thanked God. Repeatedly.

It was almost 1 a.m. when my shaking hands turned the deadbolt at home. The night had been everything terrible: scary, shocking, disappointing, sad, disgusting. I flipped on lights for the illusion of warmth as I moved through the foyer, bathroom (where I washed my hands twice), family room, dining room, and kitchen. There was no sign of Kenna, but apparently she'd been busy. Our beer bottles were in the recycling bin. The popcorn bag was trashed next to an empty pint of soy ice cream and a crinkled dark chocolate candy bar wrapper. No foul play here, just a stressed out aerobics instructor with a high metabolism.

I walked back to the front of the house and heard familiar shuffling. I peeked up and saw Jack clutching Super Teddy on the landing.

"Mommy?"

"Yes honey?" I jogged upstairs.

"Why is Auntie Kenna here?"

I wanted to pick him up and snuggle, but I hadn't inspected myself. There might be blood on me. I ruffled his hair and patted his shoulder. "I had to go out sweetie, so she babysat. Where is she?"

"She was with me because I had a bad dream. Now she's in Sophie's room."

Poor Kenna. She'd had to play musical beds. No matter what I tried, my kids woke me up with complaints, knowing I was a sucker for sleeping with them, and they disturbed each other in the process. You never knew where anyone would be in the morning. I needed someone to Ferberize *me*.

I guided Jack past Sophie's room, where Kenna and Sophie snoozed on their backs, Sophie's head in the crook of Kenna's arm. I tucked him back into bed with assurances that I wasn't going anywhere else. He drifted off in seconds.

I took a shower and dumped my clothes in the washer. (My bra didn't make it home. Hopefully it wouldn't end up in court as evidence. Talk about being tempted to lie under oath.) Dressed in pajama bottoms and a T-shirt, I tapped Kenna's arm and whispered her name. She rose without disturbing Sophie.

"What happened?" she rasped. "You didn't call, and you didn't answer, either. I was freaking out!"

"It got a little crazy."

Despite the hour, she wanted to hear everything, including what I'd told the cops. Thinking about it nauseated me. I was an honest person. I respected law enforcement. And I hadn't been straightforward.

"I was so scared of messing up your adoption. I told them I was lost and what I'd seen. They asked if I knew 'Marcus Gomez,' and I said no. I mean, I *was* lost, and I *don't* know him."

"I can't believe you saw him. And he's shot! You probably saved him." Her mouth hung open.

I was afraid probably *not*. Yes, he'd been alive enough to scare me silly and rush off in an ambulance, but he'd been shot in the head. How often did people survive that?

An image from the past filled my mind. I was working on a hospital psychiatric unit. It was my first post-college job, so I was the lowest on the totem pole: a psychiatric technician. I did everything from take blood pressure to conduct "suicide checks"—monitoring patients' safety every few minutes. One woman was admitted for shooting herself. She'd survived just fine and walked around the unit, pleasant as can be, with a telltale bandage around her head. It was bizarre.

The image switched to Marcus's injury, which in retrospect seemed rather small. Then I saw police officers fanning out, knocking on doors, questioning me. Why hadn't I been truthful? Could I have hurt Beth by holding back? If they questioned me again, would it be too late?

"I can't believe any of this," I replied.

"We should sleep on it," Kenna said.

"We should, but we won't."

We rehashed everything until my eyes closed involuntarily, right after watching Kenna walk home safely.

Four

You can't watch or listen to the news with kids. Not unless you want to explain things like murder, sexual assault and, despite the weather guy's prediction of thunderstorms, the necessity of wearing sunscreen to camp.

Yet I had to turn it on. So when Sophie poked me awake at 6:45, I put on the Disney Channel in my room and stumbled downstairs to watch a local report. Good thing, since Marcus's shooting was the lead story at seven, complete with video of his car surrounded by officers and flashing lights.

Officials say shots were fired outside a King County party last night. An eighteen-year-old victim is in serious condition, and neighbors say the shooting may have been gang related. No arrests have been made. Anyone with information should call the number on the screen.

For so many reasons, I was relieved Marcus was alive. For the sake of human life, for Beth's sake if he knew where she was, and for the baby's sake if he or she needed him in any way.

He or she. I closed my eyes and pictured a precious little one, growing inside Beth, waiting to meet the right family. I got teary and spent a few minutes asking for divine intervention.

"Mom?" It was Sophie. "What are you doing?"

"Just praying." She walked over and stood next to me. I pressed *record* on the DVR remote and clicked off the TV.

"I have a prayer."

I loved these little insights into my kids' minds. I looked into her eyes. "What is it?"

"I want to do Slip 'N Slide."

Not as deep as I'd hoped. Possibly the simplest request God would receive that day.

"We can do Slip 'N Slide. When you get dressed, put on a bathing suit instead of an outfit." She jumped up and down in her princess nightgown, making excited noises, and scurried off. "Find some water toys too," I called. Hopefully that would keep her busy for a few minutes.

As I headed toward my office, I realized I'd set an unintentional record. It had been more than twenty-four hours since I'd checked email. I knew just what I could have missed.

One of the benefits of living in King County, Virginia, is the email alert system, which contacts residents about various issues. It's a dream come true if you like technology and avoid the news.

You can sign up for everything from storm warnings to traffic reports to crime information, and sadly, there are often emails about missing kids.

Lo and behold, an alert titled "Police seek help in finding pregnant teen" had arrived the day before.

King County police are requesting the public's help in locating Beth Myers, 18, who was reported as a runaway by her family. She is 5 feet 6 inches tall, 160 pounds, with brown hair and green eyes. At 38 weeks pregnant, she is in need of immediate medical care. Beth lives in East King County and is known to have friends in Western King. She was last seen at home wearing blue jean shorts and a green tank top. If you have any information about her whereabouts, please call the number below.

Beth's photo was attached. I highlighted the message and forwarded it to Andy, since Kenna didn't use email. The phone rang almost immediately and indicated their number.

"I got that email. Thanks," Andy said.

"You're welcome."

"The police have it covered, don't you think?"

I wasn't sure what to say. "I don't know."

"I appreciate everything you're doing." He lowered his voice. "Although I really wish you'd tell Kenna to be careful. We don't want to get in trouble with First Steps and lose our chance for future adoptions. You know?"

I saw his point. But I also knew Kenna was committed to Beth—the same way Beth had seemed committed to them.

"I'm sorry. I don't want to be in the middle," I said. "I promise to talk with Kenna before I do anything else. And Andy, I'm really sorry about this situation. I know it's awful for both of you."

"Thanks. Hold on. Let me get Kenna."

He yelled for her twice and she picked up with a yawn.

"Morning," I said. "Awake?"

"I have to be. Class." She yawned again.

I updated her on the morning news, email, and conversation with Andy. She was relieved about everything and understanding about Andy.

"He just wants what's best for both of us. As much as I want to be a mom, he wants to be a dad."

I felt a surge of sympathy for him. Any guy who truly wants to be a dad, a *good* dad, gets a gold star in my book.

"Did you tell him about last night?" I asked.

"Not yet. That's next."

"He's going to be upset. I'm glad I didn't say anything."

"Good grief. Me too. Don't worry. I'll talk to him." She moved on. "So the email mentioned 'friends in Western King?' Do you think that's me and Andy?"

"I don't know. I wonder if the police are going to talk to you. Or if you should call them."

"Maybe First Steps gave them our names. If the police call us, it's okay. But I don't want to call them and upset First Steps, Beth, or her family—not to mention Andy—since everyone thinks I'm wrong."

She sounded sure, so I changed tactics.

"Do you think I should visit the hospital? I could sit in the waiting room and see who visits Marcus."

She paused. "I guess that's a good idea. Won't it be hard to tell?"

"I think it's worth a shot." I sucked in my breath at my choice of words. "I mean a try."

Kenna filled me in on her plans for the day, which included teaching low-impact, step, and body sculpting classes, plus helping with membership sales. She apologized for leaving me alone with the search.

"The manager would panic if I left him hanging right now. Everyone rearranged their schedules to pitch in when I'm...I mean if I'm on maternity leave." She groaned. "If I could quit, I would, just to help find Beth."

"I know."

"Honestly, though, you wouldn't want me around. I've never felt like this. I have to distract myself, or I'll cry nonstop. Your kids would be scared of me."

"Maybe you should call the counselor at First Steps, or someone else, just to talk. You can't live like this for long."

She was quiet. "Do you think I'm crazy?" she finally asked.

"No way. I just think you need relief."

"The only way I'll get it is if someone finds Beth."

So much for talking her out of anything. Sorry, Andy.

By the time Jack woke up, Sophie had a collection of water toys that filled two beach pails. We ate waffles with syrup for breakfast (one step away from cake and icing), so I hoped they wouldn't get sick from landing repeatedly on their bellies.

I spread the Slip 'N Slide on the grass next to our house and connected the hose. A blow-up ridge at the end collected water like a tiny pool. Nothing could stop me from laughing as the kids splashed into it and screamed with abandon. It was only 9 a.m., but so hot I could practically feel skin cancer forming on my arms. The sparkling water looked irresistible.

"You do it, Mom!" Jack urged with perfect timing.

"I don't have a bathing suit on." I surveyed my black polyester shorts and red tank top, thinking I could get away with it if I wanted to. I didn't fit the size guidelines on the box, though.

"Come on. Just do it." He must have sensed my deliberation.

"Go Mommy! Go Mommy!" Sophie chanted.

Has anyone ever compared kid pressure to peer pressure? Kid pressure must have the edge. Parents are totally disarmed by love and exhaustion.

I took a few steps back from the tarp, ran forward, and dove. Water blinded me as I flew down the mat, right over the pool into the muddy grass, where I collided like a bowling ball with Sophie's pails, water guns and plastic boats. I arose soaked, disoriented, and determined to be enthusiastic.

"Woohoo! Go Slip 'N Slide!" I rubbed my eyes and saw something blurry, yet familiar, moving toward us.

"Good one," Dean said. "You really had some momentum there."

I brushed hair clumps out of my face and forced myself to smile. "Wow. What are you doing here?" I glanced around for something, anything, to hide behind. A towel, sunglasses, a tree. Nada. I pulled my wet shirt away from my chest.

"I brought you something." He held out a book on missing children. I didn't want to take it for several reasons. I didn't want to get it wet, my hand was busy separating my shirt from my thin, clingy bra, and I hadn't showered, shaved or put on makeup. Only my mouth moved.

"Thanks. Could you put it on the porch? I don't want to ruin it."

"Yeah." He stood still, as if he was waiting for something. "Sorry I didn't call first. I was in the area, so I thought I'd stop by. I had your address from the class roster."

"That was really nice." It was also a mistake. Memo to all: Never expect a stay-at-home mom (or her car, home, children, etc.) to be ready for unexpected company. Many of us need at least an hour to stuff things in closets and make it look like life is under control.

My gaze turned to Jack and Sophie, the blessed reasons for my near-insanity, who were staring at Dean. "These are my kids, Jack and Sophie," I said. "Guys, this is one of my teachers, Mr. Summers."

"He has really big muscles," Sophie said. "Is he Superman?" I stifled some follow-up jokes and apologized for her.

"You must be strong," Jack agreed.

Dean smiled at me. "I do alright. Anyhow, here you go." He stepped away and placed the book on my porch. "See you in class?"

What? I'd almost forgotten about class. It was the next night, Wednesday. "I'll be there." I smiled bravely as drips rolled down my forehead. "Thanks again."

He waved at the kids with a wink and a bemused grin. "Nice to meet you guys." His blue eyes focused on me. "I want to hear how things are going. Maybe you could stay after class a few minutes?"

"Sure." I felt inappropriately nervous, as if he'd asked me for a date, which he hadn't.

His next three words made me want to head straight for the nearest mall, beauty salon, and fitness center. (Okay, maybe just the mall and the salon.)

"See you soon."

The sky got overcast and the kids got goose bumps, so we hung the Slip 'N Slide over a railing to dry and rushed up to the bathroom. I stripped off my wet clothes, threw on a robe and gave them a warm bath. Then, to keep them out of trouble, I sent them to their rooms with firm instructions: Dry off, put on an outfit Mommy will like, and play until I get out of the shower.

Under the hottest streams of water I could stand, I tried to scrub away the memory of how I must have looked to Dean. *It doesn't matter*, I told myself. *It's not like we have a chance of dating. He's out of my league, and he's not going to take on kids, á la the real Brad Pitt. On the positive side, if we ever do date, he's already seen me at my worst. Shouldn't that be a relief?*

By the time I dried my hair and pulled on jean capris and a pink T-shirt, I wasn't worried about Dean anymore. Maybe it was being clean, semi-presentable and deodorized, or maybe it was the distraction of kids running circles around the first floor, playing tag-and-tackle. It's undeniable that while entertaining each other, they could also seriously injure one another—accidentally of course. That was enough to worry about.

I let them play for a few more minutes, watching more carefully than a boxing referee. Finally the stress was too much and I separated them with an announcement.

"Camp time!" We'd be ridiculously early if they started getting ready now. But based on history, that wouldn't happen. We'd arrive ten minutes late after half an hour of cajoling them into outfits, shoes and sunscreen.

Thank goodness I looked decent, because we were late to camp as expected, and I had to escort them in instead of using the beloved carpool line, which allows frazzled parents to hide in the front seat while teachers retrieve kids from the back. More than once, I'd had to walk in tardy, tucked into a hat and last-minute outfit, hoping not to be noticed. Those days I'd inevitably run into Perfect Mom, some random parent who had the time and money not only to assemble stylish outfits, but accessorize them too. She'd pull off in her luxury sedan, turning the wheel with her French manicure, which she somehow afforded along with the camp fee I struggled to pay, probably off to get her hair done. *Or maybe to go home and cry about her miserable, shallow life. No, that's horribly petty,* I'd correct myself. *I hope she's happy and fulfilled and inspiration for me to get myself together.*

Today I looked presentable enough, so I used the opportunity to greet everyone I knew with confidence. Most of the counselors were experienced teachers I'd known for two years. Their assistants were college or high school students with refreshing enthusiasm. I admired their dedication to working hard instead of lounging around all summer, which is what I wished I could do. Hopefully they were having fun with the kids.

Jack kissed me goodbye and ran into class, where friends were constructing Lego spaceships. Sophie wouldn't even grace me with a kiss, demanding, "Go home, Mom!" I hid my disappointment and reminded myself that independence was one of her best qualities—one I could use more of. It would serve her well in life.

I wished everyone a good day and made my way back through art-covered walls. I scanned them for Sophie and Jack's work but didn't see any. As a passing toddler sneezed into his hands, I casually wondered where there were more germs. Here? Or in the hospital I was about to visit?

* * *

These days, when a baby is born, you might as well treat the parents for OCD. Is it possible to become a parent and not a compulsive, hand-washing germaphobe? For the first several years, you spend every day wiping snot and poop, watching commercials about the horrors of not using antibacterial soaps, wipes, and cleansers. When both kids were in diapers, I was sure our family could cause an E. coli outbreak. Finally, I rebelled, trusting good old soap and water. And what do you know? It worked!

With determination not to fear germs in mind, I walked into the hospital and allowed myself to breathe normally and press elevator buttons with my bare hands, although I did use my knuckles instead of fingertips. Visions of Marcus's dripping blood pushed their way into my consciousness, and I couldn't help wondering how many times red spots had hit the floor of the elevator transporting me from the ER lobby to the ICU, where I guessed he was admitted. I shifted my feet and replaced gruesome thoughts with images of hardworking custodians mopping away signs of suffering.

The elevator came to a smooth stop anyone in pain would appreciate. The doors slid open to reveal a placard directing ICU visitors to the right. A smaller sign informed me I was in a "quiet area" that promoted patient healing. True to this goal, Marcus's unit seemed relatively calm compared to what I expected. Last time I'd been hospitalized (to give birth) there had been no shortage of moaning and screaming.

There was a nursing station ahead, softly abuzz with beeping, ringing, and talking sounds. I had no intention of checking in with anyone there. I tried to look relaxed as I glanced around for a waiting area where I might observe comings and goings. I spotted it on the left, complete with requisite vinyl chairs, pressed wood tables, wrinkled magazines, a phone, and a TV. The room was big enough to disappear into—completely out of the nurses' view.

I was the only one there, so I had my pick of seats. Hmmm. By the entrance, where I'd see everyone and overhear staff banter? In the middle, where I could eavesdrop on visitors, no matter where they sat? Or by the TV, to catch up on soap operas?

I forced my eyes away from impossibly timeless actors and sat three seats from the door where I could fake-read *People* and real-people watch. Unfortunately, there wasn't much to see. Every visitor made a beeline for the nurses' station and didn't return. No teens in sight. With intense focus, I picked up snatches of conversation, such as "He's doing fine" and "Are you on his visitor list?"

The longer I waited, the more frustrated I got. Every minute I was here, Beth was somewhere else, surely without the support she needed. I couldn't help imagining her alone and afraid. Enough. I stood, threw my purse over my shoulder, and marched to the nurses' station.

"Hi," I said to a petite woman in blue scrubs. "I'm here to visit Marcus Gomez. Am I in the right place?"

She tapped on a keyboard and checked a screen. "Your name?"

"Nicki Valentine."

"Okay. Do you have a code?"

"No. Actually, I don't know what you mean. Marcus doesn't know me. I'm the one who called 911 last night when he got shot. I thought he was taken here, and I just want to make sure he's okay. I thought maybe—"

She held up a finger. "Hang on." She left the curved desk and padded down the hall in thick, silent sneakers. Soon after a left at the third room, she emerged with a nurse who wore no makeup and didn't bother to color, never mind comb, the wiry hair around her face. I pegged her as a veteran, the kind you'd want sticking you with a needle if necessary. Also the kind with enough authority to bend the rules.

She glanced at me and I smiled in greeting. No response. Then she reentered the room, stayed for about thirty seconds, and treaded back down the hall with nurse number one.

"You can see him," she said.

"Thank you so much." I felt like I'd been given an expensive gift I had no idea how to use. Something that intimidated me. Something like exercise equipment. "So he's totally conscious?" I confirmed.

"Yes. He's hooked up to various monitors, but he's awake, and he can talk. He's in Room Three." She pointed at the room they'd exited.

Brilliant. If only I knew what to ask him. *If you want to* be *a detective*, I reminded myself, *then act like one.* What was the old expression? "Fake it 'til you make it?" I had a lot of frickin' faking to do.

Five

Marcus watched as I bobbed past a large window that allowed for easy observation of his room. It made sense that in the ICU they'd keep a close eye on both patients and visitors.

Other than a thick, white bandage wrapped turban-style around his head, he looked good. Warm complexion. No obvious bleeding. Focused, brown eyes that locked with mine as I rounded the doorjamb. Ugh. There was no turning back.

"Hi, I'm Nicki. You probably don't remember me, huh?" I said.

"You look kinda familiar. But I don't remember nothing."

"Well, you were a little busy when we met." His lips turned up at the corners. "Did they tell you why I'm here?"

"Yeah." He stared out the window, which from our angle displayed threatening clouds. Then he glanced at me. "So thanks."

"I was worried about you. How ya feeling?" I glanced at the machines connected to his body. Pulse seventy-five and rising. Respirations fifteen. Several IV bags dripping clear goodness into his veins. If someone hooked me up to those monitors, they'd see my pulse racing and know I was holding my breath—all in fear of saying the wrong thing. I was talking to a *gang member* after all. A possible kidnapper or murderer. The birth father of Kenna's baby. *Holy crap!*

"No pain, long as they keep giving me this shi...stuff." He raised an arm toward the IV bags. I wished I could take a hit off them. "They say the bullet just grazed me, you know? But I got some bleeding in my head, so I gotta be observed for a while. Get antibiotics. Then I'm outta here." He looked around the room as if considering an escape.

I blew out a sigh of relief. "Wow. I'm so glad you're okay." I pictured his car's interior. Where had the bullet actually landed? I didn't remember any damage, but the car was a dump, and I'd been preoccupied. "Is it okay if I sit down?"

He shrugged. "If you want."

I settled into a blue vinyl chair and crossed my legs. If the kids had been there, they'd have laughed at the noises it made when I shifted to face him.

"I don't want to bother you, Marcus. I'm just worried about what happened. Last night was crazy. Do you know who did this to you?"

He shook his bandaged head almost imperceptibly. We were so close I could see black specks in his cola-colored eyes and arm veins pushed to the surface by bulging muscles. A mustache and stubble added to the misimpression he was a man, not a teen.

"All I know," he said, "is somebody's gonna pay."

How was I supposed to respond to that? Obviously, he had general ideas about the shooter, since he was planning revenge, but he didn't give specifics. It all seemed pretty gang-ish and intimidating. Part of me, though, saw past his tough-guy shell. He was really a kid. Alone in the hospital. Shot in the head. Sorry, but that had to be scary, even for a gangster.

"I really hope the police figure it out," I said. "Has your family been able to visit yet?"

"No. I talked to my ma. But her car's messed up now. I guess I hit something. You see that?"

"Yeah. You hit a car and a pickup truck that were parked. Not your fault, of course."

"Well, now she ain't got a ride since it got towed."

"Maybe the police kept it for evidence."

He bit his lip at that. Could there be proof of other crimes in there? Crimes beyond underage drinking? A light bulb went off in my head. Not exactly an Oprah "aha!" moment, but close enough.

"I could give your mom a ride if that would help. She must be anxious to see you."

"Cool." He recited their phone number, which I dutifully wrote on scrap paper from my purse, although I already had it at home. I used what was always handy, a fat children's marker that inevitably left me with stained fingers. I returned the day's selection—grape-scented purple—to the depths of my purse with the phone number, noting the predictable splotches on my fingers. If the only malady I caught at the hospital was purple marker spots, fine by me. But I did need to add "notepad" and "grown-up pen" to my shopping list.

"Is there anyone else I can help you see? Friends? A girlfriend?"

"Nope."

I was about to stand when Marcus looked me up and down and lifted his chin. "What were you doin' there anyway?"

"I was totally lost," I replied, sounding exasperated with myself. He seemed to buy it.

Frankly, *life* had me feeling a little lost. If my father were alive and in my shoes, he'd go flying, where nothing and no one stood in his way. The closest I'd come to that feeling recently was a bubble bath.

I gave Marcus a last once-over too. I wondered if he ever let a vulnerable feeling show. Maybe surviving a bullet would give him something to brag about, something akin to a scar from a dangerous sports stunt. What about killing someone—specifically a pregnant ex-girlfriend? Hopefully that would be a sign of cowardice, not bravery, to his gang buddies.

I shook his hand and wished him luck. It was comforting to know I'd return with his mom, so we could talk again.

He combined an ultra-cool "Yo, thanks" with a wink and upward nod as I left.

He's charming when he wants to be, I thought. *And that's not necessarily good. Being charmed can be the same as being fooled.*

I stopped at the hospital phone on my way out, noting the display on a giant, digital wall clock: 2:05. The countdown before camp pickup was always a ticking time bomb. Get "everything" done in an impossibly short time and hope for the best.

I called Marcus's mom, but she didn't pick up or have voicemail, which was a relief, since I needed a plan before I talked with her. I didn't want to use my cell phone since she probably had caller ID. The first time Kenna and I called their house, we'd dialed *67 first to hide my home number.

Before leaving, I washed my hands in a bathroom. Then I dashed to Whole Foods to stock up on necessities (such as ice cream and chocolate) and conveniences (such as bread and milk). Next stop was the library to check out bedtime stories and hope our old ones weren't so overdue I'd be turned away. (The librarian was lenient with me.) Finally I stopped at home, set the books where no one would trip over them, filled the refrigerator, checked voicemail, left Kenna a long message, and whizzed to camp in time to see Jack and Sophie march outside with their classmates.

Everyone was pink and sweaty, hauling art projects and heavy backpacks stuffed with soggy towels and bathing suits—all indications of a fun day.

"How about pool and pizza?" I asked when they were buckled in.

"Yeah," Jack enthused.

"Okay," said Sophie. "Can I wear my new bikini?" I'd purchased her a modest two-piece—basically a stretchy half-shirt and shorts—since it allowed her to go to the bathroom without completely undressing first. Otherwise, I wasn't thrilled with the idea of bikinis for preschoolers.

"Yep." I was happy to oblige and keep her content as long as possible. This time of day could be challenging for Sophie. *She's maturing,* I reassured myself, *and I'm getting better at tantrum prevention.*

At home the kids raced inside, eager to put on bathing suits and head for the pool. I dumped their camp gear in the hall, immediately forming a junk pile I didn't want to deal with. For that very reason, I forced myself to sift through it, carrying uneaten lunch remains to the garbage disposal and stacking various art projects on the kitchen counter to compliment later. The next day, with Jack and Sophie safely out of sight, I'd throw most of it away since I couldn't save everything, but I also couldn't bear to hurt their feelings. In a real pinch, I'd photograph adorable mementos for our photo albums.

I could hear Sophie's accusing voice upstairs. "Where's my bikini top? Jack, did you take it?"

"No, why would I have it? Gosh!" he responded.

While I certainly didn't want them arguing, I was glad they weren't ready to go. I needed to prepare myself for the pool mentally and physically. I ran through bathing suit selections in my mind. The red tankini that didn't hide butt fat well enough? The lime bikini that resulted in good tan lines but equated with wearing skimpy underwear in front of neighbors? An old reliable black one-piece? Fact is, no matter what I wore, I never thought I measured up.

I walked upstairs and past the kids' rooms. Jack was in board shorts building something with Legos. Sophie had found her bikini top and was posing in front of her mirror, confident as a Victoria's Secret model, lucky thing.

She caught my eye in the reflection. "When are we leaving?"

"Pretty soon." Translation: *It depends on a number of factors, including your ability to cooperate and my ability to get my act together and parent with authority. It could be sixty seconds, it could be tomorrow. I don't know.* I recalled hearing a joke that, thanks to parents, kids have a warped sense of time. It had to be true. I put off the bathing suit decision and headed downstairs for a quick Internet detour.

I locked my office doors with a satisfying click and spun the power dial on the baby monitor beside my computer. Ahhh, the sweet combination of separation and safety. Located between the kids' rooms, the monitor's base allowed me to listen and respond with a walkie-talkie-like feature, issuing requests, commands, and threats if needed. *Praise would be nice once in a while, too,* I scolded myself.

"Great job getting on your bathing suits, guys!" I said. "I have to do something in my office for a minute."

Out of habit, I checked email first, which included junk surrounding a recognizable address, Andy's. I frowned and raised my eyebrows. What had he sent me? I double clicked.

Hi Nicki,
You know how I feel about you and Kenna looking into things. But I couldn't help checking social networking sites. Beth's on one. Take a look.
Best,
Andy

He included a link, and I clicked immediately. A lone photo graced Beth's Facebook page, a black-and-white side view that caught just a touch of her features as she looked down to the left, sleek hair obscuring her face. It was her, though, based on the information blurb, which included *Beth Myers* and *Woodridge High School*.

I kicked myself for not checking the sites earlier. In fear the page would somehow disappear before I read the whole thing, I copied it into a file, saved it, and hit "print." Only then did I focus on Beth's words.

Sadly, she wasn't a blogger type, but she did have a list of online friends, photos and all. April was among them, but Marcus wasn't. Weeks earlier, she had posted benign references to the weather, summer school, and a song she liked.

I wanted to look up every friend and read every word on every page. And while Beth's profile looked sparse, I needed to go through it with a fine-toothed comb, scrutinizing every detail. This was going to take a while, longer than Jack, Sophie, or the pool trip could wait. I sent Andy a thank-you reply, logged off, and marched reluctantly back to my room and bathing suit decision, which, in the midst of the latest developments, didn't seem to matter a bit.

We walked to the closest pool, flip flopping our way down an asphalt path, laden with kickboards and noodles. I wore my black one-piece covered with a fuchsia cotton dress. I could pull off the dress if needed, but I hoped to keep it on and lounge by the pool, thinking, while the kids splashed around.

My favorite thing about our house is its proximity to everything. We live next to Kenna, of course, but we can also hit the pool, tennis court, and park without crossing a street. The elementary school is about a mile away. Stores and churches are a mile and a half. If we couldn't walk, we could bike. Maybe after I learned to trust my kids crossing streets on foot, we would.

"Check before you cross," I reminded them when we reached the pool parking lot. Happy screams emanated from the pool area and made me wonder if any neighborhood pals were there. If they weren't, we'd probably make new ones. Families make fast, if fleeting, friends.

Jack and Sophie dutifully swept their heads from side to side until they were sure no one was pulling in or backing out. Then they bolted for the entryway where a lanky teenage lifeguard waited to take our passes. His eyes never met mine as he filed us under V and muttered "Thanks." Was he bored? Insecure? Depressed? Angry? With teens, it could be so many things. I guess it's like that with anyone, any age. You never really know.

I thanked him and watched his bronze face and hazel eyes, a touch of sunburn on his cheeks, turn away, looking back toward the pool.

Jack and Sophie ran ahead through the women's locker room. Jack was really too old to be there, but I wasn't sending him into men's rooms alone, and I certainly couldn't go with him. I wasn't sure how to handle this problem as he grew older without a dad. Then again, it would probably be the least of my concerns.

"No running," I reprimanded as I stepped quickly to keep up. "Pull over!" I knew the out-of-place expression would get them to giggle and obey. I added a siren sound effect.

"Ha ha, Mom. The pool police." Jack dropped his shark kickboard and red noodle on a lounge chair. He kicked off his flip flops and held out a hand. "Goggles," he stated as if I were a surgical assistant.

"Goggles," I repeated while digging in the summer supply bag. The tips of my fingers identified anti-fog, UV protective goggles with a soft, foam lining. I handed them over and surveyed his look. Cool blue goggles, Hawaiian print shorts, adorable bikini-clad sister in a flotation vest, water toys galore. At times like these, when for a shining moment life looks perfect, a combination of awe, thankfulness, and guilt can strike. Is it right to have so much when others have so little? Is it wrong to savor abundance or wrong not to? The answer had to be about balance, but I hadn't found a comfortable place on the lifestyle spectrum yet.

"You guys can hop in," I said. They disappointed me by making a beeline for the deep end. No relaxation for me. I never knew when Sophie was going to pull a Houdini and free herself from the zipped, locked floatation device in seconds.

"Keep that on," I reminded her, pointing at the jacket, "or we'll have to go home." That was a threat I didn't want to carry out. I was desperate for the kids to have exercise and entertainment.

She smiled up from the sparkling water and called out an agreeable, "Okay." It was all in her tone, but something made me trust her. I could read my kids' nonverbal cues as if they had subtitles. I hoped as a PI I'd be as perceptive.

The kids swam for a few minutes and then climbed the ladder near the diving board. I sat on the side, hitched up my dress so its rear wouldn't get soaked, and dipped my legs in, allowing them to sink a few inches below the surface. Jack ran off the diving board and tried unsuccessfully to douse me with a cannonball. Sophie followed and failed too.

"Whoa! Good tries!" I encouraged. They kept it up while I envisioned the night ahead of me. I'd go online again, but if possible, I wanted the freedom to go out and investigate too. Plus, what if Marcus's mom wanted a ride to the hospital pronto? I needed a babysitter.

My mother, who lived in a condo not far away in Arlington, was scheduled to babysit the next night during PI class. I hated to ask her for two nights in a row, especially when she'd have to face rush hour traffic, but I couldn't think of anyone else who could stay late except Kenna, and I didn't want to add stress to her day. Sending Jack and Sophie to a friend's for the night wasn't an option either. They weren't comfortable spending the night alone in their own beds, never mind in another home.

I trotted over to our beach chairs and retrieved my phone from the pool bag. Keeping an eye on the kids, who had started a cannonball splashing contest with three unfamiliar boys, I dialed Mom. I tried her cell first, still thankful she had one. Like Kenna, she resisted technology until someone practically staged an intervention.

"Hi sweetie!" she answered. Clearly she'd mastered caller ID. "You'll never guess where I am."

"Where?" I asked.

"With Aunt Liz!"

Well, babysitting was out. Mom's sister Liz lived in Siesta Key, Florida, so Mom must have flown out to see her. I couldn't imagine why she was there or how she'd get back in time to babysit tomorrow. Before I could ask, she answered.

"Now don't worry about tomorrow night. I'm flying back tomorrow afternoon and can be there by six, as long as you pick me up at Dulles. My flight gets in at five. But listen, I had to fly out to see Aunt Liz last minute. She broke her ankle playing tennis, and she had a million obligations. I insisted on coming out to help."

How Mom was going to help Aunt Liz with her obligations, I couldn't fathom, since Liz is a priest and my mom can't substitute at church, handing out communion, preaching, and doing funeral after funeral.

For me, visiting Aunt Liz was like escaping to another world, and I'd done it anytime my parents would let me. She lived alone in a rectory by a tiny beachside church, where I spent hours daydreaming in creaky wood pews, deciphering stained glass windows, skipping rocks in the waves, sniffing salty air and asking Aunt Liz questions I couldn't ask anyone else—and actually getting answers. I'd never become a churchgoer, though. Maybe because nothing compared to the peace I felt with Aunt Liz. Or maybe just because I was lazy.

"Is she okay?" Aunt Liz was petite but hardy. The fact she'd broken her ankle worried me. I hoped it wasn't a sign of aging or things to come.

"Oh, you know Aunt Liz. Nothing stops her. We got her crutches and everything she needs. Problem is it's her right foot, so she can't drive. But the congregation has been wonderful. She'll be well cared for."

"I can't believe you flew down there," I said. But then again, I could. Mom was a practical, take-charge person. "I'm glad she's okay. I wish I was there too."

"So does Liz. She keeps saying how long it's been. Sophie was a baby last time she was here. We were looking at pictures."

Guilt flooded me from head to toe. I looked at Sophie waiting her turn at the diving board as Jack jumped off. They had changed so much since Liz saw them at Dad's funeral—Sophie from a toddler to a little girl, Jack from a preschooler to a kindergartener. They'd love a trip to Florida, and so would I.

"Ugh. Tell her I'm sorry," I said. We made plans to meet at the airport, and I told her about Kenna.

"My gosh! Don't you think you're taking on a little much? I mean what do you really know about this stuff?" I rolled my eyes. As relatives often do, she neglected to sugarcoat the truth.

"I'm taking on *a lot* much. But I don't think I have a choice." I glanced at the kids and waved to send a double message: *I'm here if you need me* and *I'm watching, so behave yourselves!*

"I'm sure the young woman is fine, just terribly scared," Mom said.

"I hope you're right." Here came the hard part, asking for help. "Anyhow, I might need a little more babysitting than usual."

"Fabulous, I'd love that." Considering Kenna's hardship, *fabulous* seemed a little over the top, but I was grateful.

"Thanks, Mom. I really appreciate it." We reviewed our plans to meet at Dulles the next day, and then Aunt Liz got on the line. I wished her a blessed recovery, filled her in, got updated on Florida life, and made some requests. "Could you pray for Kenna and Andy...and the birth mother and the baby? Oh, and me!" I added at the last second. "I really don't know what I'm doing."

After leaving the pool, I made another call to order a large pizza, half plain (for Jack), half veggie (for Sophie and me). The kids narrated the walk home past friends' and strangers' houses.

"Hi Jeremy!" Sophie called to a preschool buddy chasing a basketball down his driveway. She blocked it with her foot and kicked it back. "Ouch!" she said with a giggle. "I need sneakers on."

"Stop hitting me with the noodle, please," Jack told her a few feet ahead when she started bopping his head. She ignored him. "Stop!" he demanded.

"Eww. Is that a dead worm?" She was distracted by a curl of flat, dried gunk on the sidewalk, a new target for her noodle. At this rate, we'd miss the pizza guy.

"Come on guys. Let's hustle. Pizza's coming."

I surveyed the street, considering who else might be available to babysit. All the parents would be home putting their kids to bed— surely desperate to hit the sack themselves. Birch Lane looked like a too-good-to-be-true movie scene: late model cars, fresh paint, landscaped lawns, smooth, dark asphalt, sprinklers spritzing. I was about to envy it all when I realized maybe everyone was struggling to survive just like me, putting on a good face.

The long, looping road met on each end with a major artery, Berkley Ave. There were several cul-de-sacs off Birch, safe havens for street play, unlike our lot on the main stretch.

As we approached our house a brainstorm hit me. *Irene.* It would be another breach of playgroup etiquette, since parent socializing was usually confined to playtime. You didn't ring up other moms to discuss current events. You gabbed for an hour or two at playgroup, and then you waited until the next one for an update. And you never asked for babysitting. Everyone knew how worn out the others were.

But calling Irene felt right. She'd been there when Kenna called, and she knew I had some kind of emergency going on. Also, her husband worked from home, so he might be around to fill in for her, and she'd already seen my house a mess. I'd be embarrassed, not mortified, for her to see its natural state.

In case she was available, I took more care than usual in instructing the kids as we walked inside. "Put your bathing suits in the hamper. And put your toys in the basement instead of the front hall. Oh, and don't leave your flip flops in the middle of the floor please."

"Why are we being so clean? Is someone coming over?" Jack asked with the uncensored curiosity of a child.

"Well, being neat is always a good idea," I said. "But *yes*, someone might be coming over. I have an errand to do." Errand covered almost anything I ever had to do, and the kids equated it with "boredom," so they rarely asked to come along.

"Who? Grandma? Auntie Kenna?" Sophie asked.

"Nope. Grandma's visiting Aunt Liz. And Kenna's probably too tired today."

"Then who?" she pressed.

"I don't know. I'm figuring it out." I didn't think she'd like that answer, so I changed the subject. "But guess what, the pizza's going to be here any minute. So you better get dressed!" I chased them up the steps to their rooms, all of us laughing the whole way. Moments like these were treasures to savor without reservation, reasons to hope.

Irene arrived half an hour after the pizza. There was one slice left, and I offered it to her.

"No thanks," she said. "I just had mac 'n' cheese and tater tots."

I laughed. "I heard mothers' health gets worse when the kids are little. It's got to be the diet," I said.

"Or the lack of sleep," she countered.

"Or the intense stress." We could have gone on forever, but I had to get going.

It was eight o'clock, and I'd spent every spare minute reading teen profiles online while the kids watched TV. I was beyond thrilled that many of Beth's friends had mentioned a field party that night as the place to be, but worried that so few protected their privacy online. Meanwhile, Marcus's mom hadn't answered her phone again.

"Like I said," I reminded Irene quietly, "I'm helping a friend with a personal situation, but I should be available by cell, as long as there's coverage."

"Where are Ryan and Will?" Sophie asked.

"It's their bedtime," Irene said. "And yours too, right?"

"She's babysitting, honey," I reminded Sophie. "It's not playgroup. Next time she comes over, Ryan and Will can come too." I turned to Irene and pointed to a list on the counter that covered everything short of how to handle an alien invasion. "That's all the information you need, including bedtime, which is 8:30."

We walked into the living room for a quick tutorial on remote controls in case she wanted to watch TV. "The kids can look at books in bed for half an hour," I explained. "And if you have trouble with the remotes, they're experts." I smiled at Jack and Sophie, who were proudly nodding their heads, which made me nervous. What would Irene think if she discovered my addiction to reality shows? I had an entire *Real Housewives* season saved for a lonely night.

"You go." Irene said. "We'll be fine. Plus, I brought a special bedtime story for them." She whipped an unfamiliar book from her purse and presented it Vanna White style. *Knight Falls in Princessland*. Looked like it had all the ingredients for fun. I liked Irene more and more. Hopefully she wouldn't feel the opposite about me before the night was over.

Six

I had a few secrets stashed away that would have surprised Irene and the kids. That's why they were in a backpack instead of on my body. It's not like I could leave the house wearing a black miniskirt, lacy pink top, heavy makeup, and bronzer without raising questions about what kind of "emergency" my "friend" was having.

I pulled into McDonald's, where I surprised the staff by entering the bathroom as plain-Jane mom and emerging as Superslut, ordering a bottled water as payment for using the bathroom. I hoped bronzer, industrial strength concealer and cotton-candy lip gloss would help me pass as a teenager at a dark field party.

I brought along a jean jacket, black baseball cap, gum, and sunglasses in case any of them would help the cause. I also applied bug spray, since I didn't think a miniskirt was practical at a field party, what with West Nile, Lyme and all. Hopefully the pungent odor wouldn't give me away or repel everyone else.

As I reached out to pay for the drink, I noticed my nails, sans polish. Oops. Didn't most teens have manicured nails these days? Everyone I saw on TV did, so I trudged to a nearby drugstore and purchased black lacquer, a touchup pen loaded with remover, and a file. Ten minutes later, my nails were gothic, and the van was toxic. I opened the sunroof, cracked the windows, and sucked in fresh air.

While following directions to the field party courtesy of MapQuest, I prayed for a huge gathering of non-armed potential sources. I wasn't up for another shooting. Ever. I sipped my drink nervously until it dawned on me to monitor my pace, or else I'd be taking advantage of the field (and miniskirt) in ways I hadn't planned.

I imagined similar parties I'd enjoyed as a teen, wondering how I might stand out tonight, how I could prevent blowing my cover, and what the chances were of finding a porta-potty.

Arriving alone wasn't good, I worried. No one went to a party alone. Driving a minivan was a giveaway too. But lots of teens drove their parents' cars, right? I'd try to park far away, I decided, and follow the crowd.

The field party was, logically, in the middle of nowhere. I traveled past middle- to upper-class neighborhoods, into a new development, and then onto a construction site. The shopper in me couldn't help noticing model homes and signs, which advertised single families from the $700s and up.

Summer heat had dried the earth, so cars moved in a terra cotta cloud, the color of local dirt when you dug just below the surface—dirt my kids (not to mention repairmen, cable guys, etc.) had tracked into the house on endless occasions. I wondered how many parents would ask tomorrow, "Where the heck were you driving last night? I thought you said you were going..." (bowling, to the movies, to so-and-so's house—fill in your favorite lie). Maybe some kids would get a car wash on the way home.

As vehicles neared the end of the dirt road, they pulled left or right, fanning into a self-made parking lot that bordered a scrubby field. White signs with bold, black lot numbers indicated where homes would be erected and builders would have a daunting cleanup job in the morning.

Dust had settled around the first row of cars, and my headlights caught glimpses of the party in action. A boy in basketball shorts was making out with a spiky-haired brunette. Most teens were holding cups, bottles, or each other. Some puffed on cigarettes. Music throbbed from someone's car.

I had to pull in next to an SUV from which two guys sprang with surprising shouts. My stomach churned, and I reached for my shades. What if I got identified as an adult and surrounded by angry teens? Backing out wasn't an appealing option, either. There were too many cars piling in around me. I stalled, pretending I was fumbling with things in my purse. Why hadn't I brought a beer or something? That would have helped me fit in.

I slid the glasses over my eyes and touched up my lip gloss in the mirror. I made a sudden determination that my haircut, a layered bob, wasn't youthful enough, so I scrounged around for one of Sophie's ponytail holders in the glove compartment. I smoothed back my hair as well as possible, made a ponytail, and then tucked it in on itself before making the final loop.

The effect was a casual, stray-hairs-poking-out do that seemed more suitable for the occasion. The sunglasses made me look like a geek trying to be cool, but I was too scared of looking like a mom to take them off. If it got really dark once most kids parked, I could push them back on my head.

It was time to open the door. Everyone had exited the cars around mine and headed toward the field. I couldn't see much beyond the first parking line, but I assumed teens were mingling somewhere near a keg, judging from the number of red cups pressed to their lips. That was my destination too. I was about to pull the door handle when it hit me that I wasn't someone's guest here. The beer was going to cost money. For all I knew, this was a fundraiser, maybe even a gang fundraiser. My guilt alarm started ringing, but I ignored it, pulled my purse from its hiding place under the center console, and felt around inside for cash. I landed three singles and a five. That had to be enough. *It's illegal to buy beer* for *a teen*, I thought, *but what about buying it* from *a teen?*

I pushed open my door and let my feet fall to the dirt. Armed with my phone and eight bucks, I slammed it shut with confidence. If I was going to do this, I might as well act ready to party. I walked with a casual sashay-strut to a Britney Spears remix flowing from somewhere. The beat propelled me to a line of empty-handed, presumably thirsty kids.

"Hey." I acknowledged an acne-stricken boy in front of me holding hands with a pudgy, adorable girl. They nodded but mostly had eyes for each other. I took that as a good sign. They weren't rushing off to warn everyone about an intruder.

The line moved quickly, teens passing bills to a lively dude manning the keg who seemed to revel in his job, handing out sloshing cups with a smile and making everyone laugh. I wondered if his high was natural.

Belatedly, I realized I should make conversation with kids while I had the chance, so I targeted the couple in front of me, using a high-pitched voice that, hopefully, sounded like a teenager, even if she was from the '80s.

"Ummm, do you know if April Johnson is here?" I asked.

"No idea," the boy said. The girl shook her head in agreement. He gallantly paid for her drink, handing the "cashier" a ten in exchange for two frothy cups. I sorted through my bills to find the five.

"Yo," keg kid said. "What's your name? *Cool*?" I assumed he was referencing my shades. My lips formed a tight grin, mostly because teeth and gums show age. Dean's pearly whites flashed in my mind, and I added whitening supplies to my mental grocery list again. I also decided on the perfect undercover supply: fake braces.

"Funny," I said. I handed him the five.

"Cheers!" He raised my cup in a toasting gesture.

"Thanks," I said. "Um, have you seen April Johnson?"

"Another five." He held his palm out. "Kidding! I think she went thataway." He winked and fired an imaginary shot from pistol-shaped fingers at a bunch of girls. My eyes popped with excitement and fear. Was she really here?! I also felt like I'd been hit with a tranquilizer. What would I say to her, or to those girls, none of whom had April's dark hair?

"I don't see her," I said. "She was with them?"

"Yup!"

"Perfect. Thanks."

Crap. I stepped away, turned my back to him, and cleaned imaginary dust off my sunglasses. Then I sipped my beer. Blech. Skunk spray. I'd forgotten that cheap-beer taste. I grimaced and looked over my shoulder at the girls. I saw a mass of short shorts, tight shirts and caramel tans. Logic overruled emotion and told my feet to move.

"Hey ya'll," I said casually. All eyes were on me.

"Hey," one said, boosting my confidence.

"What's up?" said another, as if she actually meant the question. Like, "What's up with how weird you look?" She had wide shoulders and crispy, blond-green hair that indicated swim team participation.

Someone giggled. Probably at me.

"I'm looking for April Johnson," I said. "Have you guys seen her?"

"Who wants to know?" crispy hair asked.

Well, I'm from the SwimCap shampoo beauty squad, and we'd like to offer you a free makeover! April sent us a letter about your hair, and...

"I'm a friend," I said. "I haven't seen her in forever, and I heard she was gonna be here."

"Really? What school do you go to?"

"Saint Agnes," I said, naming a nearby private school. "Do you guys all go to Woodridge?" I looked around the group.

They nodded.

"Cool."

Maybe silence would get them to speak up.

"She was with her friend Rachael, but I don't know where they went," a third girl offered. There were a few shrugs and murmurs.

"Okay. Thanks."

"You know, you look too old for high school," crispy said, squinting at me.

Stay calm, I told myself. *They're teenagers. You wouldn't be scared of them at the mall, so don't be scared of them here.*

"I know. It sucks. I got held back," I said.

I turned, spilled a little beer on purpose, hustled to the keg, and got down to business.

"Can I get a refill?" I said. Keg kid held out the tap. "I'm still looking for April. They said she's with Rachael. Have you seen either of them?"

"Nope. But someone's sick in the woods." He scrunched his nose and tilted his forehead toward some trees.

"Oh." I frowned. "Good to know."

I took a cleansing breath and fiddled with my phone. What if he'd figured out I was an adult, and he was sending me into the wilderness to be tackled by bullies? I could always call 911 again if needed. The operator had been awfully helpful the other night.

After passing the girls and a few other kids without locking eyes, I scraped through dense brush and stared into the trees. Seeing nothing but shifting branches in the darkness, I propped my cheap glasses on my head and absentmindedly rubbed my nose where they always left an imprint. I was about to call out "April" when I heard an unmistakable, disgusting noise: retching. I squinted and poked my head forward, trying to distinguish someone in the darkness, finally seeing a patch of blue behind a tree. It moved, becoming taller and thinner, then folded back down and let loose again. This time I heard not only the release of vomit, but the landing of it, and I knew what was coming. I rocketed toward the nearest bush and gagged. I'd never been able to hear that noise without reacting poorly. Luckily my dry heaves were short lived, and I managed to blurt out April's name as a question.

"Uhhh," she responded. I approached as she held her stomach with both arms and let her hair hang toward the underbrush. The mother in me acted before I could think, gathering her hair and holding it gently behind her head. She looked at me in confusion but must have been too sick to talk. Suddenly her knees buckled, and she was on the ground in a heap.

"Are you okay?" My voice was urgent and completely adult. She brought her knees to her chest and looked at me sideways.

"Yeah," she mumbled. "I just feel bad. I wanna go home."

"Let's get you up. Who knows what's down there." Bugs. Snakes. Vomit puddles. I curled my elbows beneath her underarms and lifted. She put weight on her feet and steadied herself against the tree. "Do you have a cell phone?" I asked. "Is there anyone I can call for you?"

"No," she said. "I came with Rachael Finlay, and my phone's in her car. But she won't leave, and I'm not friends with anyone else."

"Why won't she leave?"

"She has to see her boyfriend. I did shots on the way. I'm so sick."

I nodded. I wanted to offer her a ride but feared it was inappropriate. She turned her head to the side and jerked. Uh oh. Another round.

She pulled it together after a few gasps and squeaked out, "I have to go." She sounded like she was about to cry. I thought "I want my mommy" might be next out of her mouth.

"I'm Nicki," I said. "I haven't been drinking. I can give you a ride."

"What grade are you in?"

That stumped me for a second. Lying to her felt

counterproductive. "I graduated," I said. "But I think I know you through a friend, Beth."

Her forehead wrinkled in question or physical pain.

"You're April, right?" I made sure.

"Yeah."

"I'm really worried about Beth. I'm trying to find her. Maybe you could help?"

"You can give me a ride," she said. That sounded a lot better than nothing. We'd have a chance to talk, and I could get her out of here. Plus, the thought of teens driving away from this party—and being on the road with them—was seriously unsettling.

"Come on." I linked our arms since I didn't trust her gait. All the weeds weren't going to make walking easy, either.

"I feel awful," she said as soon as we were moving. "Dizzy."

I made sympathetic noises and encouraged her. "It's not far to the car. We can make it."

I dumped my beer on the ground and, out of habit, held onto the cup to avoid littering—as if hundreds of cups minus one would make a difference.

April leaned on me heavily as we hobbled together. I shook my head until my sunglasses fell back onto my eyes. We trekked past the girls, the keg, and a group of gregarious teens, hearing shouts of "One too many, huh?" and "See ya girl!" I wanted to run when someone yelled, "Who's that? Your mom?" Where was Rachael? Making out somewhere, unaware? Would she check to make sure her friend had arrived home safely?

I loaded April into the front seat and fastened her seat belt out of habit. I was so used to buckling kids into car seats that I didn't even think about it, and April didn't seem to notice anything odd—including Jack and Sophie's seats in the back, which I should have removed before the outing.

By the time I raced around and closed my door, she'd already rested her head on the window and closed her eyes. I touched her shoulder gently, because even if I wasn't going to learn anything about Beth, I still needed directions to April's house.

"April? Hon? I need directions to your house, or at least your address." I reached onto the floor where I'd swept everything off the seat to make room for her, and I found a pen and paper.

"Mmmm," she murmured. Very helpful.

"What's your address?" I spoke up to penetrate her stupor.

"FivefifteenChesterview," she slurred. I wrote it down and looked at her slumped figure.

"Is that near a major road or shopping center or anything?"

"Mall," she blurted, as if she used all her energy to utter it.

"Brighton Place Mall?"

"Mmm." I took that as a yes.

"Okay." I started the car and looked behind me for partiers. Seeing no one, I reversed slowly and then pulled forward, on the lookout for stumbling teens the same way I checked for kids on my street. "We're on the move. Let me know if you need me to pull over." I meant it, but I also hoped my voice would keep her awake, or at least rousable. "How old are you, April?" I continued.

"Eighteen. Can't talk. Sick."

"Okay. But how many shots did you have?"

"I dunno. Four?"

I let her be while I navigated the dirt road and left the development-to-be. It took a minute to get my bearings, but after rotating an imaginary map in my head a few times, I knew which way to go. Confidence returned for a moment until I felt a burst of warm air hit the right side of my body. I turned to April, expecting to see her window open, but it was her door instead.

"My God, April! What are you doing?" The words exploded from my mouth as she struggled to release her seatbelt.

"I have to get out of here!" she yelled with more clarity than I'd heard from her yet. Her eyes darted back and forth wildly.

"It's okay," I yelled. "I promise! Close your door! Keep your seatbelt on!" My voice competed with the *woosh, woosh, woosh* of passing road sections.

"Who are you? Where are you taking me?" Her voice was frantic. Maybe she'd fallen asleep and woken up confused, like when you spend the night at someone's house and open your eyes to unfamiliar surroundings, except multiplied by ten because she was trashed.

"Remember? I'm taking you home from the party? Chesterview, right?" Recognition flashed in her squinted eyes. Under the streetlights, she looked like the portrait of an addict—smudged eyeliner, bloodshot eyes, tangled hair. She'd probably started the night gorgeous before her shot-induced makeover.

"You know Beth," she said slowly. Her hand gripped the door handle, pulling it closer.

"Close your door, and let's talk about it. I want you to be safe." I felt like a negotiator at a crime scene.

She clunked it shut in slow motion. It wasn't tight, and I didn't argue.

"Please don't take me like her." Her voice was timid.

"Like her? What do you mean *like her*?"

"Beth. Like someone took her."

I wanted to give her a lecture. *Don't ever get in a car with a stranger! What were you thinking? I could have kidnapped you and taken you anywhere.* I wanted to give myself a lecture for driving her home instead of finding her friend, Rachael.

Then again, maybe she'd just trusted her instincts and common sense. Passing out in the middle of the woods surrounded by horny guys: bad. Driving home with a silly looking female who seems to care about your best friend: not as bad?

"You have no reason to trust me," I admitted. "But I will get you home safely, and I want to help Beth do the same."

I glanced away from the road at her. Her eyes were closed again. I locked the doors with a press of a button and re-clicked her seatbelt. Then I started contemplating how to find her house and get a semiconscious teen inside.

I drove around near the mall, hoping to run into Chesterview. No luck. I needed a navigation system. *Wait a minute*, I thought, *you can do things the old-fashioned way.* I pulled into a gas station, parked in front, locked the door, and left April conked out.

"Do you know where Chesterview Street, or Avenue, or something, is?" I asked the skinny, middle-aged woman at the counter. I kept my eye on the glass entryway to make sure April didn't bolt.

"Yep." Her voice was husky and her remaining teeth were brown. She pointed a fake, red nail at the window. "You take this street here a mile. Then you take a left at the first light. It'll come up pretty fast after that. I don't know how many blocks down."

"Thank you so much," I said. "Have a good night." I gave her a smile, hurried back to the car, and slammed the door behind me. April didn't notice, which got me thinking. I used a pen to write on her hand. It was the only place I could think of where she'd definitely see it tomorrow.

"Let's find Beth," I wrote, followed by my email address. I smiled to myself, knowing it would take several hand washings for the ink to disappear. Sophie had written on herself enough times for me to learn that. Just to make sure, I traced over each letter.

I backed out slowly to keep April steady and made my way to her street. Addresses were on the mailboxes, so it was easy to find 515, a tiny single family with a long driveway—long enough that I knew April would never make it from the street. I pulled up to the garage and jostled her.

"April? April. April!"

Her eyes flew open. "What?"

"It's okay," I said. "You're home." I pointed to the house and watched her eyes register it.

I walked around the van and gave her my hand for support as she stepped down. Wobbly steps got her to the front door, where she rifled through her purse to find keys under a mountain of lipsticks.

"I like to mix the colors," she said. "I wanna be a cosmetologist."

I smiled softly at her bedraggled face and the irony of her statement. Given her state, I was impressed she'd even pronounced the word.

"The red one," she said, referencing a key, not a lip color. She handed me the set, which included only two keys, each with a different colored plastic top. It made life seem so simple. Two keys, two responsibilities, two places to be. My chain was heavy, and I didn't even know why. The red key fit perfectly in the doorknob, and I turned it gently.

"See," I whispered. "Home safe." I held her hand and turned it palm up. "Here's my information so you don't lose it." She looked at the writing in surprise. "If we can talk, maybe I can find Beth."

The cool, quiet darkness of the front porch was interrupted by a burst of light, making both of us jump, which meant April, who had begun to slip through the open door, was about to tumble. I grabbed her arm and pitched forward, looking into a face I didn't know, but an expression I did—one of a tired, about-to-blow mom.

My first instinct was to turn and run. My second was to apologize, but I didn't know for what. So I plastered on the most understanding smile I could, silently beaming the message, "It's okay. I'm a mom, too." The woman's look of confusion, annoyance and up-and-down appraisal reminded me that my appearance was more disturbing than comforting. Then again, her daughter's was worse.

"Who are you?" she demanded.

I winced. What did she want to hear?

"I'm Nicki, another mom." April looked surprised at this. "I gave April a ride home because her friend ditched her."

"Oh." She took a moment to consider this and assess me again. Her gaze shifted to April. "Rachael did that?"

"Yeah," April said quietly. She self-consciously tucked a chunk of straggly black hair behind her ear and looked down. "She saw her boyfriend and left me. I don't feel good. I'm going upstairs." April's eyes locked with mine. "Thanks," she added. She started up the steps.

Nice escape. Her mom let her go and stared at me.

"April doesn't look like she was at the movies."

"I'd rather let her tell you the story, if that's okay," I said meekly. "I don't know much. Just that she needed a safe ride. And that she couldn't drive herself." I didn't want to get April in trouble and make her angry. Yet I didn't want to piss off her mom, either.

"I don't have a clue who you are, and you brought my daughter home drunk. I'd like to know what happened. Now." Her dark eyes matched the roots of her blond hair. Its layers stood out in all directions and fit with her rumpled pajamas, the pattern so faded I couldn't make it out. She must have been sleeping or at least tossing and turning.

"I totally understand." I leaned on the door jamb. My body and brain were worn out, and the last thing I wanted to do was come in. I looked at my feet and scrunched my toes in apprehension.

"Well," I started. "I'm Nicki, and I met April at a party. I was actually looking for a friend of hers, Beth."

I watched her expression change from accusing to interested— maybe even kind. Her eyebrows were arched, but everything else had softened.

"Oh."

"I was talking to April, and it was clear she didn't feel well and needed a ride. I was worried about her, so I brought her home. You should keep an eye on her tonight because she's been throwing up." I grimaced involuntarily.

She glanced upstairs and let out an exasperated sigh. "Can you find your way to the kitchen?" she asked, motioning toward the back of the house. "I want to hear more, but I have to check on April. Make yourself at home."

I found my way to a kitchenette with a cracked wooden table and two folding chairs by a window. I turned on an overhead light and tried not to imagine how crazy I must look. I peered around in search of a mirror or powder room. A shiny toaster would have been okay, too. Nothing.

After a few minutes, April walked by with her mom, reclined in a nearby easy chair, and passed out instantly. Her mom covered her with a blanket.

"I know I look ridiculous dressed like this," I said when she returned. "I'm sorry. I was trying to fit in with the kids so they'd talk to me." I noticed she'd run a comb through her hair.

She put water in a kettle and turned on a burner. "Tea?" she offered.

"Sure. Thanks."

"My name's Jen, by the way," she said as she pulled flowered mugs from a cabinet. "And I'm confused. Who are you? And how do you know Beth?"

"It's complicated," I said while I tried to think of an explanation. She set the cups on the table and added tea bags.

"Milk or sugar?"

"No thanks," I answered. "Honestly, I don't know Beth, but I'm very worried about her situation. Even if she left on purpose, it's incredibly dangerous. I'm really just an outsider who wants to help."

She leaned against the kitchen counter and folded her arms. "Don't get me wrong. I'm glad someone's looking out for her. But again, why *you*?" There was an awkward pause. Then her mouth dropped open. "You're not the adoptive mom, are you?"

"No," I answered. "I'm investigating because..." I paused, wanting to protect Kenna's privacy. "Because someone asked me to—someone I can't name right now. But I promise you, they have Beth's best interests at heart."

"Is it her parents?"

"No," I said truthfully.

"Good. Because I have a major problem with them."

"Really? What is it?"

"They were so upset about the adoption they practically kicked her out. She came here crying a lot." She shook her head and made a *tsk* sound. "Can you imagine treating your kid like that? It's like they were so pissed about losing a grandbaby that they lost a daughter, too. Excuse my language."

I held up a hand. "No problem whatsoever. It sounds like you know Beth pretty well."

"I do. She and April have been best friends since ninth grade. And I don't think she ran away. She knows she could have come here."

"Isn't this the first place her parents would look for her?"

"Sure. It's the first place everyone, including the police, looked. Where else would she go? It kills me. Just kills me! To picture her alone somewhere." Her voice trailed off.

"You and April can't imagine *anywhere* she would go?"

"Nope. We've racked our brains. April's talked to other kids too. She won't say much about it, but that birth father, Marcus, he's bad news. You know he wouldn't have anything to do with the baby, right?"

"That's what I heard."

"Beth approached him several times. At first he got pissed and denied it, and then he damn well ignored her—acted like she didn't exist. I don't know if he ever admitted it was his."

"But it *is* his?"

"Has to be. April and Beth act tough. They try to look tough. But they keep to themselves a lot. I wouldn't be surprised if that was Beth's first time, if you know what I mean."

"Of course. So when was the last time April saw Beth?"

"A week ago Sunday. I know it was a Sunday, because April and Beth had a big test Monday. They studied here that night, and April drove Beth home—even watched her go in the house. But the next morning, Beth wasn't at school, and no one knew where she was. Her parents said they never heard her come home the previous night."

"What time did April drop her off?"

"About eleven, April said."

"And April was home on time?"

"She didn't break her curfew. I know that. I was asleep, but if she'd come home after midnight, I'd remember. She always checks in with me."

"This is so helpful," I said. "I appreciate that you're willing to talk with me. Is it okay if I call April tomorrow and talk some more?"

"Fine by me as long as you don't get her in trouble. I don't want that gangster to think April's snitching on him. She hates talking about him. She's scared. After what he might have done to Beth, what if April's next?"

She poured water into our mugs.

"I'll be more than careful," I said. "You have my word."

Just what I needed. Another child's welfare in my hands.

Seven

I had four things on my agenda the next day in addition to parenting. 1) Take Marcus's mom to see him. 2) Talk with April when she'd recovered from her inevitable hangover. 3) Get through Dean's class without making a fool of myself. 4) Remember to pick up Mom from the airport, otherwise I'd lose a babysitter and gain an angry parent.

On the way to the kids' camp, I thanked God for the umpteenth time for a place where they were happy and safe. Sure, I'd never stop worrying about them, but that was the deal I unknowingly accepted when I got pregnant. From then on, I loved so much it hurt. Good thing the realities of parenting aren't evident at conception or birth. If a screaming baby popped out right after sex, or women delivered two year olds having tantrums, the population would shrink. Sometimes ignorance really is bliss.

I dropped the kids off uneventfully and checked the sky for signs of rain. I didn't want a stray thunderstorm to force them indoors, meaning poor Jack would have suffered through sunscreen application for nothing, and Sophie's energy level could hit the danger zone.

The horizon was clear and my mind drifted to my dad, for whom a day like this was the ultimate, not because of how he could enjoy it down here with the rest of us, but because he could enjoy it alone, in a plane, with a distant perspective on the world. I smiled, thinking of the view he must have now. *I hope it's awesome, Dad. I miss you.*

I headed home to a quiet house where I could make calls in peace. The first was to Marcus's mom, who finally answered with a warm greeting.

"What do you want?" she slurred. I was stunned into silence. "Hell-o-o?" She had to be under the influence.

"Umm, hi?" I was rethinking whether it was a good idea to be in a car with this woman. "My name is Nicki, and I'm an acquaintance of your son's. Actually, I saw his accident and visited him yesterday. He said you might need a ride to the hospital, so I'm offering to take you if you'd like."

"To the hospital? Why the hell would I want to go there?"

"Well I just thought you might like to visit him."

"He's in the hospital? I thought he was hiding out 'cuz he wrecked my car."

"No one from the hospital or police station called and explained things to you?"

"Not that I know of," she said. "But I got a bad memory."

"Well Marcus is fine, but he got hurt Monday night. I have free time now, if you'd like me to pick you up. I can take you to see him."

"Sure. Whatever. I'll be here." She hung up.

I stared at the disconnected phone slack jawed. She was either drunk or on drugs, or both, and I was going to transport her in my car. And I'd been worried about April throwing up last night. I might need to buy air freshener on the way home.

I put down the phone and picked it up again. I wanted to check in with Kenna.

"Can you come over real quick?" she asked.

"Sure. But I'm on my way out, and you won't believe where I'm going."

"I'm not sure I want to know," she said.

"We'll talk when I get there." I grabbed my purse and headed out.

The air was unseasonably light, and my cotton shorts and sleeveless shirt flapped in the breeze. I hoped I wouldn't be chilly at the hospital. Oh well. I'd be so nervous I probably wouldn't notice.

I watched my sandals rush up Kenna's clean driveway. In summer, I almost forgot what it was like to have asphalt free of chalk drawings, hopscotch, and kids' scribbles.

She opened the door and smiled mischievously. "I did something," she said.

I cocked my head. "You did? What is it?"

"Come in." She led me into her sparsely decorated, meticulously clean main level. I slipped off my shoes, and we walked to the future nursery, where a shiny white crib stood next to a white bassinet, smack in the middle of the floor.

"Kenna," I said. "I'm so proud of you."

"I decided to be hopeful," she said. "And prepared."

"You've always been hopeful," I said. "But not prepared. Did you get sheets or anything?"

"Ta da!" She opened a closet door, and there, neatly folded on the plush, cream carpet, was a tiny pile of sheets and receiving blankets. Tiny, yet monumental.

"Ooh," I said, picking up a white blanket and cuddling it to my cheek. "So soft."

"I even washed it. I don't know what's gotten into me."

"I do. You're thinking positively, like always." I gave her a hug. "That's what I love about you. Any more surprises?" I folded the blanket and checked the closet corners in case a mobile, bouncy seat, or other adorable item was hidden away. I was happy, but in truth, I was also panicky. Why had she chosen now, of all times, to prepare? I wanted so badly to share her confident outlook, but Beth felt so far away.

"No more surprises," she said. "But do you have any? Tell me where you're going. Are you picking up Dean?"

"Oh, no. Nothing like that. It's Marcus's mom. She needs a ride to the hospital to see him. I'm driving."

"Marcus's mother," she repeated. "The baby's birth grandmother." She looked stunned, although she knew this was a possibility from my voicemails.

"Yes. Are you okay?"

"I just didn't think it would happen so soon," she said. "You're meeting all these people."

"Do you want to come with me?" I asked. She didn't answer right away, so I continued. "I don't have to tell you this stuff if it's too stressful. Maybe I shouldn't even be doing all this."

"No. It's okay. I need to know. And you have to do it. What else?"

"Well, I'm a little concerned, because she sounded under the influence. I'm glad she's not driving."

"I shouldn't go." She rested a hand on the crib. "I just want everything to be okay. I don't want any more bad news. I'm going to stay here and..." She looked around the room and threw her hands in the air. "I don't know."

"Make the bed," I said. "I mean the crib. And find the right spot for it. Maybe you can keep the bassinet in your room. That's what we did."

"Okay."

"It's a start. Next thing you know, you'll be buying diapers and formula."

She shook her head in disbelief. I didn't argue.

I made it to Marcus's house without getting lost, and this time, I walked right through the chain link fence and rapped on the loose screen door—the only thing between me and Ms. Gomez, who lay motionless on a sunken brown couch in front of a blaring TV. It was hard to tell through the warped screen, but her eyes looked closed.

"Ms. Gomez?" I called out. "Ms. Gomez?" No response. I took a deep breath and opened the door, which squeaked and slammed behind me, just like a cabin door. The noise didn't stir her a bit. I tiptoed over matted, gray carpet (not its original color) as a little plot formed in my head. First, make sure she's okay. Her breathing was steady—although a little snorty—and her plump body looked comfortable, as if its impression was left on the couch many naps ago. She was dressed for the hospital in shorts and a flowered T-shirt. She wore flip flops, which were askew and looked uncomfortable, suggesting she'd passed out more than fallen asleep. Her thinning, blond hair was pulled into a messy knot high on her scalp, begging to be fixed, but I resisted the urge to smooth and refasten it, instead focusing on essentials, namely snooping.

After watching her breathe for a minute, I crept away and left the TV on, dying to close and bolt the front door in this neighborhood, but not willing to make additional noise. I stayed on my tiptoes and moved further into the house. My shoulders were raised slightly, palms pressing down with each step, a technique I'd mastered over years of getting kids to sleep and sneaking out of their rooms so they wouldn't wake up.

My heart pounded as I made my way from room to room, looking for anything informative or suspicious. I didn't expect to find Beth, but I wasn't going to rule it out either. *Could I be arrested for this?* I wondered. *I wasn't exactly "snooping." But I was really breaking and entering. What if I startled Marcus's mom and she had a gun? Was she even capable of aiming?* Worry dissipated as I focused on hurrying.

The first floor, which consisted of a kitchen, den, and bathroom, was unremarkable. Nothing was cluttered and nothing was clean. It was exactly the kind of place you'd imagine a troubled mom and teenage son living. Dishes filled the sink (nothing wrong with that), but some of them were moldy, and the refrigerator was almost empty except for beer, bread, milk, jelly, and a shriveled orange. It would be hard to survive on this, so I peeked into the freezer and a few cabinets, which revealed an affinity for frozen meals and preservative-filled baked goods. No baby formula in sight.

I was afraid and eager to see the basement, where a dim yellow light shone last time I was here. It seemed like the logical place to hide someone. At least that's where it always happened on TV.

I opened a random door in the kitchen a few inches, just enough to see whether it was a pantry, closet, or steps. Steps...good—and scary. I flipped a switch that lit a bare bulb. Before beginning my descent, I double checked the door for locks. No one could hold me down here, could they?

I shivered and gripped the railing before gingerly moving from wood step to wood step, gradually seeing more of the unfinished basement with exposed pipes and white insulation. To my right was a rusty bike. Directly in front of me was a door I didn't want to open.

No matter how lightly I stepped, grit scratched beneath my feet, so I took big steps and stopped before the door. First I tapped lightly with a fingernail in case anyone was inside. Then I opened it very, very slowly, mostly because I was scared, not because I thought I'd scare anyone else. That's when I smelled something. Something I knew all too well. Something I'd rather not smell again. Laundry supplies and lint. I was in a laundry room—one used less often than my own, I guessed, because there were no clothes in sight. Maybe there was a load in the dryer, but I didn't stay to find out. The basement was obviously empty, and I wanted to leave.

Before I could go anywhere, there was a creak from above. I whipped my eyes toward the ceiling, as if I'd be able to see the source with x-ray vision. I froze in place, waiting for another creak. Then I slid my right hand into my pocket and gripped my cell phone. It always made me feel like help was on the way if needed. On the other hand, I realized in terror, I'd forgotten to turn off the ringer, so hopefully no one would call and alert Ms. Gomez to my presence with a personalized ring tone.

After a few sweaty minutes of playing statue and hearing nothing else, including my cell phone, I chose to evacuate and scout upstairs if possible. I made it up the first flight with minimal noise and peeked out the kitchen door, which, thank goodness, was still open a crack. Seeing nothing heart-stopping from my limited point of view, I pushed the door inch by inch until I was confident no one was reacting to my entrance.

In the living room, Marcus's mom was still on the couch, but she'd rolled over. That must have been the creak I'd heard. Now her back was to me, which meant I couldn't tell if she was still asleep. But her body rose and fell with such rhythm that she had to be dozing. I whizzed through the open space between her and the next staircase, taking the steps gently but two at a time, pulling myself up with the railing, just wanting to get to the top and stand still, listening. Nothing but the TV. I'd made it.

There were four doorways to check out. Two at the beginning of the hall were bedrooms, one of them obviously Marcus's, the one I wanted to see most. First I glanced into the others—a bare "guest room," a bathroom with peeling paint and hastily hung towels, and Ms. Gomez's room, peppered with knickknacks, including a photo of Marcus in elementary school, a silver brush, a jewelry stand, and a portrait of an elderly female. Although Marcus looked Hispanic, and Beth referred to him that way in paperwork, his mother and the older woman were white. I wondered what happened to his dad. Beer cans were in random spots, some on the dresser and one crushed next to a trash can.

I made my way back to Marcus's room and slowly moved around his rumpled twin bed. I approached his dresser, careful not to trip over piles of wrinkled jeans, T-shirts, shorts, tighty whities, bandanas, and sweat socks. Basketball sneakers were lined up in a doorless closet, where most of the hangers were bare. A highboy was covered with rap CDs surrounding a hefty boom box.

I opened each drawer slightly, just enough to see inside and lift whatever clothes were there. Finding nothing of interest (more clothes were on the floor than in the dresser), I checked under each side of his mattress, and *bingo*, there were fifteen little baggies of greenish brown leaves. Pot, I assumed. I wanted to use the camera on my phone, but it was set to say, "Say cheese!" when I took a photo, and I didn't have time to fiddle with its options. I'd have to rely on my crappy memory. I closed my eyes and tried to lock in the bags' image.

I took two steps toward the closet and, standing on my tippy, tippy toes, peered onto the top shelf, but I couldn't see much, thanks to my short stature. The only thing I could make out in its shadowy recesses were sports trophies with golden dudes holding footballs.

I reached back as far as I could, and my index finger caught something. I pulled it toward me, and it tumbled out at my feet, sending me hopping backward and stifling a scream. It was a gun. I'd never been so close to one, except maybe on a cop's belt or at a museum display with the kids. My eyes were fixed on its trigger. It repelled and attracted me at the same time, reminding me of evil, which made me wonder if that's what it represented—a temptation that ensnared kids like Marcus, offering a taste of power, something that may have eluded them all their lives. I had to put it back, but I was afraid of it—more afraid than I was of waking Ms. Gomez. I looked around the room for anything I could use to pick it up. I settled on a white sock under my foot, which I wrapped around the gun—one hand under, one hand over. Then, keeping the gun pointed away from me, I gently slid it back onto the shelf and backed away, dropping the sock where I'd found it.

I breathed a sigh of relief and immediately knew it was not only premature, but totally inappropriate. I was in someone else's home, illegally looking through their things, which included a weapon. A *gun*. For the first time, the comedic phrase "You better check yourself before you wreck yourself" made serious sense. I was a stay-at-home mom, for heaven's sake. What was I doing? An image of Jack and Sophie visiting me in jail slammed me back to reality. It was definitely time to rouse

Ms. Gomez. *Too late*, I realized with a jolt. Apparently I'd already done that.

There were noises in the hall and then more in the bathroom. Noises I won't—and probably can't—describe in words. Suffice it to say that Ms. Gomez's lunch, which may have been beer, apparently didn't agree with her. While she was busy, I was too, rushing downstairs and out the screen door, closing it softly and then rapping as if I'd just arrived. I looked around to see if anyone was witnessing my crazy behavior, but there wasn't a soul in sight, although anyone could be watching from a window.

I heard Ms. Gomez's unmistakable yell. "What the hell do you want?"

"It's Nicki," I called in a singsong voice, as if I was innocent and used to that kind of greeting. "I called earlier about going to the hospital to see Marcus." I opened the door and stuck my head in. "May I come in?" So polite. As if I wasn't just *all over* her house. I didn't know what to think of myself, and thankfully, I was too jittery and breathless to focus on it.

"Who?" There was some muttering. "Hold on!"

I stayed outside and tapped my foot, hoping she'd wash her hands before we officially met. I really should have given her more time.

As she stomped down in her flip flops, I smiled brightly, oozing friendliness I hoped was contagious. "Hi!" I said.

"Whadaya want?" She pulled at the door impatiently.

"I'm here to take you to the hospital to see Marcus," I restated. "Remember?"

She didn't. I could practically see her mental gears shifting, rewinding, not finding anything, fast forwarding, and finally giving up.

"Well how long have I been waiting for you?" She reminded me of an old lady trying to hide confusion with indignation, but I put her real age at about forty.

"A little while. I'm sorry I'm late. Why don't we go? Do you have everything?" Her hands were empty. "I mean do you need anything for Marcus?"

She looked down at herself and shrugged. "Huh uh. Marcus don't need nothing from me."

I wasn't sure how she felt about that, but to me, it was sad.

*   *   *

I wish I could say conversation in the car was easy and enlightening, but it wasn't. Ms. Gomez—Tracy Gomez, I learned—wasn't as outgoing when she started to sober up, which I assumed was the cause of her relative silence. Or maybe she wasn't feeling well. For whatever reason, she was frustratingly reserved.

"So Tracy," I said casually. "Tell me about Marcus. What's he like?"

She surveyed me, probably wondering why she should trust this straight-laced-looking stranger. Maybe if I'd asked what the *h-e-double hockey sticks* he was like, she'd have been more comfortable.

"He's a good boy," she responded. She looked out the window away from me. "An only child."

"No trouble?"

Her shoulders rose and fell. "Boys. You know."

"I know, but Marcus got hurt," I reminded her. "Doesn't that worry you?"

"Marcus takes care of himself," she said. "He's fine."

No, he's not, I wanted to say. That's why kids join gangs. They need family, and if they don't have it, they'll create it, for better or worse.

"It must be so hard to have a teenager in this world," I said instead. "I can't imagine."

Her eyes fell on me.

"What happened to him again?" Maybe that was why she wasn't worried. She'd already forgotten what happened. I told her about Marcus and hoped it would sink in. "Well, he's a good boy," she repeated. "Takes care of me when I can't work."

"Oh. What kind of work do you do?"

"Clean houses." That was ironic. Then again, if I cleaned houses for a living, I don't know if I'd come home and clean my own. I barely do it now except under threat of mortal embarrassment or injury.

"And how does Marcus earn money?"

"He sells CDs," she said. "Makes good money and plays them at parties. Something like that. I don't know."

My guess was those CDs contained "bonus" tracks—or tokes.

We were at the hospital, but my mind was filled with questions, so I turned into the crowded parking lot, trying for once not to find a space, buying time. I drove slowly and chose my words carefully.

"Does Marcus have a girlfriend? Anyone else who should know about what happened?"

"No. He never talks about girls. Brings 'em home sometimes though."

"I see. But no one in particular?"

"One girl used to call a lot. But she stopped."

"Why?"

"I don't know. He said she was crazy. She don't call no more."

"When was that?"

"I don't know! I got a bad memory."

"Well maybe you remember her name? I know some kids at Marcus's school. How about 'Beth'?"

"I told you I don't know." She clamped her lips shut.

"They said something on the news about gangs. Do you think Marcus could have been shot by a gang member? I think there are gangs at his school."

"Of course there's gangs," she said with an exaggerated eye roll. "They're everywhere. I told him to *stay away*," she said. "Now my car's wrecked. Frickin' wrecked my car." Was she forgetting again that her son was injured? I hoped so, because I didn't want her to be as heartless as she sounded.

I pulled into a spot. "Let's go find Marcus and see what he says."

On the way to intensive care, she mentioned the names of some local gangs, which I had to resist writing down immediately. The biggest surprise came from Marcus's nurse. Marcus was gone. Not discharged. Just moved, thankfully, to another floor because he didn't need ICU services, which were in high demand.

As we made our way to his new unit, I glanced at my watch: 3:00 p.m. Tracy would need a ride home, too, and time was running short. My breaking, entering, and stalling had taken longer than I thought.

This time, Marcus's mom was on his visitor list, but I wasn't. Before I could ask about joining her, she took off for his room, flip flops slapping down the shiny linoleum hallway. I stayed in the waiting room and considered what to do next. I didn't want to question Marcus too directly and scare him off, at least not yet, so barging in on them didn't feel right.

With time ticking away, I crossed the room to a rack of brochures on flu pandemic preparedness and tuberculosis screening—perfect for note-taking or inducing a panic attack. After assuring myself I didn't have TB and was semi-prepared for "sheltering in place" (depending on how long our family could live on O-shaped cereal and juice boxes), I was ready to call April, take notes on our conversation, and possibly order protective face masks.

I dialed the home number her mom, Jen, had given me.

"Hello?" The voice sounded young.

"April?"

"Who is this?" she asked.

"It's Nicki. From last night. Remember me?"

"A little. My mom told me this morning. And you wrote on my hand, too."

"Sorry about that. I wanted to make sure we got in touch. I know you're Beth's good friend. I'm looking into her disappearance, and I hope you can help me find her."

"Yeah. My mom said I could trust you."

"Thank you so much. I know the situation is kind of complicated."

"Uh huh."

"So if you have a few minutes," I continued, "I'll ask you some questions, okay?"

I looked around to see if I was disturbing anyone or being overheard. The coast was clear. "Let's start with Beth and Marcus. How did they meet?"

"Well they didn't exactly meet. They just kinda saw each other in the hall a lot. Then we went to a party, and he was there, and they started hanging out that night."

"When was that?"

"Maybe a year ago? The beginning of the school year. I remember because we had first period Spanish and he was always at his locker outside."

"Did he seem interested in her?"

"Yes."

"So they met at a party and 'hung out.' I'm sorry to be ignorant, but these days, what does 'hang out' mean? Talk? Make out? Have sex?"

"Jeez! No!" she said. "Beth wasn't, I mean, neither of us is like that. I guess you could say we're shy. I couldn't even believe they eventually, you know, did it."

A thought occurred to me. "Is there any chance, April, that the sex wasn't consensual? That she didn't want to do it, and he forced her?"

She was quiet. "He didn't, like, rape her or anything. But he talked her into it. Once she did it, it's like she didn't know how to turn back. She loved him. It was so stupid. I told her he was a jerk and he never deserved her."

The anger in her voice made my heart swell. "I can hear how much you care about her. Tell me more about where they hung out. Did they go on dates?"

She laughed. "Uh, *no.* He was too gangster for that."

"He's in a gang?"

"Yeah. Everyone knows that."

"Sorry. Which one is it?"

"C-16." That was one his mom had mentioned.

"Are gangs at your school violent?"

"Totally. You know who's in them, and you hear people got hurt, but you don't know exactly who did it."

"So where would they see each other?"

"Pretty much at parties."

"Like where we were last night?"

"Sorta. Like usually at someone's house," she whispered. "You know, when the parents are away. Or the parents don't care. Whatever. There's usually, umm..."

"April," I reassured her. "It's okay. I'm not the police. I just want to find Beth."

"Usually there are drugs. We don't do them," she added quickly. "But they're there." She paused. "I'll tell you something. But you have to swear you won't say I told you." She continued without stopping. "I'm positive Marcus is a dealer. He'd go off and do something and always come back with money. Beth didn't want to believe it because he sold CDs for local rappers too, but I mean he *is*. You hear things, you know? She just didn't want to admit it."

"What kind of drugs?"

"Dub bags."

I wasn't up on the drug lingo either. Maybe that was what I'd seen in Marcus's room. "I'm sorry. What exactly does that mean?" I asked.

"You know. Pot. About twenty dollars worth. Two dime bags. A dub bag."

"Okay. I heard Beth wished she could change him. Is that true?"

"*So* true! It's like he had a hold on her. Especially once they did it. I tried telling her it was *not* love. He did *not* love her. She finally saw it when she told him she was pregnant. That was it. Over. I was the only one who was there for her."

"What about her parents? Were they supportive at all?"

"At first, when they thought she was going to keep the baby, but then when she went to First Steps, they were like *hold on, no one's giving our baby away*."

"*Our* baby?"

"They said it was part of the family—that she couldn't give it away without their permission."

"Did they kick her out of the house?"

"They let her stay, and they gave her money for doctor visits. But they were always trying to change her mind, saying stuff like, 'Won't you miss the baby?' and 'Won't you be sad every year on its birthday?' So mean. I wanted her to live with me and my mom."

"Why didn't she?"

"I don't know. She always said she didn't want to cause my mom any trouble."

"Okay. Back to Marcus. When did she tell him about the baby?"

"After about five months. We read online that before three months, you don't know if you might lose the baby or something, so she waited until it was for sure. She didn't even tell her parents."

"So she didn't see a doctor for the first five months?"

"Right. And she wore big clothes so no one would know. But she took vitamins from the drugstore."

"Prenatal vitamins?"

"Yeah. She hid them in her locker."

I was relieved and thankful. "Good for her. When she told Marcus, where did she do it?"

"At school. In a bathroom." She sighed.

"How did he react?"

"He punched a door and left. Jerk. That was the last they talked. At least that I *know* about." Her tone was accusing. I wondered if all her blame was placed on Marcus, or if she thought Beth shared some of it.

"You sound angry," I said.

"Well *duh*." She took aim at me. "Someone took my best friend. Am I supposed to be happy?"

"I understand. But when you said the last time they talked was five months into the pregnancy, you didn't seem convinced of it. Do you think there was another time they talked? Like recently?"

"That's the problem—I don't know!" I pictured her eyes tearing up or rolling at me. "I mean obviously if he took her, then they saw each other again."

"You're right. But what about another time? Did she keep going to parties? Were there other times they were in the same place?"

"She stopped going to parties because she couldn't drink and she was embarrassed about getting fat. But I always got this feeling. Like if he ever, *ever* called and tried to make up with her, she'd do it in a second."

"And keep the baby?"

"No. She just wanted to be with him."

"Did she say all this to you?"

"No. I just felt it."

Something occurred to me, but I didn't want to offend her, so I tried a non-confrontational approach.

"Oh, April, I almost forgot. Do you have access to Beth's computer passwords? I think it might be really helpful."

"You mean like for Internet access?"

"No, like for Facebook and stuff."

"Oh. No. Why?"

"Those sites can be really important in cases like this. Tell you what. Could you do me a favor? Check out her pages and see if anything stands out to you."

"Like what?"

"Absolutely anything. Maybe a person or comment that's unfamiliar or odd. Anything that catches your eye. Then email me. Do you still have my address?"

"Yeah. But I already looked at her pages and talked to our friends. There's nothing."

"Okay. Well please get in touch anytime you think of something about Beth. I appreciate it so much."

Sensing time was up—in part because I couldn't imagine Marcus and his mom carrying on a long, meaningful conversation—I finished by getting April and Beth's cell numbers and email addresses, surely the most important contact information for any teen these days.

The drive back to the Gomez house was uneventful because Tracy slept most of the way. If private investigation didn't work out, maybe I could start a designated-driver chauffeur service. I managed to get a recap of her conversation with Marcus, which was loving and easy to summarize: They were both glad he didn't die. As we pulled into her driveway, she didn't invite me in, and she got out with the car running, barely giving me time to say goodbye.

In my last half-hour of free time, I raced home, played Janet Jackson extra loud, and became what I nicknamed the "whirlwind," a cleaning maniac that defies explanation since I'm always too tired for housework. Janet thrust me through the kitchen, dining room, and living room, leaving only the hidden spaces (cabinets, closets, drawers, etc.) a disaster. Hopefully Mom would incorrectly perceive our home as well maintained. At the very least, dancing through the house helped me burn off steam.

Finally, I made the same old rushed drive to camp, second-guessing everything I'd done that day, including little things, such as whether I left any embarrassing items out at home. When Jason was alive, it would have been the condoms, but there was no use for those now. The most personal item I could think of was my credit card bill, which I paid online, so there was no risk of exposing my Target, Toys "R" Us, and Whole Foods overspending.

Once the kids were in the car, we picked up drive-thru snacks (a multi-stop challenge for health nuts) on the way to the airport. Sophie chose a fruit-and-nut combo, Jack got trans-fat-free French fries, and I got a cup of pinto beans. Just enough time was wasted to put us on schedule for Mom's five o'clock arrival at Dulles. We circled past the pickup area repeatedly until we saw her waving us down. All she had was a carry-on duffel, which was great, since I'd forgotten to empty the trunk.

"Hi, Mom!" I greeted her. Being at Dulles reminded me of my dad, but I was determined to smile through it.

Mom was tan from a few days in the Florida sun, her trademark pink lipstick and favorite Lily dress extra colorful against their new backdrop.

"You got some sun," I said as I gave her a hug.

"Well, it's Florida," she said, smiling. "I couldn't help it." She slid into the front seat with her bag and turned to look at the kids. "How are my little sunshines?"

"Good," Jack answered.

"You're babysitting?" Sophie asked.

"I am," she said. "And I have a few surprises from Florida."

"How exciting," I said. The kids would love that.

"Are you all ready for your PI class?" she asked.

I looked down at myself and then tilted the rearview mirror for a glance at my face, which needed touching up.

"Almost," I said before the truth hit me. "Oh no!" I'd forgotten to do my homework.

Eight

My goal of not embarrassing myself in Dean's class was already doomed. I was supposed to have researched someone's criminal history—a stranger whose name and address I was given—and not only hadn't I done it, but I didn't remember where to start. I was hopeless.

Luckily, in addition to buying seashell trinkets for the kids, my mom had found me a pretty sundress at St. Armand's Circle on Lido Key, home to some of the best shopping on Florida's Gulf coast, so at least I'd be a well-dressed idiot. That had worked for a lot of people, hadn't it? I ironed the dress and pulled it over my head, twisting back and forth in front of my bedroom mirror and fluffing my hair. I looked okay. The brown and turquoise plaid pattern brought out my eyes without being showy, and the v-neck and cinched waist flattered curves without revealing a thing. I threw on a white cardigan and officially became the anti-Amber.

After adding blush, lipstick, eyeliner, powder, earrings, and white sandals, I was ready to go, *sans* homework, when something occurred to me. I could pay to download the criminal history online, couldn't I? Then at least I'd have something. I pulled a credit card from my purse.

"What are you doing?" Mom asked.

"Nothing." I bolted toward my office. "Just homework."

"Can I help?" she called.

"Nope!" *Just by leaving me alone*, I thought rudely. I only had a few minutes to think clearly. Otherwise I'd be late to class. Doubly irresponsible.

I did the best I could online, paying $50 to investigate Bryce Conners of King County, VA, who turned out to have a history of DUI.

Then I felt even dumber. Surely Dean would understand why I hadn't done the research properly. Now I looked like a cheater.

I grabbed the criminal history out of the printer and stuffed it into a briefcase-size purse.

"I gotta go, Mom," I called from the foyer.

"Okay." She hustled out from the kitchen. I could already smell the tofu hot dogs and mixed veggies I'd suggested for dinner. "You look phenomenal," she said.

"Thanks to you. This dress is perfect. I should be home by ten." She knew the drill with the kids, so there wasn't much to review. "Remember to cut the hot dogs longways and in little pieces," I said, giving in to my fear of losing another loved one—this time by way of choking. I'd already set out child CPR instructions, just like I did every time Mom babysat. *Maybe I should wrap them in bubble wrap, strap on helmets, hire bodyguards, and be done with it,* I thought. *I've got to relax.*

I took a deep breath and peered down the hall at Jack and Sophie, who were giggling about something in the kitchen. "I love you," I called out. "See you in the morning."

"Have fun," Mom told me. "And learn a lot."

"I'll sure try."

The night's topic was a boring necessity. The court system. I'd studied it many times before, but without using the information regularly, I always forgot it as quickly as I'd found Bryce Conners' criminal record, which Dean finally addressed at the end of class.

"So, does anyone have the lowdown on Bryce Conners?" he asked.

I did the standard look-down-and-act-really-busy move that probably doesn't fool teachers. I don't know if he noticed or not, since I was focusing intently on my notebook, pretending to review something fascinating.

A retired police officer must have raised his hand, because Dean called on him right away. "Yes, Jerry?"

Jerry listed all of Mr. Conners' "accomplishments," which were available through the court system online—completely free—so I'd wasted $50. Dean led a follow-up discussion on records research, and I stayed quiet, listening intently and taking notes, since I had nothing to contribute.

Finally class ended, and while everyone else filed out, I smiled, waved goodbye, and stayed in my seat, eating a breath mint and deep breathing. Dean sat down nearby, muscles straining against his white polo shirt. In my mind it burst Hulk-style, and I swooned. How pathetic.

"So what's goin' on?" he asked. "Give me the update."

"First of all," I said, "I have to be honest with you. I didn't do the homework. I've been really busy, but that's no excuse."

"It's a great excuse," he said generously. "You were helping someone in need."

I sighed. "Thanks. I feel bad about it."

"So tell me exactly what's been keeping you occupied, other than Jack and Sophie, of course," he said.

Aww. He remembered their names. Since he wasn't creepy, I liked it.

"They go to camp a few hours a day, thank goodness, so I had time to interview the birth father, his mom, and the birth mother's best friend. Plus I checked out some social networking sites." I gave him the details.

"You *have* been busy."

"Not busy enough. Beth's been missing more than a week, and with the first hours being critical, it's maddening."

He nodded. "I know. But how do you know for sure she's been missing that long?"

I thought for a moment. "I guess I don't. That's what April's mom told me."

"Confirm it with April and anyone else you can. Then use that as a starting point. Talk to neighbors, potential witnesses—anyone who could have been around. You got Beth's contact information?"

"Yes." I mentally crossed my fingers that he was about to offer help.

"Jot it down for me. Maybe I can work with it."

"That would be incredible." I looked anxiously at my notebook and purse, realizing that in my rush, I'd left Kenna's "case" folder at home. I wanted to kick myself and add a punch for good measure. "I left it at home. I'll email you as soon as I get there." Afraid something would distract me, such as a wayward child in need of a tuck in, I added, "If you don't hear from me, please call or email," I told him. "I appreciate your help more than I can say."

"My pleasure." He pushed up from the table. "I've gotta close up shop here."

"Oh, I'm sorry." I shoved class handouts into my notebook and pulled the bulging mess to my chest. "I didn't mean to keep you."

"I wish I could stay," he said. "But I have another commitment."

Hopefully *commitment* wasn't code for *date*.

"Of course," I said. "I'm on my way." I headed for the door and thanked him again. Amber was reading a paperback at her desk, and I desperately hoped she wasn't waiting to leave with him, although if she was, I'd totally give up. I had no desire or ability to compete with her kind of pretty.

"Keep in touch," he said. "I'll see you Saturday."

Saturdays were all-day class sessions. This weekend we'd practice surveillance. Students would divide into two-car teams and follow someone, trying not to be spotted. "Remember to email me," he added.

As I pulled out, I glanced back to see Dean turn out the lights and hold the door for Amber. Great.

My mom left on a kitchen light directly above a note that read *Leftovers in the fridge.* I found the plate of tofu, pasta, and veggies, all of which had shriveled since they were prepared, and I stuck it in the microwave for thirty seconds, hoping its beeps wouldn't wake anyone. I mixed everything and added a little tomato sauce before eating. Not bad. Not good either.

I'd invited Mom to spend the night, so it wasn't a surprise that she was in the second floor guest room, fast asleep. It was a surprise, however, that she was alone, meaning the kids were flying solo in their beds, at least for now. I wondered how she'd accomplished that.

Before anything got in the way, I slipped into my office, where the computer was on and ready to go. I sent Dean an email with Beth's and April's phone numbers, addresses, and social networking sites, thanking him again for his time.

Within seconds, I got a response. It was so fast that I thought it must be one of those auto responses—*Hi, I'm out of the office right now. Please contact so-and-so if you need immediate assistance.* But it wasn't. *Got it. Thanks*, he wrote. *I'll let you know if I find anything.* A tagline said he'd emailed from his phone. If he had a date, at least she wasn't distracting enough to separate him from email.

It was almost ten o'clock, and instead of being drained, I was unusually alert, my head practically vibrating with thoughts.

Most of all, I wanted to call April and double check who saw Beth last. I also wanted to drive to Beth's again and look more carefully at who was around at night. Last time was at the same hour as her disappearance, 11 p.m., but I hadn't paid close enough attention to the surroundings.

I opened the file and looked at my notes. If only I'd documented every house light and parked car. Maybe someone who stayed up to watch late-night TV heard something. *Fudge.*

I closed my eyes and imagined what I'd seen. Most of the lights were off. The neighborhood was quiet. Nothing stood out.

I picked up the phone and risked calling April's cell this late. I hoped her mom wouldn't mind or even notice.

"April?" I said when someone picked up.

"Yeah." She sounded wide awake.

"It's Nicki. I'm sorry to call so late, but I want to check something."

"Okay."

"When was the last time you saw or heard from Beth?"

"I dropped her off at eleven at her house, not last Sunday, but the one before that. She missed a big test the next day."

"That's exactly what your mom said. What was Beth's mood that night?"

"Her mood?"

"Uh huh. How was she feeling?"

"I told the police she was kinda down. But nothing weird. Just a lot going on. The baby, summer school, you know."

"Was she worried about the test?"

"I doubt it. We studied pretty hard."

"Was anything else on her mind? Did she mention anything?"

"Not really."

Something felt off. I didn't want to push it, but then again, teens lie a lot, and I needed the truth. I'd lied to the police without good reason myself.

"April," I said. "I know it's hard to trust me, but you've done a good job so far, and when you do, I think it gets us closer to Beth. You said you dropped Beth off at eleven on Sunday. And you told the police Beth was kind of down, but nothing unusual. Is there anything you left out? I really need to know."

She took a breath and blew it out like I do when I'm trying not to panic. A breath is proof you're okay.

My voice softened. "You can tell me."

I heard a tiny noise—something between a whimper and a cough. Definitely a precursor to crying.

"April," I comforted her. "What's wrong?"

I flashed back to high school, when everything seemed so serious, make or break, life or death, yet in retrospect forgettable. No matter how serious or innocuous April's news was, she *had* to tell me, and I think she knew it. But I was petrified she'd back out.

"I can't," she said, her voice wet with tears.

"You can," I said. "I know it's hard. I remember being your age. I had so many secrets." I paused and waited for a response. "I promise I won't tell anyone if I don't have to. I only want to find Beth."

"It's about her," she admitted. "But I don't think it matters. Oh my God, I hope it doesn't."

"Okay." *Keep going, keep going*, I urged her silently.

"It's something I told her that night. I thought she knew, but she didn't. I couldn't help it. I had to tell her. I felt like it was showing anyway."

I was starting to get a feeling, but I wasn't going to share it. April was self-conscious enough without anyone filling in the blanks.

"I think I might be..." She stopped. I sensed it wasn't *pregnant*. "Gay!" She burst into tears.

"Oh, April. It's okay." Part of me wished I was there to hug her. Another part wanted to stay right where I was—at a distance.

Everything in me wanted to trust her, but there was always a chance she was involved in Beth's disappearance, and I had to stay objective. "Is Beth the only person you've told?" I asked.

"Yeah." She let out a laugh combined with a cry. "Except for you now. Definitely not my mom. She would freak."

"But your mom seems okay."

"You don't know her."

"True," I said. "But maybe she'd surprise you."

"I doubt it. She thinks I don't date because I'm too mature for high school guys. And she likes that."

I remembered what her mom said about April and Beth being shy and keeping to themselves. I wanted to point out that April could be gay *and* more mature than guys, but I let her keep talking.

"I couldn't fake it anymore," she said. "Either I had to stop being friends with Beth, or I had to tell her. So I told her. I don't know why I picked that night," she moaned. "I just felt like it was getting obvious."

"How was it obvious?"

"I don't know. Just the way...I don't know. I can't talk about this!" More tears.

"Well, I'm glad you are. I think it would really help if you told me Beth's reaction."

"She couldn't believe it. Maybe she was disgusted. But I was totally wrong to think she knew. Then it's like she was mad, saying stuff like, 'How can we be friends now? I need to trust you, and I don't even know you.' It's not like I was any different. I told her I didn't *like* her or anything. But she didn't get it. I had to drive her home, so I did, and that was it. We didn't talk the whole way. She just got out. Didn't even say goodbye."

"Did you watch her walk in?"

"Yeah. Because I was hoping she'd turn around and come back. But she didn't. She shut the door."

"And that was the last you saw or heard from her?"

"Mmm hmm."

"Did you notice anything else in the neighborhood?"

"No."

"Any people? Cars? Lights? Anyone walking a dog? Anything at all?"

"I don't think so. All I could think about was her. I didn't care about anything else. I could barely even see because I was crying."

"So what happened next?"

"I drove home, went to sleep, and took my stupid English test the next day. When she didn't show up, I thought she was mad. I didn't even worry about her." She started crying again. "Do you think she could have left because of me?"

I wanted to say *no*, but it was more important to hear her opinion. "What do you think?"

"No," she answered.

"Why?"

"The baby. She loved it. She wanted to do the right thing."

"And to her, that was..."

"Adoption."

"April, if Beth didn't have you available, who would she turn to if she was upset? Is there anyone she could have called that night?"

"I thought of Diane, the social worker at the adoption agency, because birth mothers are allowed to call her anytime. But I asked, and she said Beth didn't call. Also the police said I was the last one she talked to."

I mentioned the school guidance counselors and "friends" I'd seen online. April assured me they weren't possibilities. Beth had withdrawn during pregnancy, not reached out.

"Okay. Last question for now. Did Beth have any marks that would stand out on her, like tattoos, birthmarks, or piercings or anything?"

There was a pause. "She would kill me for saying this, but she has a little tattoo near her tailbone. Her parents don't know. We got the same one—a rose. I already told the police."

"Do you have a picture of it?"

"Yeah. We took a picture right after."

"Could you send it to me?"

"It's on my cell. Do you want me to forward it?"

I gave her my number and watched the photo arrive.

"April, thank you so much for everything, especially for confiding in me." I considered the best words to say, but nothing seemed good enough. If I were Jen, I'd have said, "I love you" or "I love who you are," but I wasn't. So I chose, "I'm here for you. Call me anytime you want to talk. And I'll email you some hotline numbers too. When you call them, you'll see you're not alone in this. In fact, you should be really, really proud of yourself. Are you going to be okay?"

She said yes, thanked me, sniffled, and hung up. Before doing anything else, I hit the Internet and emailed her the best LGBTQ hotline numbers I could find.

Breaks from parenting are few and far between. And when they come along, sometimes it still takes a crowbar to pry me away. Never mind all those days of wishing, "If only I had a free moment." When someone offers to watch the kids for a night, I spend half the time worrying.

Technically, though, my mom hadn't offered to babysit *all night*. She was spending the night out of convenience. No matter how tempting it was to sneak out of the house for more investigation, it was also tempting to stay home, in my comfort zone, available in case my kids needed anything. But the conversation with April tugged at my conscience like Sophie pulling at my pant leg. I knew I had to do a better job of surveillance at Beth's.

I scribbled a note to Mom and left it in the guest room doorway.

10:30.
So sorry, Mom. I had to run out again. Will be back by midnight, I hope. Thanks for everything!

On the road again, I opened my window and let humidity fill the car and penetrate my skin. For some reason, it felt good—almost like company. Definitely better than being chilled and alone.

The DJs on my favorite old-school station added to the illusion. I wished I could close my eyes and float away to Freddie Jackson's *Rock Me Tonight*.

The car moved to the music, around turns and bends, finding Beth's house without my usual brain racking. The street was rectangular with five townhomes per end and ten on each side. In the center was a median with guest parking.

I chose a spot and turned off the van to think. I wanted to walk around and get a closer look at homes—maybe even peek in a few windows—but I needed an excuse to wander the neighborhood this late. Something like a dog.

Since one wasn't available, I considered undercover schemes, such as pretending to be a real estate agent or homebuyer. It was too late at night for that. I'd have to save them for daytime. Plus, there were no homes for sale on the street.

I decided to become the confident woman I'm not and simply take an evening stroll. It was plenty warm enough, and I still had my white cardigan from class. Being camouflaged with a dark sweater would have been better, but I'd based my outfit on Dean, not surveillance. I needed one of those hunting getups that looks like shrubbery. That made me smile and think of Kenna, always my partner in crime, and wish we could put this crazy situation behind us and move on to other things—*fun* crazy things. In my dreams she'd become a PI, too, and we could investigate together.

My rubber-soled sandals were almost silent on the cement that led past each house. I started at the opposite end of the street from Beth's, since that's where I parked and, honestly, I needed to gather my courage. I swung my arms as though I'd put off my power walk and was just squeezing it in before bed. Good for me! Kenna would be proud. Hopefully I looked determined enough to ward off would-be attackers. If worse came to worst, I'd press the alarm button on my van remote to attract attention.

I paused under a lamp post to scan the community mailbox, which was plastered with ads: a treadmill for sale ($100), a lost dog (a German Shepherd named Rocky), after-school childcare at an Internet café (thank goodness, because today's kids need *more* screen time), and an upcoming social event for seniors.

I continued walking past mostly dark homes with porch and foyer lights on here and there, casting a soft glow. In one house, a man watched local news on a couch, while in another, laundry hung on a treadmill in the basement. Maybe that was the one for sale? *I should buy it,* I told myself. Despite chasing kids around, doing housework, and generally being on the go, I felt bad about not truly exercising, especially since I was breaking a sweat on this little walk. I hoped fear was to blame. But calling about the treadmill might be a good way to chat with a neighbor and investigate.

When I got to Beth's row, two homes had lights on, Beth's and the one with toys in the yard. In the young family's house, curtains covered the bottom half of the windows, with only a valence over the top, which allowed me to see a heavyset woman with messy red hair and a screaming infant. She was opening the refrigerator. *Probably getting a bottle*, I thought.

Curiosity pulled me out of her sightline and closer to Beth's home, where a crack in the curtains offered a tiny glimpse inside. In an unexpected surge of resourcefulness, I slipped a sapphire ring off my finger—a birthstone gift from my father—and clutched it as tightly as possible. If anyone asked, I'd say that in the heat of my power walk, it had flown off my finger, bounced off the sidewalk, and landed somewhere on their lawn. I even felt the grass a few times with my other hand, desperately afraid of *actually* losing my ring, when it hit me. What if I knocked on their door, told Beth's parents I'd lost a piece of jewelry, and talked with them? My heart beat faster than it had on my walk. If only anxiety counted as aerobic exercise!

As quickly as I thought of the plan, I discarded it. I couldn't interrupt anyone this late at night. But I *could* drop something cheap on their lawn and come back the next day for it, something like the fake gold-and-pearl earrings I was wearing, or at least one of them. I pushed my ring firmly back onto my right index finger and reached up to separate an earring from its back. I peered through the break in the curtains and inhaled sharply. A middle-aged woman was sitting at a round, wood table, head in hands, crying. Now that I saw her, I could hear her too. A stocky, graying man sat across from her, extending his hand across the table, but she didn't take it. The moment was so personal that I felt they'd sense my presence any second. I turned and dropped my earring into the garden mulch, and then power walked my ass back to the van. There I sat, observing houses, relieved that Beth's curtains were still, wondering if I'd really have the courage to return for my earring—and hopefully something a lot more valuable.

Nine

I woke to the smell of eggs and coffee. Jack and Sophie weren't capable of creating that particular aroma, so I knew Mom was up. I looked at the clock and did a double take—8:27! She'd let me sleep in. I couldn't remember the last time I started the day after eight. I didn't even know I was capable of it anymore. I felt guilty but persuaded myself to relax. *I'll have more patience and energy,* I thought. *Everyone wins.*

Before I could convince myself to put a pillow over my head and snooze a little more, I swung my legs over the side of the bed and headed for the bathroom. *How odd,* I marveled. *Peeing and brushing my teeth in peace. Maybe I can even take a shower.* I turned on the water, threw my clothes in the hamper, and jumped in. I started off motivated (shampooed and conditioned super fast) but got lulled into enjoying the hot water and absence of worry about the kids and their activities. I took my time scrubbing and shaving. If I could have taken a nap and watched reality TV in there, I would have.

True reality hit me in the form of pounding feet and overexcited screaming downstairs. It was time to emerge from my steamy paradise into the chilly air, but before I wrapped towels around my body and head, I did a quick scale/mirror assessment: 136. *Okay.* Sinking butt and cellulite. *Eww.* I chose not to inspect wrinkles up close. I slathered on SPF 30 lotion instead and hoped for the best.

After choosing an outfit with care (criteria: anything presentable yet stainable, so I wouldn't erupt if the kids spilled something on me), applying makeup, and drying my hair for as long as I had patience, I stepped quickly downstairs to see what mischief was afoot.

Sophie slammed into me with glee, screaming, "Mommy! You're up! What took you so long?"

"Hi, Mom," Jack said. "Grandma made eggs." He didn't like eggs, but I did, as long as the chickens were organic, cage free, and vegetarian fed. Not too much to ask.

"Sorry buddy," I said, deciding to spoil him. "If you haven't eaten anything, I'll make you a bagel with peanut butter and fruit. Just be sure to say, 'No, thank you' to Grandma."

"Okay."

He did so when our trio reached the kitchen, where Mom poured me a cup of decaf and presented a plate of scrambled eggs and strawberries.

"Morning," she said brightly.

"Mom, this is incredible. Thank you so much for letting me sleep in. It's a serious treat."

"Well, you've been busy, and you deserve it."

"You've also been busy," I said.

"Jack, can I get you anything else?" She raised an eyebrow at me. "He doesn't like eggs?"

"No." I shook my head. "Sorry." He was a picky eater. As long as he ate the basics each day—with slight variations among them—I didn't mind, but with company, his rejections made me self-conscious. "I'll make him a bagel with peanut butter," I said. "And I'll share my strawberries."

"Yum," he said, plucking one from my plate. Sophie announced she'd already eaten an omelet with cheese and red peppers. Even her taste buds reflected her daring personality.

"I have to leave soon," Mom said. "I've got a mani-pedi this morning. Is that okay?"

"Of course," I said. "We've got plans too."

I wanted to see someone about the treadmill and retrieve my earring, and the kids were coming along. *Actually*, I couldn't help thinking, *they'll probably make this easier.*

"Hop in, guys!" I told them after Mom left in a taxi that had parked behind our van and saved us the drive to her condo and back.

They obeyed and peppered me with questions about our pre-camp destination. It was unusual for us to get anything done before I dropped them off. I'd made a ten o'clock appointment to see the treadmill, packed camp supplies, and sunscreened everyone with Mom's help. We were right on schedule.

"We're going to a new playground," I announced. "And I'm going to talk to someone about a treadmill."

"Like the ones at Auntie Kenna's work?" Sophie asked.

"Exactly."

"Why are you talking to someone about a treadmill?" Jack asked.

"Because I might buy it," I said. "And get some exercise once in a while."

"Weird," he said. Yup. It was.

"Anyway, I need you guys to behave when I'm talking to people, okay? No interrupting unless it's an emergency."

"Like if I have to go to the bathroom?" Sophie asked.

"Yes. If you really have to go. But you went before we left, right?"

"Yes, Mom."

"Me too!" Jack said.

Phew.

Traffic flowed and I knew the route by heart now, so I concentrated on argument-prevention through creative storytelling (Batman and Super Teddy save a stray cat!) and careful music selection (Alvin and the Chipmunks).

By the time I parked near Beth's, I had to refocus on serious issues. What would I ask (other than how can I get this enormous treadmill home)? My stomach churned. While unbuckling the kids and helping them out of the van, I took a moment to savor their relaxed expressions. How sad that youth can never be fully enjoyed. By adulthood, life's poundings finally make you appreciate innocence.

I stopped to give strict reminders about guest etiquette. *Ask before touching other people's things. If you want to say something that could hurt someone's feelings, tell me privately.* Long ago, after broadcasting gems such as, "He looks like a wolf" (he did) and "Is that a lady?" (I wasn't sure either), the kids had learned two guidelines: *whisper* or *wait.* Every once in a while, they slipped up, but for the most part, they rocked.

While I let Jack ring the doorbell, I squinted toward Beth's house, several rows away with a maroon sedan in front of a closed garage. My glance was interrupted by a woman's enthusiastic greeting as she opened the front door.

"Hi! You must be here about the treadmill." She looked fifty-ish but had more energy than I did, kind of like Kenna, which made me envy and admire her—and want the treadmill even more.

"We are." I held out my hand to shake hers. "Hi. I'm Nicki."

"And I'm Gina. Come on in."

"Thanks." I ushered the kids into the foyer. Normally I would have introduced them and removed their shoes, but she was moving so quickly all we could do was follow.

"It's in the basement," she explained, starting down carpeted steps. "I joined a health club, so I don't need it anymore. And I have grandkids now, so we need more room." She threw a smile at Jack and Sophie.

"How many grandkids do you have?" I asked.

"Two little girls, three and five. I raised three boys. So, I finally got my girls!"

We arrived at a guest bedroom with a sturdy looking treadmill, not the clothes hanger I'd seen in someone else's basement, and Sophie immediately hung on its handrails.

"No, Hon," I said. "That's dangerous. And we have to take good care of this." Maybe getting exercise equipment wasn't such a good idea.

"There's a safety mechanism," Gina said. After Sophie stepped back, Gina got the treadmill going faster than I could imagine running. Then she pulled a red string, yanking a magnet off the control panel and stopping the machine cold. "See?" she said, swinging the magnet in the air. "This has to be attached for it to work."

I'd have to hide that string where the kids would never find it. Not that such a place existed.

"Cool," I said. "Only $100 for this? It looks pretty nice." Some negotiator I am.

"It is. But it's got to go. I promised my grandkids a playroom, and this is going to be it." She hit the treadmill for emphasis. "Tell me," she said to Sophie. "What toys do you suggest for little girls?"

"Hmm." Sophie scrunched up her face in serious thought. "A pretend kitchen?"

"She loves kitchens," I said.

"Even real ones," Sophie added. It was true. Sophie would cook and try new foods—real or pretend—any day.

"That's a fun idea," Gina said. "A kitchen."

"I bet there are neighborhood kids to play with, too," I said. "Nothing's more fun than kids."

"Definitely," Gina said. "This street's a zoo on summer nights. Full of bikes, scooters, and those little pretend cars."

"Lucky," I said. "Our street is way too busy for that. And the teens drive too fast."

"We don't have that problem," she said. "I guess I take that for granted."

I saw my opportunity and seized it. "I did hear something really surprising," I said. "That a teen from your street is missing."

"Yes," she said. "I think maybe it was her choice though." She looked at Jack and Sophie as if measuring her words. "She was...with child."

"That's so sad. Did you know her?"

"Just by sight. But I think about her family a lot. I don't know them, but I left them a note passing along my support, and other neighbors did the same."

"That's nice. Did they respond?"

"No. But I understand," she said. "It must be awful." She paused. "So what do you think about the treadmill?"

"I'll take it," I decided. "My only problem is getting it into my minivan. I doubt we can lift it."

"My husband and I can get it into your trunk if someone can help you unload it."

I mentally volunteered Andy. "That would be great. Can I come back for it later?"

"You'll have to. My husband won't be home 'til five."

We walked upstairs to leave, and I mentioned our plans to visit the tot lot down the street. "Do you need water or anything?" Gina asked. "It's so hot."

"We've got supplies in the van," I said. "But thanks anyway."

We waved goodbye and carried snacks and drinks to the playground, which was shaded by a thick, leafy tree, thanks to a brilliant landscaper or community planner. I sat under it and let the kids run free. Meanwhile, I stared at the back of Beth's house, seeing it for the first time.

A wide deck with a two-level staircase rose above a small yard that looked essentially useless in the deck's shadow. The deck itself, though, was beautifully decorated with flower boxes, a stainless steel grill, sea-green furniture, and a privacy screen to block the neighbor's view. Security-wise, the deck provided another entry point and shielded the basement sliding glass door from view. I wondered if the yard was lit at night.

There were no signs of movement in the house, but I thought someone must be home, based on the car in front, a Honda Accord. I'd tried to memorize its license plate as we walked by.

After a few swigs of water and ten minutes of watching the kids, hoping bugs weren't crawling out of the grass and up my shorts, I was literally antsy. In addition to being bored, I knew if I didn't get the earring thing over with, I'd lose my courage, and anyone home might leave. Plus, I had to get the kids to camp, and that was good motivation.

I gathered our belongings and called out to them.

"Guys. Let's get ready to go."

"No!" they screamed.

"Not yet." Jack added.

"I'm sorry. But guess what, when I walked by someone's house, I think I lost an earring."

"What?" Sophie's interest was piqued. "I can find it," she said with confidence.

"Let me show you where to look," I said.

We trudged around the side of the house, and I pointed to a section of mulch where the earring hadn't fallen. It wasn't time to find it yet.

"Start here," I said. "It's a shiny gold hoop with a little pearl—a round, white thing—on it. I'll knock on the door and tell them to keep an eye out for it. Okay?"

"You're going to knock on the door?" Jack said with surprise.

"Yeah. Just for a second. You guys stay here. And yell if you find it."

Keeping them in my peripheral vision, I reached toward the doorbell and pushed it firmly, despite how much I wanted to pull back and run, screaming *Follow me!* at the kids. I'd given the situation some thought the previous night, but now I felt totally unprepared—so unprepared I wanted to forget becoming a PI altogether. It was ridiculous and insane—the most uncomfortable I'd been since childbirth. Or maybe since realizing my husband was cheating and gone forever. Or maybe since finding out my father died. Okay, wait a minute, maybe today's situation wasn't so bad. I could *do* this. I didn't need to run home to my comfy life managing kids and laundry. *I had to find Beth.*

Since I was still waiting for someone to answer, and my determination had risen dramatically, I rang the doorbell again. My reward was a shift in a curtain, a glimpse of a woman with wet hair, and an impatient call from inside: "Just a minute." Oh dear. She'd probably been in the shower.

She opened the door in a thick, white robe and matching slippers. Her hair was dripping wet but combed, and her face was red and shiny, as if she'd exfoliated and moisturized. My instinct was to hug her—the mother of a missing teen—but of course I resisted.

"Hi," I said. I sounded hesitant even to myself.

She peered around me at my kids. "Hi," she said, looking back at me. "Can I help you?"

"I hope so. I was on a walk, and I think my earring fell off in your yard. I wanted to let you know in case you find it."

"Oh. Okay." She looked annoyed. I didn't blame her. "What does it look like?"

"It's a gold hoop with a pearl on it. Just a single pearl. My kids are looking for it."

She looked at them again. "That's where you lost it?"

"I think so."

"Okay. Let me get a pen," she said. "I'll take your information in case it turns up."

"Sure," I responded. "I'm really sorry to interrupt you."

My plan was to give her my email address if necessary, which didn't have identifying information in it. When she was out of sight, I motioned the kids over. "Hey guys," I said quickly. "Try over there. Maybe it was over there." I pointed to the spot where I'd dropped it. They rushed over.

"I found it!" Sophie yelled a minute later as Beth's mom returned.

"Good job!" I said. "Bring it to Mommy!" I looked back at Mrs. Myers. "I'm so sorry we bothered you. It looks like we found it." Sophie placed it in my palm and ran to Jack, who had something more interesting in his hand—a squiggling worm. He watched it with a smile, and I saw a reluctant grin form on Mrs. Myers' lips.

"It's okay," she said. "I'm Sonja." She held her bathrobe closed with her left hand and reached out to shake my hand with her right.

I didn't think I should tell her my real name, but I didn't want the kids screaming, *Your name's not Anna!* if I lied. So I settled on a compromise—my given name—which only my parents and an occasional teacher had ever used.

"Hi Sonja. I'm Nicole."

Her eyes stayed on the kids. "They're cute," she said.

"Thanks. Actually, I was talking to your neighbor Gina today, and I heard about your daughter. I'm terribly, terribly sorry."

"Oh," she cocked her head and squinted her eyes. "Thank you."

"We were wondering, is there anything the neighbors can do to help? In talking with Gina, I got the sense people would love to pitch in, but they aren't sure how."

"That's nice, but I'm sure you heard she ran away. She wanted to disappear, and that's what she did." She pressed her lips together. It looked like she was holding something back—maybe anger, tears, or both.

"I'm sorry. I shouldn't have said anything."

"You were just being polite. Listen, my husband and I will get through this," she said. "It's not like we haven't done it before."

"It's not the first time she's run away?" I feigned surprise and didn't enjoy it.

"No, it's not," she said with a sarcastic laugh. "I figured you heard from Gina. Beth has left us twice. Came back both times. So maybe this time we and everyone else shouldn't worry so much."

I wasn't convinced. "Where did she go the first two times?"

"Oh, she hung out with friends. Then she visited my parents in West Virginia." Her voice was sing-songy as she tilted her head back and forth, giving the impression Beth selfishly took off on random vacations. "She just wanted to make a point. She says we're too strict." She rolled her eyes. "What teen doesn't say that? It's called parenting."

"I understand. It must be so hard knowing..." I mustered the courage to say it. "Knowing she's pregnant."

She closed her eyes, shook her head back and forth, and then looked at me directly. "There isn't any way she could hurt us more."

I tried not to be judgmental, but *if* Beth didn't want to live at home right now, I doubted it was just to hurt them. Who would torture themselves out of spite like that? Probably not a young, helpless teen.

"You sound absolutely sure she left on purpose," I said.

She rested a hand on her hip and shifted her feet. "I'm sorry, what was your name again?" Uh oh. I wanted to keep asking questions, to keep her talking as long as the kids were happy worm hunting, but I'd gone too far.

"Nicole. And I'm the one who's sorry. I'm interrupting your day. And I'm being nosy. I just feel awful about your daughter."

"Beth's a smart girl. She'll come home." She reached for the doorknob.

"I hope so," I said truthfully.

"Thank you," she said, cutting me off. "I've got to go. I'm glad you found your earring." The door swung closed and I almost put my foot in it.

"Sonja?" I said loudly. She stopped and looked through the small opening that was left.

"What?"

"Let Gina know if anyone can help, okay?"

"I will. And please thank her for her note." The door closed firmly.

I glanced at the kids to make sure they were okay. They were, but I couldn't say the same for the Myers' mulch, which had become a worm excavation site.

"Stop digging, guys, and start cleaning up. Fill in the holes." I walked over to help.

While talking with Sonja, I'd inadvertently tuned out Jack and Sophie. I hoped my subconscious was paying attention...that I would have noticed if either of them wandered off...but I wasn't sure. *Finding someone else's child isn't more important than taking care of your own,* I chided myself. Mommy guilt washed over me in a hot sweat.

I cleaned the kids' hands with bottled water and wipes (their fingernails remained a disaster) and showered them with hugs, kisses, and compliments while we carried our belongings back to the van. *Please God*, I begged, *don't ever let me lose one of them.*

"Enough, Mom! We get it," Jack giggled.

"Get what?" I teased, giving him another hug. "What do you mean?"

"You love us!" said Sophie.

"Oh, you *do* get it," I said, hugging her too. "Good!"

The kids spent the afternoon at camp, and I spent it confirming information. Yes, April told me, Beth had run away twice before, just like her mom said. The first time she went to a party and walked around a twenty-four-hour store, refusing to go home in protest against her early curfew, which only made her parents stricter. The second time, she surprised her grandparents with a visit to their West Virginia home, pretending her mom had suggested the trip. The next morning, Sonja had called, and the jig was up. Beth was sent home—with a few new outfits and some cash—and told not to inform her parents of the gifts. Grandma and Grandpa sympathized with Beth's teenage frustrations, but they didn't want to anger their daughter, April said, so Beth stayed quiet.

"Do you think Beth could be there now?" I asked.

"No way," April said. "Her grandparents would never hide her this long. They love her, but can you imagine how pissed her mom would be?"

April had to be right. Would grandparents do that to a daughter they loved?

"And they weren't even hiding her that time? Beth tricked them?" I confirmed.

"Totally. They had no idea. They were mad. But they got over it."

"How long ago was that?"

"Eleventh grade, over spring break."

"So she didn't miss school?"

"No. She wouldn't have missed school. I mean, we've skipped classes and stuff, but she would never leave school like everyone says she did now. We're about to graduate."

"Why did she run away back then? What was so upsetting?"

"Her parents are just way overprotective. They don't let her do anything. I think she just couldn't take it anymore. She needed freedom."

"If they're so protective, how did she go to parties?"

"Lying. Spending the night at my house. Sneaking out."

"I understand." I'd done the same things. I clung to the hope my kids never would. "Do you remember which city her grandparents live in?"

"I don't know. I think it's some town where you can gamble."

"Do you know their names?"

"No. Just Nana and Grandpa. That's what she called them."

"Okay. And can you think of anyone, anyone at all, who might be involved, whether Beth's a runaway or not?"

"You mean like Marcus?"

"Anyone."

"Marcus is the only one who would have a reason."

"And that would be..."

"Not wanting to have a baby."

After camp, a neighbor with similar-aged kids invited Jack and Sophie over for dinner and a movie—not my favorite kind of playdate since it involves no playing, but I let it slide because I loved the other family, the movie was harmless, and picking up the treadmill without kids was a giant bonus. Kids, heavy electronic objects, and my anxiety—not a good mix.

Gina and her strikingly attractive husband—one of those fit guys who would always look spry—moved the treadmill with ease. They didn't even need my help except to open the trunk. I hoped when I hit my fifties I'd be in shape and upbeat too. *The treadmill will do it,* I told myself. *I'll get in shape for the first time. Maybe I'll even lift weights! I'll be able to outrun bad guys no problem.* Just the idea of keeping up with my kids might be incentive enough. At least I hoped so.

"Did you have fun at the park this morning?" Gina asked before I left.

"We did. Thanks." I handed her $100 in cash.

"Excellent. I hear you spoke with Sonja," she said.

"Oh, yeah," I replied nervously. "Did you talk to her too?"

"She stopped by this afternoon. I guess you mentioned something about my helping?"

"I said you were concerned, and that I thought the neighbors would like to help. I hope that's okay."

"It's great," she said with enthusiasm. I'd forgotten to expect that from her. "I was so surprised to see her at my door. I've been dying to do something, and you know I wrote her a note about it. Thank you for getting her out of the house and down here."

"She doesn't come out much, huh?"

"No, and it's such a devastating situation. I think they need others, don't you? I mean we *all* do."

"Absolutely. The more people who can help, the better." That was a fact. "She told me she appreciated your note. What did she have to say?"

"Well, she still didn't want much help. But she did give me a flyer to copy and hand out. She said to leave the rest to the police."

My mind was racing. I had to see that flyer.

"She only gave you one?"

"Yes," Gina said. "But I'll make more."

"I'd love to help with handing them out or putting them up. I can take a copy with me and make extras."

"Sure. That's nice of you. I'll be right back."

I waited in the minivan, air conditioner blasting, inspecting the loading job through the rearview mirror. The back seat was folded down, and the hatchback was tied closed. Andy had promised to help me get the treadmill through the basement door, but I was having second thoughts about where to put it. The basement was cold and uninviting, not somewhere I'd want to jog every day, and my bedroom was warm and cozy. If I had to see the treadmill when I woke up, taunting me, wouldn't it be hard to ignore? So that's where it should go. My eyes returned to Gina's house.

When she bounded down the front steps with a smile on her face, waving a stack of papers, my heart sang. This was more than a way to publicize Beth's disappearance. It was an excuse to knock on doors and ask questions. I wasn't good at it, but I was determined, and hopefully that counted for something.

"Here you go. I went ahead and made a bunch." She divided the stack and handed me half.

"How about if I do that side of the street while I'm here and my kids aren't?" I asked. "It will be easier."

She laughed. "Sure. Did I give you enough?"

I counted nine. There were twenty houses on the street, including Gina and Beth's. Nine was perfect. I took that as a good sign.

"Just right," I said.

"Hold on." Gina held up a hand. "I have an idea. How about if we go together? It's a nice evening, and I could use a walk."

"Okay," I said. I hoped her familiar face would open doors—and mouths.

Ten

Gina was a talker, and I love talkers. Wait. Let me qualify that. I love talkers who discuss interesting things, and since Gina and I chatted about parenting, food, vacation spots, and the neighborhood, I wasn't bored during our hour together. I also found it easy to keep quiet, particularly about personal subjects, which I wanted to avoid. I did reveal I had a degree in forensic psychology, and that after seeing Sophie through preschool, I wanted to catch criminals and support victims.

"How fascinating," Gina enthused. "So today's a good start. Now I know why you wanted to help so much."

Sort of, I thought while I nodded.

A few residents who answered their doors were shocked to hear there was a missing teen on their street. Most had already spoken with the police. Everyone eagerly accepted a flyer and promised to look out for her. Because Beth was pregnant, people recalled seeing her walk to the mailbox or down the street, but that was about it.

The only neighbor who said she knew Beth personally was Molly, a redhead, stay-at-home mom on Beth's row, the one I'd seen through the window with her infant. She greeted Gina with a hug and explained that Gina was like a surrogate grandma, since Molly's relatives lived far away.

I smiled and let Gina do the talking.

Molly had tried to befriend Beth, offering advice, hand-me-downs, and anything else Beth needed. Beth had been polite but unresponsive, except for once, when she asked what childbirth was like. Molly had a baby boy and a four-year-old girl, and both deliveries had been difficult, so she tried not to worry Beth.

"Giving birth is the most incredible thing I've ever done," she said she told Beth. "You'll do great. I know it."

"How did she react?" I asked.

"She didn't say much. Just 'Oh, that's good' or something. But she loved looking at Michael." She indicated her pudgy baby, lying face-up on a play mat, batting black-and-white shapes that hung above him. "Anytime she'd see us, she'd come right up and ask how he was doing. She's a good girl. I can't believe she's missing."

"Did she seem like someone who would run away?"

"I don't know," Molly said thoughtfully. "Her parents seemed okay. They would say hello and stuff, but that's it. You know how they are, Gina, right?"

"Very private," Gina agreed.

"Yeah." Molly wrinkled her nose. "Nothing seemed wrong, but it didn't seem right either. Not happy. I didn't think much about it. But you know, what if she didn't run away? I mean that's *really* scary."

"She was with that one friend a lot," Gina blurted, as though she'd just remembered this detail. She looked at Molly. "Remember? The one with long, dark hair?"

"You're right. She came by a lot," Molly said. "Hopefully the police have talked to her."

I assumed the girl was April but wasn't sure how to confirm it.

"Do you remember anything else about her? Like her name or what she drove?"

They looked at each other. "Not really," Molly said. "She was about Beth's size. Pretty."

"Did the police talk to you?" I asked.

"Yeah. But I didn't see or hear anything out of the ordinary. And neither did my husband. I wish we had." Her shoulders slumped.

"Same with us," Gina added.

"Well, if you think of anything else, the number for the police is right here." I pointed to the flyer. "By the way, do you know where she was planning to deliver? Which hospital?"

"King County General," she said. "Same as me."

The ring of my phone interrupted the conversation. Just as my finger hit the "answer" button, my mind registered the name on caller ID. Dean.

"Hi, Dean," I said, turning away from Gina and Molly to concentrate. "I'm..." I floundered for a creative explanation but came up empty. "Talking to some people right now. What's going on?"

"I have a little information for you. When's a good time to call back?"

"Well," I glanced at Gina's hands. She was still holding flyers. "I'm not sure. Can I call you back soon? Or is it something urgent?" If he had big news, I wanted it now.

"No. Not at all. Give me a ring when you're done."

"Will you be at this number? The one you called from? It's on my caller ID."

"Probably," he said. "It's my home number. But you can try my cell too."

He started giving me the number, but I wasn't ready.

"Oops. Hang on a second." I asked Molly for a pen and jotted down the digits. "Okay. So I'll call you in a bit. I have a few things to tell you, too."

"Sounds good," he said.

"And you can always email me if we miss each other," I added.

"Got it." I swear I heard a smile in his voice. Could he tell I was tongue-tied?

We said goodbye and I turned to Gina and Molly, who were staring at me.

"Everything okay?" Gina asked.

"Fine," I said. "Just a friend. He'll call back."

"Your face is bright red." Molly said.

No wonder it felt like I'd stuck it in an oven. "I am a little hot. Whew!" I fanned myself.

"Or maybe *he* is?" Gina said with a laugh.

Oh my. I didn't want my crush to be obvious. I just hoped I had a better poker face with Dean.

We left Molly's and headed for the opposite end of the street, where we had one more home to visit. Gina warned me that Don Palmer, a crotchety old man, would be eager to talk, but not necessarily about Beth. She was right. His curtains parted as we approached, and he opened the door before we knocked.

"What can I do you for?" he asked Gina from his porch. I was hopeful, and a touch apprehensive, because his home was near the neighborhood entrance, where he could see everyone come and go. For all I knew, he'd seen me on my last two visits.

Gina introduced me, passed him a flyer, and asked if he knew Beth.

"Course I do," he chastised her. "The pregnant girl."

I felt for Beth. Once a teen is pregnant, I wondered, does everyone call her "The Pregnant Girl"? What was next? "The Girl With the Baby"?

"That's right," Gina started, but Don wasn't done.

"The whole neighborhood's gone down the tubes," he complained. He pointed a bony finger at me, the sparse white hairs on his bald head shaking as he spoke. "And the homeowners association doesn't do a thing about it. Gina knows what I mean." He looked at her for support.

"Don isn't happy with a few things," she understated.

I got straight to the point. "Has Beth caused any problems herself?"

"Not unless you count setting a poor example," he said. "Which I do. What about all the young ones on the street, seeing a teen knocked up, parading around? The world's going to pot." He waved a hand in disgust.

"The world *is* a scary place," Gina allowed. "And I know how much you care about the neighborhood. That's why we're here. Neighbors helping neighbors!" I wondered if appealing to his sense of community would work. "This girl ran away—or disappeared for some reason," Gina continued. "And we're handing out these flyers to help her parents, seeing if anyone saw or heard anything that could help find her. We want to keep the neighborhood safe, you know."

Don set his jaw and considered this for a moment.

"She walked a lot in the evenings. About this time," he offered. I held my breath and waited for more. I actually liked old Don for a moment. "By herself. To the five-and-dime." He pointed at a convenience store across the street.

"Did she spend long there?" I asked.

"I don't know. Never noticed her coming back."

"You never saw her walk back?" I asked. I was genuinely surprised. Don seemed so observant that if he hadn't seen it, maybe it hadn't happened.

"Young lady, it's not my job to keep track of everyone and everything."

I stifled a smirk and smiled gratefully. "Of course," I said. "You can only do so much."

"Tell us one more time," Gina said. "Did she go to the store? Or just in that direction?"

"All I'm saying is I saw her cross the street." He pointed at the store again.

"When's the last time you saw her?" Gina asked.

"Oh, I don't know. A week ago? Maybe two?"

"Her parents live at the other end of the street," Gina said. She gestured toward their house. "And they're heartbroken." Her words, not mine. "So if you see Beth again, you'll call the police, won't you?"

"I will. In fact I'll probably call them anyway. Have you heard the neighbors across the street? Putting their dogs out at all hours? Disturbing the peace is what they're doing..."

Don was still talking, but Gina was moving away. "Good evening, Don. Thanks for your help."

I followed her back to her house, where she handed me a leftover flyer.

"I can't believe you're spending all this time helping a stranger," she said. "But I sure appreciate it. Now enjoy your treadmill, okay?"

I wrote my email address on the edge of the flyer, ripped it off, and asked her to keep in touch if she heard anything.

"I sure will," she said. "And I'll tell the police what Don said, too, although I'm sure he already did. They probably got an earful."

I pulled out of her driveway and took a deep breath. I had to call Dean, but first I'd stop at the convenience store for a few things, including information.

* * *

It's a sad fact I don't want to confess. When I enter a store, even a rundown, worn-out convenience store, I go into shopping mode. It's very, very hard not to check prices and see if there's something I "need." This is true even when I'm in a rush and running late. Ridiculous.

So my goal in the mini mart across from Beth's neighborhood was to ignore everything, including an enormous display of clearance summer toys and several shocking magazine headlines—everything except the graying (hair, teeth, and skin), tattooed guy at the counter who, I hoped, had seen Beth right where I stood.

I failed immediately. If he was the owner, I reasoned, he might be more talkative if I made a purchase.

From the aisles of junk food and tiny containers of laundry detergent, mouthwash, and other necessities, I chose a pack of industrial-strength, breath-freshening gum, peanut butter crackers, and a decaf iced tea. In my defense, I did not look at the toys or peruse a single magazine.

While the clerk rang everything up, I pulled Beth's flyer from my pocket. He spoke before I said a word.

"You know her?" he asked.

"Do *I* know her? That's what I was going to ask you."

"Hell yeah," he snorted. "I hired her to work evenings, but she skipped out on me." He took the paper from my hand and squinted at it. "Are you shittin' me?" He looked up. "She's missing?"

"Unfortunately, yes," I answered.

He handed back the flyer and tossed my items in a skimpy plastic bag. I worried the bottle would break against the counter.

"That's crazy," he said, shaking his head. "You're not her ma, are you?"

"No. I'm sort of a family friend. I want to make sure she's safe. You hired her?"

"Sure did. She was supposed to start last week. She comes in all the time, so one night I asked if she wanted a job. I figured with a baby on the way and everything, she probably needed the money."

The idea of Beth working for this guy was unappealing to say the least. Even if his intentions were honorable, she'd either be alone in the store, or alone with a guy who, at the moment, was a little intimidating. He sported a fire-breathing dragon on his arm and a bunch of other faded art I couldn't make out.

"When was she supposed to start working?"

"Monday before last. But she didn't show. I was damn pissed. I'd already started training her."

He looked me in the eye, and I stared right back with a smile. I wanted to keep him comfortable and talking.

"I understand. It's hard to find reliable help. But Beth didn't say anything about going away or anything?"

"Not a damn word. Now I need someone else to fill the position. I'm workin' too much."

"Did the police come by and ask any questions? I know they've been around the neighborhood."

"Not unless I wasn't here. There's another guy works mornings. Maybe they talked to him or another part timer."

"Did any other employees meet Beth?"

"Nope. Not enough time for that."

"Okay. Could I get a card or something? A way to reach you if I have questions?"

"Sure. But I already told you what I know." He pulled a bent, fuzzy card from his jacket pocket. *Joe Shaw, Owner.*

I paid cash and flipped over the receipt. "I really appreciate your help, Joe. Here's my email address in case you think of anything. Do you email much?"

"All the time," he said.

"Great." I glanced around. "And do you have security cameras?"

"I got four. Why?"

"I'd love to see video of the night she disappeared. Even if she wasn't here, she lives nearby, and there could be something helpful on it." I shrugged. "There's always hope."

"Yep," he agreed. "But lady, it's a real pain to go through that video. I don't think there's any point."

"If you show me how to do it, I'll do all the work," I offered as a long shot. "I like technology."

He sighed and shook his head.

"Come on back. I got nothin' else to do." As he started toward a back room, I regretted asking for this "favor," which I worried could lead to finding out what happened to Beth in a really scary way.

I clutched the cell phone in my pocket and wished I'd told Gina where I was going. *Don't worry*, I told myself. *Your van is outside. Someone will know you're here.* I relaxed for a nanosecond until I realized that if anything happened to me, Joe would have my car keys, which were in my hand, so he could not only ditch my car, but also get into anything I ever locked or unlocked (including my house, my mom's condo, the neighborhood tennis court, etc., etc.). He'd also have my address from my license, pictures of my kids, everything else in my purse (a lot of junk, but still), and a treadmill. This was getting worse by the second.

I dropped the keys in my bag and heard them clink on the bottle of iced tea. *That's my weapon of choice*, I decided. *If it comes to blows, I'll swing the iced tea at his head.*

I was so busy plotting self-defense that I didn't notice Joe was sitting in front of a computer monitor with live, color video playing on the screen. I knew it was live because the date and time were listed in the corner. The screen was divided into four shots, one at the empty counter, where we'd just been, one at the store's entrance, one at the alcohol display, and one near the gas pumps, where my minivan was parked with a treadmill sticking out the back.

"I just got this setup," he said. "I can barely use it. So I sure can't teach you." He picked up an instructional booklet next to the keyboard and began to read.

My impatience and love of computers made me want to shove in and start pointing and clicking. (Maybe *he* was the one who needed self-defense.) I was sure I could figure out the program, but I didn't want to offend or further irritate Joe. Plus, I was still on guard in case this was a ruse to get me into a vulnerable spot, and it seemed smarter to stand behind him than in front of his slim but taller-than-mine figure.

He looked back at the computer and clicked the mouse. "So what day and time should I check?" he asked.

"Let's try around 10:30 Sunday night, the day before she was supposed to start working for you. Does it go back that far?"

"It better. The guy who sold it to me said it should." He typed at a snail's pace, using only his index fingers.

A slightly blurry video popped up of Joe wearing the same outfit: jeans and a short-sleeved jacket embroidered with the store logo, but the time read 10:30 p.m. on the day Beth disappeared. I got goose bumps, knowing that night, according to April, Beth was hearing April's news, and she was about to come home.

Joe figured out how to fast forward, and I watched his image hop around the store until someone walked onscreen, a woman in a dark business suit. She paid for something that looked like a candy bar and left. At 11:15, a man with a baseball cap entered, retrieved something from the refrigerated area, and approached the counter. He held out money and froze in place.

"Wait a minute." Joe had paused the video, creating a surprisingly clear picture. The man might not be identifiable, but he was Caucasian, pudgy, and certainly older than Beth. A baseball cap obscured most of his face.

"What?" I asked.

"Nothing really."

"If it was nothing, you wouldn't have stopped," I said. "What is it?"

He shrugged. "I ain't saying it means anything, but that's what Beth bought every time." He pointed at the screen. "Chocolate milk and a scratch-off lottery ticket."

"Really?" I asked. I leaned closer to the screen. "Can you play it again?"

I peered over Joe's head at the man paying for a pint of chocolate milk and a ticket, and instead of feeling afraid, I was energized, electric.

"What do you remember about him?" I asked.

He closed his eyes and rubbed his forehead. "Not a damn thing. I'm sorry."

I tried to imagine what a real investigator would ask. Age? Race? Height? Tattoos? Facial hair? The image of Beth's tailbone rose tattoo jumped to mind. Joe let the video run again.

"I can tell you he's about 5' 8"," he said. He hit pause again as the customer walked out the door, right past a measuring tape posted at the exit. Joe pointed to it. "See? We have that so we can tell how tall the bad guys are."

"Great. What about his race and age and stuff?"

"White. And he ain't no teenager."

"I agree. What about the other cameras? Do you have those views?" He consulted the booklet again and clicked. The screen split into quarters again, but the parking lot was empty. The customer, wearing a white shirt, khakis and loafers, walked straight ahead on foot, not turning toward Beth's neighborhood.

"Darn," I said. "I was hoping he drove."

"Could have," Joe said. "If he parked far off. Some spaces are out of range."

"Did you notice any identifying marks on this guy or Beth, like tattoos or anything?"

I watched him closely. If he appeared to have even a hint of knowledge about Beth's tattoo, I would die. I remembered an interview I'd seen with an expert on body language. There were so many subtle— yet detectable—signs of hiding information. I couldn't remember any of them except maybe avoiding eye contact. Joe was looking straight at me with a grin.

"Now you're sounding official," he said.

"I'm not official. Just a friend of the family. I swear."

"I didn't notice anything about her—and I would have. Look at me." He held up saggy, tattooed arms.

I wanted to ask if he could rewind further into the past—maybe find Beth shopping, training or interacting with someone—when there was a tinkling sound from the entrance. Joe clicked a tab, and live images of the store returned. There was a woman at the counter.

"Back to business," he said. His chair scraped the cement floor, and he turned off the monitor.

"What time do you close on Sundays?" I asked.

"Open every night 'til midnight."

I followed him out the door and waited while he retrieved cigarettes for the pretty, husky-voiced young customer.

After she left, I thanked him again. "Any chance I could see Beth's work application?" I added.

"Nope. That's too personal. But I'll pass it on to the police."

"Please do. I appreciate that. And I'd love to look at more footage of her. Could I get a copy of what you have?"

"I don't know how to do that yet," he said. "But tell you what. If I get bored tonight, I'll look back through the past couple weeks instead of playing solitaire. If I find Beth, I'll look through the instructions and see if I can email you a video clip. Sound fair?"

"Joe, you're my hero. Thank you so much. Maybe you could send me a clip of the chocolate-milk guy too."

Joe grinned a gray-toothed smile that thirty minutes earlier might have freaked me out. Talking with Dean would be a nice change of pace.

Eleven

"Dean?"

"Hey, Nicki. How's it going?"

I was sitting in my van in the parking lot with the doors locked.

"I guess I'm making progress." I explained what I'd been doing and said I'd call the local Crime Solvers number about Joe. I couldn't trust that he'd report what he knew. "So what did you have to tell me?"

"I put in a call to a friend in law enforcement. He was kind enough to save you a little legwork. Soon after Beth was reported missing, they checked the local shelters and hospitals, and she wasn't there."

I felt like the dumbest person on Earth. "I should have already done that."

"I assumed it was already done, and it was. Don't worry. You've done a lot. And there's more to do."

He was right. I had to put my energy toward success, not regrets. "Got any ideas for me?"

"Let's be thorough and run a background check on Beth's parents and Mr. Shaw," he suggested. I could see Joe through the glass windows, doing something at the cash register.

"Great," I said. "Should I do that?" I didn't know if I should use what I'd learned in class or depend on Dean for help. I could do a local check free of charge, but I'd need a database—and some advice—to do anything else.

"I'll do you a favor on this one," he offered. "But I expect you to be in class Saturday for surveillance practice." He was in mock drill sergeant mode. "In all seriousness, I think you'll be glad to have those skills down."

"Me too." I was tempted to request a good surveillance partner.

There were several people in class I didn't want to ride around with all day. But I kept quiet and trusted his judgment.

"I'll call if I get anything on Mr. Shaw. In the meantime I have a couple other suggestions."

"Okay." I couldn't wait.

"Let's start with the social networking sites you mentioned."

"Right," I said.

"Have you been checking those every day?"

"Absolutely. They haven't been updated."

"Have you posted anything on them?"

"Definitely not. Do you think I should?"

"I don't know. Let me think about it. Who else did you find pages for?"

"April and other kids from their school. That's how I heard about that party I went to. But I didn't see a page for Marcus."

"Those sites are gold mines. We have to keep an eye on them."

I liked how he said *we.*

"I'm worried about something you said though," I told him. "Even if the police checked the hospitals and shelters right after Beth disappeared, what if she showed up now? Would they recognize her as missing?"

"Hopefully the local hospitals are still on alert. Even if they're not, her situation would probably raise red flags, considering her age and that she might arrive alone."

"But what's considered local? I mean, what if she went to West Virginia, Maryland, or D.C.? Or what about southern Virginia, like Richmond?" I was feeling more overwhelmed and less capable by the second. Living in the "DMV" (D.C., Maryland, and Virginia) was like having three home states—four if you counted West Virginia. The area felt like one big place, even as far away as Baltimore.

"Why would she go that far?" Dean asked. "West Virginia, okay, for family. But Maryland or D.C.? For what reason?"

"Yeah." I couldn't imagine her doing that.

"If it makes you feel better to check out West Virginia, do it, especially since her grandparents are there. You should. And keep in touch with April and Marcus. See if they lead you anywhere. Have you made any progress with the adoption agency?"

"Umm, no." I was too nervous to have any contact with First Steps for fear of jeopardizing Kenna and Andy's relationship with them. I told Dean as much.

"I understand. Why don't you have Kenna or Andy work on it? There's always the chance the agency has heard from Beth by now."

"Okay." I was embarrassed to ask my next question. "You mentioned checking out West Virginia. What exactly do you mean?"

"You'll need her grandparents' names. Then you can find out where they live and check it out. Drive by, see what they're up to, just to make sure there's no sign of Beth or the baby."

"I'm sorry to sound so stupid, Dean, but how can I get their names?"

He was quiet for a moment. I hoped he wasn't thinking, *What an idiot. Has she learned anything in class?!*

"What are her parents' full names again?"

"Sonja and Bob Myers," I said.

"And whose parents are these in West Virginia?"

"Beth's mom's. Should I check their marriage license for her maiden name or something?"

"I can almost guarantee her maiden name is online. I'll text you with it."

So maybe it wasn't a dumb question. *Phew.* "Okay. Thank you so much," I said. "I'm going to head home. I'll have my cell phone with me."

"Sounds good."

"I'm going to have to start paying you for all this work," I said.

"No way," he said. "This is an opportunity to help with something unusual. Most of my cases—and don't try to deny it—are pretty boring. I'm glad to help."

Dean had a heart. Mine melted.

"Well, I enjoy your classes," I said honestly. He didn't have to know why. "And thanks again. It means a lot to me and my friend. I'll look for your text and see you Saturday."

We hung up while nervous butterflies danced in my stomach. I wasn't sure if they were from hearing Dean's ideas or hearing his voice. I had a lot to do, and after unloading the treadmill, visiting West Virginia was next.

* * *

That's what I told Andy as we (mostly he) lugged the treadmill up to my bedroom and set it in viewing range of my TV. I hid the safety strap under my mattress so the kids couldn't go for a run unattended. Attended, however, was a different story. Was it a no-no to let kids use treadmills supervised? Sophie (and I) could use an outlet for her energy.

"So you're going to West Virginia?" Andy said incredulously. I'd been reluctant to tell him much, since I preferred to talk to Kenna first, but he insisted on a heart-to-heart while we huffed and puffed.

"I hope," I said. "But what would you think about calling the adoption agency again? Just to see if there's anything new about Beth, or anything old that's relevant?"

"I guess I could. But they said they'd call us if there was any news."

"Hmmm." I mustered the strength to contradict him. "I wouldn't count on them for that. My guess is that their commitment is to Beth first. Plus, even if they're not willing to tell you anything, maybe you'll get a sense of whether they're holding back or not."

"Yeah," he conceded.

"So you'll call first thing tomorrow." We laughed at my pushiness.

"Whatever, Nicki, if it'll make you happy." I got the sense he meant if it'll make *Kenna* happy and make *you* back off. But his motive didn't really matter.

He gestured toward the treadmill. "Now that I dragged that thing up here, you better use it."

"I will. I think." I wasn't making any promises either.

The kids were thrilled to see me when I picked them up from their playdate. So thrilled they completely ignored me until I demanded we leave. Then they acknowledged me with protests.

It was straight-to-bed time, but first I asked about their evening and accidentally let Sophie see the treadmill, which meant she wanted to climb all over it and press every button. We got it out of her system for about ten minutes—machine off and safety cord hidden—and then I issued a stern warning about touching the treadmill without permission.

"I don't even want to touch it," Jack said. "I like running outside."

"I love it," Sophie said. "When I grow up, I want one too."

"Someday you can buy one with your own money," I said. "How do you think you'll earn it?" I took her hand and led her away from the treadmill.

Sophie started babbling about possible careers: running a horse farm, being a doctor, or "chef-ing" at her favorite Mexican restaurant. I took pride in successfully redirecting her toward the bathroom to scrub her teeth.

With Sophie, this was often a battle, so I took on the role of a make-believe character inspired by the late, great Crocodile Hunter. I morphed into "The Crazy Babysitter"—a jolly, overly dramatic and somewhat confused babysitter with a heavy Australian accent. The Crazy Babysitter also worked part-time as a dentist and zookeeper.

Jack was already brushing but asked for a double-check from The Crazy Babysitter. I found swamp scum in his mouth. (It turned out to be leftover toothpaste.) Sophie was next. I heard my cell phone beep and saw Dean's number pop up, but I chose to ignore it and make Sophie my priority.

"What did you have for dinner, young lady? Let me see those teeth of yours!" I demanded. "Crikey! Those teeth look stronger than an elephant's tusk. I'm afraid to get in there!"

We laughed our way through the bedtime routine and another night ended well, at least for my little ones.

Life was anything but normal, but I followed my normal routine of sitting at the computer and eating after the kids were in bed. Dean had texted the most likely last name of Beth's grandparents: Rush. He also said Joe's record looked clean so far except for a few speeding tickets. Same for Beth's parents. I texted back a quick "THANKS!" and got busy looking up West Virginia Rushes on every address site I knew. April thought they lived somewhere with gambling, but an Internet search showed several towns with casinos. Instead of calling everyone listed, like I had with Beth and Marcus, I decided this was a good excuse to call April. Maybe one of the Rushes would ring a bell for her, even though Beth referred to them as "Nana and Grandpa." April sounded wide awake when she answered.

"Hey April. It's Nicki," I said. "How's it going?"

"Fine," she answered politely.

"That's good. I wanted to run something by you. I'm going to read you some names. Can you tell me if any sound familiar?"

"Okay." She sounded skeptical.

"Annabelle Rush. Franklin Rush. Graham and Marcy Rush. Martin Rush—"

"Oh, wait, stop. Marcy is Beth's middle name. She hates it."

She was right. I remembered seeing "Marcy" on the adoption forms Beth had filled out. I mentally kicked myself for forgetting.

"Do you think she could have been named after her grandmother?"

"She *is* named after her grandmother," April confirmed. "The one in West Virginia. I forgot about that. You know her other grandparents died in a car crash, right?"

"Yes." The adoption forms had revealed that, too. Beth's paternal grandparents had died when she was young. "Thank you so much, April."

"Sure. But I didn't do anything. I mean, I doubt her grandparents know anything. You already know the story about last time."

"I know. But everything's worth a try, right?"

"I guess."

"Do you have any other ideas? I'd love to hear them. Even if they seem silly to you."

"Not really. Except to talk to Marcus."

I didn't tell her I'd already done that. What I wanted to do was follow Marcus again.

"Do you ever talk to him or see him around?"

"No. But I know where to find him."

"Really? Where?"

"Anywhere there's a party. He's always there. Probably dealing."

"So when's the next one?"

"I don't know. I'm kinda taking a break from that scene after the last one. I was seriously sick for like the whole day after that."

"I'm sorry. If you hear anything, please give me a call. You shouldn't go. But I could keep an eye on things."

"Uh huh." I heard some rustling. "My mom's coming and I'm not supposed to be on the phone," she whispered. She clicked off.

I hung up and looked at the pad where I'd written and circled "Marcy and Graham Rush."

Back online, I found something interesting—fascinating, really—about Graham Rush, Marcy's apparent husband. There was a separate business listing under his name. *Rush, Graham, MD.* But that wasn't all. Another search brought up an unexpected fact about Dr. Rush. He was an OB-GYN. Did April know this? Would Beth have turned to him for help? And would he have given it secretly? I crossed my legs protectively, aware that even though I wasn't due for an annual exam, I'd probably have to see the doctor anyway.

Twelve

I didn't want to get April in trouble, so I called her mom on the land line.

"Jen?"

"Who's calling?" She sounded understandably wary of an unfamiliar, late-night caller who knew her name.

"It's Nicki, the mom who brought April home."

"Nicki! Hi. How are things? I hope you have good news."

"Not yet, but I'm working on it. I'm sorry for calling this late. But I have a question for April if that's okay. It's about Beth's grandparents."

"Of course. Do you think Beth could be with them?"

"They don't live too far away, so I want to check. Do you know anything about them?"

"Not a thing. Let me get April before she falls asleep." She yelled for her and said it was me. We said goodbye, and after April picked up, I waited to hear Jen disconnect.

"Hey April. Sorry to call back. I came up with something after we talked, and I wanted to run it by you. Did you know Beth's grandfather is an OB-GYN?"

"A pregnancy doctor?"

"Yes. She didn't mention that?"

"No." She was quiet for a moment. "Maybe a long time ago and I forgot. But that's so weird. It's like why didn't she ask him for help? She had no money, and she was really scared." Another pause. "Then again, wait. That would be *gross*. It's her grandfather. And he'd probably tell her mom anyway."

"You think?"

"After the first time she ran away? Yeah. Her whole family was really mad."

"What about *after* she told her parents she was pregnant? Do you think she'd go to him then?"

"No, because she had a doctor by then, Dr. Ryan. And she's cool. The agency recommended her."

"Where is her office?"

"At the hospital. King County General."

"Okay. Thank you so much, April."

We hung up.

Before bed I put directions to Dr. Rush's home and office in my purse. Even though April had doubts, the Rushes were a stone I couldn't leave unturned. The trip would take an hour or so, depending on traffic, which would be worse on a Friday. If I went while the kids were at camp, I'd practically have to turn around when I got there, which would be pointless, and bringing them would be a mistake. I envisioned breaking up arguments, serving snacks, and hearing, "I need to go" several times, all while attracting attention or missing something important. No way. I'd have to get a babysitter or...I guess there wasn't an "or." I forced my brain into overdrive, a difficult task, but it responded. The best time to visit would be during the day—either when Dr. Rush was on his way to work or on his way home. I wanted to see him and his wife on the move. I called his office and listened to the recording: open from 9 a.m. to 12 p.m. and 1 to 4 p.m. Lunch from 12 to 1 p.m. That might be another chance to observe him.

Maybe Mom could come over in the morning, entertain the kids for a few hours, and then drop them off at camp. If my day was productive, she could even be "on call" to pick them up. Longing for sleep, I reluctantly dialed her number and pulled out my PI class information. I needed to review surveillance techniques, not just for Saturday's class, but for the next day's activities.

At 1 a.m., I forced myself to lie down with the light off. I still couldn't relax, since I had a mental checklist a mile long to review. Mom had agreed to babysit, and while that helped immensely, it also meant I had to straighten up the house again, pack the kids' backpacks (bathing suits, towels, goggles, lunches, snacks, water bottles), choose outfits according to the weather (which required digging through clean laundry), plan breakfast, provide tips for sunscreen application, explain the carpool lane, and set out pool passes and a movie in case Mom got desperate. I'd done most of these things already, but what else? What else? Oh! I had to let the camp know Mom would pick up the kids. I turned on the light, found a sticky note, and posted it on the bathroom mirror. "Call camp. Now!" Reminders only help if I use them *right away.* But I couldn't call at night.

I went back to bed, set the alarm for 6:30 a.m., and switched off the light, wishing I could do the same for my brain.

My shower woke Sophie, who dashed into the bathroom, where I tried the impossible—hiding in a glass enclosure. Whoever invented see-through showers didn't have kids in mind. Or modesty. I gave thanks for steam and soap scum.

"Sophie," I said. "Can you wait in my room, honey? I'm almost done." I tried to sound nonchalant. I'd always wanted to be one of those people who didn't care if their little kids (not to mention friends, sisters, mothers, locker room buddies, etc.) saw them naked. Bodies were something to be proud of, right? Whatever.

"Mommy! I see your..."

"I know, sweetie. I'm in the shower. Go sit on my bed please."

"But..."

"You can pick an outfit for me. How about that? Go in my closet and see what matches."

She obeyed, and I hustled to finish the necessities, throw on a towel, and moisturize my face.

"Wow," I said when I saw her selection. A red sundress from the depths of my closet. I hadn't seen it in years. She'd "matched" it with a pair of black velvet pumps I'd never worn. They were so out of date they needed to be shipped to a country where they were just starting to enjoy *21 Jump Street.*

"Do you like it?"

Ahhh. The familiar parenting challenge: How to be honest without being hurtful.

"I love it," I said. *On me in the '80s.* "It's a great color."

"Are you gonna wear it?"

"You know, that dress is *so* nice that I'm going to save it for a special [lonely] night, when I'm going out to dinner at a special restaurant [the drive thru]. Can you help me find something pretty, but not so fancy, for today?"

"Yes," Sophie said. "The shoes are fancy too." She sounded apologetic.

"Yes, they are. You did such a good job matching fancy with fancy! Why don't you put them away for another time?" *Like the past.* She bobbled off and tucked them in a box, which I mentally marked DONATION.

I glanced at the clock and realized I was in a hurry. Or, more accurately, I *needed* to be in a hurry. I grabbed a rumpled brown T-shirt from the closet and navy blue sweat shorts from a drawer.

"That's not pretty," Sophie noted.

"Oh darn. You're right. What do you suggest?" I slipped on undies beneath my towel, donned a bra over the towel, and then finally slipped the covering down.

Sophie paid no attention. She was focused on my open dresser drawer. If she didn't magically produce a cute outfit in seconds, I'd have to settle with my choice.

"I like these." She yanked out jean capris.

"Perfect!" I swept them out of her hands and shoved them on. "Good job Sophie. Is this brown shirt good?"

"No."

I zoomed into the bathroom and slapped on makeup while she dug through my shirts.

"Here, Mommy." She held up a T-shirt she'd made at preschool. It had colorful scribbles and handprints all over it. I was hoping for something that would make me blend in.

"Oh, I love that shirt," I said. I put it on and admired myself in the bathroom mirror. "Let's go downstairs for breakfast. Grandma's going to be here any minute."

"Yay! Grandma!"

I ushered her out and grabbed my brown T-shirt on the way.

*   *   *

Mom was holding a gift bag, complete with a giant white bow, when I opened the door to let her in. Certain it was for the kids, I turned to them and said, "Look what Grandma brought."

"Hold on," she warned. "This is for Mommy. But I think they'll like it too." She smiled and put the bag in my hand. "I stopped at Target this morning and got something you *really* need. Please don't be offended."

"Okay," I said, afraid to open it in front of anyone. We headed for the kitchen, where I showed her the day's supplies and instructions.

"Simple," she exaggerated. I wasn't sure whether that should inspire confidence or concern. "Now open your present."

After giving the bow to Sophie, I blindly reached through several layers of pink tissue paper as if we were playing the "guess what this is" Halloween game. Instead of feeling grape eyeballs or spaghetti brains, however, I felt an unidentifiable, heavy cardboard box. It took both hands to pull it out.

My jaw dropped when I saw what it was. "A navigation system! I totally need that." It had been eons, I realized, since I'd received a gift that cost money, and this was just what I wanted, right when I needed it. "Thank you!"

I tackled Mom with a hug and returned immediately to the box, noting the kids' dumfounded looks only after I'd started connecting wires.

"Do you guys know what this is?" I asked.

They shook their heads.

"It's a machine that gives us directions so we don't get lost."

"You need that," Jack confirmed.

I laughed. "It's true. And you know what's really cool? It talks."

"Make it talk." Sophie said. "Make it talk!"

"Well it works in the car," I said, "so I'll test it today, and if it works great, we'll go for a drive with it tomorrow."

We had a deal. I was on my way.

Waving goodbye to the innocent trio on the doorstep, it was hard to believe I was investigating something so disturbing. My stomach knotted as I imagined scenes I didn't want to see. *Please, please, please, wherever Beth is, let her be alive,* I begged. *And don't let her be alone. Please let her be with someone safe and caring.*

My thoughts were interrupted by a loud electronic voice insisting I turn left, for which I was thankful, as much for the directions as the distraction. Countless robotic commands later, I found myself in front of a ranch-style home that matched Dr. Rush's address. Other than being neatly mowed and mulched, with trimmed, squat shrubs dotting its perimeter, it had no personality. Black shutters. Off-white siding. Taupe garage doors and front entrance. It looked unloved.

Since it was on a corner lot, I turned onto the next street, where that side of the house had no windows, just a brick chimney. A U-turn allowed me to park in view of the garage, from which I hoped Dr. Rush would emerge. If he and his wife left separately, I realized, I wouldn't know which one to follow.

I glanced at the clock (8:24 a.m.) and the houses around me. They were small with big yards, so I hoped the distance between us provided some cover, but in case it didn't, I put the navigation system in the glove compartment and pulled out a Virginia map. If anyone got suspicious, I'd say I was lost—again. It had worked last time. Then I turned off the car, left the radio on softly, and sat watch until the last remnants of air conditioning seeped away.

I'd just cracked my window for fresh air when I heard the unmistakable noise of a garage door rising. Using the sound as cover, I started the van and saw a black sedan back out of the Rush's garage. A balding man was at the wheel with a gray-haired, female passenger, who was looking down. Neither seemed to notice me.

After they pulled onto the street and took a right, I followed, reminding myself if I lost them, I'd simply go to Dr. Rush's office. I had the address *and* the navigation system. I was set.

That didn't turn out to be necessary, since his office was only a few miles away, and there weren't many turns en route. Apparently the woman, who I guessed was Mrs. Rush, was coming along, because they parked in front of a four-story cement building and got out together. I drove by, noting their clothes for future reference, and parked a block away at a coffee shop. In my rearview mirror, I could see the couple entering the building, so I headed into the shop, where I used the bathroom, changed into my brown shirt, and ordered an herbal tea to go.

Still not feeling "gathered," I returned to the car to deliberate. I could follow them into the office and ask creative questions, such as, "I was here seeing a [dermatologist/podiatrist/psychiatrist/whatever], and I saw your sign. Are you taking new patients?" If the answer was *yes*, I'd give a sob story about being new in town with a pregnant daughter. Or maybe I should use this opportunity, when Dr. and Mrs. were out of the house, to investigate. What if Beth was there, and I was missing a chance to see her? Oh my gosh.

But here I was, and both ideas seemed important, so I stepped out of the car.

The sidewalk was wet, not from rain, but from being washed with a hose, which was coiled and dripping by the coffee shop. It created a "fresh start" feeling I needed.

I left my too-hot-to-sip tea in the car and strode purposefully toward the office building. Something helpful was *going* to happen. It had to. Kenna's image filled my mind and, corny as it sounds, my heart. Yearning for a child was primal, and she'd felt it for so long. Too long.

A well-dressed, gold-accessorized older woman—the kind who offers hope for aging gracefully—swished out the door and held it for me. I thanked her and spotted a directory of suites. Dr. Graham Rush, OB-GYN, was in 404. An open elevator stood waiting, its lighted arrow pointed up.

"Going up?" said a woman in scrubs as she stepped in ahead of me.

"I am."

I pressed *4* and was glad to see she was stopping on *3*, since I didn't want company on this mission.

We rode in silence and smiled politely when she exited. On the fourth floor, I walked around a bit, familiarizing myself with the building's occupants. Which one had I been "visiting"? The vein clinic? (I had plenty I'd love to zap.) The dentist? (Unappealing, but I did want that teeth whitening.) A hypnotist? (Sounded interesting.) I chose the dentist...Maria Brown, DDS.

Now it was time for action. I pretended to stare at a tacky, wannabe impressionist print while I rehearsed a mental script. Then I told myself *You can do this* three times unconvincingly. Sweat was forming in parts of my body I didn't know could perspire. I swallowed hard.

The glass window of suite 404 revealed Mrs. Rush, or the woman I assumed to be her, since she arrived with Dr. Rush, sorting through a stack of files at the front desk.

She glanced up and smiled, so I opened the door and dove right in, thankful I was the only "patient" around.

"Hi," I said. "I'm new in town. I was seeing someone else on this floor, but I need an OB-GYN. Is..." I paused as if double checking his name on the office sign-in log. "...Dr. Rush taking new patients?"

"Of course," she said. I'm happy to schedule an appointment for you. Welcome! Where are you from?"

"Northern Virginia."

"Oh? We have family there."

"Whereabouts?"

"King County."

"Well, that's not *too* far from here. Do you get to see them often?"

"Oh, not as much as we'd like." She was looking at her computer monitor. Her tone and expression gave away nothing. "Now let's get you set up here." She turned to me. "What kind of insurance do you have?"

"Well actually, the appointment is for my daughter." I lowered my voice. "She really needs to come in, because she just found out she's pregnant."

"Oh. How old is she?"

"Eighteen." That was a big enough lie to leave stretch marks, since that would make me eighteen when I had her. I kept my voice low. "I'm really worried. The baby's father left her, and I'm all she's got."

Something flickered across her face. Judgment? Concern? Empathy? I couldn't tell.

"Don't worry, sweetheart." Her voice was soft. "We'll take good care of her. I promise."

If I'd been telling the truth, her kindness would have lightened my heart, but instead I felt heavy. Rotten.

"Thank you so much. By the way, can you tell me anything about Dr. Rush?"

"What would you like to know?"

A woman in her twenties walked in and added her name to the sign-in sheet. We nodded at each other.

"Just a little about his personality—his bedside manner. And how long he's been in practice. And where he went to school. Sorry! That's a lot of questions."

The young woman, whose medium-size bulge under her T-shirt indicated she was pregnant, chimed in while she sat down. "Dr. Rush is so smart. You'll be impressed."

"Thank you, sweetheart," called Mrs. Rush. "I'm biased, because we're family. But he's been in practice a long time—more than thirty years now—and he went to school right here in West Virginia. He's a bit of a community fixture at this point."

"He sounds wonderful," I said. "Are you his wife?"

"I sure am."

I thanked the patient and smiled at Mrs. Rush. "Let's set up an appointment."

She booked my "daughter," whom I dubbed Melanie Smith, for the first available appointment, Monday at 10:30 a.m. I took the slot with a sinking feeling. My "daughter" wouldn't see Dr. Rush, and unless I found Beth before Monday, I'd probably be there instead.

Thirteen

Since Beth's grandparents were stuck at work, I felt more relaxed than expected about sneaking around their house—the outside of it, that is. I wanted to take a good, hard look, and based on my limited PI knowledge, I needed to stop at an office supply store first.

I tinkered with the navigation system until it listed several nearby shopping centers. It led me to an office superstore, where I parked and took a moment to make a shopping list: clipboard, invoices, pens, ruler, cold drink, big magnet.

Inside, I found everything but the magnet.

"Do you make those big, magnetic decals you can stick on cars?" I asked the copy center attendant. What would look more official than a huge sign on the van, prominently displaying the name of a fake business—a pest control company, I thought, since that would legitimize inspecting homes inside and out.

"Magnets are a special order. Did you bring art?"

"No," I answered. "I could use stock art, if you have any, but I need the magnet today."

"No can do."

I didn't want to place an order, and I didn't love his personality, so I moved on, contemplating my non-company's name. Something generic and forgettable, such as *Smith Pest Control*, was preferable to anything creative like *Bug Out*.

I'd have to make do with poking around the house with a ruler and a clipboard, pretending to inspect for termites and launching into an absurd sales pitch if anyone interfered. That gave me an idea. Maybe one of the store computers had Internet access. I could look up termite inspections so I'd appear semi-knowledgeable. All the display laptops rejected my attempts to go online. Finally I spotted a desktop clearly used by employees. After convincing myself someone *could* mistake it for a floor model, I typed and clicked as quickly as possible, settling on an article aptly titled, *Does Your House Have Termites?* I scanned and summarized its advice, committing it to memory. ("Look for termites and their piles of excrement anywhere wood touches the ground. Don't store wood near your house.") Then I walked away nonchalantly, ready to inspect the Rush home, and my own later.

I took my items to the counter and added lemonade, which I'd need if I was outside much. It was already sticky out, and my brown T-shirt absorbed heat like a solar panel. Maybe I'd change back into Sophie's handmade creation. Not exactly professional attire, but it would do, and really, how much trouble could someone in a preschooler's handprint T-shirt get in?

I parked in front of the Rush home and walked straight to the front door, hair in a ponytail, clipboard in hand, handprint shirt and all. I doubted anyone would answer the bell, although I couldn't help wishing for a miracle, so I pressed it anyway. Maybe Beth would open it herself.

All business, I filled out an invoice on the clipboard while I listened for a few minutes. No noise from inside, no barking dog, no meowing cat, and worst of all, no crying baby. I'd never have the guts to enter, but for the heck of it, I blocked anyone's view of the doorknob and gently tested it. Locked. I was disappointed and immensely relieved.

Next I walked around the house, actually inspecting the ground (I couldn't help looking for termites!), while also peering in every window, longing for a glimpse of anything that would suggest Beth was here, safe and sound. I saw nothing but mustard-colored curtains, brocade furniture that might have been elegant in the '60s, and dark wood paneling. Once in a while I made pointless entries on the invoice, put my hands on my hips, and glanced around, surveying for curious neighbors who might question my presence.

Then it struck me that maybe *I* should be questioning *them.* They'd have noticed recent changes, particularly the arrival of a pregnant teen. But what excuse could I use to talk with them? I thought about PI class but came up with nothing. We'd studied common investigations, such as workers' comp cases, but even then, investigators didn't want to tip off neighbors who might inform the subject. A terrible thought occurred to me. What if Beth *was* in her grandparents' house, and my investigation spooked her, sending her on the run again? Or what if she or a neighbor got concerned and alerted the Rushes, who zoomed home to check things out? What would I say when Mrs. Rush recognized me? ("Good news! It appears you don't have termites.")

Stomach churning, I returned to the van, where I put the key in the ignition for a fast getaway and nervously fiddled with the navigation system. It listed several things nearby, including a hospital, a post office and a convenience store. *I should call the hospital*, I thought, *and ask for Beth Myers' room—just to see if she's there.* I could also see if the convenience store was in walking distance, in case Beth still took walks. Finally, I'd keep an eye out for delivery trucks. Maybe an employee had noticed a pregnant teen around.

I tried the hospital first. No Beth. Next I drove by the convenience store, which was a mile and a half away, too difficult for her to reach by foot with busy roads and no sidewalks. But I asked about her anyway. Same result. Then I pulled into the post office and gave myself a pep talk about what I was doing for Kenna, Beth, and an unborn baby. I'd come all this way, and I couldn't wimp out now.

"Hi," I said to the woman at the counter, who was my age and overweight. "I have kind of a funny question for you."

"No problem. I've answered a lot of those."

"Great. I'm wondering what time of day the mail gets delivered to a certain neighborhood. Can I find that out?"

"Sure. Let me get a manager. Can you write down the address for me? He can check the schedule." She handed me a scrap of paper, and I jotted down the Rushes' street. She walked off and returned a minute later, alone. "He says it's a morning delivery, and the driver, Rob, is working on it now."

"Great!" I said. "That's so helpful. Thank you."

Maybe the hardest part of investigation, for me, wouldn't be getting answers. It would be mustering the courage to ask questions.

I headed out the door and back to the Rushes' in search of someone new. Rob.

I chose a parking spot where I could see the front of the house from a distance, leaving plenty of room for Rob to work, but not so far off that I'd have to chase him down. Plus, sitting here would allow me to relax a little. There was no way I'd miss a mail truck maneuvering around me.

I hoped Rob would show up quickly because it was hot, I was sweaty, and my lemonade was running low. The flags on several mailboxes were turned up, which suggested he hadn't arrived yet. I turned on the AC for a while, but then thought of the kids' environmentalism, turned off the car, opened my window, and listened to the radio on low.

Leaning my elbow on the car door, I rested my head on my hand and closed my eyes momentarily. It was so rare to get a moment of peace. The street was quiet, and the heat was draining. Even the remaining lemonade, which was positioned between my thighs like an ice pack, was sweating, leaving visible marks on my capris. I opened one eye and saw the time: 11:50. If Rob had a morning run, he was about to be late. I closed my eye for what felt like a second and then was jarred awake by the sounds of a motorcycle roaring by.

Jerk! I thought, heart racing. Why did motorcycles have to be so loud? Were all riders immature and selfish?

My cell phone indicated a new text message from Dean, and the current time, 11:58, which revealed I'd been dozing. Whoops.

I was about to read the message when the bike roared back in my direction, coming toward me this time, and parked across the street. Oh, brother. Honestly, motorcyclists intimidated me. Was I prejudiced? Or was intimidation their goal?

I put up my window, started the car, and aimed a vent my way to cool off. Before pulling forward to put some distance between me and motorcycle dude, I used my peripheral vision to ensure he wasn't walking my way.

That tiny glance caused a huge problem. The guy wore jeans, utility boots, a shaded helmet, and a white tank top that revealed muscular arms and a shoulder tattoo. I'd never seen the tattoo before, but the body was familiar. I'd appreciated it night after night in PI class. Shizzle.

I wanted to drive away in ignorance. Dean *could not* be in West Virginia, and if he was, I didn't want to know. Even more, I didn't want *him* to know this sweaty mess with melting eyeliner was me. I gently pressed the gas until I saw his undeniable wave in my rearview mirror. Shizzle again!

Instead of backing up, I took a left, as if to turn around. While I was out of view, however, I pulled into someone's driveway to mop my face with a baby wipe.

I stuck gum in my mouth and checked the text he'd sent: "Had some business in West VA and thought I'd see how you're doing. What's your location?"

Apparently he didn't need an answer. This spoke well of his investigative abilities.

I shifted into reverse and reluctantly turned back toward Dean, hoping we'd get closer to Beth, believing progress on any other front was impossible.

I plastered on a smile and pulled up behind the bike, simultaneously noticing Rob, the mailman, heading up the street, house by house.

"Dean?" I said as I got out of the car. "What are you doing here?"

He rested his helmet on his hip and squinted in the noonday sun, eyes sparkling like aquamarines.

"Where'd you go?" he asked.

"I was taking a break," I said. "But when you waved, I knew it was you, so I turned around. I can't believe you're here. How did you know where I was?"

"I called your house this morning to tell you I had business out here, and I could do some checking around. But your mom said you were already here."

"You talked to my mom?" That scared me. What else had she told him? So much for "private" investigation. I didn't remember mentioning Dean, but if I had, she'd probably seized the chance to "help" my stagnant love life.

"Yup. And I had the information about the Rushes, so when you didn't answer your cell or respond to my text, I figured out where they lived and swung by."

"Oh." I was distracted by the mail truck, now only two stops away. "Will you excuse me for a minute?"

"Sure."

Despite what I've told my kids, I don't have eyes in the back of my head, so I don't know if he watched me jog away, but it felt like lasers were burning holes in my handprint shirt and sagging capris as I waved at the dark-haired, bearded mailman and held up a "hold-on-a-second" finger.

"Help ya?" Rob called.

"I hope so," I said breathlessly. "I'll spare you the details because I know you're busy, but have you seen a young, pregnant teenager around here lately?"

"Why do you ask?" he said.

"Well, she's missing from Virginia, and she might be staying in this area. A lot of people are really worried about her."

"I'm not allowed to answer questions like that," he said, taking me by surprise. "Unless you got a federal ID or something."

"I don't understand. What do you mean?"

"You look nice and everything, but for all I know, you're out to do her harm. With all the stalkers and crazy people today, we've got rules about this stuff. To get answers, you'd have to file paperwork with my manager."

"Really?"

"Yup."

"So you can't tell me *anything*? Not even if you *haven't* seen her?" I rested my arm on his truck so he'd stay put.

"I can't," he said. "But you should ask around." He gestured toward the Rush home and beyond. I couldn't tell if that was a hint. I hadn't mentioned their family.

"I would, but I'm afraid I'll scare her away. We just want to know she's safe. She's been missing almost two weeks." I pulled a flyer from my pocket and unfolded it. "This is her. If you've seen her, please report it."

"Of course," he said. "And remember, you can file that paperwork." He made eye contact and paused. "Assuming you're someone official, which, no offense, you don't look."

"I'm not," I confessed, hoping for sympathy. "But I have good intentions. Is there any way you can bend the rules, just a tiny bit, without breaking them?"

He was quiet for a long moment, squinting and biting his lip.

Please, please, please, I thought.

"Nope," he said. "Sorry. But why don't you give me that flyer?"

"Sure." I handed it over.

"Trust me," he said. "That'll help more than anything." He shifted into drive. "Good luck."

I removed my arm from his truck. "Thanks. I really appreciate it."

He nodded and pulled away.

Fourteen

Any fear I had about talking to Dean vanished with this news. Rob had seen Beth. I felt it. And now he'd probably do something about it.

I crossed the street and resisted the urge to hug Dean and squeal.

"That was interesting," I understated. I inhaled deeply and exhaled emotion.

"I want to hear about it," Dean said. "But we should talk further away. Let's meet a few streets up."

He followed the van at a dull roar. During the short trip, reality hit hard, halting my adrenaline surge. If Beth was a runaway, it was for a reason—a reason that could devastate Kenna. I wasn't sure I was capable of breaking that news. Kenna would be relieved to know Beth was okay, and somehow, she'd recover. I had to believe that.

I stopped at an empty playground parking lot and waited while Dean secured his bike and helmet. I tried not to stare, but it was tough.

I diverted my attention to the park with a mommy eye. Was the mulch deep enough for a serious tumble? Would the slide be too hot in the sun? What was the highest, most dangerous point kids could reach—and where would they land if they fell? I sat on a bench and decided everything looked okay.

When Dean joined me, I focused on his tattoo. An angel's wings spread gracefully across his left shoulder.

"It's for my mom," he said.

"It's really beautiful." I hesitated to go on. "Did she pass away?"

"A long time ago. When I was in middle school. She's always looking out for me, so I got this when I joined the Army."

I remembered a line in his bio that said he'd been an MP. There was so much I could say but so little felt right. How awful it was to lose a parent. How sorry I was that he suffered. How much I worried about my kids without their dad. But his voice was steady and confident. He didn't want comforting.

"It's an amazing tattoo," I said. "I love it."

"Thanks." He smiled. "So tell me what you learned today. Don't keep me in suspense."

I started to fill him in, but he held up a hand when I got to the termite inspection.

"Stop right there," he said. "Wait 'til we get to trespassing and right to privacy in class. Then tell me if you should have done that." His twinkling eyes told me he wasn't upset, but I was mortified anyway. I'd never tell him the story about visiting Marcus's house.

"Good thing I'm not a real PI yet," I said, scrunching my nose. "I have a lot to learn."

"You had a great cover," he said. "I'll give you that. Termite inspector. Pretty creative. Did you get any leads?"

"Not at their house." I told him about the conversation with Rob. "I was afraid to knock on neighbors' doors," I added. "I didn't want to tip anyone off."

"I agree with that," Dean said to my relief. "We shouldn't canvass the neighborhood yet. If Beth is here, it might spook her. And if we do talk to neighbors, we need to pick them carefully, meaning we should look for people who won't spill the beans." He glanced at his cell phone. "I've got about an hour. Wanna walk around the neighborhood one more time?"

"Starting here?" I asked.

"Yeah. Let's walk back toward the house, but circle around this way." He pointed to a path that ran behind the park.

"Where does that go?"

"Through the neighborhood, right past their block."

"Oh. How do you know that?" Maybe he'd been here before.

"I check Google Earth before I go anywhere."

"Right," I said, making a mental note.

Dean stood and pocketed his phone. "You got a great lead today," he said. "Let's get some more."

I clutched my necessities—cell phone and keys, wondering what else Dean and I would discuss.

*   *   *

"So how are your kids doing?" he asked first thing.

I struggled to answer without gushing. My kids are endlessly fascinating to me, but is anyone else really interested in Jack's Lego creations or Sophie's death-defying feats? Relatives and close friends, sure. My dad liked to hear it all. Jason had been in love with his kids, just not with me. I blinked to dispel sad thoughts.

"They're great. The joys of my life."

"They're adorable," he said.

"Thanks. Do you have any?"

His bio was all professional, and since he didn't wear a ring, I assumed he was single. How many married guys ride motorcycles and have tattoos? *Not enough*, I thought, surprising myself. In a matter of minutes, Dean had transformed me from a motorcycle hater to a biker chick wannabe. His tattoo even had me thinking about one to honor my dad. A plane, maybe.

"Kids? Nope. Never married."

"I'm a widow," I blurted.

"Really?" he said. "That's unbelievable. I'm sorry."

"It's okay," I said. "It's been a while. Four years. I'm adjusting." I smiled reassuringly.

He didn't ask for details, and I didn't offer them. I didn't want to discuss Jason's death, but sometimes it was necessary, such as when I met the kids' teachers, who simply needed to know. Most people assumed I was married or divorced, and, oddly enough, I was guilty of assuming the same about others my age. Married, divorced or never married. Not a widow or widower. It just shouldn't be.

A flicker of resentment burned in my chest. It was bad enough to mourn someone you love, but being rejected at the same time— discovering infidelity—was another. Short of hiring a medium, which, believe me, I'd considered, I'd never be able to confront Jason or his mistress and get my questions answered. That was hard to swallow. Over time, I'd taken my best guesses and come to terms with it. I'd even pressed Andy about it. He swore he had no idea. That's what everyone said.

"So tell me how you got into investigation," I said.

While an MP, he explained, he'd been injured in a scuffle, leading to prolonged—but ultimately temporary—vision loss. When he left the military, that meant law enforcement wasn't an option, but he didn't want to give up the work he loved. So he took a job in security and finally settled on debugging to mix his passion for investigation and high-tech equipment.

He asked about me, too, and actually listened to the answers, which suggested that despite his amazing looks, he wasn't self-absorbed. Between his mom-inspired tattoo and friendly curiosity, I got the scary feeling he had depth and character. This could be trouble.

Who knows what he thought of me. I was so self-conscious I couldn't relax into the conversation. I stumbled through explaining why I wanted to be a PI, at one point giving the misimpression I didn't need to work. Truth was I had enough to survive and plan for the future, but not enough to open bills without anxiety. Meanwhile, I had an insatiable appetite for understanding criminal cases and making things right. Being home with my kids came first, and I was lucky to have that luxury, but soon I'd need a job with decent pay and intellectual stimulation—something that could expand when my kids were in school full time.

By now we'd reached the Rushes' street, and I wondered if Dean would notice anything I hadn't. He suggested we stay on the opposite side of the street, as if we were on a casual walk, and then circle the block so he could get a 360° view.

Oh, sure, I thought. *A casual walk? A sweaty, unkempt woman with a superhot guy? That won't draw any questioning looks. Maybe we should hold hands and make it even more convincing.*

We were silent as Dean took in the front of the home. His eyes moved slowly over the exterior. I didn't think he'd miss a thing.

"Everything's neat," he said quietly. "Fresh paint. Trimmed bushes. Smooth driveway. They have enough money to keep things nice."

"He's a doctor. His office was a lot like the house. Older. Plain. Neat. Nothing fancy."

I should have checked the waiting-room magazines, I thought. To me, a tidy, up-to-date selection shows a certain level of success and consideration for others.

"What were they driving?"

I told him the affordable make and recent model.

"Is money important in this case?" I asked.

He shrugged. "Not especially. Just noticing everything to get a feel for these people. Could they afford to take on a grandchild and her baby? They look like penny pinchers. But not hurting for money."

"Yeah. That's the way it looks," I said, thinking about my house and van. Both needed touchups and repairs. What did that say about me? *I'm busy? Tired? Short on money? All of the above,* I thought.

Dean did a lap around the house, jostled a hollow-sounding trash can on the curb, and joined me for the walk back to my van.

"Nothing so far indicates Beth is staying here except what the mailman said, or didn't say, which is huge," he said.

"Do you think she's here?" I asked.

"I'm hopeful, but I don't know."

"Meanwhile, I have no idea what to do," I admitted. "Where should I go from here? If she's here, I don't want to scare her away."

"Right. You have to be careful. Observe for as long as you can. See who you think might be willing to talk without tipping her off. How long can you stick around?"

"My mom will babysit today as long as I need her."

"Okay, then I'm going to take care of my business. You go out and get some lunch and a cold drink." This confirmed that I looked like a wilted plant. "Let's meet around the time Dr. Rush's office closes," he continued. "We'll follow him and see if it leads anywhere. If you have sunglasses or a hat, stick them on, since Mrs. Rush has already seen you today."

"You don't have to come back and help me," I said.

"Let me see how my business goes," he said. "I'll call you when I'm done."

"Can I pick up anything for you?" I said.

"No thanks. But after your break, park a ways away and keep an eye on things. Notice absolutely everything about the entire neighborhood, and write it all down. I'll touch base in a couple hours."

"Sounds good."

We returned to our vehicles and drove in opposite directions.

*   *   *

If Burger King had a shower and a hair dryer, my stop there would have been almost perfect. I briefly considered paying the day rate to freshen up at a local health club, but since I didn't have a change of clothes or makeup, I discarded the idea. Instead I munched on vegetarian fries (which didn't have "natural beef flavor" like a competitor's did) and forced down water instead of the soda I craved. By the time I finished, I felt chilly in the restaurant, so I ordered a decaf coffee to go.

My next stop was the gas station again, where I topped off the tank, not knowing exactly how far I'd drive (or how long I'd sit) over the next few hours. I bought a magazine, a cooler, ice, water, and a trucker hat.

I didn't want to go back to the Rushes' house yet, so I stopped at a drug store to pick up face powder, blush, lip balm, and deodorant. I decided to keep them in the van as "emergency supplies."

After putting them to good use, I returned to surveillance in sunglasses and the hat—same old van—to watch the home. I parked in a new location and thumbed through a magazine, keeping an eye out for Beth or any kind of movement. Who knew? Maybe I'd see a UPS delivery from Babies "R" Us.

After an hour of boredom with just a few cars passing by, I called Mom and Kenna to check in.

Mom's offer to pick up the kids from camp reminded me of Dean's loss. He couldn't call his mom for anything. Was his Dad still alive? I wished I'd asked.

Another hour later, during which I confess I left the AC on, Dean called. He had to go back to the office and couldn't rejoin me to follow Dr. Rush. But he'd see me at Saturday's class, when I'd have plenty of time to humiliate myself with inferior surveillance skills.

Seeing no one in, around, or anywhere near the house, I returned to Dr. Rush's office, where I parked in front and resolved that from now on, I was bringing audiobooks or podcasts on surveillance—or maybe I'd sign up for satellite radio, assuming my PI career didn't end before it started. Watching and waiting was boring, but reading was probably a no-no.

Finally, at 4:30 p.m. (as I dutifully noted on a surveillance log), Dr. and Mrs. Rush drove away from the office, stopped at a grocery store, and went home. This time, I wrote down their license plate number and watched their garage door open and close, again at a safe distance. It was hard to see much inside, but there were no other cars in the garage, and nothing out of the ordinary, just stacked boxes, a mower, a bike, and some kind of banner on the back wall.

I was ready to head home soon, certain the couple was in for the night, when the door reopened, and the black sedan backed out. I froze, straining to see who was inside. It was Dr. Rush, alone. I let him pull a few blocks ahead before following. From several cars back, just like I'd learned in class, I tracked his car for a few miles, until he turned into a complex of stately buildings on a beautiful, treed campus. I caught its name as I passed its closing gates: Asheleigh Manor.

I wanted to know what it was, and I also needed to check in at home, so I pulled onto a side street, struggled to load the Asheleigh Manor website on my phone, and called Mom.

"How's it going, sweetheart?" she asked.

"First tell me about you guys," I said.

"Well everyone had a great day at camp. I took them to the pool, and now we're finishing dinner. Do you want to say hello?"

"Sure. Put me on speaker."

"Say hi to your Mom," she instructed cheerfully.

"Hi, Mom!" was the united response.

"Hi sweeties!" I confirmed their day was going well and they were having fun with Grandma.

"We get donuts for dessert," Jack said. "Grandma took us to that place you never let us go."

"Really?"

"Sorry, honey," Mom piped up. "It's Grandma's prerogative." I couldn't argue.

"What flavors did you pick, guys?"

"Stwaberry fwosting!" Sophie yelled, apparently in the midst of enjoying it.

"I got vanilla cream," Jack said.

"Mmmm," I said. "Yummy! Well, keep having fun. Grandma, can you take me off speaker?" The phone clicked. "I won't be too late, Mom, but I was hoping you'd do me a favor."

"Of course."

"Can you go into my office and look up a website for me when you have a minute?"

"Oh, Nicki, you know how terrible I am at that stuff."

"It'll be easy. I promise."

"Well, the kids *are* busy with the donuts." She sighed. "I'm walking to your office."

I thanked her again for the navigation system, an embarrassingly life-changing gift. I got lost plenty in life, but at least now on the road, I knew where I was going. Then in the simplest, most patient words I could find, I reminded her how to access the Internet and type in a website.

"Asheleigh Manor provides short- and long-term care for individuals with special needs," Mom read aloud, "including complex psychiatric diagnoses and developmental disabilities." She stopped. "Nicki, I can't imagine why on Earth you need this information."

"It has to do with the investigation, Mom. It's probably not important. But keep reading if you don't mind."

She described how the Manor assured families of its commitment to "quality of life" and staff who loved their work, clients, and community. It had been founded by a local woman whose son suffered a traumatic brain injury, and now it was a major local employer.

So what was Dr. Rush doing there? Working? Visiting someone? Volunteering? Like I told Mom, it probably didn't matter, but I had to check it out.

"What would I do without you, Mom?" I asked. "Good luck tonight. I'll call you before I drive home."

"Be safe," she reminded me before we hung up. That was when I realized I *did* feel safe. Maybe I was getting too comfortable. *A real PI,* I thought, *probably shouldn't let her guard down.*

Fifteen

Instead of waiting for Dr. Rush to drive home, I headed back to his neighborhood, where as night fell, lights revealed people's indoor activities. Based on Dean's advice, I tried to notice everything about everyone. If Beth was here, neighbors probably knew, and I needed them to confide in me. It was just a matter of picking the right ones.

I took more notes than ever and actually felt a little like a PI. One thing I didn't like was sitting in the van's front seat. I was too visible through the windshield. The back seats had tinted windows, but they didn't have a clear view of the house. I knew the seats were removable—something to keep in mind for future surveillance, but taking them out myself was intimidating, not only because they were cumbersome, but also because crumbs, melted gummy bears, spilled drinks, and other unwelcome surprises had probably glued them to the floor.

My most notable observations were of people coming and going. A thirty-ish, white man in a business suit carrying a fast-food bag into a dark, seemingly empty home. A slender Hispanic woman in blue scrubs walking a pigtailed toddler to an SUV. An old man in a rusty, dented pickup flying by. While I kept watch, the curtains in the Rush home stayed tightly closed, although I saw light and occasional movement behind them. It was all I could do not to prowl around for a glimpse of Beth, but if I got caught, it could ruin things on every level.

So I kept my distance. With whom might the Rushes socialize? Who probably kept to themselves? I doubted the tailored guy with fast food knew the Rushes well. He was young. He came home late. And he lived just far enough away not to be a close neighbor. I watched him click on a TV and sink into a lounge chair. Talking with him probably wouldn't tip off Beth, but it might not yield much, either.

I was hesitant to approach the woman with the young child. She wore scrubs, so she might have talked with Dr. Rush about the medical field or having children.

Nothing else stood out except a man and woman six houses down, about my age, shooting hoops in the driveway. It struck me as a cute thing for an adult couple to do. If they spent time outside often, maybe they'd seen Beth. I wanted so badly to talk with them now, but Dean had advised me to wait, and I knew he was right.

Before calling Mom to let her know I was leaving, I had two brainstorms. I'd call Asheleigh Manor and ask about Dr. Rush. And instead of continuing to use my cell phone for investigative calls, I'd buy one of those throwaway phones I pictured criminals using. Weren't they untraceable?

The navigation system directed me back to the drugstore, where I bought the healthiest (or least unhealthy) food I could find: trail mix, whole grain crackers and extra-dark chocolate. I added an orange juice to my basket and perused the phones. The cashier rung up a ridiculously high total, and I paid it, thankful I hadn't impulse-shopped for anything else, including a digital recorder I might eventually need.

In the parking lot, I used the new phone to call information for Asheleigh Manor's number and then to reach the facility, already tallying how many minutes I'd burned.

"How may I direct your call?" the receptionist asked.

"I'm not sure. I'm looking for a doctor who I think works there," I explained.

"Okay," she said. "What's his or her name?"

"Dr. Rush. Graham Rush," I said. "Does he work there?" I bit my lip and squinted as I waited for her response. *Please be helpful!* I pleaded.

"Of course. Dr. Rush is here now, but I'm sure he's with a client. You can leave a message if you'd like."

"Hmm." I stalled for time. "What's Dr. Rush's schedule like?" I wanted to get as much information as possible without sounding like a lunatic.

"It depends. He's one of our busiest volunteers. But I'd be happy to give him a message. Are you calling on behalf of a client?"

I ignored her question and spoke in an innocent, friendly voice. "Oh, no, it's okay," I said. "I don't need to leave a message." My heart pounded as I grasped for another way to pump her for details. I heard another line ring in the background. "It's wonderful that he volunteers. How many hours do doctors typically donate?"

"Sweetheart, I don't know. But I can connect you with our volunteer coordinator."

I interpreted "sweetheart" to mean *I'm being polite, even though your incessant chatter is keeping me from other calls.* This was confirmed when I was transferred to the volunteer coordinator's voicemail, which announced she was out of the office for a week. I jotted down her name and hung up.

So Dr. Rush was charitable. That was nice. I tried to put myself in his shoes. What if my granddaughter was pregnant and I was an OB-GYN? What if she was unhappy and needed a place to stay? Would I care for her? *Yes.* Would I do it secretly? *No. I'd want my family to know she—and her unborn baby—were safe.* What would stop me from doing that? *Maybe if I thought my daughter—or her husband—was an unfit parent.*

At first glance, Beth's mom seemed impersonal, not incompetent. Maybe Beth's father was the problem. April described them as overprotective and opposed to adoption. Those didn't seem like reasons for Dr. Rush to betray them.

I called Mom to let her know I was on the way, thankful that despite typical mother-daughter challenges, we got along just fine.

I wished I could beam myself home and then skip the necessities, including small talk with Mom. There was so much to do and no time to spare.

I spaced out as I drove, letting thoughts flow without observing them, almost like meditation. Times like these often yielded the best ideas.

Finally I pulled into my driveway and parked next to Mom's car. I turned off the headlights and sat in silence, closing my eyes. I needed a minute to steel myself, organize ideas, and mentally prepare for the next day. As I took a deep breath and stepped onto the asphalt, three noises in quick succession jolted me out of peace. A roaring engine. A firecracker. And an unintelligible yell from a young man. I whirled around to see a bright red Mustang speeding away. I couldn't make out anything else.

Now my thoughts raced like wildfire. *That sounded like a firecracker. But what if it was a gunshot? Could someone have shot at me? Or am I just a basket case after Marcus's shooting?*

Moving between the van and the garage to protect myself, and thinking of Marcus's injury, I frantically ran my hands over my head and body, sensing only the pounding vibrations of my heart. No blood. Okay. Then I circled the van, heart still racing, ears on alert for approaching vehicles. I traced familiar dents and scratches we'd accumulated over the years. Nothing new. Mom's car and the garage were fine too.

Suddenly a new blast of fear ran through my veins. I'd heard stories about bullets penetrating homes and hitting kids.

I've lost it, I thought. *Those were rowdy teens. They probably had leftover fireworks from the 4th of July. Or maybe it was a backfire. Aren't there ways to make your car do that? Kids are always trying to look cool. I'm probably having some kind of PTSD-ish reaction. Plus, the stress of worrying about Beth and Kenna is getting to me.*

Calling the police crossed my mind. But it could waste precious time—theirs and mine. Instead, I'd make sure the kids, Mom, and the house were okay, and I'd give everything a once-over in the morning.

"I feel awful, Mom," I said during breakfast the next day. "I'm sorry I was late. It was a long day."

When the kids weren't listening, I asked whether she'd heard anything out of the ordinary around the time I got home. She hadn't. I called Kenna and Andy, and their answer was the same. While Kenna and I were catching up, Sophie interrupted.

"Can we do the sprinkler?" she asked.

I looked at the stovetop clock. It was still early enough that they wouldn't have to wear sunscreen, so I said yes, as long as it was in the backyard. Plus, it would keep them busy while Mom and I discussed the day. I had to take the kids to a birthday party, and Mom would meet us afterward so I could head to PI class.

She loaded the dishwasher while I urged the kids to put on bathing suits. Knowing I'd get soaked somehow, I slipped on old running shorts and a T-shirt, trusting Dean wouldn't show up again. Just in case, I pulled my hair back and rubbed on a little makeup. I grabbed study materials, put them in a safe spot on the deck, and made the kids scream with happy shock as I started the sprinkler with them in its path, each wearing a superhero-themed bathing suit.

With Mom in charge, I took a few moments to re-inspect the cars, booster seats and all, for bullet holes and suspicious scratches. Everything looked fine. That should have been a relief, but I felt queasy. What if it *had* been a gunshot? What if Jack and Sophie had been in the car? What was I doing? *Helping Kenna*, my conscience told me. *Just keep the kids out of it.* I promised myself I would.

A shriek from Sophie broke into my thoughts. I checked the backyard, where Jack was pointing the sprinkler at Sophie's face. She was standing still, taking it, water streaming eyebrows to feet.

I looked at Jack. "What are you doing?"

"I'm the Green Goblin and she's Firestar!" he said. "I'm taking away her power."

"He got me!" she blubbered.

"Stop it Jack," I said. How was she breathing with a waterfall in her face?

"I like it," she sputtered.

Okay, I thought. *She'll move when she's had enough.*

I turned toward Mom, and Jack shrieked.

"She slapped me!"

"That was a fireball," she said. I should have known. A handprint was forming on Jack's arm. Great, it would be a thrill to take him around like that. Social services, anyone?

"Sophie! You are never, ever allowed to hurt Jack. Or anyone. Unless they might harm you. Like a bad guy or something."

"He *was* a bad guy!"

"You know what I mean. A *real* bad guy."

"Like who?" she asked.

Good question.

I got the kids bathed and dressed for the party. Mom watched them while I showered, the second time in a week she'd blessed me with this enormous luxury. I took the time to iron olive capris and a navy T-shirt. I didn't paint my nails, but I filed them. That was a step in the right direction. When Dean saw me, hopefully he'd forget yesterday's sweaty mess.

On the way to the party, Sophie spontaneously apologized for her fireball. Jack checked his arm and pronounced it fine. *She's maturing*, I thought. *Parenting will get easier. I won't always worry about the kids killing each other.*

"Can I have some gum?" she asked. "Please?"

"No, honey. You'll get treats at the party."

"But I said sorry to Jack!" Oh. So she was maturing *intellectually*.

Her disappointment was replaced with excitement when I turned on the new navigation system.

With its help, we pulled up to birthday boy Justin's house, thankfully festooned with balloons so we couldn't miss it. Sophie grabbed his present and bolted to the front door. Jack and I met her there.

"He's my friend, you know," Jack said. "I should give him the present."

"Okay," Sophie conceded. She was here to keep Justin's sister company. That was more exciting than presenting a gift.

"Thank you so much for inviting both of them," I said as Justin's mom showed us in. I'd promised to stay and help with crowd control.

"Of course. You know it's easier if Ginger has a pal here. I'm so glad you're staying."

Jack joined a group of boys playing pirate Legos in the living room while Sophie and Ginger took off for parts unknown.

"Things seem pretty calm so far," I whispered, knowing the guests could turn into a screaming, group-think mob at any moment.

"It can't last," she lamented.

"If we get stuck, just yell 'Cake time!'" I said. "Even if it isn't."

While she scooted off to answer the door again, I walked around the house, looking for Sophie and admiring pirate-themed decorations, including a blow-up palm tree, a stuffed talking parrot, a treasure map cake, and booty goodie bags with chocolate coins. Justin's Dad wore a bandana, a clip-on earring, and an eye patch while tossing around pirate expressions.

"Do you know where the girls went?" I asked him.

"Aye, matey, I think they went into the ship's hull," he said, pointing to the basement. I couldn't decide whether he was awesome or weird. Or both.

I trotted down the steps and peeked around a corner. There were Sophie and Ginger, engrossed in a doll adventure involving two pools and wedding attire. An older woman sat nearby and introduced herself as Ginger's grandmother. She offered to bring the girls up when the games began.

As I started back upstairs, I heard Justin's mom call my name. Maybe the games were starting already.

"Right here," I responded, opening the door to the main level.

"Do you drive a silver van?" she asked.

"Yes. Why?"

"Someone said it has a flat tire. Do you want to check it?"

"Oh, I can't believe this. I'm so sorry. I'll be right back." Great. I really needed my car for PI class today. Much worse, I feared this wasn't a coincidence. It was best to trust your instincts, I believed, and last night, mine had shouted, "Someone just freaking shot at you!" Unfortunately, it was easy to confuse instincts with panic attacks.

Looking at the front left tire was confusing, too, especially for someone who knows nothing about cars. It was about one-third flat. There were no obvious problems with it, such as a gash or protruding nail. I had tire sealant in the trunk, so I could probably make it to a gas station, if I could figure out how to use the gunk. I didn't even know if I had a spare. Pathetic.

I opened the trunk and poked around under the carpet. There was a tire in there, but it wasn't normal size. How far would it get me? Certainly not through a day of surveillance. If nothing else, I'd be spotted immediately. Like it or not, I definitely had to ask for help. And promptly sign up for one of those "I'm a woman, so no one ever taught me how to take care of essential shit" classes. I vowed to pass on whatever I learned to Sophie.

Pirate Dad walked up just in time, sans eye patch and pirate accent.

"Need a hand?" he asked.

"I'm embarrassed to say I do," I said. "But it can wait 'til after the party." It really couldn't, or I'd be late.

"Don't worry about that. I'm just the cheap entertainment. What have you got in there?"

I showed him the mini tire, some tools I couldn't name, and the sealant. "Please ignore the mess," I added, waving at a laundry basket full of jumper cables, flares, baby wipes, first aid supplies, recently purchased makeup, and practically everything recommended in case of a terrorist attack. The car was a rolling surplus store.

"I could put on the spare," he said, with a glance toward the party. He picked up the sealant. "Or we could shoot this stuff into the tire, and that'll hold you for a while. At least it should. Only problem is it tends to piss off the tire repair guys."

"Why?"

"It's messy stuff."

"Oh." I wasn't thinking about the tire repairmen. I was imagining evidence technicians. If the van had been shot, I had to preserve the proof.

"Do you think I can drive on it? Just to get home? I'm about two miles away."

"Maybe. It looks like a slow leak. But I wouldn't advise it." I decided Pirate Dad was cool, not weird. At least not in a bad way.

"Okay." I considered my options. "Let me think about it." I knew what I had to do, and I'd have to talk myself into it. Maybe some birthday cake would help.

Sixteen

AAA towed us to a nearby service station, where I rented a car, moved our stuff into it, and started for home. I'd asked the police to meet me there. The kids were ecstatic to see a cruiser in our driveway when we arrived. I tried to act excited, but I was anxious. On the way, I viewed every car I passed as a possible threat. If someone had shot at me, would they try it again? Was someone trying to scare me off the case? Or was it because I'd witnessed Marcus's shooting? Did someone think I'd seen the shooter?

I didn't want the kids to overhear this conversation, no matter how fascinating police, bad guys, bullets, and tires might be to them. Come to think of it, I didn't want Mom to know what happened, either, because she'd probably try to talk me out of helping Kenna. I couldn't hide the truth from her, though. She and the kids had to be safe.

Tears eked their way out of my ducts as I forced myself to sing along with the kids' made-up song, "The police are at our house! The police are at our house!" to the tune of *The Farmer in the Dell*. My voice cracked as I pulled up to the curb and considered the possibility of these perfectly innocent kids getting hurt by my snooping around. Even if they were fine, what if something happened to me? They'd already lost one parent.

"Are you okay, Mommy?" Sophie asked. "Your voice sounds funny."

"Yes, sweetie. I'm fine. I'm just thinking about how much I love you and Jack. So much!"

I slid her door open and prayed I'd do the right thing, whatever that was. The kids bounded toward the officer with so much enthusiasm he could have claimed self-defense. Instead, he chuckled as I cautioned them to slow down and walk with me. He introduced himself as Detective Walters and shook our hands.

"Mrs. Valentine?" he asked.

"Yes." I preferred Ms., but I didn't correct him. "I'm sorry to keep you waiting, but I need to get them settled inside, and then we can talk. Feel free to have a seat on the porch, and I'll be right back. Is that okay?"

"Yes ma'am."

While he waited, I ushered the kids inside to the only child care available: snacks and TV. I moved a baby monitor to the den and carried another outside so we could talk in private.

Detective Walters had the law enforcement look. Buzz cut. Trimmed mustache. Respectful but stern expression. He appeared in his fifties and exuded fatherly vibes that put me at ease.

I told him the story and handed him a card from the auto shop. "So what do you think?" I asked nervously. "I know it sounds crazy. But it's true."

"Let's call them," he said, pulling out a cell phone. "See what they have to say." He squinted at the card, dialed, identified himself to someone, and listened without giving anything away.

"You're right," he said when he hung up. "Your van was shot." It was exactly what I expected, and yet I couldn't believe it. He probably couldn't either. "The bullet went right through the tread and into the wheel well, which is great, because the bullet's intact."

My mouth hung open in what must have been a particularly attractive look.

As he asked questions and I answered honestly, I realized he was focused primarily on physical evidence (he mentioned casings), potential witnesses, and gangs. We discussed Marcus's shooting and the little I knew.

The subject of Kenna's adoption didn't come up, and although it was potentially relevant, I was too scared to go there without her permission. Plus, gangs were infamous for intimidating witnesses, Walters said, and I couldn't imagine anyone thinking I was a real threat to find Beth. Who knew I was even looking for her? April, April's mom, the convenience store owner, a mailman, her neighbors, and anyone those people told. Uh oh. The list was longer than I thought.

"Ma'am?" Detective Walters got my attention. "Is there anything you'd like to add?"

I took his card and promised to call if there was.

"I'm going to have someone from the gang unit get in touch," he said. "They'll give you advice on dealing with this stuff. And we'll probably send someone from the lab to check around for casings or bullets. Meanwhile, be smart. If you don't have to be alone, don't be. And see if the kids can stay somewhere else."

By the time Mom pulled up, Walters was gone, and my nerves were raw. Unfortunately, as much as I wanted to miss PI class and stay home with the kids, I had to go. There were no makeup classes. And I needed to talk to Dean.

Mom was understandably panicked by the entire thing and begged me to give up. She even played the Mommy card—mine, not hers. "What about Jack and Sophie? You're willing to put them in danger over this?"

"I know. I know." I put my head in my hands. "I think it's too late to turn back. I was already at Marcus's shooting, and I'm sure that's what this is about. I can't turn back time and *not* be there. And I don't think looking for Beth is going to hurt anyone. But *not* looking for her could hurt a lot of people."

Mom shook her head in disapproval. "I don't like what you're doing," she said.

"I don't either. But you'll help me—and Kenna and Beth—anyway?"

"No." My stomach dropped. "But I'll help the kids. Lord knows what you'd get them into without me."

A wave of heat rose from my chest to my face. *I'd never knowingly put them in danger,* I wanted to argue. But truthfully, I wasn't sure I could defend my choices, and without her help, I'd have to quit. I bit my tongue and said, "Okay."

Mom followed up with an offer I wanted to refuse but couldn't. She'd take the kids to her un-childproofed, full of fragile objects, "be quiet because the neighbors are grumpy" condo, and they'd return when the coast was clear. I couldn't bear the thought of turning them over. She was a wonderful, caring grandmother, but she hadn't raised a kid since babies slept on their stomachs, kindergarteners walked to school alone, and superhero cartoon characters had values. There was a steep learning curve and big margin for error.

After packing, transferring car seats to her Lexus, and deciding how the visit would go (trips to the park, eating out, swimming, watching too many DVDs, and sleeping in Mom's bed so everyone would stay in one place), I released the kids into her care. I cried as they drove away, waving enthusiastically, as if I—and everything else— was okay.

I showed up at PI class a mess. An emotional mess at the very least, but not physically impressive, either. I'd broken into multiple sweats through the day, driven a stinky rental car, and "freshened up" by throwing on blush and face powder.

Dean, meanwhile, looked so good I wanted to crawl under my desk and hide. At the same time, I knew I'd have to do the opposite— approach him after class for a serious face-to-face, so I might as well buck up and act confident. As long as I learned something and he didn't visibly recoil, I'd consider the class a success.

"We'll divide into pairs today," he told everyone. "Each two-person team will take a car. You'll link up with another two-person team by walkie talkie. It's your job to cooperate with your partners and trail our volunteer targets today. But you can't let them spot you. If they identify who's following them, or you lose them, *not good*."

The first target, Dean explained, was a female FBI agent driving a silver Ford SUV. The other was a retired police officer with a black GMC pickup. Both were parked on nearby major roads waiting to be followed. They'd cruise around for a while and finally lead the teams back to the academy.

I braced myself as Dean called out assignments. I was fine with almost anyone in the group except Jeremy, a kid in his twenties who asked too many questions and never had the right answers. He was also obsessed with cop shows and talked about them incessantly. I'd heard there were a lot of law enforcement wannabes (or can't be's) in the PI and security industries, and maybe he was one of them.

The other guy I wanted to avoid was Scott. He was a quiet, mop-headed security guard who was already looking at me every time I glanced his way. Creepy. My only comfort was that in Virginia, becoming a PI requires a thorough background check, including fingerprinting. I tried to forget that plenty of horrible criminals had clean records before they were caught.

Early on, Dean called my name and first choice for a partner, Dorothy, a retired accountant with a tell-it-like-it-is attitude and special interest in financial investigations. We didn't have much in common, but we were the only women in the class, and that was bond enough. I desperately hoped she'd drive, because I was too preoccupied to focus well. I also wasn't familiar enough with my rental car.

We were teamed with a retired DEA agent and Jeremy, with whom we'd follow Ginny, the FBI agent. She was described as 5'10", 130 pounds, blond and wearing a pink sundress. Sounded like we might not be the only people checking her out. We were given her license plate, location, and expected departure time.

"Let's go out to the parking lot," Dean told everyone. "Take your valuables with you and give me a head start. I'm riding with Ginny." Amber, the receptionist, would ride with the other target.

The pressure was on as Dorothy and I headed out. She asked if she could drive while I worked the walkie talkie and navigated.

"Sounds good to me," I said. "Where's your car?"

She pointed to a dark green Honda CR-V. Not the best in terms of visibility, but not the worst either.

I climbed in and admired what I didn't see: trash, juice boxes, receipts, pens, change, coupons, snacks, CDs, library books, barrettes, and other items that resided in my van. Not even dust! I expressed my awe.

"It's retirement, honey," she explained. "I'm so bored that cleaning is fun." Boredom was a foreign concept to me. So was organization. I doubted either one would change.

"Is that why you're becoming a PI?"

"That's part of it," she said as she checked her rearview mirror.

I wanted to know her other reasons, but we had to focus on the task at hand. I contacted Jeremy and Brent.

"We're pulling out," I told them.

"Right behind you."

I swiveled my head and saw Jeremy driving a blue sedan. At least Brent would do all the talking.

"We have the eyeball," I reported, using lingo we'd learned in class. That meant we had the target in sight. "She's parked at a convenience store on the corner." I glanced at Dorothy's navigation system and called out cross streets.

"We'll pull into a lot across the street," Brent said. "You take her side. No matter which way she goes, someone can follow her."

"Sounds good," I replied. Dorothy pulled into a nearby lot in view of the store's exit. We didn't have a direct sightline to Ginny's car, but there was no way she'd leave without being seen, unless she was on foot. Jeremy and Brent confirmed they'd watch from across the street.

When Brent said Ginny was on the move, we waited until she'd pulled into traffic, and then we hung several cars back at a stoplight. Once she was a little further ahead, we practiced surveillance tricks, such as pulling over briefly so Brent's car could take the eyeball while we tailed him.

When Ginny turned, Brent went straight and did a U-turn, and we took the eyeball. Switching back and forth was so helpful that it was daunting to imagine doing mobile surveillance alone.

It was my job to be especially observant while Dorothy drove, so I couldn't help noticing Dean laughing a lot with Ginny. She mostly kept her eyes on the road, but he kept turning to look at her. Occasionally she'd throw her ponytailed head back to guffaw.

"So do you think you'll do much surveillance as a PI?" I asked Dorothy. I had the impression she was destined for bigger things.

"Not a chance," she answered. "Too much time on my ass. I've already got hemorrhoids." We laughed. "I want to do undercover corporate work. What about you?"

"I'm not sure yet." I needed to give it more thought. I told her what interested me so far—background checks, process serving, and surveillance. I longed to help with criminal investigations, too, but I wasn't qualified. Looking for Beth drove that point home.

"What do you think about infidelity cases?" Dorothy asked, stopping my heart.

How could I separate Jason from my answer? Truth was, I'd been an idiot about him. The clues had been there, and I'd ignored them. I was so busy parenting that I'd been resentful, not suspicious, when he "worked late" or went out with "friends." When we didn't have sex, I was relieved. My days were full of breastfeeding, doing laundry, carrying kids, managing tantrums, drying tears (sometimes my own), and feeling mortified by the state of my house and body. If he wasn't interested, I understood, and I assumed we'd work it out when life calmed down. Eventually the kids would go to preschool, I'd get the house and myself in shape, and we'd reconnect. Ha.

If I'd given our marriage the attention it deserved, maybe we would have been okay. At the very least, I wouldn't have been blindsided. Sucker punched. Decimated.

Poor Dorothy had no idea she'd opened a can of worms.

"I've got some personal feelings about infidelity cases," I confessed, a rare occurrence for me. "So I probably wouldn't be the best investigator for that job."

"Oh. I'm sorry, hon. It's not my business, but whatever some two-timer did to you might make you a better PI." She gave me a sympathetic glance. I looked out the window.

"I think it brings back too many...," I choked on *memories*. How embarrassing. I hardly knew Dorothy, and here I was on the verge of tears. I thought I was over this. Or getting over it. As much as anyone can get over loss and betrayal. "You know what?" I said. I forced my eyes back to Ginny and Dean's car. "You have a point. I have to be optimistic."

Eventually Ginny turned back toward the academy, followed by us and then Brent and Jeremy. We parked a good distance from the strip mall and watched her and Dean walk into the office—all smiles.

"They're hot stuff," Dorothy said. "I wonder if they're an item." She wiggled her eyebrows comically.

I smiled, feeling a little depressed. I hoped not.

Seventeen

Back at my desk, I listened to Dean evaluate the teams. I also unsuccessfully searched Ginny's appearance for flaws. Tall, blond, athletic, tan, a sprinkling of freckles across her cheeks and shoulders. She looked like she belonged on a surfboard, not in the FBI.

"Okay. Team one. Nicki, Dorothy, Brent, and Jeremy. Nice job. Ginny never spotted you."

I perked up. We hadn't been seen! I was proud until I realized that with Dean in the car, it would be hard for Ginny to notice much else.

"Anything to add?" he asked her.

"Nope." She wagged her perfect ponytail. "They did a great job."

"We'd like to hear a report from you guys, though, about what you observed." He looked at each of us. "Anyone?"

Brent spoke up, thank goodness. He described where Ginny and Dean had driven and when. He even identified the candy she'd bought at the convenience store. (Snickers.) He must have used binoculars.

"Looked like you two were having fun," he threw in.

"More than we were," Dorothy added. I wasn't sure if I should be insulted.

Dean launched into a short lecture on the realities of investigation. *Most cases require patience and persistence. Surveillance can be boring and uncomfortable. If you want a car chase or shootout every week,* he said, *watch TV.* That must have resonated with Jeremy.

Dean congratulated our team and sat down while Amber and her partner, who had spotted the other team, gave constructive criticism.

One of their cars had gotten lost while the other followed too closely. I guess we'd done well.

Dean suggested everyone take a break while he walked the targets out. After eating two maple-nut granola bars and checking my appearance in the bathroom, I chatted with Amber in the reception area, hoping I'd see Dean say goodbye to Ginny—preferably without much affection.

"Did you guys have fun today?" she asked.

"We did. I still can't believe Ginny didn't spot us."

I glanced out the window and saw her talking with Dean and giving him a quick hug. Hmm. Inconclusive.

"Do you know what she does for the FBI?" I asked.

"I think background investigations. She's really sweet." Hmm again.

Dean was approaching so I squeezed in one more question. "How did you guys get her to help with this?"

"I don't know."

He pulled open the door. Somehow his muscular arms didn't rip it off its hinges.

"Hey Dean?" Amber asked. "How'd we get Ginny to help today?"

He shrugged. "I just asked." I bet he was used to that.

The afternoon flew by since I was worried about talking with Dean after class.

"Nicki," he said as I slowly got up from my desk, letting the other students filter out. "First, congratulations on your mobile surveillance today." He pulled chairs together for us.

"Thanks." I sat down and put my shoulder bag on the floor. "But I bet you saw us, since you knew who was following Ginny. How'd we really do?"

"No, you did great," he said. "Really."

"Well I've gotten some practice lately."

"I know. What's the latest on West Virginia?"

I described observing the Rush neighborhood and following Dr. Rush to Asheleigh Manor.

"I'd give it one more night," he said. "If you don't spot anything, you're gonna have to talk to people. You're just running out of time."

That sounded awful. *Beth was running out of time.* And I had no experience interviewing people. I admitted my lack of confidence.

"If I could go with you," he said, "I would. But my schedule is crazy. I'm teaching classes and my caseload is full."

"Don't worry," I said. "I wasn't asking you to go with me. But there's something else I need to tell you. It's kind of shocking."

He raised an eyebrow and tilted his head.

For some reason I lowered my voice to a whisper. "Someone shot my car."

"What?!" I was right. It was shocking.

"It's okay. I mean I'm okay. My kids are okay, thank God. Even my car's okay." Without thinking, I reached out and touched his arm reassuringly. Then I realized what I'd done and retracted it as if I'd burned myself. Smooth. "The bullet just went through my tire."

He leaned forward and spoke decisively. "Tell me exactly what happened."

"Okay." I inhaled. "Someone drove by my house, and they shot my van. It was a red Mustang. Two door. Like maybe from the '80s. I heard someone yell something, though. It sounded like a young guy."

"You saw it happen?"

"I was getting out of my van. In my driveway last night."

"Whoa," he said. "It's time to back off." He made sure I'd reported everything and asked how I was doing.

I explained that somehow I was adjusting to the idea, that the crime was probably related to Marcus, and that the police were taking care of things. I also told him the kids were staying at Mom's house just in case. That was probably the biggest relief of all.

"So you're still looking for Beth?"

"I have to. Honestly, I doubt it has anything to do with her. And based on what that mailman said, maybe she *is* just a runaway who's staying with her grandparents. But I really appreciate your concern."

I didn't like my next thought. Many runaways fled homes that weren't safe. Maybe Beth had escaped a terrible situation. Finding her might be her worst nightmare. Then again, Kenna was convinced Beth wanted to stay in Virginia, and April agreed. They might be right, but what if April's house had been her only safe haven? Learning about

April's sexual orientation might have been the last straw that made her run.

"What are you thinking?" Dean asked.

"That I have to keep looking," I admitted. My gut and heart felt it, I told him, and when I had that feeling, I couldn't ignore it.

"You're big on gut instincts?"

"Yeah."

"Me too. But you're in danger. And my intuition says let the police handle it and keep your family safe."

I didn't know what to say. *I trust myself more than I trust you? My intuition says you should move in as my personal security guard?* I settled on, "I hear you. But I can't let go. I totally understand if you need to stop helping, though. You've been great."

"Take some time," he said. "Think about what I said. And keep me posted no matter what. Don't go this alone."

I left the academy with good wishes from Dean and paperwork on interviewing witnesses. The suggestions were pretty logical. Briefly establish rapport. Ask open-ended, non-leading questions. Listen closely to answers. Notice non-verbal cues. And clarify information. As a parent, I'd had some practice.

I stopped at home before heading back to West Virginia. I was nervous, truth be told, to go anywhere gangs would expect me to be, and it didn't look like Kenna or Andy was around. I parked in the garage, watched the door lower behind me, and felt trapped. What if someone was waiting inside? *If they wanted to kill you, they would have done it already*, I told myself in vain.

I felt alone. Really alone. And scared. The only person you could count on—or ask to be involved—in a situation like this was a spouse, parent, sibling, or best friend. None of those was available. So I said a prayer and called Aunt Liz.

"Hi, sweetheart!" she greeted me loudly. My impulse was to shush her, since I was in self-protection/hideout mode, but that was ridiculous.

"Hi, Aunt Liz." My voiced cracked along with my emotional armor. I couldn't hide anything from her. That's probably why I called.

"I'm having a hard time." Tears started to flow.

"What's wrong?" she asked. "I'm here. I'm listening."

I told her what had happened since we last talked. I confessed to being frozen in the driver's seat, afraid to enter my house, afraid I'd waded in too deep, afraid more than two lives were at risk, and afraid it was my fault.

"You never intended any of this," she said.

"I probably deserve it. I'm such an idiot." I'd made big mistakes in the last decade. Believing in my marriage. Putting it on the back burner. Not pushing Dad to take better care of himself. Trying to do things I didn't know how to do. Screwing them up.

"You're not an idiot. You're trying to help people. And cruel punishment isn't how God works."

She'd told me this before, but it felt good to hear it again. *God is forgiving. He wants good things for us. His ways are always loving.*

"Will you stay on the phone with me while I go in the darn house?" I said with a tearful laugh.

"Honey," Aunt Liz said, "I'll go anywhere with you."

The house was empty. I knew because with Aunt Liz on the line, I checked every closet, nook, and cranny. I also turned on lights in every room and inspected every lock. After that, part of me wanted to crawl into bed—or at least distract myself with Internet research, because if I went to West Virginia, I'd have to be brave *and* recheck the house when I got back. But a bigger part of me knew plunging forward, not hiding, was the only real solution.

Aunt Liz made me promise to eat a meal before heading out, and although I lacked energy or desire to cook, she was right, so I deposited frozen lasagna in the microwave. *5-0-0*, I jammed into the keypad. Watching the seconds tick away worsened my mood, so I went online to research Marcus's—or C-16's—rivals. The big one was Los Reyes, which meant the "The Kings." Maybe they were my rival, too. The microwave's shrill timer broke the silence and seemed to warn, *You're alone. Eat and get out.*

* * *

"I'm going to find Beth. I'm going to find Beth," I chanted on the way to West Virginia, committing myself to the task. The more I said it, the better I felt. Sure, I was vulnerable and ignorant, but that wasn't going to stop me. Aunt Liz had said something that gave me strength: *Replace fear with faith.* By the time I reached the Rushes' neighborhood, I was so pumped that I couldn't imagine sitting still; I wanted action. So after double-checking the notes from my last visit, I decided to take an undercover walk.

It was still light enough that I could get away with wearing sunglasses, so I put them on, parked several blocks away, and added a hat. I was incognito. At the last second, I thought of wearing my iPod with the sound off.

Walking briskly through fading rays of sunlight, I compared the neighborhood to mine. Smaller, older houses. Bigger, better yards. More diversity among developers. Less diversity among residents. Safe, but not as safe as my neighborhood, at least before yesterday. Despite being a vegetarian, I couldn't help enjoying the smoky aroma of a cookout, wishing I was at home grilling with Kenna, Andy, and the kids.

None of the neighbors looked familiar. No Hispanic woman leaving for work, businessman returning home, or couple playing basketball. This time I saw a middle-aged guy flipping burgers, tweenage boys on bikes, and an elderly woman gardening—no one I'd approach yet. When I finally reached the driveway where the couple had played basketball, I noticed a house for sale half a block away. Had I missed it before? I doubted it. Maybe it had just gone on the market. No matter what, it provided a good excuse to stop and look around.

When Jason and I were house hunting, we'd walked up possible streets many times, chatting with neighbors, asking about the area. One woman, I recalled, told us about a hard-partying family with untrained dogs. Disaster averted! In the end, we built a new home, knowing nothing about who would join us on the street, except Kenna and Andy, and that was enough.

Now I had a perfect excuse to approach someone. I looked around and set her in my sights.

Eighteen

"Excuse me," I said to the old woman tending flowers in her front yard. Her short, white hair set off eyes so blue they distracted from her soft, deep wrinkles. She was beautiful, and her smile exuded kindness. She had to be in her eighties.

"How can I help you?" she asked in a wobbly, confident voice.

"I was looking at the home for sale up the street," I said pointing to it, "and I'd love to know a bit about the neighborhood. Are you happy here?"

"Oh I am," she said. "I'm an original owner." She gestured to her white ranch with freshly painted black shutters. Alone, it would have been ordinary, but surrounded by colorful flowers, it was a cheerful oasis. White Adirondack chairs were strategically placed on the lawn to admire the view.

"Your garden is incredible," I said.

"Thank you. It's my pride and joy. Flowers are great company."

I took that to mean she lived alone. "They're gorgeous," I enthused. "Your neighbors are lucky to have you next door. What can you tell me about living here?"

"You're welcome to have a seat," she offered. "If it doesn't interrupt your workout." She eyed my iPod, and I removed the earbuds.

If I sit down, I might be here a while, I thought. *But if I don't, I might miss something.* I sat.

"Thank you," I said. "So you really like the area?"

"Nowhere is perfect," she said diplomatically. "But it's certainly nice enough. Safe. Do you have children?"

"I do," I said. "They play outside a lot, so good neighbors are especially important to me."

"That's where kids should be," she said, "not in front of the TV. When I was a girl in Colorado, I spent every waking hour outside. It's how I learned to respect nature. Of course we didn't have TV or computers back then." She smiled at her flowers.

I thought about my kids. When they were outside, it was often on pavement or in a pool. And my only efforts to garden were trimming bushes that came with the house. Until now, I'd never given it a second thought.

"Are there many kids in the neighborhood?"

"We've got some that live there." She aimed a garden-gloved finger at a house near the one for sale. "Precious little preschoolers."

She went on to name other families with kids, but she didn't mention the Rushes. I considered Beth a child, but technically she was an adult.

"How about teenagers?"

"Not many of those. We have mostly older folks and young families. Which is nice."

"You know, I think I may know someone who moved here recently. She's a young woman who's pregnant. Have you noticed anyone like that?" I asked.

"The only pregnant girl I know is Dr. Rush's granddaughter." She pointed to the Rush house. "I'm not sure of her name."

My stomach flipped, but I hid my excitement, paced myself, and asked when she'd seen her.

"Oh, I don't know," she said. "Certainly in the past month. I just returned from my daughter's in Cleveland, and it was before that. When did your friend move here?"

"About two weeks ago." That's when Beth had disappeared. "Are the Rushes friends of yours?"

"I wish I could say so, but they keep to themselves. I can't fault them though. He's a busy obstetrician, and I hear his practice is excellent."

It was crucial to wait until I found the right source—someone in whom I could confide—to reveal why I was here, but I felt like I'd found her, and I had to pounce. I hoped it wasn't a huge mistake.

"Please don't think I'm crazy, but I'd like to confide in you about something."

"I can't imagine what, but I've kept many a secret over the years. Go right ahead." Her blue eyes sparkled.

"I *was* looking at that house for sale and getting to know your neighborhood, but not because I might move here. I'm actually looking for a missing, pregnant girl. She disappeared from Virginia two weeks ago, and her grandparents are the Rushes. So if you've seen her since then, it will be a relief, because we'll know she's with them. Is there any way to pinpoint when you last saw her?"

"Heavens," she said. "My memory is terrible." She sat and pressed shaking fingertips to her temple. "Let me think."

I waited patiently but tensely, feeling sweat leaving my pores. "Maybe you remember the weather, or what she was doing. Anything that might indicate the time."

"Oh my goodness." She frowned. "I just don't know."

"It's okay," I said. "Don't worry. We can probably figure it out. But please don't mention anything to the Rushes or their granddaughter. If she's here, it might scare her off, and in her condition, she needs to be somewhere safe."

"She'd certainly be safe with him, since he's a doctor," she said. "But why would she leave Virginia? And why wouldn't her parents know if she's here?" There was concern in her voice and eyes.

"I don't know," I said. "I'm hoping to find out."

"Is she running away from something?"

"Other than the stress of being young and pregnant, I'm not sure, but a lot of people are worried about her. They just want to know she's okay."

"Are you working for them somehow?"

"Well, it sounds funny, but I'm training to be a private investigator, and I have a personal connection to the case. So I'm working on it with one of my teachers."

"Oh! A private investigator? I don't think I've ever met one of those. I wish I could help. When I saw the girl, she looked fine, if that's any consolation."

"It's wonderful. What was she doing? Do you remember?"

"Just coming and going from the house to the car. I've seen her on and off over the years, but this time stood out because of her condition." She pulled off her gardening gloves and reached a hand toward me. "I don't think we've properly met. I'm Edith Huggins."

"Oh, I'm sorry, Edith. I'm Nicki. Thank you so much for taking all this time to talk with me."

"It's my pleasure," she said. "Now let's figure out how I can help."

We decided Edith would notice when the Rushes came and went and make a point to say hello. She even said I could observe from her house.

"Sometimes I make cookies and deliver them to neighbors," she said, "although they're not usually among them, unless it's a holiday. I could do that tomorrow and ask all about their granddaughter!"

Her enthusiasm was contagious. Who better to ask about a granddaughter than a grandma? I felt like I needed to pull back the reins, though. If Beth was here, I should notify the police and let them handle the recovery. I shared my concern with Edith.

"That's sensible," she agreed. "I wish I knew when I saw her. That's going to drive me nuts."

"Tell you what," I said, "I'll ask one of Beth's friends if Beth visited her grandparents before she disappeared. And you can notify the police that you may have seen her. I'll give you the number to call. Meanwhile, if you run into the Rushes, you might ask some key questions."

I listed them for her. *Was Beth there now? If not, when was she last there? Had she given birth? How was her health—and the health of the baby?*

Edith went inside to take notes and returned with her shakily written name and number on floral stationery. I tucked it deep into my pocket. It felt like gold.

"You may have solved this case, Edith," I said. Yet it didn't feel solved. As she said, if Beth was here, why wouldn't her parents know? I gave her a flyer about Beth and added my contact information. "Let's talk tomorrow," I suggested. "It was a blessing to meet you."

"Lovely to meet you, too," she said. "Wait just a minute." She retrieved shears from a bucket and snipped four large blossoms—

fuchsia, orange, white, and yellow—from a long row of flowering plants. "Take these home."

"Thank you so much." I held them out for a good look. "I love them."

"Know what they are?" she asked.

"No," I said. "But I'd love to."

"Zinnias." She leaned in closer. "Now I'll tell you a little secret."

"Okay," I said.

"They're a lot easier to grow than they look."

It was almost dark when I got to my car, and officially night when I got home. I'd stopped on the way to drop off the rental and pick up my van, which now sported a new tire. As I pulled up, Kenna's porch light blinked on and she tiptoed out, barefoot and in a bathrobe. I put down my window.

"Come over," she hissed.

I was tired, but she needed an update, and I was scared to enter my house. I grabbed the essentials, including Edith's flowers, and dashed over to Kenna's steps.

"Hi," I said. "Where's Andy?"

She looked me up and down, incredulous. "Have you been exercising?"

"Just walking. This investigation stuff requires it." I handed her the flowers. "Let's talk and you can put these in a vase."

"Andy's working late tonight," she said over her shoulder as I closed her door and turned the lock. "It's baseball season." Andy specialized in writing about baseball and football. "I'm so glad we can talk. But where are the kids?"

"They're at my mom's. Special treat." I didn't have the heart to tell her about my tire. Not yet.

We turned left into her kitchen, which she'd upgraded with cherry cabinets and dark, speckled granite, leaving me in the dust with builder-grade oak and white laminate.

Pulling a stool to the counter, I assessed Kenna's face as she filled a vase with water and arranged the zinnias. Dark circles gave depth to her eyes, and her cheekbones were sharp. If she was too depressed to eat, she'd hit a new low, and I couldn't imagine telling her Beth might be in West Virginia, planning to raise the baby—never mind that my car had been shot.

Ignoring the pit forming in my stomach, I got up and opened the refrigerator, hoping she'd join me. "What sounds good?"

"Help yourself," she said. "I just want to know what's going on."

I turned to face her. She'd moved to the table and was resting her chin on a palm, expectant.

"I'm worried about you," I said. "You look thinner than usual."

"It's just stress. I need this to be over. Have you made any progress?"

I closed the fridge, leaned on it, and crossed my arms over my chest. "Nothing concrete."

"Anything *iffy*? I can tell you're holding back, so spill it. I want to know."

Of course she did. She was Kenna. Unfazed. But she was crushable, too, and I had information that could take her down.

"I'm going to be honest with you." I looked at the flowers. "You know those flowers?"

She glanced at them and back to me. They looked so innocent. "Yeah."

"They came from a neighbor of Beth's grandparents. The Rushes."

"Uh huh. In West Virginia."

"Right. I was asking this elderly woman about the neighborhood." I moved to sit with her. "She told me the Rushes' granddaughter is pregnant and that she's actually been there."

"Oh my God! When?"

"That's the part I don't know. There's a chance she's been there all along." I squinted in anticipation.

"What makes you say that?" Her words were measured. Careful. As if she was avoiding a land mine.

"Well, the woman who gave me the flowers, Edith, wasn't sure when she'd last seen her, but it was in the past month. And you know the mailman may have spotted her, too."

"Oh my God."

"I know." I held her hands and squeezed. "I wish I knew exactly what it meant. But at least Beth might be okay. You know?"

"Yeah." She pulled her hands away and covered her face. "I'm relieved. But..."

"I know," I said. She wept almost silently. "You don't have to explain unless you want to." Feeling helpless, I retrieved a box of tissues from the living room. "I promise, Kenna, I'll do anything I can to help make this adoption work."

She wiped her eyes and nose, crumpled the tissue, and grabbed another.

"I wish it was that easy," she said. The tears kept coming. "But if wishing—or trying—could fix this, I'd already have a baby." Her eyes searched mine. "Do you think Beth changed her mind?"

I looked down and rubbed my temples. "I honestly don't know." Desperate, I thought of Aunt Liz, the most comforting person I knew. What would she say? And what would Kenna think of it? Neither of us talked much about faith, and rarely did we say anything like, "I'll pray for you." I plunged forward anyway.

"I talked to Aunt Liz today," I said.

Kenna knew who she was and nodded.

"She reminded me of somewhere in the Bible, I have no idea where, where Jesus says something like, 'Ask and it will be given to you.' I think we should ask, ask, ask. It can't hurt, right?"

"Doesn't it also say 'Seek and you will find'? And something about knocking on a door?" Kenna asked.

"Kenna," I said with a smirk. "I have no idea. But it sounds good."

"We are so clueless," she said, smiling back. "It's embarrassing." I loved how even our most difficult conversations could end with humor. What's better than that in friendship?

I sent a quick SOS to heaven and hoped Kenna did too. Then she grabbed my hands. "You know what we should do?" she said, wide eyed.

"No," I said. "Buy a Bible? Go to confession? Wait. I know. Get baptized!" Now she was laughing through her tears.

"Seriously," she said. "Let's have a sleepover. We can talk all night."

"Andy might not like that plan," I said.

"Oh, come on." She dismissed me with a wave. "He'll be glad to have a break from me. I'm a downer." She wiped away a tear.

"Well, you better tell him to ignore our shenanigans," I said. "And we *have* to get some sleep." I knew it was unlikely unless we passed out involuntarily.

"We'll try. And we'll stay in the guest room so we don't keep Andy up."

That room was beautifully decorated with white twin beds, floral bedding, and cozy, cottage furniture. I'd stayed in it before and loved it.

"First you're going to keep cheering me up though," she continued. "Hand me some chocolate ice cream and a spoon, and tell me something exciting about Dean. Order pizza, too. Then we'll get serious again."

Exhaustion didn't stop me from being happy to oblige.

Nineteen

We didn't get a whole lot of sleep. But we did get a whole lot done. Kenna ate most of the pizza and all the ice cream. We joked about my fantasy future with Dean. And we short-sheeted Andy's bed.

More importantly, though, we talked a lot about Beth, Kenna's future, and how she couldn't imagine anything other than adopting Beth's baby. She relived their conversations, remembering new details, which I wrote down for my file. The agency didn't have news about Beth, she said, and they didn't want to give her false hope. I also checked in with Mom, Aunt Liz, and my voicemail, where I had several messages, including one from the county gang unit and another from April. She mentioned sending me an email. It was too late to return calls, and since Andy was asleep and we couldn't use his work laptop, Kenna wanted to go over to my house.

"I can check email on my cell phone," I told her, angling to stay where we were—relatively safe and comfortable.

"You know my love of computers," she said dryly. "But I think we should check Beth's Facebook page or whatever it's called again."

Bless her technology-phobic heart, Kenna was right. We needed to check Beth's page and all her friend's pages. I also needed to search for the Rushes. People of all ages were on Facebook, why not them?

I broke the news to Kenna about the tire. She was appropriately horrified and characteristically fearless.

"Let's sneak over," she said. "Like the old days."

"The old days" were our teenage years, when we pretended to be investigators, usually in pursuit of a cute boy, whose activities we'd observe with incredible focus.

I agreed only because I wanted my toothbrush, makeup, and a

change of clothes. And because we could go in the back, where passing cars couldn't see us. I also couldn't bear to crush Kenna's sleepover high.

Kenna went upstairs to whisper to Andy that if we weren't back in forty-five minutes, we were in trouble and he'd have to play hero. She set an alarm to blast him out of bed in case we didn't return.

We exited Kenna's back door, locked it behind us, and tore across the grass to my patio—armed with cell phones, Andy's softball bat, and forks. Thankfully our yards bordered trees, so no one would see us looking foolish. But the sound of rustling branches, which was usually soothing, had morphed into something ominous and prickly, and I couldn't wait to get inside.

"I'm fencing in my yard," I grumbled as we burst into the kitchen. "I want a barrier between me and that forest. How 'bout you?"

"Too expensive," Kenna said. *True.*

I was fumbling for the light when I heard another unexpected noise. My free hand, which was holding a fork, flew back to stop Kenna from taking another step.

"Shhh," I said. "Listen."

She inched backward, perhaps in case we needed to evacuate, or maybe to escape my utensil. The sound of her slippers on the floor was so loud compared to the silence that I couldn't hear anything else until she stopped.

Then I heard it again. *Squeak. Squeak.* I knew that sound. It was the front door moving—either opening or closing. Was it possible I'd left it open earlier? Or not closed it properly? *No.*

My eyes locked with Kenna's.

"What is it?" she whispered.

"The front door is moving. Let's go!"

I pushed her toward the patio door and saw one of her hands glowing with the light of a cell phone, rising to her ear. As I turned the door handle, I heard someone answer her call.

"911. What is your emergency?"

While waiting for the police to arrive, Andy was jolted out of a short-sheeted bed by an oddly armed wife, who was panicked and blabbering about her best friend, a shooting, and a squeaky door. Understandably, he was annoyed. Kenna focused on damage control while I peered out the front windows, intent on seeing whoever had been on my property, hoping I was invisible to anyone outside.

Kenna had been impressively calm on the phone with 911, so I was surprised and mortified by the collection of police cars that pulled up. I was even more taken aback by what emerged from them. Not just people, but a dog. A big, intimidating German shepherd. I was nervous to step outside and greet them.

"Officers?" I called politely as I peeked out Kenna's front door. "That's my house. I think everything's fine."

One left the group and approached me. He introduced himself as Officer Suarez, took my name, and asked what happened, which was basically nothing. It took some effort to explain why I was staying at Kenna's and how we'd visited my house in the middle of the night.

"I'm glad you called," he said generously.

"It was my friend who called," I clarified. "She's with her husband. Should I get her?"

"Yes. And while you do that, we're going to search your house, just to make sure there's no one inside."

"Oh, okay." I couldn't argue with that. I *could* mentally run through what the dog and its handlers might find on this unexpected tour of my home's hiding spots. I didn't ask if they'd open closets and look under beds, or if they'd use high-beam, dust bunny-revealing flashlights. Some things are better left unsaid.

Kenna and Andy arrived wearing sweats, a step above the old pajama pants and T-shirt I had on. Andy had thrown on a baseball cap. I gave him a raised-eyebrows, *please-don't-hate-me* smile.

"Hello, Ma'am. Sir," Suarez said. He asked Kenna to come outside and give her version of events, leaving Andy and me to avoid eye contact in silence.

"I am so sorry," I finally said quietly. "I'm sure everything is fine and we're just overreacting. But with all that's happened..."

He took off his cap and ran a hand through his dark, disheveled hair.

"This whole situation is crazy," he said.

"I know."

Kenna returned with Suarez.

"Your house is clear," she said before he could. "No one's there."

"We don't see any signs of a break in," Suarez added. "Although your lock is pretty shabby. Builder grade. You should replace it. Does anyone else have keys to your house?"

"Just them," I said, gesturing to Kenna and Andy. "And my mom. She's babysitting my kids tonight. I guess there's a chance she came by earlier when I was gone, but I think she would have told me."

"All right. We're having the crime lab process the scene. They'll fingerprint possible entry points. And we'd like you to take a look around, make sure nothing's missing or disturbed. Can you do that?"

"Of course. Can I bring my friend?" I looked at Kenna. Andy and Suarez nodded their permission.

"Okay," Kenna said. "Let's go."

"Everything looks out of place like always," I joked as Suarez, Kenna, and I surveyed toys on my living room floor. I hoped the officers had made it through without injury.

An uncomfortable feeling hung in the air. In a small way, it reminded me of when I'd lost Jason, not just in an accident, but to another woman. Before then, life was like a jigsaw puzzle with all the pieces locked in place. Complete. Suddenly some were gone, and their replacements were ugly, jagged and awkward. Yet they were part of my life. I had to make them fit.

Something was wrong now, too, I sensed. There was no denying it. Looking at Jack and Sophie's belongings created a volcano in my chest that threatened to erupt and spew anger at whoever might have invaded our space. I pictured a stranger moving among our things. What had he seen? What had he touched? I could barely think about it.

Embarrassed to tour the house with Suarez, even though his colleagues, human and canine, had just turned it inside out, I asked if he'd mind waiting in the living room. I pushed aside a pile of *Bob the Builder* DVDs to make room on the couch.

"It's better if I go with you," he said. "I may have a few questions."

I hid my disappointment with a shrug. "Okay. No problem." I led the way to the kitchen.

"Some common items to steal are drugs, weapons, money, jewelry, and tech gadgets," he informed us. "But check your food and alcohol too, and remember sometimes these guys actually *leave* something. Look at trash cans and toilets, just in case he availed himself of the facilities."

Oohkay, I thought, curious if poop and pee yielded DNA. If so, would the kids and I have to submit samples for comparison?

Everything seemed pretty much the same. Crumbs were on the kitchen floor where I'd left them. No one had loaded the dishwasher or made our beds. Jack's Legos had not been organized or put away. And Sophie's devotion to creating the perfect outfit was still evident from rejected options on the floor. All the toilets were flushed (a miracle), and the sinks were dry. (I was used to checking for splashes as proof the kids had washed hands or brushed teeth.)

My biggest concern was the computer. If anyone had stolen it, I was in big trouble. I'd never backed up the photos and documents saved on it. I tensed as I peered into my office, and then relaxed when I saw the computer sitting atop my desk, intact and lovely. I pressed the power button, remembering our original intention to check email. While it hummed to life, I ran through a mental checklist of other valuables. My engagement and wedding rings, along with critical family documents, were locked in a small safe in the basement. We trudged downstairs to find everything there, along with other items, including my camera and video camera. My iPod and purse had been with me all day, so they were okay.

"Did you notice if the kids' videogame system was by the TV?" I asked Kenna.

"Still there," she confirmed. "I saw it. Along with the basket of games."

"Then I think we're done."

I'd have to let Suarez go. He'd certainly been patient.

"Are you going to spend the night next door?" he asked when we got upstairs.

"I sure am," I said. *Maybe two nights*. I hoped Andy would tolerate me.

"Okay. We'll drive by periodically and keep an eye on things," he offered.

"I really appreciate that."

"Please don't hesitate to let us know if anything else comes up."

That would be sooner than any of us expected.

As soon as Suarez left, Kenna and I returned to my office to check email. We wanted to do it quickly and get out of there. Andy was probably waiting up for us, and the longer we took, the less sleep he got. I wiggled the mouse to wake the computer while Kenna called to update him.

"Hey," she said. "It's me. We're just..."

"Oh my God," I interrupted. "Look!"

The computer must have been on when I pressed the power button earlier, because my word processer was open, and someone had created a document with only a few words in a huge, red letters: "BITCHES GET STITCHES AND SNITCHES GET DITCHES."

I yanked my hands away from the mouse and keyboard. Maybe someone had left fingerprints. Now I *knew* someone had been here, and we'd have to call the police again. I couldn't check email or Facebook, either.

Kenna explained my outburst to Andy and hung up without saying goodbye. I didn't want to know how he looked or sounded on the other end.

"He's on his way," she said. "I *cannot* believe this."

Me either. I was speechless. Just the way someone wanted me to stay.

I wore bright yellow rubber gloves to open the front door for Andy, who surprised me by acting supportive, not angry. I still had them on when Suarez returned with new friends—no dogs this time, just more evidence collectors. I didn't want to be the cause of any lost clues.

The stress of having a stranger—and now many strangers—in my house was draining, so I asked Andy if we could go next door and use his laptop. Hopefully it would encourage him to go back to bed, considering it was now 4 a.m., and he had to be up at seven. Kenna's first class was at nine. I couldn't imagine how she'd teach it, but work was more than a job for her. It was a distraction and stress reliever. Just like reality TV was for me.

"Sure," Andy said. "I'll write down the password for you."

Suarez approached and looked at me.

"We swabbed your computer for DNA and processed it for fingerprints."

Embarrassingly, I'd also seen them turn the keyboard upside down and shake it over paper—and then save what they found. Gross. I preferred not to know the results of that test. "I'm sorry, but we have to take it in and make sure no one put malicious programs on it. That okay?"

"I guess so. Thank you." I thought of how much I used it and all the personal information it contained. It was unpleasant, but necessary, to let it go.

"We also need your fingerprints for comparison purposes. Does your friend spend a lot of time here too?"

"Kenna? Definitely. But not on my computer."

"Let's get her prints anyway before we leave. And first thing tomorrow, you'll meet with Sgt. Dwyer from the gang unit. Can you come to the station around ten?"

"I'll be there," I promised.

Twenty

"Don't get mad," Kenna told me. "But I don't know where to turn this thing on."

She fiddled with Andy's laptop, which was open, but off, on his desk. I took over and found the power button illogically placed on the side of the computer. I hoped the rest of our time would go more easily and boost Kenna's confidence. Over the years, I'd enabled her by finding anything she needed online, and Andy did the same. We'd definitely done her a disservice.

"I wonder if his password is case sensitive," I muttered as I typed in the mix of letters and numbers. I was honored he'd shared it with both of us.

"What does that mean?" Kenna asked.

I explained while I accessed my email. April's message was simply titled *Beth*. It read:

Hi,

Thanks for the 800 number you gave me. The people there are really nice. I also want to say there's rumors going around about Marcus. Since he got shot he's kind of a hero, but I still hate him. Supposedly, Los Reyes still wants to get him because he's a leader who's taking a lot of their drug business. I thought you should know. Have you gotten any good information yet? I hope so. My mom wants to know too.

April

I looked up at Kenna.

"What do you think?" I asked.

"I like her," she said.

"Me too. I want to trust her. What do you think I should write back?"

"Hmm." Kenna rubbed her eyes.

"Maybe we should get some sleep before we do anything," I said. After all, there was nothing urgent in April's message.

Kenna agreed. "Let's look at Facebook though," she suggested. "And then go to bed."

We found Mrs. Rush, not Dr. Rush, on Facebook, but her full page wasn't accessible unless we friended her, which I wasn't sure we should try, certainly not as ourselves. All this was way too complicated for Kenna, who had never seen a Facebook page. Under different circumstances, we could have stayed up all night looking up former classmates and having fun, but no matter how much I wanted to cheer her up, we just didn't have time.

Instead we read about Marcy Rush, including her location and interests. Apparently she was a fan of cooking shows. Her birthday was January twenty-first. She was a registered nurse. And she had a grand total of twenty-eight friends, one of whom was Beth. We clicked on relatives' and friends' pages, and then returned to Marcy's page for a last look.

"This is so bizarre," Kenna said. "This lady is the baby's birth grandmother. I just never imagined seeing her. I wonder what Andy would think." She moved closer to the screen and squinted. "It's frustrating that her picture is so small though."

"I know. We can't see bigger pictures without friending her," I said. "But I saw her in person. I can tell you anything you want to know."

"Maybe later, I guess," she said. "What should we do with all this online stuff?"

I tried to barrel through exhaustion and think. How could we learn more about Beth's contacts without creating a new Facebook identity and trying to friend them? Two ideas came to mind. 1) Guess Beth's password so we could see her friends' postings. 2) Start a

Facebook page in her honor, where friends could post whatever they wanted.

That woke me up. I knew there were cases in which online posts made a huge difference. In one kidnapping, the victim managed to post on a page dedicated to his recovery. I tried to explain the idea to Kenna.

"So if *anyone* can post on a page in her honor," she said, "could I post on it?"

"I take it back," I said. "I didn't mean *anyone*. I meant anyone with an account."

She nodded. That didn't include her.

I wanted a caffeinated soda so badly I could almost taste it. I squeezed my eyes shut and reminded myself that I wanted to live a long, healthy life with my kids. Soda wouldn't help. Neither would staying up all night.

"Kenna, I want to research this a little more, but you'll be bored sitting here. You wanna go to bed?"

Her hesitation was an answer.

"Go," I encouraged. "Please go to bed." I rose to get a glass of water and prodded her ahead of me. "I'm getting a drink," I told her. "Now off with you!"

She raised her hands in surrender.

"Where are you sleeping?" I whispered as we entered the hallway.

"Not with Andy," she whispered back. "I don't want to wake him up. I'll be in the guest room. Don't worry about waking me up, though. I better not find you on a couch in the morning."

Don't worry, I thought. *I'm too scared to sleep alone.*

I stayed online for a while testing various ideas. If someone, maybe April, set up a social networking page in Beth's honor, what would it look like? Similar pages had meaningful posts from all kinds of people. But they didn't list the members. We'd have no idea who'd been there unless they posted something. Creating a simple web page dedicated to Beth, on the other hand, would probably be time consuming and expensive. But at least it would allow us to track visitors. I wished I could talk to Dean's computer-expert colleague.

While I kept brainstorming, I absentmindedly typed possible passwords into Beth's Facebook account. I used the email address I had from April as the logon name, but not surprisingly, none of my password guesses worked. I took paper from Andy's desk and jotted a reminder to myself: *Ask April about passwords and accounts.* She denied having direct access to Beth's email or social networking pages, but I wanted to double check anyway.

I checked my email again and saw something from Joe Shaw. He'd finally sent the convenience store video. Apparently he was up late—or early—too. I felt bad about downloading it to Andy's computer, just in case it had a virus or took up too much space, but I had to see it again. Nothing stood out except the sinking feeling it gave me. Maybe it was because I'd spent the evening in fear, but everyone looked suspicious to me now, even Joe, who had also attached a two-minute clip of Beth working at the store. In it, he showed her how to use the cash register. She was looking down, clearly pregnant, and just as beautiful as I expected. Seeing her on video, right there, just inches from my face, was surreal. I wanted to reach back in time and stop the clock. Change everything.

I gave all the video to the police, Joe wrote, *and they're reviewing it.* I'd turn it in too, just in case Joe wasn't being upfront. I wiped away a tear and responded with thanks.

In that state of hopelessness, a wonderful thought occurred to me. I was spending the night at Kenna's and using Andy's computer. Beth had spent a lot of nights at April's, and maybe she'd used a computer there—and logged onto personal accounts. Could her passwords be stored at April's house?

I replied to April's email and sent Dean one too.

Hi April,

Thank you for your email. I'm glad you called that number and got help. I absolutely know you're not alone in how you feel.

And thanks for keeping me updated about Marcus. Every bit of information helps, even if it seems really minor. You're being a great friend to Beth.

I'll give your mom a call, and I want to talk to you, too. Call me anytime that's good for you.

All the best,
Nicki

Hi Dean,
Thanks for all your help lately regarding Beth. There have been some developments I should tell you about. Also, I remember you have a colleague in computer forensics. Any chance you could ask him a question on my behalf? I'm sorry to ask another favor. I'll give you a call tomorrow.
Thanks again,
Nicki

It took me a few minutes to review the email to Dean. Communicating with him still made me nervous, but less than it had in the past. Finally I pressed send, shut down the computer, and went to bed.

There was an alarm clock in Kenna's guest room, but she hadn't set it, I realized as warm sunlight penetrated my eyelids. According to my cell phone, it was 8:15.

Someone was showering, I could hear, so I pulled on yesterday's extra-wrinkled outfit, made the bed, and crept down the hall to the guest bathroom. I didn't want to be seen yet.

I did the best I could with what was there, including my reflection in the mirror. Washed my face. Ran fingers through my hair. Swished mouthwash longer than recommended. Used a tissue to de-smudge my eyeliner. I still preferred not to run into Andy like this.

I returned to the bedroom and hoped Kenna would check on me. When that didn't happen, I called her from my cell phone.

"Hey," she said. "Are you still in the guest room?"

"Yeah. And I look like crap."

"Andy left for work already." She read my mind. "Don't worry."

"Where are *you?*" I asked her.

"Getting dressed in my room. I'm hanging up. Come in."

Kenna had never been modest about getting dressed—or undressed—in front of others. She didn't parade around naked in locker rooms, thank heaven, but she didn't hide her body, either, the way I had since puberty. The exception was during breastfeeding, when I was so tired and desperate to meet Jack and Sophie's needs that sometimes I forgot to think before releasing a boob.

"That's cute," I said while she pulled on skintight navy shorts and a matching sports-bra-passing-as-a-shirt. She was so thin her stomach was concave. *How many new moms actually need to gain weight?* I thought. "Why are you working on your day off?" I asked instead. She rarely worked on Sundays.

"We're short-staffed, so I'm teaching step and boot camp." She smoothed her wet hair into a ponytail. "And I'm interviewing new teachers. I'll definitely call you though. I want to make sure you're doing okay."

"Me?" I said. "I'm fine. I'm worried about *you*."

"Stop. I could do these classes in my sleep." She put on ankle socks and did a final mirror check.

"No need to rub it in," I teased. We both knew I couldn't watch a class without feeling winded.

"Listen, I have to go, but stay as long as you want. Andy won't be home 'til tonight." She grabbed a CD off the dresser and led the way out.

As tempting as her offer was, the kids were at Mom's, and I had to make the most of it.

Light streamed through the windows of my house too, giving it less of a crime scene—and more of a homey—feel as I locked the door behind me and slipped off my shoes. Before showering, I took a quick tour, looking for evidence again, straightening up, and wiping down surfaces as I went. Fueled by disgust, I also mopped and vacuumed. An intruder had been in my home. I wanted every trace of him out.

Freshly showered and fortified with a bowl of whole grain cereal and chopped banana, I sat at my empty desk and took a deep breath. Without my computer, I wasn't sure where to start.

I recalled copying and printing critical Facebook pages when Kenna first told me about Beth. They were the only case-related information anyone could have found on my computer. But I had an entire paper file devoted to her. Where was it? I opened and closed desk drawers frantically until I remembered that I'd left it, along with my PI class materials, in the car. Kenna had called me over to her house before I ever came inside. Phew.

The more I thought about it, the more creeped out I was that someone had used my computer. In seconds, they could have copied every file, including family photos, tax records, and letters, onto a thumb drive. When I got the computer back, I'd protect it with a password. And a backup hard drive. And anything else I could find. I also needed to install new locks and an alarm system in the house.

My immediate priorities, however, were talking with April, Edith, and Dean. I looked at the phone reluctantly. I was nervous to call them. *I'm not capable*, I worried. My eyes floated up to my father's model airplane, gliding above my desk. I knew what he'd tell me. The same thing he said after I lost Jason. "Life is what you make it." He was right. I could choose to give up, or I could go on, and I believed he was there to help—even from afar.

As I reached for the phone, the image of an intruder doing exactly the same thing flashed through my mind. What if he'd called someone? I stopped myself from dialing and pressed redial instead. I should do this on every phone in the house, I thought. It was unlikely, but possible, that one of them had been used.

My office phone displayed the last number called and started dialing before I hung up. It was Kenna's number. Dang. She'd called Andy before we could see if anyone else had used it. I got up and walked to each phone, pressing redial and noting the number dialed. Everything was familiar. I checked caller ID to see if any strangers had called, too, just in case someone checked to see if I was home before breaking in. Nothing suspicious there.

It was a little early on a Sunday to call Dean, I decided, especially since someone like him had a good chance of enjoying Saturday nights. So I started with Mom, with whom I chatted while collecting trash around the house for Monday's pickup. While listening to an adorable story about Sophie getting a tour of the restaurant where they'd eaten dinner—simply because she was brave enough to ask—I noticed the recycling can in the garage smelled good. That was odd. Curiosity got the best of me, and I poked around to find a donut box dotted with powdered sugar and frosting, left over from my mom's visit. Inside it was a beer can. Normally I'd think it was Kenna's, but neither of us buy malt liquor. Mom confirmed—with a slightly offended chuckle—that it wasn't hers. I left a message on Kenna's cell to see if it could be Andy's.

That was all I could do. It was time to call Dean.

"Hey, Nicki." His voice was gravely. I hoped I hadn't woken him. "What's up?"

It took a few minutes to fill him in, answer his questions, stop imagining him in bed, and get to the point.

"I'm going to talk to April today," I said. "I bet she might have some of Beth's passwords. Even if she doesn't know them, maybe they're on her computer. Do you think your computer forensics investigator could tell?"

"I don't know. But I'll be happy to put you guys in touch. He's teaching an upcoming class anyway. His name is Darrell." He gave me Darrell's extension and suggested I call him Monday. "So, you doing okay?" Dean asked.

"I'm trying."

"You're obviously strong and independent, and that's great, but anyone would be scared right now. I'm scared *for* you. You should let the authorities handle this. That's what I'd do."

I appreciated his attempt to protect my dignity.

"I'd be lying if I said I wasn't freaked out," I admitted. "Especially because I'm a mom." I needed to change the subject. "If this is Marcus's rival gang, Los Reyes, intimidating me, how do you think they know where I live?"

There was silence on the line. "When Marcus was shot, your car was on the scene, right?"

"Yeah. For a while."

"Maybe someone paid forty bucks to look up your license plate."

"Can anyone do that?"

"The law's pretty strict about it, but certain people, including PIs, can do it at certain times. And your name would be on the police report—again, private information, but certain people have access to it.

It's hard to believe a gang could get hold of it, but stranger things have happened."

"Or maybe someone just followed me home. I was pretty distracted. I wouldn't have noticed."

"True," he said. "And wasn't there an accident that night?"

"You mean when Marcus hit some parked cars?"

"Yeah."

"There's probably an accident report from that, which would be easy to get if your car was involved. But yours wasn't, was it?"

"No. And I have no idea whose cars were hit. One was a black pickup truck. The other was a sedan." I should have paid more attention. I was too panicked.

"The fact is someone found you. Do you have a security system?"

"No. But it's on my to-do list. I'm supposed to meet with someone from the gang unit, too. So I better get going."

Twenty-One

It's strange how intimidating small tasks can be. My to-do list was short because I wasn't sure how to proceed, yet it felt daunting. What would I say to April and her mom? Should I have trusted Edith? How would the gang officer treat me? And what kind of security system did I need? Imagining Beth waiting for me to make progress was like pressing a launch button. Time to move.

To give Edith as much time as possible to watch the Rushes, I tried April's cell first. She had a laptop, she told me, and Beth used it regularly. Hesitation in her voice gave me a familiar feeling. She was holding back.

"Is this an okay time to talk?" I asked. "I'm not sure where you are."

"I'm home," she said. "It's fine. My mom's downstairs."

"Okay. I just want to make sure you're comfortable." I started with a softball question. "Do you know when Beth last visited her grandparents?"

"I don't know. Maybe the last time she ran away. I think it's been a while."

"So if anyone had seen her there recently, would it be a surprise?"

"It would be to me," she said. "Why? Did anyone?"

"I'm trying to figure that out." I wasn't ready to discuss Edith or the mailman yet. "Anyway, do you happen to know any of Beth's online passwords? I'm hoping you do."

"I already told you I didn't," she answered slowly.

"I know. But that was a while ago," I said, giving her an out, "and you didn't know me as well. Hopefully now you trust me more."

"Uh huh."

"So maybe you can share more with me."

"Yeah. I guess so. I might be able to remember some of her passwords."

"That's great. It might really help us."

"Okay. Do you need to come over and look at my computer or something?"

"Maybe. But if you give me the passwords, I can start checking her accounts from my house. Would you be okay with that?"

"Sure," she answered without elaborating.

Time and patience were slipping away.

"What's wrong, April?" I asked. "Please tell me so I can help."

"Remember I told you that I didn't *use* her accounts? I didn't really. But I read all her emails. I'm really sorry. I was just so curious and I wanted to help. I also sent some emails to her, especially right after she disappeared. If you find them I'll be embarrassed. And please don't tell my mom about them."

"I'll do my best to keep them private," I said. "Is there anything else you can tell me?"

"I don't think so."

"Did you send any emails from her address?"

"No," she said.

I wasn't sure I believed her, but I didn't want to upset her, so I left it alone. Instead I tried to put her at ease.

"If I were you, I'd have read her emails too. They could provide great clues. Did any of them stand out?"

"No. I was hoping I could figure out where she is. But I couldn't."

I asked if Beth had created any documents on April's computer. She hadn't, April said.

"April?" I asked. "If Marcus did take Beth, why do think he did it?"

"To get rid of the baby."

"Do you think that's what happened?"

"I don't want to think about it."

I empathized. Neither did I.

April's Mom was next. She answered their home number, and our conversation was brief, but friendly. I apologized for not having anything concrete to share. I hoped my call to Edith would change that.

"Hi, Nicki," Edith greeted me warmly when she answered.

"Hi, Edith. I wanted to check and see if you'd noticed anything with the Rushes."

"Well, not yet. I went to church this morning, and I'm baking cookies now. I'd like to bring them some, along with other neighbors, so it looks natural. What do you think?"

"I don't know. They might think it's strange, since you don't normally socialize with them."

"Yes, but old ladies can get away with a lot without looking suspicious," she said.

She had a point. I confirmed that she still had my numbers and reminded her what to ask the Rushes. Then I paced the room, wondering if they were home, regretting I hadn't checked before calling Edith, and willing her to call me back quickly.

I also considered alternatives. Maybe April could call and ask for Beth—with me listening in, just to see how the Rushes responded.

And if I didn't get anywhere today, what then? *I'll have to talk with Dr. Rush tomorrow at that 10:30 appointment,* I realized. *That won't be fun.*

While I waited, I used my cell to check Beth's email using her password. The only thing better, I imagined, would be complete access to her Facebook page, which I'd check next, and her text messages. I really needed my computer back. My phone made this process nauseatingly slow.

Beth's old emails, it turned out, were a gateway to her past social networking messages. Anytime someone had posted on her wall, it showed up in her email, along with responses to any messages she'd left online. I scrolled down, looking for standout names or subjects. Unfortunately, most of it was teen talk and inside jokes that didn't make sense to me, and if April hadn't noticed anything suspicious, I probably wouldn't either.

I focused most on emails around the time of her disappearance. The day before she disappeared, she'd exchanged messages with the adoption social worker, giving the clear impression she had no plans to back out.

Dear Beth,

I hope your OB visit went well. Please call and let us know. We also need to arrange a meeting for you and the adoptive parents. They're really looking forward to seeing you.

Talk to you soon,
Diane

Hi Diane,

The appointment was good. Everything's fine. I'll call you soon about the meeting. I can't wait until this is over! Who is allowed to be with me at the hospital?

Beth

I wondered if she'd ever made that call. Once, Kenna had mentioned that being in the delivery room was a possibility—a choice that was up to Beth. I couldn't imagine being in Beth's position. Marcus was out of the picture. Her parents weren't supportive. She'd fought with her best friend. I wouldn't be surprised if she'd turned to her grandfather, a relative and expert, for last-minute support.

April's emails after Beth disappeared were nothing to be ashamed of, although I appreciated her concern. She pleaded with Beth to understand that yes, she was gay, but she had a crush on a girl at school—not on Beth. Beth's friendship meant everything to her. She wanted and needed her friend back. It was heartbreaking to imagine April coming out for the first time only to be rejected. Her emails sounded sincere, but I reminded myself to be objective. Only Beth and April knew the truth about their relationship.

Reading email and arranging a same-day home security review passed the time before Edith finally returned my call.

"Hello, dear," she greeted me. "It's Edith."

"Hi Edith," I said. "How did it go?" I sounded relaxed but wanted to shriek, *What happened?! Tell me everything!*

"Well, I talked to Dr. Rush about his granddaughter, and he said she's not there currently," she said. I was dumbfounded. Edith had gotten somewhere. She'd spoken with Dr. Rush.

"You mean she's not home? Or she's not living there?" I talked as quickly as I wanted Edith to reply.

"She's not living there now, but she visited three weeks ago, which must have been when I saw her. He said after her visit, she went missing, which confirms what you told me. That was about it. He was rushing out the door so fast he barely remembered to take the cookies I brought."

My heart dropped. I'd been hoping for an answer. A miracle. This wasn't it. I felt like a popped balloon.

"I appreciate this so much, Edith," I said. "You've been an incredible help. You don't need to do anything else except stay in touch if you see any sign of Beth—or anything else notable. And keep this whole thing just between us." I gave her all my phone numbers. "I'll always be happy to hear from you."

I arrived at the police station at 10 a.m. sharp and asked for Sgt. Dwyer. His greeting was so friendly I could almost ignore his imposing height and stocky build. He led me to a bare interview room and asked me to review the whole story, start to finish. This time, I had Kenna's permission to explain what I knew about Marcus, which was a relief.

Dwyer's gaze was a disarming mix of intense and understanding. I kept reminding myself to stick to the basics, but I ended up feeling lucky to escape without confessing my life story. I was thrilled when he stopped asking questions and walked me out.

"Let's go over it one more time," he said, referring to anti-gang precautions I should take. "Tell me what you're gonna do, and what you're not gonna do."

I held up a hand to tick off four essentials. "I'm going to change my routines, relocate, avoid being alone, and stay accessible." I pulled out my cell phone and wiggled it for emphasis. Dwyer wanted me reachable—and able to call for help.

"Did you know that *any* cell phone with power should be able to dial 911—even old ones without service?"

"No. I didn't." I hoped that tidbit would never come in handy.

"Now you do. So take care of yourself and your family, okay?"

"I will."

"These gangs are into drugs, weapons, prostitution, and more. Let us handle it. Just look out for number one."

That didn't sound like advice a good PI would take.

Before pulling away from the station, I left Kenna a message about the beer can. Part of me wanted it to be hers or Andy's so I wouldn't have to report it. Another part was hopeful it would show which lowlife had been in my house.

So far, Dwyer had told me, none of the fingerprints in my house matched anyone on file. The DNA swabs would take a lot longer to process, but they kept hope alive.

Halfway home, Kenna returned my call. I pulled over to talk.

"What's this about a beer can?" she asked.

I described what I'd seen in the recycling.

"I don't drink that, and Andy doesn't either. That's weird. It has to be from the break-in."

"That's the only explanation," I said. "But a criminal who recycles? Come on. I hope it has fingerprints. Or maybe the recycling can will."

We hung up so she could teach and I could get home to meet the security company. If the salespeople preyed on fear, I was in trouble.

I got home with a few minutes to spare and called Dwyer to report the can. He advised me not to touch it, and said he'd send evidence techs out. He'd also update Suarez and Walters, the officers who'd responded to the shooting and break-in.

"Fingerprints aren't the only thing they can get from a can," Dwyer reminded me. "They can swab for DNA, too."

"Isn't it weird that I found it in the recycling?" I asked.

"Sure. But stranger things have happened. Criminals aren't known for their smarts."

I excused myself when the doorbell rang and explained it was a two-man security team. They walked around the house, inside and out, and noted just how poorly I was protected. Where were my motion sensor lights? Prickly shrubs? Upgraded locks? Industrial-strength window and door hardware? Opaque curtains? And of course they wanted to install a system that would alert the world if it was breached. It would also alert Visa that I'd officially gone mad by adding the equivalent of a car payment to my monthly bill.

I couldn't afford what this company was selling, and the more I listened, the more vulnerable I felt—even *before* their speech about fire, carbon monoxide, and medical emergency features. Had someone told them I was an overprotective widow being stalked by gangsters? Because they had a way of hitting every nerve.

When the doorbell rang again, it was the evidence techs, and the security guys looked surprised when I introduced them.

"What?" I teased. "Is this the first evaluation you've done at a crime scene?"

We laughed, but I could have cried. I wanted this process to make me feel better, not worse. Reassured, not frightened. I let everyone finish their work and sent them packing. I needed some time to think, I explained, before committing to a year of "alarming" monthly bills. I also wanted time to check out do-it-yourself systems at the local home improvement store.

After my Dad passed away, I was forced to get comfortable with home improvement. When something needed repair, either I had to do it, or I had to pay someone else. Often I procrastinated until a problem became dangerous, unlivable, or embarrassing.

I thought I'd seen alarm systems in the aisle with child-proofing supplies, so I headed there first and found two options. One had cameras, and the other didn't. There were also single-room motion sensors and accessories, including outdoor signs and window decals. I wished the alarm company had let me buy those. ("Sorry guys. I can't afford the system, but how much are those stickers?") Maybe I could find some online.

For ease of installation and affordability, I chose the non-camera system with a door alarm, window alarms, and a motion sensor for the basement. It also had a chime feature, so anytime the front door opened, I'd know. A great feature with a potential escapee like Sophie.

*   *   *

It took two hours to install the system and test every sensor. I might have sustained hearing loss during the process. Afterward, I called Mom to check on the kids, hoping I wasn't distracting her from their needs. We agreed to meet the next day for dinner at a mall restaurant. I'd make every effort not to be followed.

The longest they should stay with her, I thought, *is one more day. But what if they're still in danger? I have no way to "quit" this case or stop being a witness to Marcus's shooting. Unless someone stops me themselves.*

I ended the day by reviewing my file about Beth. I read every detail and added anything I could think of. Then I set the new alarm system and went to bed, hoping I wouldn't hear any unexpected noises, yet missing the familiar interruptions of precious kiddos.

Twenty-Two

It was a relief when the light of Monday morning arrived, although I couldn't cancel my 10:30 appointment with Dr. Rush, since his timeline differed vastly from April's. But I wasn't going to get an exam today. He was.

"My daughter Melanie couldn't make it due to a last-minute work conflict," I told Mrs. Rush when I arrived. "I'm so sorry. But could I ask Dr. Rush some of her most important questions?" I offered to pay out-of-pocket and was grateful when she said new-patient consultations were free.

"Your daughter can fill out paperwork when she comes in," Mrs. Rush said kindly. She was just as nice as the first time we'd met. "You can take a seat for now." She nodded toward the waiting area.

What a relief. I didn't want to fill out a clipboard full of lies. I also wanted to review my notes. I sat a few chairs away from a woman who appeared in her thirties and flat-stomached. We exchanged smiles and returned to our respective tasks. She watched a video about prenatal nutrition while I ran a finger along every line of my interview plans for Dr. Rush. Hopefully I looked like an organized, prepared patient.

I also inspected degrees and awards on the wall, including a plaque that listed him among the area's "most respected" doctors for the past ten years—with plenty of space for future honors. Also framed were two news articles about Asheleigh Manor. One named Dr. Rush's aunt as its founder in 1980. She and a young Dr. Rush were at the ribbon cutting. Her son, Dr. Rush's cousin, had fallen from a ladder and suffered a devastating brain injury, which inspired her to open the center. I wondered if he was still alive and living at the Manor.

The other article named Dr. Rush "volunteer of the year" for his work with patients there. Apparently he held certifications in internal medicine and obstetrics/gynecology. Impressive.

"Mrs. Jacobs?" the nurse called out, looking at each of us. The other woman got up. *Don't hesitate when she calls Mrs. Smith*, I reminded myself. *That's you today.*

When it was my turn to get settled in a room, I happily shunned the exam table in favor of an upholstered chair. Dr. Rush entered a few minutes later.

"Hello," he said brusquely, glancing at a thin chart and then at me. "Mrs. Smith?"

"Yes," I said. "Nice to meet you."

"You too." He pulled up a rolling stool. "How can I help you?"

"I'm here on my daughter Melanie's behalf," I explained. "She's eighteen and pregnant, and she wanted to be here, but she got stuck at work, so I'm here to get some information for her."

"Okay. And when is she due?" His pen was poised over the chart.

"November," I lied. "Is there a certain hospital where you recommend delivering?"

He named two where he had privileges. "I assume you're local?"

"Yes. We're new in town. I know there are risks to having a baby so young. Can you tell me about those?"

"Has she been getting good prenatal care?"

"Yes. Before we moved."

"Good. You probably know teens are at higher risk for complications like anemia and premature labor. High blood pressure can be a problem too."

"Uh huh." That was news to me. I wondered if Kenna was aware.

"Their babies are also more likely to weigh less, so that's another concern. Does your daughter smoke?"

"No," I said firmly, remembering the agency forms Beth had filled out. She'd indicated clean living except for drinking a beer before knowing she was pregnant.

"How about you or anyone else she spends time with? Any smokers?"

"No." I wondered if Beth's parents, April, or Dr. Rush himself smoked. I definitely hadn't smelled it on anyone.

"Good," he stated.

He asked about drug use, drinking, diabetes, and lab work. When he started to discuss prenatal vitamins, I turned the focus to him and tried to seem legit.

"Before we run out of time," I said, "I need to ask, when you aren't available, who covers for you?"

He explained that although he ran a solo practice, an excellent local physician took call for him. I wrote down her name: Janet Lawrence.

"Dr. Rush, my daughter is scared and embarrassed about being young, single, and pregnant. In fact she's still in high school. Have you worked with patients like that before?"

He stared at me for a moment. I held his gaze and waited.

"I have," he said with what sounded like confidence. "Fear is normal at her age, or at any age for that matter. I'm sure your daughter will do fine." He closed the chart unceremoniously. "Any other questions?"

Yes. But now wasn't the time.

Dr. Rush said all the right things, but his emotion was flat. I hoped intelligence made up for his lack of bedside manner.

Out of curiosity—and to buy more time in his office—I asked Mrs. Rush if I could borrow her phone book. I wanted to see how many OB-GYNs were listed in the area. To my surprise, there were almost forty.

I jotted down Dr. Lawrence's contact information, returned the phone book to the front desk, and made a follow-up appointment I hoped to cancel. Mrs. Rush was friendly the whole time, which continued to reassure me about how she'd care for Beth, but it made me feel bad about fooling her.

Back at the car, I took out my disposable cell phone and mulled an idea that was potentially horrible. I'd make a similar appointment with Dr. Lawrence. In conversation with her, I could casually mention Dr. Rush's granddaughter and see if I got a reaction. If I got desperate, I could call the other OB-GYNs with an innocuous question and see if Beth was a patient. I thought of what I'd ask my own doctors' offices without raising suspicion, such as "When was my last appointment?" or "Could you check some lab results for me?" But since Beth might have been in recently, I couldn't ask that. They might respond, "Umm...you were just here yesterday" or "We delivered your baby Tuesday. Are you okay?" Although I guess that would still be helpful.

Maybe I could say, "I'd like you to check my chart for some test results I just had sent." That might fly. The worst they could do was hang up on me. Or maybe that wasn't the worst. Could I get arrested for impersonating a patient? This couldn't be proper PI protocol.

First things first. I'd try to see Dr. Lawrence and pretend to be Melanie's mom again. That couldn't get me in trouble, could it?

I put a little pressure on Dr. Lawrence's receptionist to see if she could squeeze me in for a fifteen-minute "meet and greet," as she called it.

"My eighteen-year-old daughter is pregnant," I explained, "and I'm really anxious about finding the right care for her. If Dr. Lawrence has just a few minutes to talk, that would make a huge difference."

"Hold please."

I obeyed.

"She can see you at 2:30."

"That's wonderful! Thank you." I hung up and looked at the phone's time display. I had one hour to prepare.

Seeing two OB-GYNs in one day could be a lot worse, I consoled myself as I waited in Dr. Lawrence's exam room, reviewing my notes and listening for the chart to rustle outside the door. *You're just here to talk.*

I looked to God for help and saw a poster on the ceiling above the exam table, designed to relax nervous patients (not nosy investigators), but it helped anyway. It was a picture of a cat stuck in a tree with the caption, "How did I get myself into this position?" Funny. Maybe. Unless you were there for something like crabs or herpes.

There was a "knock, knock" at the door and Dr. Lawrence burst in.

"Hi, Ms. Smith, nice to meet you!" Dr. Lawrence said. Darn. It was so much easier to lie to unfriendly people. Even her appearance was likeable. Neat, gray bob, crisp lab coat, lively green eyes and a warm smile. She was someone you'd want to greet your newborn.

I reached out to shake her hand. "Thank you so much for seeing me on short notice."

"Oh, I didn't even know it was short notice. You can thank my staff for that. So what brings you in today? I see you're here about your daughter?"

"Yes. She's a teenager, and she's pretty intimidated by being pregnant, so I'm helping her pick a doctor. We're new in town, and while I was talking with Dr. Rush, he mentioned you take call for each other. My daughter might be more comfortable with a female physician."

"I understand. I'd love to meet her. So she's feeling overwhelmed by being pregnant, huh?"

"Very."

"That's obviously normal." She smiled. "How old is she? And how many weeks pregnant?"

"Eighteen. And about twenty-six weeks."

"Ahhh. Well, if she comes in, make sure she brings all her records from her past doctor. Then we can go from there. Do you have any specific questions for me?"

"Not really. I just really wanted to get a sense of your personality, which seems great. One of my friends mentioned Dr. Rush has a pregnant young granddaughter, and I figure if he trusts you, that makes me feel better."

Her eyes widened slightly, and I strained to interpret her expression. Surprise? Surprise that I'd mentioned this detail? I couldn't tell.

"Good. Well Dr. Rush and I have worked together a lot over the years."

"That's great." I wrinkled my nose. "You know, maybe I shouldn't have mentioned his granddaughter. It's kind of personal. I heard it from a mutual friend, and I assumed it was public knowledge. Maybe it isn't?"

"Oh, I don't think he'd mind," she said. "It's exciting news! So, he's going to be a great grandpa? We must be getting old. We've been doing this a long time."

"Experience is a good thing," I said, wishing I had more of it.

*   *   *

Dr. Lawrence didn't seem to know about Beth, so I wrapped up the appointment and called Kenna, who unexpectedly picked up her cell phone.

"Hey," I said. "Can you talk?"

"Yes. I'm on a break." She was crunching on something. That was a good sign. I hoped it was fattening. "Tell me everything."

I disappointed her with my dearth of information and decided not to share my view of Dr. Rush's personality yet. It was too depressing. But she was thrilled I had the guts to visit two doctors. That wasn't like me.

"What do you make of Dr. Lawrence not knowing about Beth?" I asked. "Do you think it means anything?"

"If Beth was there, you'd think, or you'd hope, Dr. Rush would pick the best to work with her. Do you think there's another doctor he trusts more?"

"I have no idea. I wish I knew. Maybe I could call and ask."

"Where are you going from there?" she asked.

"Home," I said. "I want to—"

"Oh, Nicki," Kenna interrupted. "I almost forgot to tell you. Andy and I are meeting with the adoption agency tonight."

"About what?" I asked, hopeful.

"They want to talk about moving on. Showing our profile to new birth mothers."

"How do you feel about that?"

"Confused. Not ready. I'll listen to what they have to say though."

"I hope you call me afterward. If you can, try to see what they know about Beth. I keep wondering if they're protecting her in any way."

"Me too. I can't imagine they'd do that though. But don't worry. I'll pull out all the stops. At least it's one thing I can do. And you know what? If anything, I'll put pressure on *them* to find her. They probably have more information about her than anyone else."

"That's true. I mean, she was getting counseling there, right?"

"Definitely. For months."

"Well, call me as soon as you can. What time is your meeting?"

"Seven."

"Hey Kenna," I said, "My other line is ringing." I looked at caller ID. Oh my. It was Dean. Kenna loved that.

"I gotta do an interview anyway," she said. "Go!"

I clicked over.

"Hi, Dean."

"Hey, Nicki. I talked to Darrell, and he's willing to take a look at that computer you mentioned. He's got some free time today."

"That's great. I was able to get the passwords from Beth's friend," I said. "But he could take a look anyway if I can get the computer from her."

"Sure. Just drop it off with Amber when you can. In fact..." He paused. "I'm looking at my schedule. I'll be here between four and six if you want to fill me in on things. Then I've got a VIPA meeting."

"Okay." Our class had learned a lot about VIPA—the Virginia Investigative Professionals Association—and I planned to join. It was a great resource with plenty of retired police and FBI members. Its dinner meetings were known for their intriguing speakers.

"You know," Dean said, "you're welcome to come along. I can introduce you to a lot of veteran investigators."

I wasn't sure what to say. It was a good idea that made me really nervous.

"Let me think about it," I said. Dinner together would be nerve-racking, and possibly a waste of precious time, but it also might help. First I had to meet Mom and the kids for dinner at five. "I'm pretty busy between four and six. But the VIPA meeting might work. Thanks for mentioning it."

To get to the restaurant on time, I had to fly home from West Virginia, convince April to let me pick up her laptop, and deliver it to the PI Academy.

"This is for Darrell," I told Amber. "Do you have a sticky note I could put on it?" She handed me one, and I jotted down a request to talk with him before he delved into the computer's contents. I added my phone number, visited the bathroom, and bravely asked if Dean was around.

"Sure," Amber said. "Hang on." She picked up a multi-line phone and pressed a couple buttons. "Dean? Nicki's here." She said he'd be right out.

I sat on a couch in the reception area, anxiously tapping one sandal against the other. I only had a few minutes to say hi, but it was important to keep him posted.

When he came down the hall and saw me, his smile was genuine, as if we'd developed a friendship. Oddly, instead of making me uncomfortable, it was relaxing.

"Hi there," he said. "Come on back."

He led the way to an office I'd never seen. He took a seat behind a mahogany desk covered with stacks of paperwork and folders.

"Welcome to my world," he said, spreading his arms and leaning back in his chair. "Sorry it's not more presentable."

"It's fine," I said, taking it all in. A matching bookcase was filled with reference books. He had a trio of framed photos on a windowsill, one with his arms slung around two men, one as a child with a beautiful woman, and the last with a group of Army buddies.

"That must be your father and brother," I said about the first. The men looked almost identical, although Dean's hair was the lightest and his build was the thickest.

"How can you tell?" he joked.

"And that's your mom?"

His eyes rested on the photo. "That's her."

"She's so pretty," I said. Dean looked about ten years old in the photo, his blond hair several shades paler than hers. "What was her name?" I asked.

"Jacqueline," he said with a French accent.

"Even her name is beautiful. Was she French?" I asked.

"Oui," he said proudly. If Dean spoke French, I wasn't sure I could handle it. That would just be too much. "She was fluent, so I picked up some of it." Oh. My. Gosh.

"That's amazing," I said, realizing the polite conversation had to end. I had to go. "Okay, so, I dropped off the computer for Darrell, but I didn't want to leave without checking in with you." I glanced at the time on my cell phone. "But my mom and kids are expecting me soon."

"Oh. Okay. Are you staying at your house?"

"I am. But not my kids. They're still staying with my mom. We're meeting at a local restaurant tonight so I can give them some supplies."

"Are you sure *you* shouldn't stay with your mom too?"

"It's tempting," I admitted. "But it's a drive. I can always stay with Kenna or in a hotel if I really need to." I told him what I had (and hadn't) learned in West Virginia, glossing over any questionable details. We agreed there was still a chance Beth was there.

"Why don't you come to the VIPA meeting tonight?" he asked. "There are a few FBI guys who might have some good advice. I'd be happy to pick you up."

My heart raced and my temperature rose, flushing my cheeks and, less appealingly, my armpits.

"Okay," I heard myself say. *What?*

"How about 6:30? The meeting runs from seven to nine."

"Sure." I sounded more comfortable than I felt. "Do you remember where I live?"

"I do."

Eeek.

I rushed home to gather the kids' necessities and meet them at a Mexican restaurant—keeping an eye out for stalkers on the way. I soaked in their hugs and love and listened to every word they said. I also thanked Mom for her amazing generosity.

"Aren't you exhausted?" I asked her. "Be honest. I know this isn't easy."

"Not yet," she said. "So keep doing your thing. But don't tell me anything I don't need to know. Just promise you'll be okay."

"I'm fine," I exaggerated. "And tonight, Dean—that teacher from the PI Academy—is taking me to a dinner for investigators. So I'll be in good hands and hopefully make some connections."

"Is that like a date?" she teased.

"No." I grinned. "It's like a meeting."

"Hmm." She wasn't convinced. "Well, there's no need for you to eat here then, unless you're hungry." I was. But I didn't want bean breath. "Give the kids some more love and then go before I don't let you out of my sight."

* * *

I knew how to dress for the meeting: business casual. Problem was I only had casual casual. I frowned at the dress Mom had given me. It wasn't business-y. It was soccer mom-ish. And I'd just worn it. I pulled out the black outfit I'd worn at my first meeting with Dean, which I'd actually washed and hung carefully. I added the infamous fake-pearl earrings (which had been cleansed of mulch residue) and a soft, violet cardigan in case I was cold in the air-conditioned restaurant. I freshened my breath, brushed and sprayed my hair into place, and applied makeup more carefully and liberally than usual—all the while hoping the restaurant was dimly lit.

Dean rang the doorbell promptly at 6:30. He'd changed out of his work khakis, I noticed immediately, and into black pants, a charcoal dress shirt, and a black belt with a tasteful, silver buckle. More of him was covered than usual, yet everything highlighted his physique. The dark colors also set off his blond hair and bright eyes. If we were on a date, I would have said, "You look great!" (and thought *Holy shit!*), but we weren't, so I kept quiet.

"Thanks so much for the ride," I said. "I really appreciate it." I grabbed my purse from the foyer, knowing that if he stepped too far inside, he'd see the pile of junk I'd dumped out of it at the last minute. I'd also added a ballpoint pen—no writing in crayon or marker tonight—and paper for taking notes. If this didn't impress him, what would?

"It's good to see you," he said. "You look nice."

I felt myself blush as I thanked him, locked the door behind me, and tested the knob. The last time a guy complimented my appearance—other than Andy, who didn't count—was...well, a distant memory.

I tucked a lock of hair behind my ear and peered at my driveway, where a shiny blue roadster—definitely not Dean's motorcycle—was parked next to my van. "Is that your car?" I asked dumbly. I'd seen it in the academy lot but never knew it was his. "What kind is it?"

"An Aston Martin." I didn't know what that was, but I knew it was ultra expensive. "It's my Dad's car," he explained, "but he's overseas. So he's letting me enjoy it."

"It's gorgeous." Its lines were so sleek I wanted to run my finger along them. Suddenly men's obsession with cars made sense.

Dean opened the passenger door for me, a chivalrous gesture I appreciated but never liked—right along with pulling out chairs and helping me out of coats. It made me want to explain the obvious: Thanks, but I'm capable of getting in and out of things like cars, chairs, doors, and coats pretty well. I've had some practice, and I've actually mastered it. "Helping" just complicates things.

I slid into the passenger seat, and as Dean stepped around to the driver's side and opened the door, I formulated my next question.

"What's your dad doing overseas?"

"He's an actor," he said, resting a hand on my headrest while glancing behind us to back up. My stomach tingled. "He's doing a play in London."

"Wow. That's neat." I recalled the picture I'd seen on Dean's desk. Other than resembling Dean, his dad didn't look familiar.

"Has he been in anything I would have seen?"

"He's had small roles in big things," he said. "But you probably wouldn't remember them. He's great though."

"That must be so much fun. Have you seen his play in London?"

"Not yet. Hopefully I'll go in the next couple months."

I wanted to ask more questions. How long had his Dad been acting? Where did his Dad live full time? How did Dean end up in D.C.? With bigger mysteries at stake, though, I minimized the small talk.

"So who's the speaker at tonight's meeting?" I asked.

"A former hostage negotiator. It should be really interesting."

"Sounds great." I smoothed my pants and fiddled with a sweater button. "I should join VIPA while we're there," I said. "Although it's hard to imagine making it to meetings. The kids keep me so busy." I looked at his strong, angular profile. "It's even harder to imagine getting beyond this situation with Beth," I said honestly. "You know?"

Our eyes met for a second before he refocused on the road.

"Let's see what we can do about that tonight."

Twenty-Three

As far as I could tell, no one followed us to the restaurant, and although I should have focused on protecting myself while exiting the car, I was more worried about somehow damaging it. I'd forgotten what it was like to preserve a vehicle's appearance.

Inside the restaurant, Dean led me to a room reserved for VIPA where we signed in, paid a dinner fee (Dean insisted on covering mine), and donned nametags. I picked up a membership application and stuck it in my purse.

I couldn't imagine anywhere I'd feel safer than in a room brimming with law-enforcement types, many of whom I guessed were packing. Most were retirement-age men, but a few women dotted the room, which was crammed with tables for six.

"I'll let you pick where to sit," I said to Dean, in case he had favorite tablemates.

He chose a table near the podium with two unoccupied, front-and-center seats. They reminded me of empty front pews at Aunt Liz's church.

"How's this?"

"Good." We were surrounded by a group of gregarious men laughing.

"Hi," one of them welcomed us. "Sit down."

If Dean was going to pull out my chair, I didn't give him a chance. I sat and slid my purse under it, resting the cell-phone pocket against my foot, where hopefully I'd feel vibrations if it rang silently. Then I politely put a cloth napkin in my lap.

Almost immediately, a waiter appeared to take our orders.

"Chicken, salmon or vegetarian?" he asked.

"Vegetarian, please," I said, curious what that would mean. Too often it was a pile of vegetables.

Dean ordered chicken and asked if I ate meat or fish.

"No." I hoped that wouldn't scare him off.

"Is it okay to eat meat in front of you? I don't want to upset you."

"Of course. It's not like that," I laughed.

"What's it like?" He seemed genuinely curious.

"Well, I don't eat meat, fish, or shellfish. I eat dairy sometimes, especially if it's organic. But I don't push my diet on anyone except my kids. They're veggies too."

We busied ourselves with pouring drinks, passing rolls, and dressing pre-dinner salads, which were already at each place. When I saw our meals on the way, I introduced myself to the man on my right, giving Dean a chance to eat in peace.

"I'm Julius Wagner," the man said. "With Julius Security."

I made small talk and listened to other guests discuss local security and terrorism issues.

"Nicki's working on an interesting case," Dean interjected. He'd already finished his meal, and I'd barely started the ravioli I'd been served. "George," he nodded to a silver-haired, black man across the table. "You might be interested." George raised his eyebrows, and all eyes were on me. "Want to tell them about it, Nicki?" Dean asked.

"What's the situation?" George said in a gentle voice.

I cleared my throat and considered how to summarize the case without monopolizing the conversation.

"There's a pregnant eighteen-year-old who's missing," I started.

"Did an email go out about her?" George asked. "King County?"

"Yes."

"Is she a runaway?"

"That's the big question," I said. "Almost everyone, including her parents, thinks so. But there are a few holdouts. My closest friend is one of them, so I'm trying to help. Dean has been really supportive." I gave him an appreciative look. "There have been sightings that suggest she might be with her grandparents in West Virginia. But I haven't been able to confirm them yet."

"When's the baby due?"

I took a deep breath. "In a week."

"Are you keeping an eye on the social networking sites?" George asked.

"Definitely."

"Nothing helpful there?"

"Not that I've found lately. But I haven't had time to research many of her friends."

He reached into his pocket, pulled out a business card, and passed it around the table to me. "I'd be happy to talk with you about this," he said. "Will you call me after tonight's meeting? Maybe I can help."

"Of course. Thank you so much." I looked at the card. *George Gray. President, NOVA Investigations. Specializing in missing persons.* Then I looked at Dean, who was beaming.

A rush of prickly heat swept over my body. I had a feeling George didn't just want to help. He *would* help. I tucked the card into my wallet for safekeeping.

While listening to the former hostage negotiator speak, I was hyperaware of Dean facing the podium, his hair brushing the neckline of his shirt, his sculpted arm resting on the table. Good thing I was sitting behind him. If things were the other way around, I'd be hyperaware of the back of *my* head, which I hadn't checked in the mirror before leaving home.

When it was time for Q&A, I raised my hand. Most people had asked about police negotiation, but I wanted to know something else.

"What if you *are* a hostage?" I asked. "How can you keep yourself safe?"

"Try to connect personally with the hostage taker," he suggested. "You might talk calmly about your family, for example. Humanize yourself."

Logical advice, but even if I could share it with Beth, would it matter? The chances seemed high she was with someone she already knew.

After saying goodnight to everyone, Dean and I walked to his car.

"It'll be worth it to call George tonight," he said while opening my door. "I don't know him well, but I know he's passionate about his work."

"Does he work missing children cases?" I asked.

"He did with the FBI." He walked around to his side and slid in. "It's lucky he was here."

"I know. Everyone was so nice. Thanks for bringing me."

"My pleasure."

The Aston Martin purred to life. Each time Dean accelerated, I wished we were on open road, not in overcrowded suburbia. The car was like a restrained jungle cat. Other drivers craned for a look as we passed them.

"I can't believe you drive this all the time. Aren't you afraid it'll get damaged?"

"Sure. But my Dad says—and I agree with him—it's made to be enjoyed. Plus, it's insured."

"Weren't you driving something else when you dropped off that book at my house?" I asked. "It wasn't your motorcycle, was it?"

"It was a gray SUV," he said. "Good for surveillance."

He could have picked me up in that, I realized, and he hadn't. It probably meant nothing, but a girl could dream.

"Let me walk you inside," he offered as we pulled into my driveway. *Ugh.* I hadn't had time to clean. There was no way I'd let him in.

"You don't have to do that," I said, wishing he could search the house for bad guys. I put my hand on the door handle and locked eyes with him. "Thanks again. I'm going to call George first thing."

Instead of staying in the car, he stepped out and waited for me on his side, where my stomach did flips.

"Come on. I have to make sure you get inside okay," he said.

As we walked up the brick path to the porch, I felt a light touch on my elbow. He was guiding me toward the door. Goosebumps rose up my back.

"So why don't you email me after you talk with George?" he suggested after his arm dropped away. "I'm curious what he has to say."

"Sure. I'd love to." I fumbled to get the key in the lock. "And don't worry about me. I'm sure Kenna will come over in a little bit. She had a meeting tonight too." I opened the door a few inches and flicked on the porch light. Dean brushed his hand through his hair and shifted his weight. Either he was a little uneasy or he had to pee.

"Take care of yourself, Nicki," he said. "Don't be too brave."

"Okay, but if the alternative is giving up," I said, "I'm not doing that." My eyes scanned the street. I didn't like being out in the open, and if anyone even slightly suspicious drove by, I might overreact and yank Dean inside.

"Don't get me wrong," he said. "Finding Beth is important. But it's not worth your life. Or someone else's."

I wasn't sure if he meant Jack or Sophie, but that's who came to mind, and my stomach sank. I leaned on the doorjamb. "I think I know what you mean." But I was too scared to ask.

After thanking him for dinner, I closed the door, reset the alarm, and listened to the Aston Martin back out with a growl. I was alone. The house was silent.

Instead of walking further inside, I turned the deadbolt, sat in front of the door, and called Kenna.

"Hey," I said when she answered. "Where are you?"

"Picking up Chinese food. I'll be home soon. Where are you?"

"Home. Hoping you'll come over. I just got here."

"Where were you?" she asked.

I decided to give her a thrill. "Out to dinner with Dean."

"What? Oh my God. Hold on." I heard her pay for the food. "I'd ask you if you want anything," she said, "but you just went out with Dean!" There was rustling as she walked.

"It's not what you think," I said. "But I knew it would make you smile."

"But you *did* have dinner with Dean?" she confirmed.

"I did."

"Tell me everything."

I made her wait until she got home.

"Don't you want to eat with Andy?" I asked when she banged on my door.

"I eat with Andy every night," she said. "This is more important." I knew she was joking, but at times, our friendship annoyed him, just like it had Jason. Waiting for women to stop blabbing about apparently meaningless (but truly life changing!) stuff isn't fun—especially when it prevents another activity, such as watching a movie, sleeping or—less frequently—having sex. Sometimes it was just impossible to hang up. There was always one more essential thing to say.

Kenna ate her beef-broccoli lo mein while I talked. Then I asked about the First Steps meeting.

"The agency thinks she ran away, and they're clearly worried about her. But their job is to protect us from situations that don't look good, and this is one of them. So they want to show our profile to other birth mothers. Andy wants to do it, but you know how I feel."

"That must have been a hard conversation. Is Andy frustrated with you?"

"Not about that. But I did something that really pissed him off. I don't know how you're going to feel about it, either."

"Uh oh. Tell me."

"First you have to listen to a couple things."

"I'm all ears."

"Number one, the social worker, Diane, said it's not unheard of, or even uncommon, for a birth mother to quote 'disappear off the radar.'"

"What does that mean?"

"Like some birth mothers become homeless or get arrested and put in jail. The agency makes reasonable efforts to find them and make sure they're safe, but people have the right to disappear."

"Okay."

"Number two, Diane had concerns about Beth before she disappeared. She still seemed to care a lot about Marcus, and there were some questions about her past."

"What do you mean 'her past'?"

"The agency asked for a copy of Beth's birth certificate, but her parents wouldn't hand it over because they didn't support the adoption."

"Uh huh."

"So the agency helped her get one on her own. But when it arrived, Beth was confused by it."

"Why?"

"Something about it didn't match what Beth knew about herself. Diane didn't think much of it until the police started asking questions."

"What questions? And what didn't match?"

"I don't know. She didn't want to go into detail. I can tell she's just throwing out anything that will steer us in another direction. I mean, we don't even have Marcus's cooperation yet. From First Steps' standpoint, the whole thing is kind of a mess."

"What about from yours?"

"I'm not giving up. You know that. I could never forget about this." She avoided eye contact and pulled something from her purse. "So I got this."

"Kenna. What's that?"

"Beth's birth certificate."

"Is this the part I'm not going to like?"

"Maybe. Or maybe you'll love it." She smiled hopefully. "At one point, Diane left the room to get Andy some coffee, and I checked her file cabinet under Myers, and I made a copy."

"You didn't." No wonder Andy was pissed. In addition to being ethically reckless, what if she'd been caught? That would end their relationship with First Steps—and potentially a lot more. "What the heck did Andy do?"

"He couldn't decide whether to tackle me or look innocent. Actually, he tried both." She held out the paper. "Take it." I froze. "Nicki. Come on. Andy will forgive me, and I think it was worth it. Decide after you read it."

I gingerly unfolded the sheet. *"West Virginia Delayed Birth Certificate,"* I read aloud. "What does that mean?"

"Check the date on the bottom. The certificate was issued when Beth was fifteen. She wasn't born at a hospital, so it looks like her parents had to prove it really happened."

"Where was she born?" I saw the answer before Kenna provided it. Dr. Rush's address was listed as the place of birth. I read aloud to Kenna and told her what I knew.

There was a small section labeled *Abstract of Supporting Evidence*. It listed her parents' marriage application, a copy of her newborn checkup, and a statement from the physician who attended her birth: Dr. Rush. Yuck.

"It must have been an emergency," Kenna said. "But here's the thing. Beth told me her mother had a short labor at the hospital, and that Beth's father missed the delivery because he was stuck in traffic. I specifically remember her saying that because she wanted her delivery to go that quickly, too."

"That explains why she's confused. Plus, why wait to get a birth certificate? That makes no sense. You need one for registering for school, getting a social security card—everything."

"Do you think maybe her parents were hiding something from her?" Kenna asked.

"I guess. But what?" Feeling clueless reminded me to call George while it was still early. I encouraged Kenna to stay. "Don't mention how we got our information," I said. "We don't want to scare him off."

Kenna pushed aside her food, and I picked up the phone.

"Nicki," George greeted me after I reintroduced myself. "Tell me more about this missing young lady."

"If you don't mind," I said, "I'm going to put you on speakerphone. My friend Kenna is with me, and she's much closer than I am to the case," I explained. "Is that okay?"

"Sure, sure," he said graciously. "Go right ahead."

I pulled a marker and paper out of a nearby drawer and prepared to take notes. Kenna said hello and expressed her gratitude.

"Before we start," I said, "Why don't you tell us about your background? Dean says it's really impressive."

"I came up through the ranks in the FBI," he explained, "and ended up with a unit that handles crimes against children." Ended up? I was sure he'd worked hard to get there. "I worked a lot of missing children cases. Now I volunteer to help with cold cases. It's incredibly fulfilling and intense. I also own an agency, as you know, Nicki. I guess retirement just isn't for me." He laughed softly.

"Lucky for the rest of us," I said. "I feel like it's a miracle we met you."

I looked at Kenna. She was wide-eyed, slack-jawed and nodding.

"So tell me again what you're working with. Hopefully I can lend a hand," George said.

"Well I'm completely new at this," I said, quickly reviewing my lack of expertise. Then I expanded on what I'd said at dinner, including the fact I was probably being pursued by a gang. It was awkward discussing the details of Kenna's life in front of her, but it was also a relief, since she could chime in anytime. Instead, my talkative friend surprised me with silence.

"I'd like to make you an offer," George said. This gave me pause. I hoped I hadn't misunderstood this whole thing. I looked at Kenna, who couldn't afford to pay for more than an hour of George's time, which, given his background, had to be expensive.

At the same time, with his skills, I wanted to hand over my life savings if it would bring Beth home and give Kenna the baby she longed for. I focused on a mental picture of my kids so I wouldn't go overboard.

"Sure," I said to George. "Go ahead."

"My heart and soul are in this business," George said. I already felt tears coming to my eyes. His voice was so warm that something good had to be coming. "Dean told me that hiring an investigator isn't something you can consider right now. At least not for the amount of work this kind of case requires. And Nicki, you've got a lot on your plate, not to mention two children, I hear."

"Yes," I confirmed, dumbstruck.

"I can't promise you anything," he warned.

"We understand," Kenna interjected.

"It sounds like you especially need someone in West Virginia, plus some research here. I'm able to provide that at a very, very low cost. I mean minimal, just so we can make things official. It's not something to concern yourselves with. Believe me, nothing would make an old guy like me happier than bringing home a child. I'm sure the local investigators feel the same way, but they're limited by time and resource restraints. I guarantee you, their hearts are in it."

Kenna and I stared at each other, and then the phone, in disbelief.

"I don't know what to say," Kenna told George. "My husband and I thank you from the bottom of our hearts."

"We'll never be able to thank you enough," I added.

"Hold your applause," he said. "I don't have results yet. We'll hope for the best. Meanwhile, I've got some questions for you."

Kenna and I spent an hour on the phone being interviewed by George. As a budding investigator, I couldn't help savoring his style, which was incredibly detailed. Afterward, I faxed him everything we could think of that might help, including Marcus's address, the adoption paperwork, and Beth's birth certificate. I also emailed April for permission to pass along her contact information. I'd call her mom the next morning.

"We should have made that call from my house," Kenna said. "It feels creepy here. Someone could be outside spying on us. I'm scared to walk home."

She was right. On the phone with George, I felt okay, but once we weren't distracted, I got chills. It was as if the temperature had suddenly dropped in the house. I didn't want to spend the night at Kenna's again, but resting here might be impossible.

"You should stay with us," Kenna offered.

"I'm worried about Andy," I said. "He's going to hate me."

"Think about the good news we're bringing him," she said, although I wasn't sure he'd see it that way. "He won't mind."

"Maybe I should go to a hotel," I said.

"That's ridiculous. Get your butt in pajamas and come over. If you're going to spend money on anything, it's not that."

I went upstairs obediently, put on sweatpants and a T-shirt, grabbed a hair clip for morning bed head, and brushed my teeth. Then I collected a handful of toiletries.

"Ready," I told her when I returned downstairs and dropped everything in a plastic bag. "Wait." I picked up my cell phone from the counter. "Before we leave, I have to email Dean and tell him about George. And there's one more thing."

"What's that?" she asked.

"We should thank God. I think George was heaven sent."

"That's so true," she agreed.

I'd never prayed with Kenna, quietly or aloud, but we'd asked for help, and God's answer was better than anything we could have imagined. I took a deep breath.

"Thank you, God, for George," I said simply.

"And for Dean," Kenna added, raising an eyebrow. "I mean it!"

Twenty-Four

After waking up at Kenna's feeling refreshed, I called Mom first thing. I was dying to say good morning to the kids, find out how (and where) everyone slept, and tell them I loved them. Now that George's team could cover West Virginia, I felt obligated to help with a dreaded family commitment—attending a Pizza Arcade birthday party for Sophie's friend Megan.

I swung my legs over the side of the bed and made the next call to April's house. She and her mom agreed to talk with George, so I touched base with him, too. Everything was a go.

I set my phone on the end table, stood up, and made the bed. The door was closed, so I listened for signs of life outside. None. I opened it a little, and seeing no one, hustled to the guest bathroom with my toiletry bag. When I came out and listened again, Kenna and Andy were talking in the kitchen. I couldn't help hearing their conversation as I moved down the hall, still in my overnight sweats and T-shirt.

"This guy George better be careful he doesn't screw things up," Andy was saying. "You can't imagine life without Beth, but *I* can't take starting this whole process again. You almost ruined everything last night, and now this?" He made a dismissive noise.

I wasn't sure whether to announce my presence or do a one-eighty and tiptoe away.

"Hi guys," I called out. "Sorry to interrupt."

Kenna's back was straight and tense, and her arms were folded across her chest. She was wearing her usual exercise clothes—black lycra shorts and a body-hugging shirt. Andy wore dress pants and a pink button down, and he was holding a bowl of something. They both turned to me in surprise.

"Morning, Nicki," Andy mumbled.

"Hi, Nicki," Kenna said. "I'm sure you heard what we were discussing."

"A little," I admitted. "Is there anything I can do to help?" Stupid question. In Andy's eyes, I'd done enough. Or too much.

"Maybe you could reassure Andy that George is incredible," Kenna said.

"You just met him last night," Andy said, rolling his eyes. "No offense. How do you even know he is who he says he is?"

"Dean, my PI instructor, knows him," I explained self-consciously. "I'm sure George is for real."

Andy considered this for a moment. He looked at Kenna. "Did you explain that we want him to be extra discreet so First Steps doesn't think we're nuts?"

Kenna was quiet. "No. I didn't think of that."

"We can call him right now," I jumped in. "I just talked with him."

I turned back down the hall to retrieve my cell phone. When I returned, Kenna was pouring orange juice, and Andy was eating. No words or eye contact.

"Want some OJ?" Kenna asked me with a forced smile.

I accepted and handed her my cell phone. "There's George's contact info. I'll let you guys copy it down and give him a ring. I'm going home to freshen up. Okay if I go out the back?"

"Of course," Kenna said. I took a few sips while she noted George's number and unlocked the patio door. "I'll watch you walk." She handed over my phone.

"More like run," I said. "You guys, thanks so much for letting me stay again." I looked back and forth between them.

"Anytime, Nicki. Thanks for everything," Andy said. I didn't detect sarcasm, but I couldn't be sure. "Hey, speaking of running, how's the treadmill?"

Ugh. He had to know the answer. "Lonely," I confessed. "But that's going to change."

"Good," said Kenna. "Call me. I'll be home for an hour."

"Will do. Bye guys."

I hoped she wouldn't be crying when we talked again.

*   *   *

Since I was technically running from a gang, jogging on the treadmill seemed like a good, totally unappealing idea. Maybe pounding on the equipment would take the fear out of being home alone. With that kind of racket, I wouldn't notice every strange noise the house made.

I attached the magnetized end of the safety strap to the treadmill and the clip to my sweatpants. With my cell phone in the drink holder, I started walking and progressed to running five minutes later. After two minutes of that, about to collapse, I walked again. I continued the two-on, two-off pattern for thirty minutes and went two miles total. Weak. At least it was a start.

It was time to think birthday party. Since I'd be seeing lots of other parents, I put extra effort into visualizing an outfit while showering. I finally settled on jeans and a black T-shirt, just in case pizza, soda, or worse headed for me. Mini gold hoop earrings would dress things up and make me feel presentable.

On the way out I had a last-minute thought. I'd bring a baby monitor with me and turn one on inside. Then, when I came home, I could listen for suspicious noises before coming in. I dashed upstairs, turned on the hall monitor, and grabbed the base from my office.

As soon as I got in the van, my dark outfit absorbed the sun's heat. I blasted the AC and hoped it would work quickly.

Seeing no one around, I pulled out as fast as I dared, always on the lookout not just for gang members, but also neighborhood kids. At the same time, I kept an eye on the rearview mirror. The minute I let my guard down, I feared, someone would strike, and unlike last time, maybe they'd succeed. A terrible thought occurred to me. What if someone tried to shoot me, but hit an innocent bystander instead? This was all too much. And there was no way out. Maybe the kids and I should go stay with Aunt Liz for a while.

The AC was pumping, but my wandering mind made me sweat. I actually *wanted* to be in the safety of a germ-infested, infantile crowd. I shook my head at the irony of parents telling kids to ditch their intuition and cozy up to giant mascots. "*Come on.* He's just an overgrown animal. He's nice!" Same with Santa. "Stop crying! Sit on the fat guy's lap, tug his weird facial hair and tell him your hopes and dreams. Sure, you've never met him and he's dressed like a maniac, but he's going to give you presents and candy, so it's okay!"

The parking lot was jammed for a Tuesday morning, I thought, but maybe it was birthday party prime time. I searched for Mom's car and anyone remotely suspicious—especially a young male without kids. Unfortunately, the "restaurant" was next to a convenience store, which attracted all types.

I spotted Mom's car but had to park in the next row, further away than I liked. I couldn't wait to get inside and hug the kids. I stuck some extra wipes in my purse, locked the car, and dashed to the entrance, where my hand was stamped with the appropriate symbol to match Megan's party. Her parents had been kind enough to invite Jack too. My stamp wouldn't match Jack and Sophie's by number, I realized, but Mom's would.

I pushed through the turnstile into a madhouse of screaming kids, blaring games, and lines of people waiting for tokens and food. The place was rockin'. I spent a few minutes observing, but Jack, Sophie and Mom weren't anywhere in sight.

Sauntering through the main entrance behind me were two teenage boys with sideways caps and sleeveless shirts. I didn't like their looks, but maybe they were just here to hang out, as humiliating as that should be for self-respecting high schoolers.

I looked around and saw plenty of other teens, boys and girls, tossing basketballs into hoops, rolling skeet balls into holes, and carrying strings of prize tickets. Maybe I was overreacting. Plus, they could have younger siblings here.

What I didn't see were people I knew. After watching the guys behind me check in and head for the hoops, I moved to the back room where party tables were set up. I found Megan with some buddies, wished her a happy birthday, and hoped Mom remembered to bring our present.

"Have you seen Jack and Sophie?" I asked. "I think they're here somewhere."

"I don't know where they went." Megan was adorable in pigtails, a red plaid shirt and white shorts. A little country girl.

"Do you think they're playing games?"

"Uh huh."

"Okay. Thanks, sweetie. Have fun!"

I wandered through the games with no luck, finally deciding to check the bathroom, where I found them washing hands.

"Hi, honey," Mom said when she saw me.

"Mom?" Sophie said. "Why are you here?" She stomped a foot.

"Sophie!" Jack scolded, giving me a hug.

"Sorry," Sophie grumbled. "But Grandma's taking care of us. And she does a good job."

I knew why she was upset. With Grandma, the kids got more freedom. I appreciated, but didn't rely on, the hand-stamp security system, and chose to follow the kids around instead. That meant they had to stick together, which they despised.

Jack wanted to play racing games, and Sophie always wanted to ride the three-seat merry-go-round. I wished I could enjoy letting my kids roam, but I wasn't ready. Not yet. It was one of the countless times I missed having a partner.

"Grandma does a great job," I agreed. "And since she's with us, you guys can separate. We'll each take one of you."

"I get Grandma!" Sophie yelled, her voice echoing painfully off the bathroom walls.

"No fair," Jack said. Then he looked at me. "Sorry, Mom."

"It's okay." I glanced at Mom, who was trying not to grin. She couldn't help basking in her popularity.

"Come on, Sophie," she encouraged. "Let's go play. Then we'll wash hands again before pizza." She took a cup of tokens from the counter and met eyes with Jack. "Have fun, honey. After lunch, we'll switch, and you can come with me."

"Okay. Come on, Mom." Jack picked up his tokens and led the way to a pair of life-size jet skis in front of a video beach scene. "Wanna race?" he asked.

"Let's do it."

Every time I saw Sophie, she was with a friend, and Grandma was chasing after her. I kept an eye on Jack and everyone else, still wary of the teens who had walked in behind me. They kept looking at me, I thought, but maybe because I kept looking at them.

After pizza, cake, soda, and mascot singing, it was back to the games, this time with Sophie.

"I wanna climb," she said, pointing at a network of slides and ceiling-high netting. This was my least favorite area because I couldn't follow my kids or tell where they'd end up. It was probably their favorite for the same reason.

"Go ahead," I told Sophie, who was already shoving her shoes into a cubby. "If you come out and can't find me, meet me at this shoe rack." I pointed to it. "Remember, it's blue."

"Okay. Blue." She scampered up a slide the wrong way, immediately breaking the rules and putting herself at risk.

"Sophie," I warned, knowing she wouldn't turn back. "Don't go that way again."

"Okay!" I heard from somewhere above me. I watched her crawl through a cylinder made of thick, black rope. Then she entered a yellow plastic tube that forked at the end. From there I lost track.

I looked around at other parents nearby. They all seemed relaxed. Okay, that's an exaggeration. They looked frazzled and exasperated—like normal parents—but comfortable with the climbing area. Meanwhile, their kids were just as ornery, if not more, than Sophie. *Everything with Beth is making you tense*, I told myself. *Take a few breaths. Chill.*

Before I could exhale peacefully, a teen who'd followed me in climbed into the suspended tube structure, which was not meant to support, accommodate, or entertain someone his size, not to mention anyone with shoes.

That's not right, I thought as he scrambled up two netted levels with ease. No one else seemed to notice. I caught one mom's eye who was tying her kid's shoes. "Some older boy just went up there," I said with a sigh. "And he's wearing shoes."

She rolled her eyes. "Kids," she said. "Good luck. I'm outta here."

"On your way out, would you mind telling someone who works here?" I asked. "I just feel bad for the little ones up there. I don't want anyone to get hurt." Truth was I didn't trust him, which is what I should have said, especially since she wasn't appalled by his behavior.

"Umm, sure," she said. "Come on, Taylor." She walked off with her toddler.

"Excuse me!" I called to the teenager, who was crawling close to Sophie's likely vicinity. "You're too old to be up there. You need to come down *right now*." I used my firm Mommy voice, which tended to work with everyone's kids but my own. He ignored me and disappeared into a tube.

"Hey!" said a faint voice that sounded like Sophie if she were in a plastic bubble, which she probably was.

"Sophie?" I called.

"No!" she said.

"Sophie?" I said again more loudly. No one looked concerned. I squinted at a red plastic bubble at the end of a tube. It had a little window from which kids could peer. Instead of seeing Sophie peek out, though, I saw the teen, who nodded at me without smiling. Oh my goodness.

"You're ugly!" I heard Sophie yell with confidence. "And you're wearing shoes!" Then she said something I'll never forget. "Stop!"

I was so upset I almost launched off the floor like a Sophie-seeking missile.

"Sophie!" I yelled. "Get away from that boy! And you get away from her RIGHT NOW!"

Everyone around me froze. *He's not going to do anything terrible up there, is he?* I asked myself. *With me right here?* "We have to get that boy out of there," I said while diving into the slide. "He's bothering my daughter!"

It was a tight squeeze, but I made it up, pushing hard with my sandals' tread and hooking my fingertips into the slides' grooves, calling Sophie all the way. *Just let me get to her before anything happens*, I begged. *Please!*

By the time I reached her, she was alone, and we were in the plastic bubble together. I looked out the cloudy, scratched window at all the faces pointed our way.

"What happened?!" I asked. She wasn't crying, and she looked okay.

"He said he was gonna get me!" she said. "I don't want to play that game!"

"Did he touch you?"

"No." She shook her head. I didn't know how to make the sign of the cross, or even what it meant, but my instinct was to do it. My thankfulness was beyond words.

I pulled her into my lap for a cuddle. Tears were in both our eyes. "I'm so sorry, honey. He's gone now." I wanted to tell someone to get him, but I wasn't leaving Sophie. Hopefully security cameras somewhere had captured the boys' images. Yet it wasn't like I could report a crime. *Hello, 911? Someone tried to play tag with my daughter at Pizza Arcade! With high-tops on!*

"Did he say anything else?" I asked her.

"No. But I called him ugly. His teeth were gold and scary and gross! And he tried to grab me. But I kicked him. Hah!"

"Then what happened?"

"He went away."

"Good for you. Well, you're safe now. Let's get out of this thing." I was starting to think—and worry—about Jack's whereabouts.

"I don't want to leave," she said.

Maybe she was afraid. "You don't want to leave the tube...or the party?"

"Both," she answered. "I want to play."

I decided the best route was bribery, not arguing.

"Don't worry. You're going to get a lot of playtime," I promised. "We'll get lots of tokens. But let's find Grandma first." And an ugly teen in need of dental work.

Twenty-Five

Sophie was determined to exit via the slide, so I dutifully followed, shocked by the scene at the bottom. Three moms surrounded the kid, encouraging him to explain himself. His friend was nowhere in sight. Meanwhile, the play area was strangely quiet. A male employee blocked the exit, armed with a hand stamp and black light.

"What happened?" one of the moms asked me. "Is your daughter okay?"

Sophie ran to my mom and Jack, who were standing nearby.

"She's fine. That guy was just chasing her." I pointed at him. "It was really weird." I wished I could add, *And I'm being chased by a gang, so I was extra freaked out*, but I didn't think that would go over well. "What were you *doing*?" I asked him directly. "Bothering a little girl."

"Is Pizza Arcade," he said with a Spanish accent, raising his hands in innocence. His teeth were nightmarish. "Is playtime, right?"

"Hey," said another male employee, who broke into Spanish and gave the teen a hard time.

"Please ask if you can see his ID," I said to the man. "I'd like his name." I turned to the kid and held out my hand. "Can we see your ID?"

The employee translated my request.

"No, man," the teen said. "I leave. No problem." He looked at me for a long moment. "But she need to watch herself. She don want nobody hurt." He brushed past everyone and out the door. This had definitely spoiled the party atmosphere.

"I'll be right back," I announced.

I saw Mom's shoulders sag.

I hurried after the guy I was already nicknaming Gold Tooth, sure I wouldn't catch him, but hoping to see a glimpse of him pulling away. I wanted a license plate number or something concrete.

After being indoors, the sunlight was blinding, and I could barely see. I held my hand over my forehead as my eyes watered in protest. The lot was still full. Logic told me to look for the sports car that had pulled away from my house Friday night. Instinct turned me toward the exit, which was next to a stoplight. There, at the red light, was someone who looked like Gold Tooth, staring out the window of a battered, navy SUV. I was too far away to do anything, but I ran toward it anyway as the light turned green and the SUV pulled off. I couldn't make out the license plate except that it started with an X.

Lately, I'd been terrified in open spaces, but turning back toward the party, heart pounding and sweaty, I felt like the enemy was moving out of reach, and it was upsetting. I wasn't scared; I was pissed.

Mom met me in the lobby with the kids. It was comforting to see them holding hands.

"Nicki!" Mom said. I braced for a reprimand. "You're going to be so proud of me!"

Huh? "Why?" I asked.

She held up her cell phone. "I got a picture." Gold Tooth was proclaiming his innocence, hands in the air.

"You don't know how to do that!" I said.

"Well, that didn't stop me. And Megan's mom got video. I told her to. She's emailing it to you. We'll text this picture to your phone."

"Mom, I'm beyond proud of you. And when did you even learn to text?"

"Megan's mom is teaching me. I get the concept, but I don't know how to do it yet."

Pretty much how I felt about a lot of things.

After the adrenaline drained from my system, I thanked Megan's mom and the restaurant staff, and Mom insisted I report what had happened to the necessary people. I couldn't imagine leaving Sophie and Jack for a moment, but I knew what I had to do.

"Can I spend the night at your place tonight, Mom?" I asked while we stood near the exit. "I don't want to be away from the kids all night."

"Do you think that's a good idea?" she asked in a low voice. "What if someone follows you or something?"

She was right, and it hurt so much I got teary. Someone could even follow her from here. The tears came faster. I covered my face with a nearby napkin and pretended to blow my nose, hoping the kids wouldn't see I was crying. How could I keep them safe?

"You know what? Let's all meet at a hotel tonight and collect ourselves," Mom said brightly. "That would be fun."

I let the idea sink in. If we stayed at a high rise and were careful with our room numbers, it was doubtful anyone would follow us by elevator. And I could sleep with the kids by my side.

They showed their approval by jumping up and down and yelling, "Yay! A hotel!"

"That's a pretty good idea," I said.

"Then I'll make arrangements," Mom offered.

"No thanks," I said. "I'll do it." My brain was already working on how to keep us incognito. Pay cash. Use an assumed name. I wasn't taking any chances. Plus, I wouldn't feel right about Mom paying. "Do you have a hotel preference?" I asked her.

She didn't, but her tastes, I knew, could afford to be nicer than mine. I'd have to find somewhere upscale enough to have security and big enough to hide in.

We stayed at Pizza Arcade long enough for Sophie to fulfill her dream of spending $20 worth of tickets on a lollipop she'd been eyeing. Instead of taking the kids to camp, Mom left straight for her condo, where she could personally keep an eye on them. I notified the camp and agreed to check in with Mom when I'd made a reservation. I also called Sgt. Dwyer with a full update. He said he'd make a special trip to Pizza Arcade and see if they had footage to add to my picture and video.

I was dying to text April the picture of Gold Tooth to see if he looked familiar, but I felt like it should stay in my possession. So I drove to her house after making sure she was home.

"Do you know this guy?" I asked when she answered the door. I handed her my cell phone and wished it had a bigger display.

"I totally know him. That's GT."

"GT?"

"Yeah. Short for Gold Teeth."

"Makes sense," I said. I'd been close.

"Where'd you get this?" she asked.

"I'll tell you, but I need to know what you know about him first."

"Well, he's high up in a gang," April said. "It's called Los Reyes."

"Are you sure?" I asked.

"Totally. Everyone knows him. Look at the burn mark on his shoulder if you don't believe me."

I saw three dark circles on his shoulder. "That's their thing?" I asked.

"Uh huh."

"They're rivals with Marcus's gang, C-16, right?"

"Right. That's who was fighting when Marcus got shot. So where did you get this picture?"

I told her the basics.

"That's crazy. Pizza Arcade?"

"Crazy," I agreed, shaking my head.

Would one gang kidnap another gang member's pregnant girlfriend? That's what I was wondering when I called George from the car to update him on the latest development, hoping I wasn't already driving him nuts.

"There is no such thing as too much information, Nicki," he assured me. "In fact, if you don't think something's likely to be important, tell me about it anyway," he said. "We don't want to overlook anything."

"How often do you check your email?" I asked. "Because I can email information instead of calling."

"I check it constantly." He recited the address I'd seen on his card.

He had one investigator heading to West Virginia soon, he explained, and another would watch Marcus's house—and hopefully

Marcus himself—by the next morning. My job, he said, would be to stay safe.

"You need to lie low," he said.

"That's hard to do. But now that you're helping, I can relax a little."

We promised to keep in touch.

I checked my email to see if Megan's mom had sent me the video. She had, so I forwarded it to Dwyer and George without even seeing it. Downloading or watching it was impossible on my old cell phone. Belatedly, I realized I was probably in it—coming down the slide flat on my back, awkwardly slipping off the end, obviously not looking my best. I hoped George didn't lose respect. Or forward it to Dean.

Instead of driving all the way home, I parked a street away to see if anything looked suspicious. I was totally uncomfortable with guns and worried that if I owned one, it might be used against me, but the PI Academy was having an effect on me. Lots of PIs, especially if they were retired law enforcement, had concealed weapons permits. There was constant talk about firearms courses and firing range practice. Right now, the thought of "carrying" was scary, but tempting. The image of Marcus's gun flashed through my mind. What were the logistics of being an armed gang member? How did you learn to shoot? Did you practice anywhere? Or was your first shot always at a victim? Thinking about it made me want to get rid of guns, not buy one. It was so confusing.

I chose a parking spot where I didn't know anyone living in the surrounding houses. I didn't feel like explaining my actions to anyone. I turned on the baby monitor and listened in silence, hearing nothing but the sound of a neighborhood dog barking.

After about five minutes of that, I tucked the monitor into my purse and got out. *You're fine,* I assured myself. *It's broad daylight. Nothing's going to happen.*

I hustled down the street with sunglasses on, peering behind me and hoping I didn't look as paranoid as I felt. A familiar car approached from the opposite direction, not Dean's Aston Martin or the Mustang seared in my memory, but Marcus's mom's car, and it slowed in front of my house. I couldn't stop in my tracks, and I didn't think I should turn around and miss what was going on.

Should I hide behind a tree? I wondered. I looked around, knowing there wasn't a public bench nearby, but hoping for one anyway. So I kept moving forward—very, very slowly—stopping once to pretend something was stuck in my sandal. The car revved forward. I'd been spotted.

It idled parallel to me, and I could see Marcus with one hand on the wheel. I stepped back from the curb, ready to roll down a nearby hill if threatened. He put down his window and let a tattooed arm hang out.

"Hey, Miss," he called.

"Yes?" I said. I wasn't ready to show recognition.

"You know me, right?"

"What's your name?" I stalled. I did a furtive look around to see if potential help was anywhere close. Nope.

"Marcus," he said. "Come on. I been looking for you."

How did you find me? I wanted to know. I asked something more critical instead: "Why?"

"Somethin's going on you should know. You helped me. I'm payin' you back. Get in."

"I can't," I said. "Just tell me here please."

He glanced at an oncoming car behind him. "It ain't safe. Come on."

I shook my head. "Pull over and park."

Where could we talk that was out of sight but safe? I saw wrought iron chairs on someone's lawn. The driveway was empty. Maybe the owners wouldn't notice, and if they did, I'd be glad someone was around. I could tell them I was exercising and got too hot. Come to think of it, I was feeling woozy at the thought of talking to Marcus.

"I'll meet you over at those black chairs," I told him, pointing. "In that yard."

Confusion crossed his face, but he nodded his okay.

While walking quickly, I surreptitiously called Kenna and left a fast-talking message. "If anything happens to me," I said, "I want you to know I'm meeting with Marcus in our neighborhood." I glanced up at the house number and relayed the address. "We're gonna talk on the lawn with iron chairs," I said. "I was on a walk when he pulled up. Maybe he wants to talk about the shooting," I said. "I think it'll be okay."

I clicked off as Marcus approached. Instantly I regretted it. I should have let her voicemail record our conversation.

"Looks like you're healing well," I said. "I'm so glad. But why are you here?"

"Stop playin'," he said. "You know people are after you, right?"

"If you say so. Why? Can you help me?"

"I dunno. I gotta try. At least warn you. You had my back. Now people want you dead 'cuz of it. That's not right."

Dead? I knew they wanted me *scared*. But *dead*?

"So is it Los Reyes that's after me? Because I saw you get shot?" He nodded.

"Some guy named GT?"

"Could be."

I took in his appearance—blue basketball shorts, white T-shirt, backward cap hiding his fresh scar. *Thanks for the warning*, I thought. *Better late than never*. "I appreciate your concern. But I don't know what you can do. People think I know who shot you, but I really, really don't. I wish I did, but you probably know a lot more than I do."

"I'm workin' on it."

"With the police?"

He laughed under his breath. I couldn't blame him. The guy was armed and dealt drugs. He didn't keep the police on speed dial.

"Marcus," I said, trying a different tactic. "Is there anything I can do for you?" He cocked his head and squinted at me. "You live a dangerous life," I continued. "Don't you ever want out?"

"Lady," he said, shaking his head, "That's an effed up question. You're askin' if I wanna leave my family. People who take care of me." He stood up. "I gotta go."

"Wait. Don't go." I held out a hand and motioned for him to sit again. "Hold on," I said. "Please. I'm sorry. Let me hear you out. How did you want to help me?" He put a hand on his hip.

"I'm just warning you, this is serious shit, and you better stay outta the way. That's about it." He turned and started walking toward his car.

"Do you think anyone would actually kill me over this?" I called.

He turned back. "You wanna find out?"

Maybe I was starting to fall for Marcus's charm, but I thought he was trying to do the right thing. Either he had a sense of justice or another motive I couldn't identify—I just wasn't sure which. If he had a conscience, too, maybe Beth was okay.

I desperately wanted to ask about her and gauge his response. It might be my only chance to question him again. But if I scared him, and he was keeping her somewhere, he might hurt her, and he'd certainly steer clear of me. I decided on a positive approach.

"I believe you're trying to protect me. Honestly. That's extremely admirable. I hope you'll let me help you, too."

"I told you I don't need help. I'm good."

"Well, I heard a rumor your pregnant ex-girlfriend is missing. Maybe kidnapped. Is that true?"

He shifted back and forth on his feet, sniffed, and looked away. Sweat glistened on his forehead. He wiped more from his upper lip.

"You heard that, huh?"

"I was asking about you, and it came up a couple times, actually. I guess it's old news."

"You know, you better back off. You're gettin' in a lotta people's shit."

Whoa. I'd hit a nerve. "Okay," I backpedaled. "I just figured you'd be worried about her and especially the baby."

"No shit. But it's not your fucking business." He pointed at me. "Stay. The fuck. Out of it."

Oh my gosh. He was convincing.

"I'm sorry. I was just trying to help you, Marcus, like you did me. I see you have a good heart. I know you're mixed up in some stuff. But you wouldn't be here if you didn't have good intentions."

"You're the one in trouble," he warned again. "Good luck."

Twenty-Six

Talking with Marcus took some fear out of being home alone. I couldn't withdraw; I had to take action. First thing, I called Sgt. Dwyer from the gang unit with another bulletin: *Somehow Marcus knows where I live, and he swung by to tell me that, yep, I'm being targeted by Los Reyes. Witness intimidation has been confirmed. I'm a witness, and I'm officially intimidated.* Dwyer's advice was to stay calm and stick with my relocation plan. He also said Marcus's sense of justice—choosing to warn me because I'd helped him—was plausible. Gang members aren't automatically heartless.

"Stay out of trouble," he reminded me. "Let us do our jobs."

We hung up, and I got to work leaving Kenna a new message and browsing hotels in the yellow pages, all the while considering how Marcus's visit related to Beth.

If Marcus doesn't know where Beth is, I thought, *who does that leave? Beth. A gang. A stranger. Beth's family. Maybe even April.*

I saw an ad for a decent hotel—complete with restaurants, a pool, and a workout room I wouldn't use—and called to make sure there were plenty of vacancies. After checking email, I carried Beth's case file up to my room, where I let my mind drift while packing an overnight bag. *What if Beth had returned home, and I didn't know it?* I shook my head at that unlikely, but possible, outcome.

After overstuffing the duffel, I sat on my bed and reviewed everything in the folder. Now that I had a few extra moments, it was time to follow up with people I hadn't talked with in a while.

Instead of calling Beth's parents, I dialed April's mom and asked when she'd last talked with them. Although they weren't friends, Jen said, she called Sonja occasionally out of concern, and they'd talked in the past couple days. It was a short conversation because there was nothing new to report. I wondered if Beth's parents would even tell her if Beth had been found.

Gina, meanwhile, said she hadn't heard anything about Beth since we'd canvassed the neighborhood. She said Molly, Beth's neighbor, would have told her if Beth was home, and she promised to alert me to any developments. She wrapped up by saying she hoped the treadmill was running well, no pun intended.

"I used it this morning," I was glad to say. "It's working great."

I was about to start calling hospitals and shelters when the phone rang. It was April.

"Hi, April. I just talked to your mom."

"I know." She sounded out of breath. "Nicki, you're not going to believe this. I think Beth just called my cell phone."

"What?!"

"I missed a call, and it's from her number!"

"Her cell phone?" I asked.

"Yes!"

"But there's no message?"

"Just a missed call. I got out of the shower and saw it. What should I do?"

"Don't delete anything related to it. And call the police right away."

"I can't believe I missed it," she wailed. "I should have kept the phone nearby. I'm freaking out."

"Don't worry! Just call the police with your mom." I opened Beth's file and found the investigator's number on her missing-person flyer. "Call this number, unless you have another one," I said, repeating it twice. "Then call me back."

During the interminable wait for April to get back in touch, I called Edith.

"Hello, dear," she greeted me. The sound of birds chirping told me she was outside or near a window.

"Hi, Edith. I'm just checking to see if anything has happened over at the Rush house."

"Other than the police yesterday, no. But you already know about that."

I uttered my second *What?!* of the day. "No, I don't know about that! Tell me."

"Well, I called the police as you suggested, but I thought you were in touch with them too. They visited around, oh, I don't know...noon?"

"What did they do?"

"I saw them at the door. Then I checked my mailbox to get a better look. They talked with Mrs. Rush, and she let them in. I don't know if Dr. Rush was home."

"Did you see the police leave?"

"Oh yes. I wasn't going to miss that. They were alone—two officers in front seat, no one in the back."

"Do you think you could ask the Rushes about it without raising suspicion? I mean, it's natural for neighbors to ask about police activity, right?"

"Well, sure. Especially old ladies who live alone."

Goosebumps covered my arms. She was joking, but it scared me. I'd involved an innocent elderly woman, and if anything happened to her, I'd blame myself.

"Be careful, Edith," I warned. "Listen to your instincts and don't do anything that makes you uncomfortable. We don't know what happened to their granddaughter. I don't want to involve you in anything dangerous."

"Don't be silly," she said.

"Just take care," I said. "And please call me right away if you talk with them. I'll be eager to hear from you."

"I'll do all of the above," she promised.

April hadn't returned my call yet, but I didn't want to interrupt whatever conversation she might be having with the police, so I emailed George and worked up the courage to call Dean.

"Do you have any connections with law enforcement in West Virginia?" I asked him.

"Not personally," he said. "Why?"

I relayed the latest developments. "I'd like to know what they found when they talked with the Rushes," I said.

"Let me talk to some people and call you back," he said. I told him how many calls I was expecting and encouraged him to leave a detailed message if I didn't answer.

"I hope you make it to class tomorrow," he said. "Nighttime surveillance—video and photography—remember? It's gonna be interesting."

"I can't wait," I said, ready to hang up.

"Hey, Nicki?"

"Yeah?"

"I admire what you're doing. Kenna's lucky to have a friend like you."

"I'm the lucky one," I said. It was strange to say that in the midst of so much stress. But I meant it.

I frittered around the kitchen, so anxious I hardly noticed I'd swept and mopped the floor, scrubbed the stove and started a job I'd only done once in memory—washing the cabinet doors. My self-imposed distraction was interrupted by the sound of a car pulling into Kenna's driveway. I peeked out and saw her Solara. Before I could get out the back door to see her, she was at the front. I disabled the alarm and let her in.

"I just got your message," she said. "Are you okay?"

"I'm fine," I said, pulling her inside. "Can you stay? I've got a lot to tell you."

She looked at her cell. "I have half an hour before Andy gets home. I'm making his favorite burgers tonight."

We sat at my kitchen table with glasses of water. As I described the day's events, starting with Megan's party, I was startled by how much had happened—all before dinnertime. I also realized I should be hungry. I hadn't eaten—or thought about food—since breakfast. I grabbed random items out of the refrigerator while we talked. Multigrain bread, almond butter, honey and blueberries. Everything looked good.

"What are you making?" Kenna asked.

"I don't know. I think I'm going to combine all this." I piled everything into a sandwich that looked amazing and filling. I'd just finished a bite when the phone rang.

"Hello?" I answered.

It was April, and before I heard anything significant, Edith called on the other line. I asked April to hang on. Edith hadn't learned anything yet, she told me, so I asked to return her call. Then I switched back to April.

"Beth's call came from West Virginia!" she told me. "The police are totally jumping on it. She must be with her grandparents!"

Now I really needed to talk with Dean. I prayed his contact would have information.

"Beth's call came from West Virginia?" I repeated aloud for Kenna's benefit. "That's amazing!"

"I know!"

"I'm so glad you called. Thank you. Is there anything else you can tell me? Did the police say anything else?"

"No. They just thanked me. I bet they're going to find her today. I can't believe this."

Her joy was infectious. It also reinforced my sense that April wouldn't hurt Beth. But I couldn't get carried away.

"I'm happy too, April," I said. "But I'll really celebrate when I know she's safe. Let's stay in touch if either of us hears anything, okay?"

"Of course!"

We said goodbye, and I looked at Kenna, who was crying softly.

"Oh my gosh, Kenna," I said. How could I tell her not to be happy or sad? We hadn't found Beth yet. All we had was another clue. There could be countless explanations for a call—especially an incomplete one from West Virginia, and some might not mean anything about Beth. Maybe her family found her cell phone and checked out her contacts. Or maybe she'd visited her grandparents and left it there. Or maybe... I stopped thinking and wrapped my arms around Kenna.

"We don't know what this means yet," I said. "What are you thinking?"

She cried harder and rested her cheek on my shoulder. Her arms were around me, limp.

"I'm so selfish," she said.

"What?" I pulled back to read her expression. She bit her lip, looked down, and fiddled with her wedding ring.

"I just realized I'm hoping for a happy ending for me as much as Beth," she said. "Maybe more. That's horrible."

"You're human," I said.

"You know how much I care about Beth, right?" she asked, lifting her head.

"Kenna. I absolutely know," I said, meeting her gaze. "This search wasn't about you. I remember how it started. It was more about her than anything else. You *knew* something was wrong."

Saying that was like dropping a weight into my stomach. Kenna *had* known something was wrong. Something beyond running away. And I trusted that. If she was right, the explanation for Beth's call might not be good.

Dean was successful in gaining some information. The West Virginia police had, in fact, visited the Rushes and determined Beth didn't appear to be living there. There was no sign of her, and the Rushes were cooperative.

Beth's call added a twist Dean couldn't explain any better than I could. We could only speculate and hope George's team and the police would make progress.

While Kenna went home to freshen up and make Andy's burgers, I worried about his arriving home to find her a teary, splotchy mess, thanks to being with me. Hopefully he'd take comfort in recent developments.

Meanwhile, I set the house alarm, put my bag in the van, and dialed Edith before starting the engine. When she didn't answer, I left a message and turned the ignition, mentally preparing to back out of the garage. I'd been in a quandary about where to park. Inside, I couldn't see much before leaving. I could unknowingly back into a barrage of gunfire. But I liked the privacy and protection of the garage. Next time, maybe I'd back in, facing out, although I didn't like the idea of staring into trouble, either.

The street was busy with commuters returning from work, so I entered the fray when there was a break in the action, scanning oncoming cars from both directions. Feeling relatively secure since no one was in close range, I sped toward the hotel where I'd meet Mom and the kids, constantly checking for anyone suspicious.

The hotel garage was like any other. Deserted, dim, and devoid of cell phone reception. I parked and stalled for a few minutes, hoping to see someone friendly, especially a woman, who would ride in the elevator with me. How could there be so many cars and so few people?

When my patience wore out, I gripped my keys like a weapon and marched toward the elevator, feigning confidence. Knowing I was headed for the kids gave me an extra shot of courage. Unfortunately, that didn't help when I heard a male voice call out, "Lady?"

Fight or flight kicked in, and instead of turning around to see who'd spoken, I bolted toward the elevator, punched the "up" button, and hopped in. Then I pressed the symbol for "close these frickin' doors!" and watched them slide together—only then noticing an attendant by my car. Apparently I'd parked in a valet zone. Oops. My nerves had gotten to me. I let the doors close anyway.

On the main floor, I saw Mom and the kids in the lobby before they saw me. Normally I'd sneak up on them in surprise, but that seemed wrong today. Instead, I strolled up and called lightly, "Hi, guys!" The kids turned and ran toward me, arms outstretched. *Ahhhh.*

"Hi, sweetheart," Mom said. "Have you checked in?"

"Not yet. Why don't you guys have a seat and I'll take care of it?" I motioned to maroon loveseats and a huge TV. I knew it would mesmerize Jack and Sophie even though it was tuned to a stock market report.

While they sat, I paid cash for a room with two queen-size beds. I didn't think Mom would mind bunking together. I also apologized to the clerk about my parking error and wrote down my license plate number, requesting a few minutes to settle in before braving the garage again.

"If you like, you can give me your key, and I'll have the valet guys park properly for you," the clerk offered. In my state of fear, that sounded great.

"Super," I said, detaching the key from my chain. "Thank you."

"Here are the keys to your room, Ms. Baker." He handed me two cards tucked into an envelope with our room number—311—written on it. It was awkward to hear him use the fake name I'd chosen for the reservation. *Sharon Baker.* "Would you like help with your luggage?"

"No thanks."

We carried our bags—one each—to the elevator. This time it was a calm trip, filled with talk about what to order from room service for dinner. The only consensus was on dessert. The kids agreed it shouldn't be delivered to the room. We should get it from the most awesome source around. The vending machines.

The next hour felt like a mini vacation. We ordered food, perused TV channels, poked around the minibar, and jumped from bed to bed. Mom sat that part out, but I spotted the kids, desperate to burn off tension myself. The whole time, I kept my phone in earshot, hoping to get news from George or anyone else.

After dinner arrived (broccoli, breadsticks, and pasta), my phone rang, and I took it into the bathroom. Thankfully, the kids were relatively quiet with food in their mouths.

"George?" I answered based on caller ID.

"Nicki. I've got a little news. Are you sitting?"

I glanced at the toilet and stayed upright.

"I'm fine," I said. "Tell me what's going on."

"My guy's at Beth's grandparents' house, and there's an ambulance at a nearby home."

"Uh huh." Was this the kind conversation where someone starts with "There's been an accident" and then drops a verbal bomb? I was familiar with that approach. If so, I had no idea what was coming next.

"It's there for your source, Edith. Apparently she took a fall. She was temporarily unconscious but managed to call 911."

"Oh no! Is she okay?" Edith was more than a source. She felt like a friend. I kept my voice down to avoid worrying Mom or the kids. I caught a glimpse of myself in the mirror, eyes wide, pale.

"We don't know. They took her out on a stretcher. We'll find out where she's going and let you know."

"Okay," I said. "George, this doesn't feel like a coincidence, does it?"

"It's odd," he admitted, "given what we know. I suggest that if possible, you get down here and visit Edith while you can."

While I can? Did he mean she might not make it? Or before it got too late at night? I opted for late at night.

"Call me when you know where she is, and I'll be there." Now I felt rushed to eat a few bites and take the kids to the vending machines. I'd never make progress unless I knew they were tucked in for the night, tummies full, doors locked. I felt awful about leaving Mom again, but if the past was any indication, she'd understand. I guess that's what moms do best.

With more leeway than I usually allowed at vending machines, each kid got to pick a dessert, pay for it, and press the corresponding button. My priorities were keeping them safe and getting to West Virginia. I could live with a one-time nougat bonanza.

Mom and I walked the kids back to our room and discussed my plans. I'd keep in touch by cell phone, and she'd brush the kids' teeth, read them stories, and tuck them in. Then she'd watch TV. I gave her a thankful squeeze.

After painfully rejecting requests for teeth-brushing by the Crazy Babysitter, I peed, grabbed my purse, and left, suddenly remembering I no longer had my car key. I'd have to wait for the valet. At least I wouldn't be alone in the garage. And I'd tip him well for the trouble I caused.

Ten dollars later, I was cruising to West Virginia with the navigation system on. George had texted me the address of a local hospital, and I imagined what I might find there. Edith in the emergency room? Admitted? Sent home? Since she'd arrived by ambulance, hopefully she'd gotten immediate treatment and skipped the waiting room.

Jumbled thoughts collided as I considered what might have happened to her. Edith was shaky when I met her, yes, but I didn't buy that after investigating a little, she happened to fall and get knocked unconscious. If she'd learned something sinister—something that would endanger her life, maybe she'd told the 911 operator or someone else. Most of all I prayed she was okay.

By the time I arrived at the hospital, my mind was weary but still racing. An ER nursing assistant brought me to see Edith, who was propped up with an IV in her arm and a monitor on her thumb. She was perfectly still and much paler than I remembered. Her blue eyes had lost some of their sparkle.

"Hi, Edith," I said softly. "It's Nicki. I hear you've had some trouble. Are you okay?"

"I'm fine, dear," she said unconvincingly. I wanted to ask someone how she was really doing, but everyone was bustling around too quickly to be interrupted.

"What happened?" I asked.

"I don't know," she said. "They tell me I fell."

"Who tells you that?"

"These people," she said, gesturing vaguely at no one.

"Do you remember who I am?" I asked.

She shook her head back and forth. *No.*

"Well, how about if I keep you company here for a while?" I asked. "I'm a friend."

Even if Edith couldn't say much about her fall, hopefully I'd be a reassuring presence, and maybe I'd learn more about her medical condition.

I also wanted to reach her family. Her daughter was in Cleveland, I remembered, but surely she had friends or family closer to home. No one should be in the hospital alone.

Gentle quizzing didn't reveal anything about loved ones, except her daughter's name—Meredith Hall. I didn't have a phone number, so I asked what church Edith attended, hoping a pastor might fill in some gaps. *St. Francis*, she told me.

We sat in silence for a bit, and I reached out to hold her hand until a doctor introduced himself so enthusiastically it jolted Edith out of a restful state.

"Hi, Dr. Swanson," I responded, standing to shake his hand. "I'm a friend of Edith's. She seems to be having trouble remembering things. But she does know the name of her church and her daughter."

"Thanks," he said. "I'll get right on that." I hoped he wasn't kidding. But since he might have a coronary patient or worse in the next room, I wasn't sure.

"I can call if you'd like," I offered. "If it's okay to use my cell phone in here."

"Go right ahead," he encouraged. "Just give the information to the nurse, too." He turned his attention to Edith. "How are you feeling, Ms. Huggins?"

"Okay," she answered. That was good news, but it didn't seem meaningful, considering she looked and sounded awful.

"We're going to admit you and keep an eye on you tonight," he said. "We're just waiting for your room to be prepared. But all your tests have come back normal."

"Good," she said. I nodded in agreement.

Dr. Swanson told Edith he'd check on her again before she was admitted, and I said the same, and then followed him into the hall.

"Dr. Swanson," I started. "Is memory loss normal after a fall like this?"

"It can be," he said. "There are various causes, but after an accident, sometimes people just forget the event. Sometimes they forget people, too."

"Yeah. She doesn't remember me right now. Do they remember everything eventually?"

"Sometimes yes, sometimes no," he said. "Time will tell."

"Do you know anything about how she fell?" I asked.

"Nope," he said. "Just that it was down some steps. Were you there?"

"No," I said. "But I want to make sure it doesn't happen again. And honestly, I want to make sure it was accidental."

His eyes widened. "Do you suspect it wasn't?"

"Not really, and I know falls are common at this age. But she can't remember what happened, so I have no way of knowing. She's old and lives alone, so she's vulnerable. And one of her neighbors is iffy. The police were there, though, so I'm sure they checked things out.

"If they had any concerns," he said, "they would have told me." He scratched his beard. "You know, at her age, it's amazing she didn't have *worse* injuries."

"I agree. Thank you so much for taking care of her. I'll call the pastor and hopefully he can reach her family."

"Sounds good," he said. "Good luck."

Twenty-Seven

Pastor Greg Williams didn't have information about Edith's daughter, but Edith had friends on the grounds committee, which kept the church gardens beautiful. He'd contact them to see if they could help.

"I'll notify the healing prayer and pastoral care teams, too," he said. "They can offer other things she might need." We agreed to touch base the next morning.

Before leaving the hospital, I accompanied Edith to her private room on a regular patient floor. The transfer went smoothly, and since Edith was ready to close her eyes for the night, I said goodbye and spoke with a nurse about her care. He assured me Edith was in good hands and I didn't need to worry about leaving. I wrote down my number just in case.

I'd arrived at the hospital frantic, but sitting with Edith had been almost meditative, so my thoughts were clear when I called George to catch up. Dr. Rush was driving somewhere, he told me, and the PI was staying on site to observe the house.

"Don't ask how," George said, "but we know where Dr. Rush is too."

"Okay," I said. "That's good. I'm in the car, trying to decide what to do next." I shared the little I'd learned from Edith. "I'm still worried this wasn't a fall."

"I understand," he said. "So just for a moment, assume she was pushed. Who would do it? And why?"

"Your guess is far better than mine."

"I'd like to hear what you think," he said.

"Well, she's been asking around. And the only place she's been asking is at the Rushes' house, I think. So it would have to be them or someone who knows them."

"But why would they react that way?"

"I guess maybe she learned something or came close to learning something that threatened someone."

"Okay."

"And even if being pushed didn't seriously injure her," I continued, "it might scare her off. Except she doesn't remember being pushed or even falling. So it's definitely not scaring her now."

Edith's memory could return at any moment, it occurred to me. Someone should be there to listen and protect her. I needed to call the nursing station so they'd note anything she remembered. I also wanted to know when she woke up.

"You're doing fine, Nicki," George said. "And since I'm an old geezer, I'm going to bed. I gave my investigator, Steve, your number. You can coordinate with him the rest of the night. We'll talk in the morning. Be safe out there."

Steve was a friendly guy who suggested I keep an eye on Dr. Rush, who, according to his resources, was headed South on Windham, which rang a bell. Maybe he was going to Asheleigh Manor. I still had the address in my case file, so I programmed it into the navigation system and double checked the directions. *Yup. He was probably headed there.* I told Steve my theory.

"It's a charity he works for," I explained. "So he's there a lot. I can watch the entrance and let you know when he arrives or leaves. I'm not far from it right now."

"Are you sure you want to do that? It's late, and George said you have kids."

I thought of Sgt. Dwyer's warning to mind my own business.

"I'm good," I decided. "I drove all this way. I want to make the most of it."

"Okay then. Keep in touch. You got my number?"

"I do. Is it okay to call? I don't want to interrupt what you're doing."

"Don't worry. I'll have it on vibrate or off if needed," he said. "And you can always text me. I'll do the same for you."

We hung up and I pressed "Go" on the navigation system. Asheleigh Manor was about a mile from the hospital. Following Steve's lead, I set my phone to vibrate and pocketed it so I wouldn't miss anything.

Listening carefully to the navigation prompts, I arrived at Asheleigh Manor in a few minutes, hopefully before Dr. Rush, if that's where he was going. The gates were closed, so I passed it, did a U-turn, and parked a block away. Before I had time to get bored, Dr. Rush drove by, but instead of turning into Asheleigh Manor, he passed it. I gave him a head start and pulled out, lights off at first, and then on after I did a U-turn and saw him take the next left. I turned left, too, and watched him take another left down a tree-lined, gravel road that ran toward the manor. The navigation system insisted I turn around, but I tried to ignore it, finally jabbing it off in annoyance.

My eyes strained to see Dr. Rush's taillights as he drove down the road, which felt more like a long driveway. I turned off my headlights and pulled over momentarily to give him more room, afraid he'd be suspicious of anyone behind him on this deserted lane. When I pulled out, I used parking lights instead of headlights to see. I held my breath and gripped the wheel as the road opened into parking spaces and a loading dock flanked by dumpsters. If Asheleigh Manor were a person, this would be its unattractive backside. Dr. Rush's car was parked, headlights off, at the far end of the lot near a door marked "EMPLOYEES ONLY."

I stayed near the road and backed into a space for an easy exit. Pulse thumping in my ears, I considered two options. Wait for Dr. Rush to leave. Or take a look around. Everything in me wanted to keep moving in hopes I'd get closer to Beth.

As I was about to dial Steve for advice, Dr. Rush got out of his car. Whoa. I'd assumed he was already in the building. I pocketed my phone and watched as he stood by his car for a moment, a glowing gadget in his hands, which had to be a phone. I unbuckled my seat belt stealthily, as if he could somehow hear it from across the lot.

When he used the employee entrance, I opened my door, pressed "lock," and closed it gently. I impressed myself by doing a quiet tiptoe-run across the lot, although I had to catch my breath afterward. I leaned down, not sure if I was panting from exertion or stress, and envisioned what was next. I was going inside. I was following Dr. Rush. And if anyone stopped me, I'd say I was out exercising and had an asthma attack. That wasn't quite true. Panic attack, asthma attack...close enough.

While I still had the nerve, I gingerly opened the employee door, which led to an empty break room. Vending machines brought the kids to mind, so I forced myself to refocus and step further into the building.

Seeing no one, I followed a sterile basement corridor lined with closed doors and empty rooms until I spotted Dr. Rush in the distance. The sight of him was a terrifying relief. I was glad to know where he was, but being in the same empty hallway was freaky. At any second, he could turn around and catch me. Much worse, he might remember me. What would I do? Pretend to be a visitor? The whole acting part of investigation was so unpleasant.

Thankfully, Dr. Rush turned and closed a door behind him, still unaware of my presence. Most of the rooms I'd passed looked like treatment rooms or offices, empty for the night, but with the lights dimmed, it was hard to tell. The one he'd entered was unmarked and had a windowless door. A rectangle of chipped paint indicated where a plaque had been removed. I walked by, listening intently and noticing the door's latch hadn't caught. I moved closer to a sliver of light emanating from the room. Perfectly still, I turned my head, ears perked. I heard one word in a female voice, "Grandpa," and that was all I needed.

I put a touch of pressure on the door, and although it didn't squeak, it opened way more than I intended, exposing four things through the gap. Dr. Rush. Beth. Me. And a game of checkers.

What was the most appropriate response in this situation? "Can I play?" "Sorry! Wrong room." Or maybe, "Did anyone here order pizza?"

Both of them looked startled, but Beth didn't seem afraid or panicked. She didn't look like a prisoner, either, although she was in a hospital bed, attached to an IV. Best of all, she looked pregnant. She held a black checkers piece over a board being set up for play.

I wanted to run outside and alert 911. *Beth is okay! She's here! Come and get her!* But I was afraid Dr. Rush would follow and things wouldn't go well. Maybe I could "pocket dial" 911 and get attention by saying Beth's name and location.

"Beth?" I said while fingering the buttons on my phone. *Over three. Down three.* I pressed 9 and returned for 1. "Send" was hardest to find, but I was pretty sure I hit it.

"Yes?" she answered.

Dr. Rush's eyes slid to me, squinting with what I feared was recognition. "Can I help you?" he said.

"Beth Myers?" I asked loud and clear, hoping 911 was listening. "The missing girl from Virginia?"

She looked quizzically at Dr. Rush.

He stood, and I didn't back away. I wanted to protect Beth.

"A lot of people are worried about you," I said to her. "Are you okay? Don't worry, the police are on the way."

Maybe that would reassure her and scare Dr. Rush. If he got violent, I couldn't take him, since the closest I'd come to physical confrontation was roughhousing with the kids, and if anyone got hurt, it was me.

"The police?" she asked. "Why?"

"Because he's keeping you here, isn't he?" I asked, looking at Dr. Rush.

"No." Her voice was firm. "He's *protecting* me."

"From what?" I asked. "Or who?"

"Who are *you*?" Dr. Rush interrupted. "Aren't you one of my patients?"

"Not exactly," I said. "Beth, why are you here? Is Marcus after you?"

"No," she said. "Grandpa, what's going on?"

This wasn't how I thought things would play out. I'd found Beth, and that was supposed to be a good thing. I felt like I was being Punk'd.

"Then why are you here? Did you change your mind about the adoption?"

"No!" Beth said. "How do you know about that? Who are you?"

I wanted to keep running down the list like Twenty Questions. *Your parents? Is it them?*

"Get out," Rush said, extending an arm, as if he was going to personally escort me. I mentally glued my feet to the floor. Then his eyes refocused on something behind me. Maybe the police were here!

"I told you to stay out of this, bitch."

That didn't sound like the police. It sounded like Marcus. He pushed me aside, and I stumbled into a chair next to a silver tray of examination supplies, including gloves and lubricant. Eeek.

"Beth," he said, darting to her. "Are you okay?" His voice sounded almost...*loving.* He glanced at Dr. Rush. "Hey, Grandpa."

"She needs to leave," Rush told him, pointing at me. I shrunk into the chair beside the door, hoping to become invisible.

"She's harmless," Marcus said, waving his hand. "Remember her, Beth?"

I felt like I'd entered the Twilight Zone. How could Beth *remember* me?

Beth shook her head *no.* At least that made sense.

"Kenna's neighbor," he said under his breath. "From when we checked the house. The one who called 911 when I got shot."

"What house?" I interjected.

He shrugged. "We didn't want to pick parents for our kid without checking them out. So we looked at the profile pictures and figured out where Kenna and Andy live. We saw you there too. A couple times."

"I'm sorry," Beth said, wincing. "I felt bad about it."

"It's okay." I looked at Marcus. "Did you recognize me in the hospital?"

"I thought you looked familiar. But it didn't hit me 'til later. I thought maybe fate put you there to save me. A sign about the adoption. But then Los Reyes put a hit on you. I tried to keep you safe. So why are you in my business again?"

"First, I don't get why *Beth* is here. Did you change your mind about Kenna and Andy?" I asked her.

"I told you no." Tears came to her eyes. I'd obviously said the wrong thing, and I was thankful when Marcus patted her head. She touched his hand. "We were protecting the baby. Los Reyes wants Marcus dead. And me and the baby. We broke up, but we got back together and didn't tell anyone. Then Los Reyes put a serious hit on Marcus, and he told me to get out of town fast. My grandfather helped."

"He picked you up the night you went missing?" The man in the convenience store video looked enough like Rush to make sense.

"Yeah."

"Do your parents know?"

"Yes."

So that's why they were so uncooperative. They didn't want Beth to be found. And since they didn't support the adoption, they probably hoped this would delay or prevent it...that First Steps would give up and move on.

"Why couldn't you go to the police? Wouldn't they protect you?"

Marcus laughed. I thought of his gun, gang leadership, and pot supply—not to mention the possibility Beth's family was hiding something. "All kinds of reasons," he said.

"So you're Kenna's friend?" Beth asked. "She told me about you."

"Yes," I said. "She's been incredibly worried about you."

"I tried to tell her everything would be okay. Did she believe me?"

"She did," I said. "Always. But she wanted to make sure *you* were okay. She asked me to find you."

Beth closed her eyes and sank into the bed, turning to Marcus. I was starting to relax, too, but I wanted to know the whole story. Why would Dr. Rush keep her here instead of getting real protection from the authorities?

Suddenly all eyes turned my way, or that's what I thought until the door next to me moved again. It had to be the police this time.

"Oh shit!" Marcus yelled. That seemed like an overreaction. "Cover Beth!"

Dr. Rush jumped on the bed and threw his body over hers. That seemed excessive too. Marcus stepped away from the bed, dumped the checkers game, and held the metal table like a shield.

I instinctively put my hands in the air and looked left, still expecting to see cops with guns drawn. Instead I saw GT with a pistol aimed at Marcus, who'd been smart not to protect Beth himself. From everything he'd said, Los Reyes would love to take them both out. I watched GT alternate pointing the gun at Marcus and Grandpa/Beth.

For the moment, sitting slightly behind GT and the open door, I was as good as invisible—at least to GT, the one who mattered most.

Slowly, I lowered my hands and made the "shhhh" sign to everyone else. Then I surveyed my immediate surroundings. Beside me was the table with lubricant and gloves. If only it had something like a syringe. I scanned cabinets and drawers, all labeled with unhelpful medical terms, until I spotted something familiar, metal, a little pointy, and definitely uncomfortable. I'd never seen one up close, but I'd experienced its torture: *the speculum.*

In that blessed moment, Marcus distracted GT with a question. "How'd you find me here?"

I hoped GT would take a moment to brag.

"Was easy to follow a stupid fuck like you," he cackled. I slid open the drawer, lifted the largest speculum I saw, and marveled at its gun-like shape.

"I got somethin' for you to tell your boys," Marcus told GT.

Me too, I thought. *Tell all the boys.*

Screams erupted as GT fired, leaving an unmistakable hole in Beth's hospital bed. I jumped onto the chair and, with every ounce of mama bear in me, shoved the speculum at his temple, brought it back up again, and speculum-whipped his face. *How'd that exam feel?* I thought as GT's gun dropped from his hand and he looked at me in terror.

Marcus and I jumped on the pistol at the same time. Within seconds, he picked it up, raised it, and chased GT into the hall, which was easy, since GT was dazed and wobbly. Then, without hesitation, he shot GT in the leg. Sometimes it pays to be a badass.

With GT down and Marcus in charge, I turned back to Beth. She was breathing hard, and Grandpa was hooking her up to a monitor.

"She was already in labor," he said. "Now she's over the edge."

"She's not having the baby here, is she?" I asked. He didn't answer. I ran out of the room, past Marcus holding GT at gunpoint, past GT bleeding on the floor, past empty rooms, all the while checking my cell phone, which had no signal.

Just as I got to the "employees only" door, it burst open, and in came the police. *Finally.* Someone else must have called them.

I froze in place and explained where to go. Two officers stayed behind, asking questions and reporting to their colleagues. They already knew about Beth. Apparently they'd tracked her cell phone signal here. She'd tried making calls when she went into labor, but the reception was awful. Almost immediately, I saw paramedics removing her on a stretcher.

"Is she okay?" I asked frantically.

"She's fine, ma'am," a female paramedic reassured me. "She and this baby are gonna do great."

"Is there anyone I can call for you, Beth?" I yelled through the fray.

"They won't let Marcus come." I doubted they'd let me go either. "Call Diane at First Steps," she said. "Tell her I want April. I don't want to be alone!"

Beth was out the door, so I turned to an officer. "Where should I say they're taking her?" I asked.

"I don't know," he said. He looked unsure about telling me anything. "The closest hospital is Westridge."

Done.

Beth's words haunted me as the police insisted I answer their questions. *I don't want to be alone.* All this time, I'd feared her isolation, and now that I could do something about it, my hands were tied.

At least I could provide them with Beth's medical records, which the agency had given Kenna, and I'd kept in my case file. While retrieving them from the van, I noticed several gangish-looking dudes in the backs of police cars. Apparently GT had brought backup. I tried not to make eye contact.

Once the police were sure I was physically okay and being truthful (giving them George's number seemed to help, as did the story Rob the mailman had called in), they escorted me to the hospital. I'd already called First Steps and April's house, where Jen screamed with joy and said she'd call April, who was out with a friend. The woman I spoke with at First Steps had been elated too. Thank God they had an overnight answering service.

My final call was to Kenna, who picked up on the first ring, drowsy and afraid of what she'd hear. Late-night calls were typically bad news, but tonight was the best possible exception.

"Beth's okay!" I said in a restrained yell. "She's still pregnant, and she's going to deliver the baby in West Virginia." The background was too complicated to explain, so I simplified it. "She was with her grandparents after all. I don't know if you should come or not. Call the adoption agency right now and see what they say."

Kenna let out an excited yelp, thanked me, and promised to call back.

"I'll be at the hospital," I said, "and I won't leave until everyone's okay."

"She's doing fine," a young, female OB reassured me when I asked about Beth. "She's having regular contractions, and her water broke earlier, so this baby's on the way."

"Wow," I said. "I know she really wants someone with her. How is she doing emotionally?"

"She's okay. The nurses are taking good care of her. I'll let her know you're here."

"She barely knows me," I said. "But tell her April's on the way."

"I will. She'll be fine. She's a brave young lady, that's for sure."

I couldn't agree more.

April arrived an hour later with Jen, and they were ushered to Beth's room immediately, but not before April whispered to me, "I was on a date when you called."

"I'm so proud of you," I whispered back.

I never heard back from Kenna, and when I called her, I got no answer. Instead, I saw her beaming face next to Andy's when they arrived in the maternity waiting room, where I sat with other families awaiting news.

"Surprise!" Kenna told me with tears in her eyes, arms extended. "Beth wanted us here!"

Any residual tension escaped with sobs I couldn't hold back as we hugged.

"This is the best news I've ever gotten," I blubbered. I smiled at Andy over her shoulder. Was a miracle really going to happen for them? Now, like Kenna, I couldn't accept it until I knew it was real.

"We have to go," he said. "She's waiting for us."

"Next time I see you, you might be parents," I said. I couldn't stop the tears, but I had to stop talking. "Go! Go!"

I watched Kenna squeeze Andy's hand as he pushed a button to gain entrance to the delivery rooms.

"Take pictures!" I called.

Andy pulled a digital camera from his pocket and waved it at me.

"Got it!" he said. Good, because in Kenna's hands, it would be useless.

Hours later, when I thought I might pop with anticipation, I saw the OB-GYN walking toward the elevator.

"Wait," I said. "Is Beth okay?"

Andy and I had been texting, and I knew the time was near.

"She's wonderful. Mother and baby are doing great." Goosebumps rose along my arms and legs. The baby was born! "Do you know boy or girl yet?" she asked.

Did *I* know? "No," I said. "What is it?"

"I'll let them tell you."

The next message from Andy was one I'll save forever. It was Kenna holding a baby girl, smiling next to the most loving and generous woman I'd ever meet: Beth.

Sky Bethany Moore, said the caption. *7 lb. 10 oz.*

Another text arrived minutes later, apparently dictated by Kenna. *Sky loves her Aunt Nicki and her cousins very much. See you soon!*

Epilogue

In the month since Sky entered the world, GT had been released from the hospital and charged with gang participation, attempted murder, use of a firearm while committing a felony, and brandishing a firearm, among other things. His DNA matched the stray beer can at my house.

During the time Dr. Rush and Beth spent together, she'd demanded to know why her birth certificate was odd. Eventually he'd broken down and confessed the truth. A comatose patient at Asheleigh Manor had become pregnant, clearly the victim of rape. Instead of reporting the crime, he and his aunt had gone to great lengths to cover it up. Mrs. Rush, RN, had helped.

When the baby was born, they placed it with an infertile couple: Beth's parents. Sonja and her husband Bob took her home to Virginia, believing the birth certificate Dr. Rush provided was real, and that one of his office patients had chosen adoption.

They also followed Dr. Rush's terrible advice not to tell Beth she was adopted. The fake birth certificate worked for years, but Dr. Rush got worried when the DMV needed it for Beth's driver's license. So he confessed to her parents, and they lied to get a new one, using the excuse that Beth had been born at home. Dr. Rush begged Beth and her parents not to tell anyone. His job and life would be in jeopardy. Beth's parents could lose her. Now that he was protecting Beth, couldn't she protect him, too?

The staff at Asheleigh Manor only cooperated because Rush and his aunt told them to, purporting that Beth couldn't afford medical care, and that they were doing a community service by allowing her to stay there, closely monitored. With their jobs at risk and devotion to Dr. Rush, it was hard for anyone to say no.

Dr. Rush confessed to everything except pushing Edith down her stairs. He was arrested and then investigated for a myriad of crimes, the least of which was falsifying a birth certificate—a felony in itself. Edith had fully recovered and called me several times with gardening tips. She didn't remember why she fell.

Most importantly, Beth had visited Kenna, Andy, and Sky, signed adoption papers with Marcus's cooperation, and started working on reconciliation with her parents. First Steps arranged for intense counseling to help with the discovery that she was illegally adopted—even encouraging her to wait to relinquish custody of Sky. This baby was the first biological relative she'd met, they told her, and it was natural for that to affect her decision.

But Beth remained steadfast, saying she'd proceed with or without First Steps. So the agency conceded. Beth was temporarily staying with April, who said she would come out to her mom when it felt right. Beth was sorry for being angry with April, but when she needed to trust April most, she felt betrayed. And in leaving April in the dark, she thought maybe it protected her from harm.

I thanked Mom constantly for her help—so often that she eventually corrected me.

"I love spending time with the kids," she insisted. "It's a gift to *me*." I believed her.

So when Dean asked me out for celebratory drinks with George and Steve, I accepted, and she babysat. And when George and Steve left after the first toast, I had a good feeling—either from the champagne or the idea that Dean might have encouraged them to go. Or both.

"You have three weeks left in PI class, and your first case is already solved," he said with a friendly nudge.

"I know," I said, dizzied by his turquoise gaze, glowing smile, and edible-smelling aftershave.

I hadn't solved the case alone, but I'd taken a literal stab at protecting Beth's life, and I was humbled to know it had earned Marcus's respect and strengthened Beth and Kenna's bond. *Without you*, Kenna said, *Beth might not be here.* We knew what that meant, and it was too unthinkable to discuss.

Dean and I were side-by-side in a restaurant booth, just where we'd been when George and Steve left. He hadn't moved an inch, and I was more than fine with that, as long as I had fresh breath and something to say.

"This could be the start of something big," he continued, raising his glass a second time.

"Why not?" I concurred. "To big things!" Oops. That was an inappropriate toast. I wasn't feeling myself. Or maybe I was *too* myself. Too comfortable. Was that good or bad? I didn't know. I tried not to care.

Dean laughed, and I joined in.

"I haven't studied as much as I should have," I admitted. "And I missed one class. I've got some catching up to do."

Jack, Sophie, and I had been so obsessed with blond, blue-eyed Sky that other cares faded into the background. All we wanted to do was join in Andy and Kenna's bliss. Just hearing Sky's name, Kenna knew, reminded me of Grampy and peace. It reminded her of beauty and freedom.

"I'll have to tutor you then," Dean said. "What are you doing tomorrow?"

"Tomorrow?" I tried to focus. "Tomorrow is camp for the kids. They have a recital at three, and I have to be there."

"How about before the recital?"

"Nothing much" was my answer. *Laundry* was the truth.

"Great," he said, setting down his champagne. "Let's make it a date. Meet me at the academy for lunch, and I'll make sure you don't miss a thing. This time I'm buying."

"I'm a vegetarian," I reminded him.

"I know," he said. "Don't worry."

"For once," I said, "I'm worry free."

I looked into his eyes for a long moment until they closed.

"Perfect," he whispered before he kissed me.

And it was.

Susan O'Brien

Susan has been passionate about reading and writing since childhood, when she started a neighborhood newspaper and escaped tween stress with mysteries. Since covering her first big story (the birth of gerbils next door), she has worked with USA TODAY, *PI Magazine*, The Parent Institute, and others. Susan has an M.A. in forensic psychology and is a registered private investigator in Virginia. Among her diverse interests are photography, gardening, loud R&B music, healing prayer, and reality TV. She lives with her husband and children in the D.C. suburbs and donates part of her earnings to missing children's organizations. Susan can be reached at www.SkywritingSusan.com.

Henery Press Mystery Books

And finally, before you go...
Here are a few other mysteries
you might enjoy:

PILLOW STALK

Diane Vallere

A Mad for Mod Mystery (#1)

Interior Decorator Madison Night has modeled her life after a character in a Doris Day movie, but when a killer targets women dressed like the bubbly actress, Madison's signature sixties style places her in the middle of a homicide investigation.

The local detective connects the new crimes to a twenty-year-old cold case, and Madison's long-trusted contractor emerges as the leading suspect. As the body count piles up like a stack of plush pillows, Madison uncovers a Soviet spy, a campaign to destroy all Doris Day movies, and six minutes of film that will change her life forever.

Available at booksellers nationwide and online

Visit www.henerypress.com for details

DOUBLE WHAMMY

Gretchen Archer

A Davis Way Crime Caper (#1)

Davis Way thinks she's hit the jackpot when she lands a job as the fifth wheel on an elite security team at the fabulous Bellissimo Resort and Casino in Biloxi, Mississippi. But once there, she runs straight into her ex-ex husband, a rigged slot machine, her evil twin, and a trail of dead bodies. Davis learns the truth and it does not set her free—in fact, it lands her in the pokey.

Buried under a mistaken identity, unable to seek help from her family, her hot streak runs cold until her landlord Bradley Cole steps in. Make that her landlord, lawyer, and love interest. With his help, Davis must win this high stakes game before her luck runs out.

Available at booksellers nationwide and online

Visit www.henerypress.com for details

DINERS, DIVES & DEAD ENDS

Terri L. Austin

A Rose Strickland Mystery (#1)

As a struggling waitress and part-time college student, Rose Strickland's life is stalled in the slow lane. But when her close friend, Axton, disappears, Rose suddenly finds herself serving up more than hot coffee and flapjacks. Now she's hashing it out with sexy bad guys and scrambling to find clues in a race to save Axton before his time runs out.

With her anime-loving bestie, her septuagenarian boss, and a pair of IT wise men along for the ride, Rose discovers political corruption, illegal gambling, and shady corporations. She's gone from zero to sixty and quickly learns when you're speeding down the fast lane, it's easy to crash and burn.

Available at booksellers nationwide and online

Visit www.henerypress.com for details

BOARD STIFF

Kendel Lynn

An Elliott Lisbon Mystery (#1)

As director of the Ballantyne Foundation on Sea Pine Island, SC, Elliott Lisbon scratches her detective itch by performing discreet inquiries for Foundation donors. Usually nothing more serious than retrieving a pilfered Pomeranian. Until Jane Hatting, Ballantyne board chair, is accused of murder. The Ballantyne's reputation tanks, Jane's headed to a jail cell, and Elliott's sexy ex is the new lieutenant in town.

Armed with moxie and her Mini Coop, Elliott uncovers a trail of blackmail schemes, gambling debts, illicit affairs, and investment scams. But the deeper she digs to clear Jane's name, the guiltier Jane looks. The closer she gets to the truth, the more treacherous her investigation becomes. With victims piling up faster than shells at a clambake, Elliott realizes she's next on the killer's list.

Available at booksellers nationwide and online

Visit www.henerypress.com for details

THE DEEP END

Julie Mulhern

A Country Club Murders Mystery

Swimming into the lifeless body of her husband's mistress tends to ruin a woman's day, but becoming a murder suspect can ruin her whole life.

It's 1974 and Ellison Russell's life revolves around her daughter and her art. She's long since stopped caring about her cheating husband, Henry, and the women with whom he entertains himself. That is, until she becomes a suspect in Madeline Harper's death. The murder forces Ellison to confront her husband's proclivities and his crimes—kinky sex, petty cruelties and blackmail.

As the body count approaches par on the seventh hole, Ellison knows she has to catch a killer. But with an interfering mother, an adoring father, a teenage daughter, and a cadre of well-meaning friends demanding her attention, can Ellison find the killer before he finds her.

Available at booksellers nationwide and online

Visit www.henerypress.com for details

BET YOUR BOTTOM DOLLAR

Karin Gillespie

The Bottom Dollar Series (#1)

(from the Henery Press Chick Lit Collection)

Welcome to the Bottom Dollar Emporium in Cayboo Creek, South Carolina, where everything from coconut mallow cookies to Clabber Girl Baking Powder costs a dollar but the coffee and gossip are free. For the Bottom Dollar gals, work time is sisterhood time.

When news gets out that a corporate dollar store is coming to town, the women are thrown into a tizzy, hoping to save their beloved store as well their friendships. Meanwhile the manager is canoodling with the town's wealthiest bachelor and their romance unearths some startling family secrets.

The first in a series, *Bet Your Bottom Dollar* serves up a heaping portion of small town Southern life and introduces readers to a cast of eccentric characters. Pull up a wicker chair, set out a tall glass of Cheer Wine, and immerse yourself in the adventures of a group of women whom the *Atlanta Journal Constitution* calls, "... the kind of steel magnolias who would make Scarlett O'Hara envious."

Available at booksellers nationwide and online

Visit www.henerypress.com for details

CPSIA informatio
Printed in the US,
.VOW07s00262:

$1142LV

6303